Energetic Processes

Interaction Between Matter, Energy & Consciousness

Volume I

Library of Congress Number: 2001119877
ISBN #: Softcover 1-4010-4113-2

The views expressed are those of the authors and do not necessarily represent those of the United States Psychotronics Association (USPA); of its directors, officers, or staff. The USPA does not manufacture or sell any devices, equipment, or services.

Audiotape and videotape copies of all conference lectures may be purchased from the USPA.

To order additional copies of this book, contact:
Xlibris Corporation
1-888-7-XLIBRIS
www.Xlibris.com
Orders@Xlibris.com

Contents

13927-VALO

PROJECT DIRECTOR	Peter Moscow
ASSOCIATE PROJECT DIRECTOR	Robert Beutlich
EDITOR	Thomas Valone
CONTRIBUTING RESEARCHERS	Glen Rein Jon Klimo Barbara Hero Laverne Denyer Fran Ehrlich Eldon Byrd

United States Psychotronics Association

13927-VALO

United States Psychotronics Association

P.O. Box 45
Elkhorn, WI. 53121
Phone: 262-742-4790
Fax.-262-742-3670
E-mail: uspa@elknet.net
Web: www.psychotronics.org

INFORMATION ABOUT USPA

The U.S. Psychotronics Association covers a broad spectrum of interests. The Association defines psychotronics as the science of mind-body-environment relationships, an interdisciplinary science concerned with the interactions of matter, energy, and consciousness. Our annual Conference is an open forum for any aspect of psychotronic research. Conferences are usually held in July at various colleges, universities or retreat centers around the United States. Audio taping of the annual Conference presentations began in 1978, and video taping in 1982. A catalog of the tapes for sale is available for $2.00.

USPA has evolved from a meeting in Indianapolis, Indiana, in 1975, organized by the late J. G. Gallimore. A talented psychic and scientific researcher himself, Jerry sought to understand the rules governing the energy fields and currents he could see and feel around people, objects and machines, and to develop ways of constructively applying those rules. The meeting drew over 80 people and led to a second meeting in Washington, D.C., the following year where the decision was made to form a registered non-profit organization under Section 501(c)(3) of the IRS Code, as the U.S. Psychotronics Association. The USPA was incorporated in the District of Columbia in August, 1977.

Our basic premise is that ESP is a natural occurrence. We seek to understand how it occurs, and to use that understanding for the benefit of mankind. USPA is not an experiential group; our orientation is towards the technical and scientific aspects of

13927-VALO

psychotronics and its practical applications. Quantum mechanics has provided a "scientific" basis which allows the existence of psychic phenomena and unconventional energy effects. Members are on the leading edge of the new paradigms in science—theory and instrumentation. This is the physics of the 21st century.

Because we are an open forum, the USPA has no single viewpoint Our greatest strength lies in the interdisciplinary nature of our Conferences, where Ph.D.'s sit down with interested persons—regardless of background or formal education—and discuss their theories and research openly. In the process of explaining complex subjects to lay persons and scientists of other disciplines, a synergistic effect takes place.

The Association does not sell any radionic, TENS, ELF, or other devices. We publish a list of manu-facturers who seem to provide the necessary training and have demonstrated some ethical stan-dards in dealing with their customers. Warning: There are manufacturers of psychotronic and radionic devices who make unreliable products and unsubstantiated claims. Before purchasing a device from any manufacturer, make sure they offer a 90 day money back guarantee, that their training is adequate for your own purposes, and that they deliver exactly what is promised. If necessary, ask them for letters of reference.

USPA publishes a quarterly Newsletter for members. We have local chapters throughout the United States, generally meeting monthly.

List of *Proceedings of USPA Conferences*

	MEMBER	*NON-MEMBER*	*US SHIPPING**
VOL.# 1,1985	$20.00	$30.00	$3.50
Peer reviewed & edited, 268 pgs.			
VOL.#2, 1993	$35.00	$45.00	$4.50
Unedited, 394 pgs.			
VOL.#3, 1994	$35.00	$45.00	$4.50
Unedited, 389 pgs			
VOL.#4, 1995	$35.00	$45.00	$4.50
Unedited, 376 pgs.			
VOL.#5, 1996	$35.00	$45.00	$4.50
Unedited, 327 pgs.			
VOL.#6,1997	$30.00	$45.00	$4.50
Unedited, 192 pgs.			
VOL.#7, 1998	$35.00	$45.00	$4.50
Unedited, 258 pgs.			
VOL.#8, 1999	$40.00	$50.00	$5.50
Unedited, 486 pgs.			
VOL.#9, 2000	$35.00	$45.00	$4.50
Unedited, 406 pgs			
VOL.#10, 2001	$35.00	$45.00	$4.50
Unedited, 316 pgs.			

Please circle volumes ordered, allow 6-8 weeks for delivery if temporarily out of stock, shipped via US mail, book rate. *All other destinations please phone for shipping fees.

13927-VALO

Check______ Visa______ MasterCard______

Card # ____________________ Exp. Date______

Signature:____

Name____

Address____

City ______________________________

State/Province ______ Zip ______ Country______

Phone#____

E-mail____

Make check out to USPA, or use Master/Visa charge card, send to: USPA PO BOX 45, ELKHORN, WI. 53121, or PHONE: 262-742-4790; FAX: 262-742-3670 E-mail: <uspa@elknet.net> WEB SITE: <www.psychotronics.org>

AUDIO TAPES ARE FROM 1978 ONWARD @ $8.00 EA . + SHIPPING.

VIDEO TAPES ARE FROM 1982 ONWARD @ $20.00 EA. + SHIPPING.

Discount: –10% for set of two. *Special discount:* –30% for ordering a complete year's set.

Tapes orders are filled at:

USPA , c/o Katherine Larsen,
993W—1800N, Pleasant Grove, UT 84062
Phone: 801-785-7416

Foreword

Twenty-seven years ago an accomplished Radionics researcher, Jerry Gallimore, founded the United States Psychotronics Association. People from US, Europe and beyond joined the organization which holds a major annual conference and promotes education and workshops through various chapters as well as providing a major archive of videotapes, audio tapes, *Journals* and *Proceedings* for sale to members and the general public.

The glue that binds the researchers, lecturers and lay public is a tremendous desire to explore the margins of reality through frontier sciences. Thus, participants in the group get to experience first hand the remarkable discoveries in Quantum Holography and Radionics, the latest research in Over-Unity machines, new theories about Time and Space, the latest research on Cold Fusion, Distant Healing Studies and Techniques, Magnetic Machines, ESP and Survival of Bodily Death, Bio-Dynamic Farming methods using Subtle Energy devices and much more.

The Association welcomes innovative papers and presentations and has therefore attracted important and unusual work over many years. Original thinking and research is the hallmark of the large archive which has been built over nearly three decades. Recognizing that the public today demands a greater depth of understanding than ever before and also that the professional and academic communities worldwide are becoming more aware of the need to understand the universe in non conventional ways

13927-VALO

the USPA has decided for the first time to publish it's very first book. In this way many more people can get a taste of the enthusiasm, excitement and depth of study that permeates the work of each of these truly independent researchers.

In most cases the authors did not receive grants, funds or paychecks to sustain their interest. In many ways they are like the early pioneers in this country staking out claims in new territory with a sense of wonderment and respect for the newly found land, hoping and expecting that it will be fertile ground for an unknown future. At the same time their work is built on the foundations laid down by the great scientists of the late nineteenth and twentieth centuries.

It is in this tradition that this compendium is presented to you. I believe that you will enjoy the variety and perspicacity contained therein.

Peter Moscow
President, USPA

July 2001
Louisville KY

1

Psychotronics: Yesterday, Today and Tomorrow

Henry C. Monteith, Ph.D.

Reprinted from the *J. of the U. S. Psychotronics Association*, Nov., 1988, p.3

Beginning at the very moment when a newborn baby takes its first breath, there appears to be an innate urge which propels it to reach out and learn. Accompanying this desire to learn is the need to love and be loved; therefore, from this observation one readily concludes that the purpose of man must be intimately related to learning and loving. Here, one is reminded of the immortal statement which was given by Orfeo Angelucci: "In the final analysis, there is but one virtue, the love of pure learning; and all else is but procrastination and dissipation in the eyes of the Eternal One who patiently awaits our evolutionary awakenings."

Thus it appears that there can be no happiness in man unless his life is filled with learning and loving because only in this way can the purpose of his existence be fulfilled. The major purpose of psychotronics is to study the means by which man can be brought to a realization of his higher nature so that he might feel the impulses of the cosmic mind and sense that finer thread of consciousness which permeates all of space, time, and matter. In psychotronics, one studies not only the material universe – the vehicle through which consciousness expresses itself – but also seeks to discover the invisible cause from which the universe began.

A Brief History of Psychotronics

Where and when did psychotronic investigation begin? There is no concrete answer to this question because aspects of the psychotronic art and science have existed as long as man himself. At the dawn of such investigations psychotronics and natural science were mutually inclusive. The high priests, the philosophers, the astrologers, and the soothsayers were also the scientists. When the prophets of old worked their "miracles," when Moses parted the Red Sea with a touch of his staff; when Christ walked upon the water, healed the sick, and raised the dead – all were practicing psychotronics.

Psychotronics was part of religion until religion became dogmatic. Where absolute truth was proclaimed and belief was considered knowledge, there was no place for those who sought for higher awareness. There was no alternative but to break off from established religion. Thereafter, psychotronics expressed itself very strongly within magic, witchcraft and alchemy. This trend of affairs continued, in the Western world, until the 16th Century when investigators such as Copernicus and Galileo began developing the scientific method, which ultimately led to the discipline of physical science as it is known today.

In the Eastern world, focusing primarily on China, the development of psychotronics followed quite a different path. Acupuncture has been practiced in China for more than five thousand years, long before Western civilization had its birth. Those who practiced this art believed that a subtle energy, intimately associated with the processes of life, flowed with great intensity along specific pathways in the human body and that this flow could be influenced by inserting needles into the various points of the body where this energy enters and exits. The Chinese believe that this living energy has two poles-the positive referred to as Yang, and the negative called Yin. Since the scientific method did not exist when acupuncture was developed, and since the Chinese firmly believe that this energy is influenced by mental processes, acupuncture fits firmly into the domain of psychotronics.

The actual origins of the concept of a subtle energy, more refined than electricity, is lost in history. However, certain documents which were found in India and Tibet indicate that this concept was passed down from a great civilization which existed on Earth previous to recorded history and which was destroyed around fifteen thousand B.C. Apparently, these ancient peoples referred to this living energy as *vril*.

Physical science relies entirely upon gathering facts through experiment, forming an hypothesis based on those facts, and then testing the hypothesis until it can be confirmed as a law of nature. Psychotronics, on the other hand, does not reject the technique of physical science, but considers it to be only one road to knowledge among many. There is no known scientific instrument which can directly detect the *vril*. Consequently, its secrets can only be unlocked through psychotronics.

Psychotronics began to become an organized discipline in the West when the Society for Psychical Research was established in London in 1882 (Jane Oppenheim, 1986). Many of the 19th Century's most famous scientists joined this Society. Among them were such noted scientific giants as Lord Rayleigh, J. J. Thomson, William Crookes, and Sir Oliver Lodge. In 1922, Sir Oliver Lodge wrote an article presenting his views on psychic science (J. Arthur Thomson, 1922), which were strongly influenced by his belief in the ether. The concept of an ether is experiencing a great revival at the present time, so it is of interest to consider the following quote from this 1922 article:

13927-VALO

"Some of us are beginning to suspect that these psychical entities are able to utilize the properties of the ether, too—that intangible and elusive medium which fills all space—and if that turn out to be so, we know that this vehicle or medium is much more perfect, less obstructive, and more likely to be permanent, than any form of ordinary matter can be. For in such a medium as ether, there is no wearing out, no decay, no waste or dissipation of energy such as is inevitable when work is done by ponderable and molecularly constituted matter-that matter about which chemists and natural philosophers have ascertained so many and such fascinating qualities. Physicists, chemists, and biologists have arrived at a point in the analysis of matter which opens up a vista of apparently illimitable scope. Our existing scientific knowledge places no ban on supernormal phenomena; rather, it suggests the probability of discoveries in quite novel directions."

It appears that to Sir Oliver Lodge, psychotronics was merely an extension of physical science.

Even though the term psychotronics has been constantly used in this article, it was not coined until the 19th Century – when it appears to have originated with the Soviets, who began very active research in the late 1950's in an area they referred to as *psychoenergetics* (Krippner, Rubin, 1974). To the Soviets, however, psychotronics was merely a subset of psychoenergetics. In America today, the I term psychotronics is being used to include all phenomena I which the Soviets referred to as "psychoenergetics."

One might define the area of psychotronics as that domain of human inquiry which includes the study of all phenomena that are created by the direct interaction of the living force, *vril*, with the ether medium. Here, the term *vril* is far more inclusive than the term "bioplasma" which is only a certain expression of the *vril*. To the psychotronic investigator, *thoughts are things*, and they lie at the foundation of all phenomena, physical and non-physical.

The development of psychotronics in the United States is of recent origin. In December, 1969, the American Association for the Advancement of Science formally admitted the Parapsychological Association into its ranks. Thus the of study of paranormal phenomena can henceforth be I pursued with some official sanction, a blessing which has been hard to win.

Prior to 1972, if one was asked about the state of psychic research in the United States, about all that would s come to mind would be the work of Dr. J. B. Rhine at Duke University which began in the 1935 time frame. Indeed, until the early 1970's, work in psychotronics was kept alive in the United States only by a very few devoted scientists and laymen receiving little or no support, official or otherwise. Even today, support for such work is difficult to obtain. However, there is now a much larger number of dedicated researchers painfully advancing the state of the art.

I believe that the initial impulse which started serious development of psychotronics in the United States was the publication of the book *Psychic Discoveries Behind the Iron Curtain* (Ostrander & Schroeder, 1970). This book stimulated private researchers in the United States to organize and attempt to reproduce Soviet work in psychotronics. Ken Johnson, Howard Burgess, and I nearly simultaneously reproduced the Kirlian camera in early 1971. Controversy still surrounds this device which is reported to be able to detect the living "bioplasma field" around the human body by causing a high voltage electrical corona to interact with it, an effect which reminds one of the interaction of iron filings with a magnetic field.

On November 15, 1971, the American Society for Psychical Research held a symposium on " Advances in Psychical Research" in the Soviet Union. At the invitation of Dr. J. G. Pratt, then a parapsychologist at the University of Virginia, I demonstrated my Kirlian device and showed photographs that had been taken with it. Dr. Pratt had just returned from a visit to the Soviet Union and gave a report on the many startling psychotronic experiments he had witnessed there. At the conclusion of the formal talks, a panel discussion was held with the panel consisting of the following members: Dr. J. G. Pratt, Parapsychologist, University of Virginia; Dr. Bernard Aaronson, Psychologist, Princeton University; Dr. Lyman Fretwell, Physicist, Bell Laboratories, Whippany, New Jersey; Dr. Gary Gruber, Physicist, Hofstra University, New York City; and myself, Engineering Physicist, Albuquerque, New Mexico. (The management of the laboratory for which I work strongly objected to its name being associated with psychotronic research.)

In the audience of this symposium was Max Toth, an American pioneer in psychotronics, and of Czechoslovakian heritage. He later met with Dr. Zdenek Rejdak, a Czechoslovakian researcher associated with the Department for Psychotronic Investigation, affiliated with the Czechoslovakian Society for Applied Cybernetics, not long after the New York symposium. It was the collaboration between these two men which laid the foundation for the historic Prague Conference – perhaps the most significant event to occur in the entire history of psychotronics. [In 1993, Dr. Z. Rejdak also participated in a Joint Conference of the International Association for Psychotronic Research and the USPA, at the U. of Wisconsin, Milwaukee. Other foreign speakers included Gabrial Christeller, Prof. Chanceverov, Toshia Nakache, Dr. Ivan Ploc, Dr. Yvonne Duplessis, Prof. K Kademova, Ing. L. Keclik, Ing. S. Starman, Dr. Victor Adamenko, and Dr. F. Karger – Ed. note]

The Prague Conference

This unique conference was held in Prague, Czechoslovakia, in June of 1973. The basis for all of the recent advances in psychotronics was laid at this event, and international cooperation in this field of research was at a level never obtained before or since. Nearly every country which was performing psychotronic research to a significant degree was represented. Approximately fifty-two of more than 250 total attendees were Americans. Only five Soviets took official part in the Conference, but more than two dozen submitted papers. The most important Soviet researchers, such as Vikton Adamenko, Viktor Inushin and Semyon Kirlian did not appear in person; however, some of the Americans who visited Moscow later were able to meet and talk with Viktor Adamenko and his wife. Czechoslovakia, of course, was heavily rep-resented by the most noted researchers alive today such as Julius Krmessky, who has been investigating and demonstrating the radiation of bioplasmic energy from the human body; and Robert Pavlita, a very important Czech inventor who had developed material devices which are capable of concentrating and manipulating the bioplasmic or *vril* energy to a degree powerful enough to actually run small motors.

Pavlita demonstrated at the Conference –without any doubt— that bioplasmic energy was polarized. His daughter projected her bioplasmic energy into various devices which were designed to produce specific physical effects such as motor action, precipitation of solutes from solution, stimulating or destroying plant growth, and the killing of insects. Pavlita told of an accident which occurred during his experimentation when his daughter was partially paralyzed and her life placed in great danger by being exposed to a negative form of bioplasmic energy. He had to work feverishly without stopping for over two days in order to build a device which would reverse the negative effects produced by the one which did the damage. As a result of this experimentation, Pavlita found that he could build devices of sufficient scale that they could project enough negative energy to kill human beings. [The Spring/Summer 1988 issue of *Artifex* (published by Archeus Project 2402 University Avenue, St. Paul, MN 55114), carried an article titled "Experimental Investigation of Biologically Induced Magnetic Anomalies," by G. Egely and G. Vertesy. The authors worked with Robert Pavlita, who has apparently effected various magnetic anomalies by means of "concentration and a small metal device." –Ed. note]

Brazil was represented by Dr. Brenio Onetto-Bachler, a professor of parapsychology at the University of Chile; Canada was represented by Dr. and Mrs. Duncan Blewett, both psychologists at the University of Saskatchewan, where they developed a mathematical formula for "psychic energy" which explains its characteristics and dynamics. Also from Canada came Dr. Edward Mann, who lectured on experimentation with orgone blankets.

After the lecture of Dr. Alexander Grigorievich Bakirov, a professor of mineralogy at the Polytechnical Institute in the Siberian City of Tomsk, there was no doubt in anyone's mind that the Soviets had a deep interest in dowsing, one of the oldest psychotronic practices. He represented the Soviet Interdepartmental Commission for the Study of the Bio-Physical Effect, and stated that he and other Soviet dowsers have used various kinds of dowsing instruments to locate bodies of ore as deep as 3000 feet below the Earth's surface and to make geological maps. He said that they have worked both on foot and from helicopters traveling at 200 kilometers per hour at a height of more than 200 meters have ground. He believed that in the USSR the dowsing technique had been perfected to such an extent that it rivaled all existing scientific prospecting methods, and is certainly far less expensive than any other conceivable detector.

One surprise at the Conference was the presence of the noted Soviet psychic Tofik Oadashev, who –without question— exercised genuine psychic capability. Oadashev is a highly developed telepath. From a crowd of more than 300 persons he arbitrarily selected a woman to help him carry out his demonstration. She was asked to choose another person from the crowd but not to inform anyone present –especially Oadashev –whom she had chosen. Oadashev was then tightly blindfolded and hooded with a thick, dark material. He proceeded to walk through the crowd with the chosen woman following three to four meters behind him. He asked that she send him mental commands to aid in finding the person that she had mentally selected. After about five minutes of effort, Oadashev located the individual whom he believed had been chosen by the assistant and brought the indi vidual on stage. He then asked if this was the person she had chosen and she answered that it was. Needless to say, the crowd was astonished at this feat of telepathy. Oadashev has been written up in the Soviet press and Soviet scientists have tested him repeatedly and verified his authenticity.

The Conference was divided into six working sections; however, the one devoted to psychotronics and physics was by far the most popular. In this section, my talk on "Consciousness and Theoretical Physics" followed that of Julius Krmessky. Or. Yurii Andreyevich Kholodov, a Soviet biophysicist, reported on the extensive work he was doing concerning the effects of electromagnetic fields on the central nervous system. Without a doubt, the Soviets are the world authorities in this field of research and they have learned to use some of the knowledge they have obtained to perform feats as yet unknown in the West. For example, a side effect of a device built to aid them in espionage was the increase in the white blood cell count of workers in the American embassy. It appears that the American Intelligence Community still has no real understanding of the nature of this device or its purpose, only that it somehow utilizes electromagnetic energy, in a special form, which adversely affects the human body.

Dr. Alexander Oubrov gave a stimulating talk on his new theory of "biogravity" which he believes can explain the mysterious solid and liquid phase changes that occur in living cells. He referred to startling experiments which have been performed at the institute of Clinical and Experimental Medicine in Novo-Sibirsk which indicate that cells themselves can converse by coding messages in the form of a special electromagnetic ray with frequencies in the ultraviolet. It was found that cell structures which were dying communicated the death signals to other cells of the same type which in turn began to die as they frantically attempted to re-adapt themselves in a manner that would make them more resistant to that which was killing them. Here also lies the essence of a very terrible weapon which the Russians may have already perfected and tested. It is possible that such a weapon was tested in Afghanistan in 1981 when, after an attack from Soviet helicopters, several resistance fighters died instantly and their bodies did not decay for more than 30 days. Apparently every cell, bacterium and virus in the body had been instantly killed. If such a weapon exists, it would not be continuously used in order to avoid compromising it to the West. However, it should be remembered that in January, 1960, Khrushchev announced to the Presidium that a new, fantastic weapon was in development-so powerful that if it was used without restraint it could wipe out all life on Earth. He was not talking about the nuclear bomb or conventional biological weapons.

International Association of Psychotronics

At the Prague Conference, Dr. Zdenek Rejdak was elected president for the Eastern Division of the newly established *International Association of Psychotronics*, and Dr. Stanley Krippner was elected president for the West.

The results of the Prague Conference and all of the reports being brought back from Russia by visitors which concerned psychotronic research in that country spurred the Defense Intelligence Agency to conduct an investigation into Soviet and Czechoslovakian parapsychological research. The results of their investigation were published openly in two documents (which are given in the references). Classified versions of these documents were also written. In spite of the alarming information set forth in these documents, there is little or no evidence that it significantly stimulated research in the United States. In addition, several Jewish scientists who were allowed to leave the Soviet Union openly warned the West about the tremendous advances being made in the Soviet Union in the field of psychotronic research.

One must wonder how Soviet leaders, all of whom are sworn materialists, got such a driving ambition to investigate psychotronic phenomena. I believe that it was due to the relentless efforts of Dr. Leonid L. Vasiliev. After the death of Stalin and the overthrow of Lysenko's biology, Vasiliev found that the time was ripe to make an attempt to reestablish psychotronic research in the USSR. A major impetus was given to this desire when he heard that the United States Navy was conducting telepathic experiments between a land installation and the submerged submarine Nautilus in 1959. (The story has long since been denied by the United States Government, and considering the sad state of psychotronic research at that time in the United States, the government denial was probably true. I was later told by my sources that the story was concocted by an overly zealous reporter and widely published in the United States.) However, the Soviets believed the story to be true. Vasiliev confronted the Soviet leadership with this story and suggested that the West was getting ahead of the Soviet Union in a new and potentially lethal area of research. Since the Soviets were taking no chances of having America come up with another "battlefield surprise" after the atomic bomb, they immediately provided Professor Vasiliev with all he needed to start a laboratory for psychotronic research which today has no real counterpart in the West.

While talking with Soviet researchers in Moscow after the Prague Conference, I was thoroughly convinced that Soviet scientists are certain of the existence of all forms of psychic phenomena and no longer find it necessary to try and "prove" its existence – as is still the case in the West. [A television broadcast on the ABC World of Discovery, March 25, 1993, entitled the "Powers of the Russian Psychics" showed trained psychics disrupting chess matches and causing physical distress on subjects at a distance.—Ed. note] They are hard at work attempting to develop and apply the bioplasmic energy which they believe is the source of all such phenomena. To stress this fact, one of the members of our team, Marcel Vogel, who was at that time a senior research chemist working for IBM in San Jose, California, was invited to speak to a select group of Soviet scientists, including Nobel Prize winners – and perhaps the world's greatest expert on electromagnetism and its effects on life, Dr. A. S. Presman. Such an invitation is not arbitrarily extended by the Soviets. [Marcel Vogel, IBM scientist and inventor of magnetic tape, became a regular speaker at the USPA soon afterwards and established a psychotronics laboratory attached to his home when he retired. – Ed. note]

Recently, Dr. Rusell Targ, an expert in remote viewing, has been invited to the Soviet Union on several occasions to participate in their local psychotronic conferences. Also, his former colleague, Dr. Harold Puthoff, has been closely communicating with the Chinese in their psychotronic research. Needless to say, psychotronics is now a respectable field of research in all major Communist countries (and some Western countries.) However, in America, it still lags behind.

Physical Science and Psychotronics

Domains of gender exist in knowledge just as they do in material creation. Unfortunately, this concept is still alien to modern man—who continues to overemphasize the masculine while suppressing his female counterpart. Physical science is masculine in nature, while psychotronics and religion are feminine. Physical science depends heavily upon the conscious mind and uses hard data, experiment, and reproducibility of results as its criteria for determining truth. However, physical science often ignores the material evidence which exists openly around it. For example, the underwater man-made walls which have been discovered off the coast of North Bimini in the Bahamas; the high technology devices found fossilized in stone; the thirty foot iron pillar in New Delhi, India, which does not rust; the giant 70 ton stone blocks, cut and smoothed by some unknown process, that lie mysteriously in the desert of Baalbek, Lebanon; and many hundreds of other mysteries, have all failed to convince physical science that at least one great civilization existed here before.

While examining the magnificent crystal skull which was discovered intact and undamaged in South America, a physical scientist simply murmured to himself, "The damn thing should not even exist." Even with today's technology, the magnificent feat of producing such a skull from a single piece of quartz, with moving parts, cannot be reproduced. Such scientific anomalies are simply being ignored by physical scientists because they do not fit into their beliefs.

When the scientific technique cannot be utilized, it becomes necessary to rely upon intuition. Even from ancient times, men have always marveled at "feminine intuition." The wonder is not misplaced because "intuition" has always come more natural to the feminine aspect than to the masculine aspect. Therefore, it is absolutely necessary that the "intuitive" approach of psychotronics be combined with the masculine "conscious" approach of physical science for a full comprehension of nature to be obtained. In other words, it is time for a proper marriage to take place between the masculine and feminine approaches to the obtainment of universal knowledge.

Finally, I will list certain discoveries I believe have been obtained through psychotronic means but which are still far out of the reach of the physical scientific technique. Some of this knowledge will be learned through physical science only after it is 100 late to do anything about it. The price which must be paid for ignoring the feminine aspect of knowledge is already beyond measure. That which has been unbalanced must, of necessity rebalance itself. In the process of this rebalancing, the forces of Mother Nature have always, unwittingly, wreaked great havoc and destruction upon the civilizations of man. The time of rebalance is again at hand.

13927-VALO

Summary

1) Since 1900, the biosphere of planet Earth has been reduced in its life-giving functions by more than 60%. All life on Earth is under increasing threat because of its continuous weakening by man's pollution-forming activities.
2) All sources of energy which science has produced to date produce by-products which are destructive to life and are opposite to the energies of the positive ray, called *vril*. The most destructive of these energies, by far, is that energy derived from the fission of the atom. The continuous testing of nuclear weapons, and the so-called peaceful uses of nuclear energy, have already caused immense damage to the Earth and her biosphere. Nostradamus correctly called nuclear energy the "anti-thesis of the positive ray."
3) About 19% of the damage done to the biosphere has been caused by the launching of rockets. The massive amount of pollutants ejected by each rocket launch is far more harmful than physical science yet realizes. If a star wars-type race is continued, the huge number of rocket launches which will be necessary to implement it could possibly deal a death-blow to the Earth's biosphere and ultimately to man himself.
4) AIDS is not a natural creation but is a direct result of tampering with the mechanisms developed by nature to create and sustain life. In addition, man's inability to control his population on the Earth has presented to this virus a vast field of propagation enabling it to recycle at an enormous rate and adjust to any condition man might create in an attempt to eliminate it. It can only be defeated through a psychotronic energy approach; chemical methods simply will not work because it is a greater chemist than man.
5) Another horrible threat is man's development of genetic engineering. Unfortunately, certain nations are already hard at work using this technology to create lethal agents for use in war. A high probability exists for both accidental and inten-

tional release of extremely lethal agents into man's environment, which could threaten life more seriously than a nuclear war.

6) Even the physical scientists realize that the West Coast is due for a devastating earthquake at any time; however, they are divided on how destructive it will be. Nostradamus stated "So great will be the deluge that there will be no spot of earth for a firm foothold." Edgar Cayce stated that the oceanfront would approach the state of Nevada. If Nostradamus is correct, the great earthquake and tidal wave destruction will occur between 1988 and 2000.

Psychotronics of today must now take a place alongside the science of yesterday. If true knowledge is to be obtained, there is no room for dogma, nature sets the rules, and man can only follow if he has an open mind.

References

1. Ostrander, S., and Schroeder, L. *Psychic Discoveries Behind the Iron Curtain*, Prentice-Hall, Inc., 1970, Englewood Cliffs, New Jersey.
2. Vasiliev, L. L. *Mysterious Phenomena of the Human Psyche*, University Books, 1965, New Hyde Park, New York.
3. Krippner, S., and Rubin, D. *The Kirlian Aura*, Anchor Press/Doubleday,1974, Garden City, New York.
4. Thomson, J. Arthur. *The Outline of Science*, G. P. Putman & Sons, 1922, New York and London.
5. Oppenheim, Janet. "Physics and Psychic Research in Victorian and Edwardian England," *Physics Today*, May,1986, pages 62-70.
6. Bird, C. "Mind over Matter in Prague", *The East West Journal*, July 1974, Volume 4, Number 6, pages 18-21.
7. Angelucci, Orfeo. *Son of the Sun*, DeVorss and Company, 1959; 516 West Ninth Street, Los Angeles, California.

2

Engineering the ZPE from a Post-Cartesian Unified-Field Idealist-Monist Perspective

Jon Klimo, Ph.D.
The American Schools of Professional Psychology, San Francisco Bay Area Campus
Annual Conference of the United States Psychotronics Association, 2001, Columbus, Ohio

Introduction

This interdisciplinary paper provides a model of how the so-called zero point energy vacuum (ZPE) can be embedded within a multidimensional post-dualistic, essentially idealist mental monist, cosmology that reframes contemporary notions of the internal, subjective, experiential, mental-spiritual domain, on the one hand, and the domain of external, objectively real objects, events, and energies, on the other. It is argued that how we may be able to engineer the ZPE must be looked at in new, more inclusive top-down consciousness-centric ways. Rather than consciousness being an emergent epiphenomenon of brain/body physicality, physicality is reconstrued as being an emergent epiphenomenon of the underlying all-constituting consciousness field. The unified-field character of the model draws from the meaning of Carl Jung's term "psychoid," as that which possesses the characteristics of simultaneously being both internal/subjective and external/objective in nature. Further, and especially, the philosopher Hegel's concept of "Absolute Spirit" and an extension of the psychological concept of dissociation are used. Within this model, local sentient beings, seats or foci of consciousness and intention, and groups of such beings state-specifically sufficiently similar to each other to give rise to and maintain shared consensus realities, interact with each other and with their common ground of being, which is partially comprised of the ZPE (supplemented by higher-dimensional, higher-frequency, more-consciousness-characterized superordinate components), in a variety of modes that reflect different levels of evolution of consciousness and resulting technology with regard to the local environment. Some beings, and entire consensus realities of them, are already elsewhere in the universe, and someday will be here on Earth, capable of what could be considered feats of post-dualistic unified-field engineering as seen from the frame of reference of the consensus reality of the mostly physical-reductionist-oriented inhabitants of present-day Earth. What may be deemed paranormal or miraculous in one context may be normal in another more-inclusive one. What the field of parapsychology terms anomalous cognition, telepathy, clairvoyance or remote viewing, and pre-or retro-cognition may be the norm for how more evolved beings within a higher-dimensional, non-locally correlated experiential domain communicate and access information from their environment. What parapsychology considers to be the still-rare psychokinetic anomalous effects of mind on matter on Earth may be at the heart of how beings interact with and effect their environments by way of the ZPE in more evolved consensus realities. What parapsychology deems to be the mysterious and rare out-of-body experience on Earth may be the dominant in-subtler-body mode of movement in a higher-dimensional reality. What today's parapsychology considers to be the hypothesized non-physical afterlife realm our still conscious and experiencing essences go to after the deaths of our physical bodies on Earth may be the normal experiential realm for countless beings more advanced than we.

In this modeling, the ZPE will be portrayed as the domain with respect to which all particles (or as I will tend to call them, wavicles) comprising all current Earthly spatiotemporally contained mass and energy emerge, are maintained, and may be transmuted into one another, from heavy mass hadrons and fermions to electron and related leptons and massless light-type bosons, to superluminary tachyons and excitation pattern wavicle systems closer to pure living consciousness itself. Higher dimensionality, higher vibratory frequency, and the more mental/consciousness/spirtual character of the psychoid unified field are argued to be deeply interrelated and maintain a superordinate relation to what we think of at present as physical reality. This presentation asks: How is our species changing and learning with regard to our own birthright potential and how we relate to the ZPE, to higher-dimensionality, and to the post-dualistic unified field?

Note: The present article stems in part from (among others) the following five earlier publications by the author: "Cosmological Dissociation: Toward an Understanding of How We Create Our Own Reality," *Paranormal Research '89*: Proceedings of the 2nd International Conference on Paranormal Research, Colorado State University, Fort Collins, CO, June 1989; "Overcoming Cosmological Dissociation, *1989 Annual Conference Proceedings of the U.S.P.A.*; "Toward a Universal Grammar," *1996 Annual Conference Proceedings of the U.S.P.A.*; "The Role of Consciousness in Emerging New Paradigm Science: Toward an Idealist Paraphysics," *2000 Annual Conference Proceedings of the U.S.P.A.*; "Otherworldly and Interdimensional Realities," *UFO: The Science and Phenomena Magazine*, June/July 2001, Vol. 16, No. 3.

What is the Zero-Point Energy (ZPE) Vacuum?

As an extraordinarily energetic latter-day all-pervading all-constituting ether, the seething creational cauldron of quantum potential, of random self-cancelling stochastic energy of the electromagnetic field in the vacuum averages to zero over long periods, but fluctuates wildly on very short time scales. It fluctuates with the presence of virtual photons and the creation and annihilation of electron-positron pairs out of and back into what has been called the "Dirac sea" surface of the ZPE. The ZPE (also termed the ZPF, or zero-point frequency) exists in a vacuum, in which all know extant particles and forces have been extracted, and even at absolute zero temperature this vacuum is homogenous, isotropic, and Lorentz transformation invariant. Calculations show that there is virtually infinite energy in each cubic centimeter of this vacuum; but, due to the extremely varied fluctuations and wave-cancelling negative interference of resonant frequencies of the oscillations within this ZPF field, and due to the continuous changes in energy state of particles, and of particles moving from actual to virtual states and back again within a minute Planck's constant interval, according to Heisenberg's uncertainty principle, there is very little to detect or measure, let alone to access or manipulate. Yet what a ground of being—at least of physical-level being— it is! It is comprised of endless quantum-level virtual states transforming into locally objectively real states and back again; ground states moving into excited states and back; potential energy states into kinetic ones and back. The ZPE energy is being constantly absorbed and emitted by local wavicle matter and energy excitations in an endless dance of the ZPE appearing to be the womb, preserver-sustainer, and destroyer (dissolver and absorber) of all components that make up what we know as locally real, as it makes up the underlying ground for all that can possibly locally exist and be objectively real.

Let us try to get a better sense of this ZPE. Under emptied, laboratory-controlled ZPE conditions, the space or cavity between two electrically neutral close-together metal plates introduces an anistrophy of the ZPE, with certain ZPF resonant modes being excluded in the cavity but not outside of it, with less wavicle excitations between than outside, resulting in more pressure from the ZPE being exerted against the outside of the plates than between them, giving rise to a force attracting them together, which is known as the "Casimir" effect or force. At the same time, there is an interaction of the underlying ZPE with the proton-and-neutron-constituting quarks and the electron-type leptons, together comprising what we know as matter, giving rise to the changes in resonance and a "zitterbewegung," or vibrating, buffeting, buzzing jitter, in a quantum-level micro-version of the more-macro-level Brownian movement arising from minute particles knocked around randomly by the movement of neighboring air molecules. As a result, changes in mass result from changes in the amount of energy involved in the ZPE-quark interactions brought about by changes in resonance.

Any symmetrical or spin movement of a homogenous portion and aspect of the ether field upon itself gives rise to inertia and hence mass. Simple rotation, revolution, or spin about an axis is one such endophasic, intrinsic, intra-field motion. More complex movement gives rise to the basal building blocks of orbital paths, curved vectors and geodesics, vortices, toruses, and plasmoids. Theosophy's heart-shaped many-layered "fundamental atom," the "anu," is a still-more-complex recursive flow system of basal substance on itself . Other physical or mathematical self-contained forms may also be related, such as solitons, twistors, flexors, torsion fields, et al. All could be seen as potentially local inertia and mass generating wavicle systems of contained excitation (and/or quiescence) out of a process of a kind of cosmological "incestuous intercourse" within the basal ground, such as the ether or ZPE in motional self-interaction. As surface waves modulated out of their carrier background, as in-turning centripetal convolutions, conscriptions, and scriptings of local form writ out of the undifferentiated underlying waters. Chladni and Jenny vibratory excitation patterns created by the most-manifest node points of standing wave systems out of the same underlying waters are another version of this process. All inward turnings of the underlying fully open, unconstrained, and radiant pure creational field are responsible for all local existents, forms, patterns, and manifestations, and, more densely, for all inertial, mass, and matter systems which we currently deem necessary prerequisites for being objectively real. Then, there is spin-spin and other isomorphic relations among such internal flow forms of the basal ether operating co-extensively within its different carrier-wave-like differentiated strata, and across such strata, operating by harmonic resonance coupling relations as well as by the ubiquitous non-local correlatedness always the case with respect to the relations among all creational sibling offspring of the common quantum ZPE field.

Recently, Haisch , Rueda, and Puthoff have made a case for how inertia, mass, and even gravity, stem from the effect of the background ZPE, due to the kinetic energy that fluctuations in the ZPF induce on the quarks and electrons comprising matter. Also, the changes in oscillation of matter particles effect the adjacent virtual particles of the ZPE which in turn influence the matter particles. The rest mass of an otherwise massless particle would then come from interaction and energetic exchange with the vacuum. Any accelerated motion through the zero-point field of the quantum vacuum would therefore result in a reaction force, with mass and inertia being a kind of electromagnetic drag force. And, due to relativity theory's equivalence principle between inertia and gravity, gravity could also be seen to arise from this interaction of matter systems with the ZPE. The subcomponents of any mass-possessing frame of reference on a Poynting vector accelerating with respect to the quantum vacuum will generate interactive friction with the local "Planck oscillators" of the vacuum and will create a "Rindler flux," asymmetrically scattering them in a bath of radiation known as the "Unruh effect," and will experience radiation coming at them from in front and providing a retarding force against their accelerated motion proportional to the acceleration and creating what we know as inertial mass for that system moving with respect to the ZPE. Also, since Einstein pointed out that light follows curved space-time geodesics in the presence of matter, objects within a gravitational field will experience a similar flux and asymmetric behavior.

Stable electron lepton and proton-and-neutron-comprising quark elementary particles, and the massless energetic messenger boson (photon, gluon, graviton, Higgs, and other) "gauge" particles mediating their interactions, are all seen as local excitations, standing wave systems, or wave packets, arising out of, being sustained by, and interacting back with the background quantum ZPE field. These fluctuations of the quantum vacuum field are irregular, but are averaged out using quantum field theory. The interaction of electrons with photons are studied by quantum electrodynamics, and gluon/quark interactions studied by quantum chromodynamics. One theory for how massless particles acquire mass, or how immaterial substance becomes material, is a form of what in grand unified theory (GUT) is called spontaneous "symmetry breaking" of the vacuum. As a result, hypothesized "Higgs bosons" are said to arise in the ZPE and cluster around matter particles creating the "color field" force of gluons binding quarks and giving rise to the property of mass out of lepton-quark and boson source force fields. The summation of the energy density of this entire quantum vacuum is called the "cosmological constant."

Also, the nature of local particle or wavicle systems arising from and maintained within the quantum field ZPE, due to their common quantum ZPE origin, are in a state of quantum entangled superposition and coherence such that all probabilistic states of such particles are simultaneously coexisting until a conscious observation or measurement collapses the wave function representing those states (except in Everett's Many-World's theory of quantum mechanics), which renders decoherent the formally quantum-coherent state, creating a single concretized, singularized version that can be experienced and measured as objectively real. Part of this picture includes what is called nonlocality, meaning that there is a now empirically proven nonlocal correlation found to exist between individual wave systems sharing a common quantum system of origin. Nonlocality means that there is an instantaneous causal or measurement relation between any two such systems no matter how spatially separated. This appears to violate the Einsteinian limit that the fastest correlating, causal, or informational linkage between any two physically real systems must be limited to speed-of-light signal propagation. Nonlocality is another way of looking at the essentially non-separated nature of components within the quantum field, including the ZPE. For example, the geometrodynamic shaping of the space-time metric through controlled quantum action at a distance would be possible through nonlocality. Also, if information could be modulated on one of a set of quantum entangled nonlocally correlated systems, that information would be instantly available anywhere else in the set if it could be successfully demodulated and decoded.

Selected Currently Understood and Hypothesized Modes of Interaction with the ZPE

Some of the modes to be described here are as yet only theoretical, but are generally receiving increasing acceptance in the mainstream physics community, while a few modes to follow have actually been successfully applied. Probably the best known mode is the ability to be able to engineer the ZPE through the earlier-mentioned Casimir effect by placing two uncharged metal plates very close together so that the subtle pressure of the background ZPE on the outsides of the plates is greater than on the insides. This gives rise to an exceedingly subtle force, seen either as a pushing pressure against the outsides of the plates or as an attractive force between them. Currently this force is too weak to work with in any realistic engineering way, but its proven existence may someday be usable. For example, very small, perhaps nanotechnology-scale objects, including curved ones, in sufficiently close proximity to each other could experience the Casimir effect and be spun in a kind of generator-type energy-creating, or cohering, polarizing manner. Cavity quantum electrodynamics is another somewhat related way of working with the ZPE. A small enough cavity can suppress the natural inclination of the ZPE, getting the trapped excited particles to give up some of their energy as they drop to a lower energy state, as the cavity partially controls the ZPE vacuum fluctuations and allows a tapping of the change-of-energy-state emissions. Also, the Casimir effect, by attesting to the existence of the ZPE, makes a strong case for resurrecting the concept of an all-pervading underlying "ether" that earlier was supposedly disproven by the Michaelson-Morley experiment. Working both theoretically and empirically with a real ether, banished for the past 100 years, may prove revolutionary in our understanding of the universe and our place within it. So, the ZPE can now be accepted as a real, Lorentz-transformation-invariant ether capable of exerting pressuring or attractive force on the matter-possessing objects arising from and sustained within it, by means of the Casimir effect, and within which any accelerating body with respect to it requires properties of mass, inertia, and gravity as a function of asymmetrical interaction with it. The question then becomes how to interact with the ZPE in order to interact in turn with the matter and energy systems that have and maintain their existence in interaction with that ZPE?

Miguel Alcubierre's hypothesized "warp drive" starship propulsion system is one of many examples of trying to engineer the ZPE and its additional relatively-theory-based geometrodynamic gravity-space/time relations. From Alcubierre's metric engineering perspective, the region directly in front of a ship could hypothetically be contracted, while the region behind could be expanded, propelling the ship in a weightless geodesic path through space-time. The fabric of space-time would push the ship away from its origin and pull it toward its destination in a kind of relativistic geodesic version of the ZPE's push-attraction Casimir force. This is a subtler variation of the hypothesized engineering tactic of generating a cosmological black-hole-out-into-a-white-hole-type wormhole that could join our location within four-space (three spatial and one temporal) dimensionality with another location within it or joining our location in 4-space with a location in a higher-dimension, allowing for shortcut hyperspatial leaps out of and back into the constraint system of our known space-time reality. If, as Haisch, Puthoff, and Rueda postulate, mass, inertia, and gravity all stem from the Unruh radiation and Riddler flux frictions and drag relations of the interaction of material systems generated from the background ZPE and interacting as accelerating frames of reference back with respect to it, then there may be related modes of working with the ZPE that might be able to manipulate and reduce, or cancel entirely, the properties of mass and inertia, and the presence of and relation to gravity for the matter particles comprising a spaceship and its passengers, for example.

Current GUTs work with anywhere from six to dozens more dimensions than the four currently familiar to us (our 4-space). Those higher dimensions lie somehow within, by way of, or through and beyond the extraordinarily dense, opaque seething plenum potentiality of the ZPE. These higher dimensions tend to be depicted as being incredibly compacted, curled up into domains smaller than the less-than-atom's-diameter Planck length where our usual understandings of space, time, and causality break down entirely. Essentially, with higher dimensions come higher degrees of freedom. An inhabitant of a higher-dimensional world than ours would be able to do more within his world that we can within ours, and he would be able to know more about and do more within our world than we can. As pointed out by physicist Michio Kaku in his book *Hyperspace*, "The laws of physics appear single and unified in higher dimensions." Edwin Abbott's 1884 novel, *Flatland: A Romance of Many Dimensions by a Square*, has long been helpful for speculating on higher dimensional reality in relation to ours. For example, a sphere slowly moving through two-dimensional flatland is experienced by the flatland inhabitants as a slowly expanding and then contracting circle, beginning and ending with a point. How can the person in Flatland know that the four separate circles he sees before him are actually the four legs of a three-dimensional creature standing in Flatland? In that next higher dimension, what was locally separated in Flatland is joined as part of a single coherent body. In this sense, lower dimensional domains in relation to adjacent higher-dimensional ones may serve as projection systems, with the lower dimensional world comprised of shadows cast, as in the parable of Plato's cave. We in our relative three-dimensional flatland, related to the experience of the shadow projections on the wall, are as yet developmentally unable to turn around and see the higher-dimensional cave with people moving freely around the fire carrying objects and what we can know of them only by way of their lower-dimensional shadow aspects. The question then remains for us: if there are higher dimensions within or beyond the ZPE, what goes on within them and what relationship, if any, do they have to what is going on within our lower-dimensional world and its physical reality environment ongoingly riding the womb of the underlying ZPE? Some reported extraterrestrials have been said to move freely through homeland higher dimensions and to project at will into our lower-dimensional world so that we can experience them and their ships alongside the other shadow-level objects and events available to our current consciousness and environmental dimensionality: Abbott's Lord Sphere as ET visiting our Flatland. Then what is objectively real, and to whom, and what is only imagined or dreamt? "I see them coming through the solid wall of the bedroom," reports the abductee. "They are now levitating me up and I pass right through the ceiling, with their reassurances telepathically resounding in my head."

Also interesting to note is the equivalence relationship long intuited to exist among velocity, vibrational frequency, and dimensionality. Physicists today tend not to include frequency vibration in their multidimensional formulations; but Tesla-era early-20th-century physics and more-recent perennial philosophy and New Age literature, with its channeled and ET experiencer messages and insights, is filled with references to how frequency is the key to cross-dimensional relations, and of how processes within, or more likely beyond, the ZPE effect the local physical systems arising from it. One way to consider frequency is as the measurement of how many moving waveforms pass a fixed point in a given amount of time. One can put an enormous number of vibrations in a very small space and time. There could be an informationally rich world, even an experienceable world, residing in regions smaller than the Planck length, if basic frequencies of the carrier being modulated were high or fine enough. There may be a relationship between velocity with respect to a point of measure and frequency. For example, there has always been speculation about how ETs, or us someday, need to be able to break through the barrier of the speed of light for our mass-possessing bodies and vehicles to be able to bridge the light years of distance. Once they have broken through, they are probably operating within a superluminary or hyperspatial domain. Maybe then, the particles comprising their bodies and ships have been turned into tachyons (superluminary or hyperspatial wavicles); or, in reverse, perhaps they originally have evolved to be made out of such stuff and have developed the post-dualistic unified-field technology to phase or state shift the macro aggregate system of particles/wavicles to enter and be co-extensive for a time with our level of reality made out of mass-possessing quarks or near-massless leptons and massless bosons.

Supersymmetry and Symmetry Breaking

This brings us to what is called supersymmetry, which is broken by the strong dynamics of gauge (mediating force particle)

13927-VALO

theory, with supersymmetry relating, and theoretically allowing transformations across, particles of different spins. Supersymmetry needs a balance of massless light-force bosons and mass-possessing fermions, which can be invariant under exchange for the two into each other. For example, quarks (three of which comprise each of the protons and neutrons in the atomic nuclei of matter) and leptons (comprising electrons, neutrinos, and other small mass, 1/2 spin wavicles incapable of strong, nuclear interactions) can transform into each other by the exchange of gauge bosons (massless force-mediating wavicles); and different kinds of quarks, such as "up" and "down" ones, can transform into each other through charged-current weak interactions mediated by a somewhat different kind of gauge boson (called W), which can potentially thereby change the fundamental nuclear nature of the mass-possessing world. The question then is: who or what can purposefully control and manipulate such systems of gauge bosons so as to alchemically work with physical reality in a more direct reality-creation way? What is the mechanism of coupling interaction with respect to gauge bosons to control them? Simply other coextensive, same ontological-level bosons? Or could they be potentially directly controlled by wavicle fields of ether excitation superordinate with respect to them that we would tend to currently construe as being coextensive with and nonlocally coupled to a consciousness field characterized by such qualities, and possibly causal energies, of thought, ideation, desire, belief, intention, expectation, et al? I believe so.

The gauge principle allows change of phase of quantum-mechanical wave functions or quantum fields locally. Such modern-day GUT transmutational alchemies depict spontaneous symmetry and local symmetry breaking processes that can generate massless bosonic field oscillations out of the quantum vacuum, which in turn could be symmetry broken to generate fermionic mass-possessing field oscillations or wave systems, in a kind of local physical-reality-creation out of the ZPE. Then, more speculatively, further symmetry breaking might, in reverse, generate hyperspatial superluminary tachyons out of bosons, and perhaps even oscillating wave packet systems beyond tachyons more in the region of a pure consciousness realm comprising things such as "thoughtforms." In cross-dimensional trans-octave harmonic, cascading, downstepping, entraining relations, such thoughtforms may give rise to their counterparts in lower-frequency, yet still higher-dimensional, vibratory form, which, in turn, give rise to "light body" bosonic versions, which, in turn, give rise to mass-possessing fermionic wave systems. Then, the reverse process could be conducted, moving from extremely physical to extremely mental/consciousness appearing versions of whatever localized, individualized informational, organizational pattern, template, signature, or identity print. But what might then account for such transmutations, translations, or transformations from one kind of a relatively objectified and localized wave system to another? It might be that we change the orientation of the particle-like individual waveforms with respect to a dimension higher than the one in which they exist. Changing orientation, spin state, rotation, frequency or velocity, hydrodynamics of the flow patterns comprising an individual complex waveform, changing chiraltry or handedness of orientation or flow, or changing the scalar or vectoral relation of local dimensional system with respect to a higher, subsuming, embedding constituting frame of reference, all could be ways of looking at how manipulation of ZPE-based components can occur. Generating or changing symmetry fields moving on themselves in charge-generating asymmetric flows and flows between fields in the ether that constitute charge is another mode. All of these modes of interaction presuppose superordinate dimensions, forces, and wave systems capable of effecting and manipulating lower-dimensional and more constrained wave systems. Implied in these speculations is that processes construed as originating ontologically more on the consciousness end of a post-Cartesian unified field monist spectrum would exercise a non-locally correlated, probably directly causal, relation to processes existing more on what would be traditionally construed as the physicalist objectively real end of that same psychoid spectrum.

Superstring Theory

In contrast to supersymmetry theory, superstring theory sees the underlying ground state riding and moving in and out of existence on the surface of the ZPE giving rise to an infinite number of infinitesimal-length mathematical strings that vibrate according to discrete resonances. Combinations of such vibrations then give rise to all the mass and energy particles responsible for our level of reality, with the higher the frequency, the more massive the particles. Superstring theory can in turn be extended into what is called "d-brane theory" where strings are seen as connected to "world sheets" and hyperspatial membrane-like "branes." The presence of open strings attached to d-branes gives rise to gauge fields living on the brane. What is called a Higgs field breaks the vacuum symmetry, which corresponds to separating the branes, and higher dimensional objects are comprised of such branes to which are attached the variously vibrating strings comprising matter and force wavicle systems. Pure energy force mediating bosons are depicted as closed loops of superstring that do not and cannot attach to such branes. Only recently have string excitations and extra dimensions been brought out of hiding from the incalculably tiny and short Planck domain. All gauge (mediating force) and matter fields in such latest thinking inhabit the inside of 10-dimensional hyperplanes.

As an aside, we can ask: Do our reported extraterrestrial visitors now—or will we in the future—see things in such a GUT-type engineerable way? Do the strings on their level of reality simply vibrate at a different, much-higher octave than ours do? Have they found a way to raise or lower the superstring frequencies responsible for their bodies and ships so that they can move at will between the higher octave carrier wave their reality is modulated within and the one ours is modulated within? Can they simultaneously phase shift the open string brane-attached superstrings of their more-fermionic more-matter-type local systems into closed-loop more-light-type bosonic ones not attached to such branes, to free the internally consistent variegated aggregate of their string frequencies and interrelations from local quantumly decoherent constrained frames of reference, activity, and manifestation? Have they learned to carry out transubstantiations with respect to the ZPE, and of the ZPE extended and embedded in a more consciousness-characterized underlying potentiality that all beings are given to work with, so that they can turn mass-possessing quarks and fermions into leptons and bosons of the essential light, and then translate such in turn into superluminary tachyons, and on even higher? A true post-Cartesian monist unified field technology probably will involve such conversion abilities whereby what we have thought of as mind and its ilk, as creator mode, is more nonlocally entangled and coherently superposed and at one with the negotiable artist's clay of creation and its underlying ground of being.

Superconductivity

Creating quantum isolation in a system sufficient for quantum entanglement, superposition, coherence, and non-locality to occur within it can lead to a variety of desirable results and uses. However, the wave function representing any system will automatically be collapsed not only by any intervention of conscious observation or measurement, but also by macro-level near-enough ambient decoherence environmental effects on it. That is, the presence of nearby physical systems, already wave collapsed to their currently focused states, can collapse the quantum wave function for a neighboring system just as much as the more-familiar process of this version can occur from observation or measurement. Even an atom or photon colliding with another can constitute a wave-collapsing act of measurement, collapsing the superposition of quantum mechanical states into one objectified, delimited and constrained, experienceable state. To get the benefits of using a maintainable isolated macro-level quantum coherent system is not so easy therefore, but it is already being explored in the development of quantum computers. Such quantum computers must be separated from their surroundings to maintain quantum coherence. Magnetic fields can trap and cool charged particles into pure quantum states for use as computing q-bits. A thimbleful of liquid brought to the right isolated coherency conditions could be used for quantum computation, programming initial conditions and conducting logic operations on the quantum entangled superpositions to get the result.

So, superconductivity and superfluids are potentially very useful ways of cohering or polarizing local portions of the ZPE vacuum. Superconducting systems offer no resistance to current flow, and although it was once thought to be possible to attain only at very stilled, near-absolute-zero temperature conditions, there is now evidence that superconductivity is possible in high-temperature systems, including living biological systems such as the human brain. In this regard, we may discover that the experienced qualities of our own subjective consciousness is associated with conditions sufficiently coherent to allow a superposed sensation of flowing and changing possibility structures accounting for the rather vaguely experienced only partially quantumly decohered contents and objects of our ideation, mentation, intention, imaging, desiring, et al. Superconductors and superfuids possess giant quantum wavefunctions allowing their separate subcomponents to be quantum entangled, superposed, nonlocally correlated and acting essentially as a single entity, rather than myriad separte micro-level entities each with its own quantum wave function. The so-called Bose-Einstein condensate is another example. And there are a number of other attempts to engineer with superconductivity, only one of which is now being able to partially levitate heavy trains. Also, certain gravity shielding experiments have been done, placing small weights on very sensitive strain gauges with rapidly rotating super conducting ceramic disks underneath which are capable of levitation because of the superconducting "Meisner effect."

The "Scalar" Domain

As Tom Bearden has pointed out, when Oliver Heaviside tried to simplify and make more-wieldy Maxwell's original, demanding electromagnetic "quaternion" equations, he deleted the complex-number scalar part, leaving only the vectoral components. Thereafter, for a long time researchers tended to ignore the possibility of there being standing and longitudinal scalar stress waves with respect to the ether or to what could be approximately conceptualized as the—or a—membrane of the ZPE, and clearly related to relativity theory's view of how "flat" space-time can become geodesically deformed, curved, or locally convoluted inward upon itself. E.T. Whittaker, Bearden and others have theorized about how to work with the ZPE using scalar engineering. For example, it has been found that "bucking" or "zero-summing" two rhythmically varied traditional vectoral, transverse Hertzian electromagnetic wave sets that are 180 degrees out of phase with each other will cause negative wave interference cancellation, leading to no remaining electromagnetic energy/force; but in the process scalar waves or potentials are induced with respect to the ether of the ZPE. Perhaps even more interestingly, conversely, superimposing and interfering such scalar potentials can in turn generate vectoral fields. That is, vectoral EM waves can be replaced by scalar interferometry and EM waves can be used to produce standing wave force potentials. In this way, manipulation can translate into and out of the ether ZPE background with respect to the local space-time vectoral/Hertzian EM energy domain we normally operate within. This is now a proven process for manipulating local available vectoral forces to reach up into, couple and work with, the locally underlying ether ZPE to generate causal forces to bring back into our own familiar experiential regions, which themselves are locally generated and sustained by that same ether ZPE, and by what, I believe, lies superordinately beyond the ZPE, in turn. In addition, what Bearden calls "Whittaker" structures or potentials are conjectured to be two-way, bidirectional, harmonic pulsed vectoral EM wave sets wave-interfered into rhythmic force-field-free standing-wave potential or scalar systems that can then be worked with back in relation to the vectoral fields of our local reality. Such "Whittaker structuring" of the ZPE vacuum potential thus structures the vacuum's virtual particle flux exchange with local-reality matter systems and this process can be purposefully engineered as well.

In such thinking there is a more-varied relationship between our local space-time matter-energy domain and a transcendent adjacent region giving rise to and maintaining or changing it. Bearden and others speak of a process of hyperspatial cross-dimension "cross-talk" energetic local virtual photon flux that flows rotatingly, spinningly, in and out between the quark/nucleon wavicles of our local domain and related hyperspace dimensionalities by way of, or through and beyond, the ZPE. Each wavicle in our local region, riding and fed by the underlying ZPE, experiences an "orthorotational" flow-through between itself and the creational ground. Nuclear wavicles stemming from the ZPE can then be "pumped" via their derivative relation to the potentials of that ground. Also, there are nesting virtual levels within the vacuum that can be structured and, in turn, accessed. There is a tuning relation between ground and local configurations that maintains—and is capable of being worked with to change—discrete wavicle forms in our local space-time region. Potentials within the ZPE can cohere or constructively interfere to breach the quantum threshold, moving from a virtual to a locally objectively real state. This breaching is another perspective on moving from quantum coherence to delimited, constrained, and localized decoherence, from a state of quantum entangled superposed co-existence of many probablistic states at once to a focused, finite local manifestation. It is also a re-framing of the traditional notion of the process of "collapsing the wave function," that represents the underlying probability distribution, by an intervention of consciousness, an observation, a measurement, or even the effect of nearby already-decoherent, seemingly already collapsed, existents.

In addition, a time-reversal and back-tracking, mirroring "phase conjugate" relation is hypothesized to exist with regard to mass-possessing (fermion, hadron, and some lepton) wavicles that emit and absorb photons with other such locally reality occupying wavicles and that emit and absorb virtual-photons with the underlying ZPE vacuum. A nonlinear material may emits a photon signal and can also emit a phase conjugate replica of the photon it absorbed through reflection back from its own signal emission. This conjugate process involves signaling waves and their reflections, time reversal signaling, 180-degree-out-of-phase relationships, and being in or out of phase relation with the underlying time flow. A phase conjugate replica wave can be in-phase spatially with a signal wave, but 180 degrees out of phase with the underlying time flow, and a usual vectoral force wave gets translated into a scalar stress wave on the time flow parameter. This gives rise to a variety of kinds of electrogravitational, spacetime geodesic curving, and related GUT-type engineerable relationships. Bearden points to the former Soviet Union having learned to engineer such phase conjugate relationships, along with being able to interferometrically add and manipulate both EM fields on our physical-reality level and scalar ones in the vacuum so as to program the ZPE and then target cascadingly downstepped collapsed quantumly decohered potential systems into actual locally real ones, though unfortunately usually done by the Soviets only for weapon-creation purposes. But one can see the potential positive uses of such ZPE engineering tactics.

Nikola Tesla was certainly the father of this realm of thinking and doing. Much earlier, he conceptualized similar engineerable systems that could tap and download local vectoral, usable force field energies from potential, scalar, longitudinal, standing-wave, or hyperspatial states or realms. More recently, James Wheeler and Richard Feynman conjectured about "advanced waves" that can propagate backward in time from their own future absorption point to their past emission, and how consciousness may operate backward in time by effecting photons and other wavicles that will act in the past—which could be construed as one's own present at the time one thinks about this—as a function of the future choice made by that same conscious observer. So we can add this rather mind-bending thought experiment to the rest of our "mirror" and "phase conjugate" type thinking. Still more recently, W. Schemp, Edgar Mitchell, and others, have developed a sub-field called "quantum holography," where the experiencing observer is pictured to be in "phase-conjugate-adaptive-resonance," or "PCAR," with the object he is observing within the quantum hologram. Such resonance requires a virtual path that is mathematically equal but opposite to the incoming sensory information about the object being perceived, with the phase conjugate reversal mirroring path of perception flow going from the object to the observer and the attentional/intentional flow going from the observer to the object.

Recently, biologist Glen Rein has taken this scalar context and successfully brought it to bear experimentally on living systems, showing the efficacy of laboratory-generated scalar systems on local standing and vectoral wave force fields comprising targeted biological systems. Rein does his Whittaker-type structuring of the ZPE vacuum by zero-sum bucking rhythmically pulsed normal EM waves nearly 180 degrees out of phase with each other through using a helical "caduceus coil" electrical wire-winding system, and then under controlled conditions exposing biological systems to the result and noting the changes that occur that are not attributable to any other forces. Again, it is conjectured that in such processes, the tuned balanced destructive wave interference in turn generates ether/ZPE stress standing scalar potential waves that can be manipulated to interact back with our EM vectoral level of energies and constituted structurings of such out of the vacuum ground. Or, we can talk in terms of higher-dimensional quantum-conceptualized subtle or potential fields residing within, or by way of, through, and transcending the ZPE vacuum, in superordinate relation to forces, wavicles, and fields comprising our physical-level reality. Created scalar quantum systems that can interact with EM ones, can interact, in turn, with what Rein and so many others today refer to as "biofields," or "bio-energy fields"— the subtle or pre-or trans-physical organizational fields that are responsible for the structure and function of living systems. Change the quantum/scalar superordinate system and you change the system based on it stemming from the ZPE that, in turn, effects the biofields similarly originating, and thereby you can maintain or change living, and for that matter non-living, systems. Healthy structure and function is a probably God-or at least "Nature"-given tuning relation between the ZPE and the local system, from the platonic or "thoughtform" higher-dimensional ideal that can be cascadingly downstepped or resonantly cross-harmonically attuned to move orthoginally through the ZPE and into our local space-time matter-energy domain drawn from and based on such superordinate systems. Hopefully we are in a state of normally being resonantly entrained to be, in phase with, coherent, aligned, and attuned with respect to the natural or "God-given" optimum functioning health-providing informational patterns or organizational fields responsible for organisms on our physical-level reality. But when we fall out of such alignment with respect to certain aspects of healthy structure and function, it would be good to be able to trace back up the aforementioned causal or correlated chain to a point where, top-down, change could be engineered with respect to the living system to bring it back into alignment. Virtually all alternative approaches to biomedicine, healing, and wellness maintenance today use some version of this process either directly or indirectly, with the developmental paradigm-shifting flow moving toward ever more direct versions.

The "Fallacy of Misplaced Locus"

Finally, before leaving this area of considering some selected existing and hypothesized modes of interacting with and engineering the ZPE vacuum, I want to make an observation that may also provide a segue to the remainder of this paper. It involves what I call "the fallacy of misplaced locus." That is, we are putting the eye on the ball of, and as, where the action is because we are used to looking at ball-like things with our usual ball-based eyes and thinking; but what might be a more direct and veridical view? There is a strong disposition or conditioning, even in much forward-edge new-paradigm, as well as more-mainstream post-classical quantum physics, thinking to still retain a physical-reductionist-type Newtonian causal "billiard ball" approach to construing reality. For example, gauge theory and related GUT thinking seem to need to picture virtual particles being emitted and absorbed by other particles in locally linear vectoral mapping connectivity paths in a busy and ubiquitous swap-meet process of exchanging particles. Each of the four known forces needs to have its own respective "gauge particle" to run back and forth, being emitted and absorbed, mediating the respective electromagnetic, strong nuclear, weak radioactive decay, or gravitational force with respect to the other systems they are respectively coupled with and effect. All force needs to be quantized into such "force carrying" particles. Also objectively real mass-possessing particle-wavicles seem to need to be pictured as experiencing constant interactive exchange of "virtual photons" or virtual wavicles. That is the nature of the quantum world, I suppose: to quantize, quantify, pin down, and trace everything into discrete, discontinuous bits or particles (or at least wave packets or "wavicles") that then interact with each other in mini atomic billiard-ball-type depictions, including "spooky" at-a-distance" versions where we picture two separated particles (in the manner of the Einstein-Podolosky-Rosenberg/Bell/Aspect modeling) that are nonlocally correlated and coherently quantum entangled though still thought of as separate. The anchoring, delimiting, focusing, reifying disposition stolidly maintains itself, localizing process and event, choosing the particle rather than the spread-out diffuse not-as-easily-localizable and identifiable wave version that may scare us and seem to be impossible to live with unless one lives within, or from, a place (an ontological locus) that is itself in a non-focused uncollapsed, relatively all-containing, quantum superposed coherent entangled ubiquitously nonlocally correlated at-one-ment unity state. Pilot waves, quantum waves, quantum potentials, vector potentials, magnetic vector potentials, and related hypothesized billiard balls or manipulatable local fields of force, or at least informational or probablistic influence are pictured to nudge, push, steer, guide, dispose, delimit, inform, or in other ways causally or a-causally influence, or even constitute, all real-world building-block particles or wavicles. Why the need for this doppleganger twin relationship? Why the need for this one-to-one bit-to-bit "big brother" type shepherding of real-world local micro systems by hypothesized systems one or more hyperspatial or ontological removes from them? Fallaciously, the locus of control, responsibility, and causality, is placed in such hypothesized quantized billiard-ball pairings.

Another version of what I'm calling this fallacy of misplaced locus can be found in some of the late Marcel Vogel's work, which can also be used to represent a number of other new-paradigm thinkers' modeling before and after him. Vogel would say that he intentionally would put information from his own system into a quartz crystal. He would then see the crystal lattice structure of the quartz as being modified and modulated by what he put into it, such as by causing or modifying the subtler higher-harmonics of phonons or other oscillating systems already indigenous to the lattice structure. Thus the crystal had been causally transformed and informed by what he put into it. Then he would, say, circulate water around the crystal and then see the water as having causally or in other ways by contiguous association taken on the information that had earlier been in the lattice and before that had been in and of himself. Next he would look at the tetrahedral lattice structure of the water molecules and see the water as having been structured or informed as part of this increasingly passed-on causal chain. Then he would treat a human subject with the water and see this as a process of the informed, structured condition of the water effecting and structuring/informing the water-based person or in other way effecting his/her system. The misplacing of locus here, for me, is tracing the locus of causal action, the local placing of effective information and structure variously in himself, the crystal, the water, the client, et al. The information, for example, was seen as being in the piece of quartz, not as always or only in his own consciousness, or by way of his own mind nonlocally correlated with and quantum coherently entangled and superposed with a larger, less constrained, more inclusive, and more knowing and containing consciousness. What if the true locus of all was in such a place, consciousness, or being? Endless little pilot waves (et al) matched up with having to steer endless little real-world wavicles, or mad-scientist movements of globs of information, invariant local structure, or configured local causal force fields from one receptacle to another like a stage magician and his hidden rabbit, once more, for me at least, continues a kind of antiquated Newtonian causal chain way of thinking.

But what, then, would be a possible alternative view that would not be, in my terms, fallacious? To answer this, we must move to the rest of this paper. But, suffice it for now to say that, in what I call a post-Cartesian unified-field idealist-monist view, everything may be embedded in the one underlying unity state of one Universal Being and we and all we can interact with, work with, think with, think about, and experience, is part of a single continuous, living nesting self-creating, maintaining and changing infinite unity system of ideas in the mind of God, to cite the philosopher George Berkeley. So, for example, Vogel's passing on the locus of causal focus across different things "out there" in the world is a function of his frame of reference only. It is actually occurring simultaneously "in here," within an extraordinarily higher-dimensional universal Mind/Being and is being tracked, localized, quantified, quantized, tracked pulled apart and mapped back together solely as a function of how we causal, consciousness subsets of that Universal operate with respect to its own larger being grounds and creative self-possibilities. I will try to spell out this perspective in a little more detail in the remainder of this paper.

The Need to Add Consciousness for Any Truly Efficacious GUT ZPE Manipulation

Current science has three presuppositions that make it difficult to accept the reports and claims of ufology, for example:

1) nothing possessing mass can ever reach the speed of light;
2) nothing, not even light, can go faster than that; and
3) it would take a prohibitively huge amount of energy—such as existed in the first few seconds of the hypothesized big bang origin of the universe before the initial "singularity" that was all there was, spread and cooled—in order to alchemically engineer at will state and phase shifts of wave system subcomponents out of the ZPE so that they could transform into one another across the mass macro-level aggregate systems that comprise human bodies or space ships.

Yes, conceptually we can see how we may be able to change the frequency, phase, or state of constituent subcomponents by manipulating local symmetry breaking, changes in resonance of the underlying superstring raw material of local creation, engineering transductions and translations across local wavicle characteristics out of and upheld by an underlying ZPE, and any number of other related approaches; but we have not reached a true post-Cartesian unified field understanding and technology until we have brought in the other half of the traditional Cartesian, dualistic, equation: the realm of what we have traditionally termed the inner, the subjective, mind, consciousness, intention, etc., even, dare we, say it, spirit.

Quantum physicist David Bohm was unusual in his attempt to picture the universe as being comprised of an underlying "implicate order" (and nesting "super-implicate" orders within that) that gives rise to an "explicate order." This implicate order lies outside of all time and dimensionality and is the grounds not only for all objective realities but for all local consciousnesses that can experience such realities. Therefore, his implicate order is a non-dualistic unified-field ground of all subjective and objective being. He pictured the implicate order as a pure "frequency domain" made out of all building-block pre-spatiotemporal waveforms and their phases. This is essentially the picture of the underlying nature of the universe as being a holographic-process reality prior to any local holograms being generated by it. What he calls the explicate order is the generation of all local spatiotemporal, dimensionally constrained, mass and energy containing realities as well as the local, individuated consciousnesses to inhabit and experience them. There is also a "holomovement" process whereby explicate-order local realities can be generated out of the underlying implicate order, maintained with respect to it, and returned back into it. What are called "Fourier transforms" allow for the adding together or superimposition of simpler waveforms (which may include vortices, toroids, plasmoids, et al, of the universal ether moving with respect to itself across different velocities, vibratory frequencies, densities, temperatures, charges, viscosities, and other qualities, qualifications and quantifications of itself). Also, such Fourier transforms can break down into, or tune for, separate componential waveforms that make up any complex wave system. Bohm's system is closer to helping us find a true unified field technology because of its inclusion of consciousness along with the objects, events, and world such consciousness may experience, and by introducing, in his later work, a domain of experiential subjective meaning-making to place in working relationship with the objectively real system known to physics from which such meaning is made. But we do not really have any more of a clear idea of how explicate-order systems are created or changed from and by implicate order systems, or where the latter reside in relation to our own human intention and causal efficacy, than we do about exactly what goes on in the process of collapsing the quantum wave function, who or what collapses it, and from where that collapsing is taking place with respect to the level of local physical reality comprised of the products of such wave function collapse.

It was quantum mechanics itself in the 20th century that started this paradigm shift toward a post-dualistic unified field by pointing out that any "real" particle, or real-world aggregate of them, is really only in a virtual state of probabilities of local experienceable existence. This virtual probablistic state associated with any potentially objectively real thing is depicted in terms of the "wave function" representing it. Any observation or measurement, any decisive intervention of consciousness, to determine the local objectively real nature and properties of a thing causes what is called a "collapse" of the wave function. This is said to instantaneously replace the spread-out probability distribution of all its possibilities with a single concretized, focused, experienceable version. Quantum physics no longer allows consciousness to be left out of a unified field view; and yet it is still struggling to understand the relation between consciousness and the seemingly objectively real objects it experiences. If there is this ongoing quantum interaction between consciousness and what it is experiencing as objective and separate from itself and its kind, then there may be some kind of continuous process of collapsing the wave function responsible for maintaining, or changing, what is experienced. The psychokinesis phenomena studied by parapsychologists may involve ways of collapsing the wave function done differently than normal, giving rise to non-ordinary data and experiences. Perhaps extraterrestrials have become, and we in the future will have become, adept at changing the parameters of the process of continuous wave function collapse in order to engineer shifts in phase and state between local consciousness and its experienced environment.

We still must figure out the inter-relations among velocity, frequency, dimensionality, consciousness, and what that consciousness experiences. Is operating at a sufficiently higher frequency the same as operating within a higher dimensional system? Can you increase dimensions by increasing frequency? Can shifting the phase relationship of the constituent components of a lower dimensional system raise it into a higher dimension, by transforming fermions of mass into bosons of light into superluminary tachyons of ever higher octave until one reaches the domains of living, causal mind/consciousness itself? Recall that with higher dimensionality come higher degrees of freedom for anyone or anything operating within it. The higher the frequency of a carrier wave of energy, the more quickly and efficaciously modulations and operations may occur because of and with respect to it. But how do we increase frequency? Probably by bringing to bear superordinate forces capable of driving or resonantly entraining the system into the rarified octave of its own higher harmonics. What are the forces available to us that lie outside the box of our "four space" of three dimensions in time and of the four forces in nature we currently understand? We are going to need to examine the "inner" side of our traditional dualistic pre-unified-field perspective.

My Own Post-Cartesian Idealist-Monist Unified-Field Perspective

In closing this consideration of speculations on how to manipulate the ZPE, with its related inter-dimensional and cross-world relations, I want to briefly share my own view, which I have published elsewhere. Recall that in psychology the term "dissociation" means any experience of disconnection or lack of flow with respect to conscious awareness, cognition, information processing, or causal or motor control. The left hand doesn't know what the right is doing; someone's left hand can be taking part in automatic writing while the person is totally unaware or is doing math problems with the other hand. Within the larger consciousness field of which I am comprised, which my consciousness can access or of which I am a part, part of me is not aware of what another part of me is thinking or doing. Part of me has ideas or consciousness this moment that the part of me that is writing is nor aware of or does not have access to. I cannot access the contents of most of my own unconscious right now, but it is still there and maybe is even cooking away and effecting conscious me this moment, for all I know. I am dissociated with respect to myself in such ways. Now let us take this process or condition of dissociation to a universal level. Consider the metaphor that the Universe, or All-That-Is—creator and creatable aspects both (what I call "Absolute Spirit," based on the philosopher Hegel's thinking)— is something like a vast dissociated multiple personality, as experienced from our frames of reference as Its own sub-or alter-personalities. Because we are dissociated away from this host all-containing, all-creating all-sustaining Personality/Being, we tend to only be able to experience It as dissociated as well, as a function of our own dissociation. We experience the Many, not the One. There seems to be this presenting problem for us humans: we seem dissociated on three levels: 1) we are dissociated intrapersonally, across levels of ourselves, conscious with respect to the unconscious, mind with respect to body, et al; 2) we experience dissociation interpersonally, between ourselves and others like us, and even others not like us, and, except for occasional ESP and more familiar compassion, empathy, and love, it is difficult to make the normally impermeable membranes surrounding each of us more permeable to better share our own respective inner states and experiences with another, to be more in a kind of identical-twin identity (or ET "hive mentality") condition with each other; and, most relevant to this discussion, 3) dissociation is experienced by us with respect to the Universal, the one all-uniting, nonlocally self-correlated, self-entangled, superimposed, and coherent Being or ground of being—God, if you wish, or my Hegelian Absolute Spirit.

This metaphor of what I call a state of experienced "cosmological dissociation" gives rise to two related concepts. The Universe, or Being, is a unified field comprised of both Creator aspect and Creational grounds for all that can be created, is comprised of being both ultimate experiencer and meaning maker and of being all that can be experienced and from which all meaning can be made. This Universal Being is a living, conscious house of many mansions, the ultimate ghost infinitely and eternally imbuing, constituting, and experiencing the machinery of its own creating. This Being is filled with endless varieties of what I call relatively dissociated "cosmological sub-personalities." Each individual sub-personality, and each consensual reality comprised of sufficiently similar such sub-personalities, live with their own degrees and kinds of cosmological dissociation across those three levels just mentioned. Because we're talking about everything, in the same way Bohm was with his super-implicate order giving rise to all explicate systems of experiencers and experienceable and objective realities—all cosmological subpersonalities of the One are "psychoid" in nature, to use Jung's term: there is always some local ratio of phase relation between psychological, inner, consciousness characteristics and objectively real, external and seemingly autonomous aspects with respect to attending consciousness. So cosmological subpersonalities range across the old inner-outer, subjective-objective, mental-physical spectrum. Cosmological subpersonalities can then include physically embodied human beings on Earth; other physical-level plants and animals, and even rocks; non-physical-level human spirits who have survived bodily death; physically based extraterrestrials; non-physical-level extraterrestrials, those living in other dimensions, times, parallel universes; ascended masters, light beings, gods, and angels— all explicated variously out of the underlying super-implicate order, or, for me, Absolute Spirit, responsible for all that is or could ever be. We are all sibling beings, sons and daughters (and others) stemming from a common Creator, all of us taking our bodies, our vehicles, our daily lives and environments from the underlying ground of all Being; and the essence of the Infinite Creator in those of us with a higher consciousness-to-material ratio is the in-kind creator spirit core that uses the denser lower vibrating sheaths of body, vehicle, and local dimensional environment in which to operate and through which to experience, learn, create, and make meaning. And this includes all the ZPE-engineering possibilities mentioned earlier in this paper. So I call this first concept the presenting problem of the condition of "cosmological dissociation" that gives rise to the activities of all religion and science, and this is followed by the related concept of "cosmological sub-personalities" that arise from such dissociation.

The other related concept in this extended metaphor involves the related process of what I call "overcoming cosmological dissociation" across all three earlier-mentioned levels. For example, the more dissociation is overcome on the interpersonal level, the more telepathy and other ESP anomalous cognition and shared mental space and its contents can occur. The more dissociation is overcome between oneself as an individual cosmological subpersonality and the parental Creator-Creation underlying ground of being—only one thin stratum of which is the currently understood ZPE—the more, for example, one may engage one's individual consciousness and intention in psychokinesis-seeming activity with regard to the surrounding environment; the more one can consciously exercise causal efficacy with regard to one's surrounding in a truly local reality effecting and creating manner. As one overcomes the presenting problem of one's (and one's species') kinds and degrees of cosmological dissociation, accessing of the Universal Being's, Absolute Spirit's, omniscience, omnipotence, omnibenevolence, omnispatiality, and omnitemporality occurs until eventually one reaches, essentially, identity condition with the Universal, or God. One can only wonder how much more some of our extraterrestrial cosmological subpersonality siblings have overcome their cosmological dissociation than we have. They may have been able to engineer the ZPE to transmute mass and exceed light speed; they may have become able to move in and out of our lower-octave dimensionality and frequency domain through apparent superluminary or hyperspatial shortcuts and materialization and de-materialization processes involving post-Cartesian unified-field technologies related to adjusting particle-pair creation, engineering local symmetry breaking, changing the resonant modes of underlying superstring frequencies, or other related GUT tactics, but none yet may evolutionarily involve the direct use of superordinate, causal mind/consciousness. Or, if they have learned about and use more of this latter domain, they may have become able to pull us telepathically into their mental space where they co-dwell among themselves in their own hive mentality, having increasingly overcome their level of interpersonal cosmological dissociation; or they can create and mentally control their vehicles that are living in-kind extensions of their own psychoid level which has a higher mental-to-physical ratio than ours. And some ETs appear to overcome their cosmological dissociation, especially on the third level with regard to our common source, that they communicate to us, as contactees, abductees, and through channeling, experiences and knowledge of a much more spiritual nature. How we learn to bootstrappingly overcome our own individual and species-specific kinds and degrees of cosmological dissociation, including to be able to catch up technically to our extraterrestrial siblings, will include learning to engineer the forward-edge of present-day GUT-oriented theoretical physics approaches to working with and through the ZPE. And, eventually, I believe this will have to include opening to, accepting, and learning to control, our own local relatively dissociated consciousness fields which I believe to be superordinate and causal with respect to the fields comprising the creational ground and responsible for our local individual and consensual-reality shared experienceable reality.

The process of overcoming cosmological dissociation will also manifest in higher-order telepathic connection and at-one-ment of local mind with (in Huxley's tems) "Mind-at-Large" omniscience through dilating the reducing valve, in a mode of personally reclaiming quantum coherence out of a prior constrained, dissociated, quantum decoherent, and thermodynamically branch-systemed state, returning to experienceable and accessible states of quantum entanglement, superposition, coherence, and non-separated, non-local correlatedness. The process of overcoming cosmological dissociation will also involve higher-order psychokinesis experience as perceived causal self-efficacy transmuting and transubstantiating as a function of individual will, consciousness, and intention, for example aggregate Hamiltonian-type phase shift of states of particles/toroidal anu from fermionic/quarkian to leptonic/bosonic to tachyonic and beyond toward pure causal consciousness.

"The Hard Problem"

As I have written elsewhere (*Proceedings of the USPA Conference*, 2000), consciousness is held by the vast majority of scientists attempting to study it today as being only an emergent epiphenomenon of living brain/body. What is called "the hard problem" then becomes how the entirely physical domain of known biological matter and energy can be solely responsible for giving rise to human consciousness as we are each the case of it and experience it with awareness in all its ideational qualia (experienced qualities) so difficult to reduce to the realm of artificial-intelligence-type material and analytical relationships alone.

13927-VALO

How can something so non-physical, so Cartesianly unextended, or, conversely, so infinite-seeming in what it is capable of extending into experienceable existence out of and for itself to experience, how can this immaterial consciousness come only out of a purely material womb of non-conscious matter and energy? How can consciousness as we know it arise from pure, non-conscious physicality?

One of the most sophisticated recent attempts to address this hard problem has been conducted by scientists such as Roger Penrose, Stuart Hameroff, Jack Sarfatti, and others. They picture the locus of dualism-bridging activities lying, along with other similar-size places, in tubuline molecules only a few nanometers long, only slightly larger than the crucial Planck length. These tubulines comprise the inside walls of the hollow microtubules that lie in turn within the elongated axon portion of the body of brain neurons. These molecules, packed like corn kernels on the concave "cob" of the microtubule interior are small enough and numerous enough, millions or billions of them within each of the billions of neurons within each brain, to constitute wave-function-collapsable fire-or-not-fire binary bits, or "q-bits" in a quantum-level biocomputer. Hameroff and company then add further related concepts, such as higher dimensional configuration space, a quantum information field, quantum pilot waves, magnetic vector potentials, emergent self-organizing systems, feedback and reflection processes arising from the detection of phase changes in the interpretation of arrays of the microtubule molecules acting as phased nanoantennae, et al. The concept of computing waveform phase changes adds interferometry and the holistic notion of quantum holography to the picture as well.

But all this just sends me back to my earlier sense that the fallacy of misplaced locus is at work here once more. For, what, who, or where is it that is responsible for throwing the q-bit switches in such a quantum computer? What is the causal lineage and ontological locus of current information and intelligence that is the ghost that runs the machine? Is it totally coextensively within and operating at the level of the machine? It seems that we continue to fight the cultural and paradigm-specific disposition to always slide down the gradient toward physical reductionism capable of satisfying causal and critically analytical and quantitative parsing deep-seated programs and allegiances. Thus we can be relieved when everything can be traced back, for instance, to a ZPE that has no subjective or living, conscious, creative intelligence aspect to it other than emergent negentropic nonlinear far-from-equilibrium emergent self-organizing systems and made from the known forces, fields, and particles that can bootstrappingly be cooked up out of the ZPE alone. Even Bohm's supposedly all-containing, all-generating superimplicate order seems reducible to a simple vibratory phase-relation frequency domain. While I suppose one could revisit it and reconstrue all of its wave systems as being panpsychist or psychoid in nature, there still seems to result thereby only a disappointingly reductionist smeared-out and diffuse subjective, causal, aware, etc., presence remaining. Meanwhile, someone like me is disposed to slide down the opposite gradient toward philosophical idealism and mental monism. There the ultimate locus of explanatory power is pure living, experiencing, meaning-making consciousness itself, ultimately the one Absolute Spirit. There, once more, all physicality can be seen as being emergent epiphenomena arising from and sustained within a universal consciousness field that I admittedly conceptually extrapolate upwardly and ever more inclusively toward increasingly less-cosmologically dissociated sub-personality anthropomorphizations. I do this until I reach the all-subsuming and embedding Being from whom/which all us cosmological subpersonalities arise and with respect to which our localized beings are maintained, and to which, upon local dissolution, we return into underlying oneness and identity condition that passes all understanding, but which would certainly appear to be the ultimate in having overcome cosmological dissociation on the part of any local being.

But, as I already started to do, let us go now to the opposite end of my post-dualistic unified-field spectrum: to mental monism or idealism, whereby all that exists is seen as being fundamentally comprised of consciousness, even, dare we say, pure spirit. From this frame of reference, physical reality is an emergent epiphenomenon of consciousness. Here, then, a very different, but no less hard, problem arises: How does what we experience as physicality arise from consciousness? This hard problem is 180 degrees out of phase with our original hard problem of how pure subjective consciousness arises from pure objective physicality. Yet, for me, it is easier to try to explain this new hard problem, based on an idealist perspective, than it is to try to explain the old hard problem, based on a physical monist perspective. I cannot satisfactorily explain for myself how consciousness can come entirely from a non-conscious physical reality, but I can, for myself at least, satisfactorily explain, or at least understand, how what is experienced as physicality can arise from consciousness.

If, in the idealist view, all is consciousness and all is contained within and as part of consciousness, then anything that can be differentiated, distanced, and experienced as physical and other, out of and for that consciousness, will account for a subject experiencing something as physical object, where both subject and object arise from and are held within the one all-inclusive field of consciousness. Accounting for how consciousness is there on the part of the subject in the first place is certainly not a problem, then, since the eternal (or at least timeless) Ground of Being is consciousness itself. So the local experiencing subject as focal self-aware consciousness merely rides and partakes of, is fed by and imbued with, the background reality of consciousness and awareness as the superordinate containment space, living, aware, experiencing semantical or meaning space, not just the lower dimensional syntactical and surface structure space and its contents which the consciousness of the former space creates, contains, and with which it interacts in its awareness-experience-, and meaning-making. As conceptualized before, one is a relatively cosmological dissociated sub-personality of the universal consciousness field of the one Creator/Sustainer Being. Having to turn a portion of the one consciousness field into what is then experienced as a passive, inanimate, non-conscious object to be experienced as such by another portion of that same consciousness field is not as easy. Consciousness is as capable of experiencing something within its field of consciousness in terms of its being experienced as a physical object, and seemingly external to and other than that consciousness itself, in a state-dependent manner as a function of the belief, expectation, and information processing and experiential-object-generation program that such local consciousness has access to do so with, as it is capable of experiencing remembered, imagined, or dreamt objects. Probably how, and what, the local more-subjective aware consciousness aspect of the larger field experiences as objects, contents, and events with respect to itself is a function of the post-Cartesian unified-field psychoid phase relations among the oscillating excitation patterns of standing and moving wave systems and basal substance flowing and moving on and with respect to itself within a deeply relativistic manifold supporting infinite frames of reference of localized consciousness and their objects and contents, of localized experiencers and objects and events experienced, of individualized meaning-makers and materials they generate from which all meanings are made.

The conjugate portion of the consciousness field—what we might call the "objective correlative" or conjugate of the subject's experiencing frame of reference as subjective correlative—could be seen to cooperate, as self-same consciousness, in and of the same mind, so to speak, to make the dyad of experiencer and experienced be of the nature of the one encountering the other as something we call and know as physical. In this scenario, all is contained within one consciousness, one multidimensional domain of experience. This is one first-approximation way that the idealist would explain how what is experienced as physical by consciousness can arise from the same non-physical, pure consciousness field. The object would arise from and be maintained for awhile within one portion of the consciousness field to be experienced by another portion of that same field which/who probably would not have the kind or state of consciousness at the time to be aware that the object came from the same consciousness field that it, the subject, comes from and is made out of as well. This, of course, is a process of cosmological dissociation itself; so it would seem that positive experiential worlds within which life, local consciousness, experience, and meaning can occur must come from a process of cosmological dissociation, or symmetry breaking process also. Dissociation at the same time then becomes the creative problem to be overcome or solved by Absolute Spirit from its now dissociated endless relativistic cosmological subpersonality frames of reference, to return to full consciousness, self-identity, self-awareness of Itself as Absolute Spirit. Thus the Universal Humpty-Dumpty gradually puts Itself back together again, only to break Itself apart once more, in cycles of self-creation, self-concealment, self-reflection, and self-revealment. So all is Lila, or the one cosmic, divine play of which we are forever a part, even as we are Absolute Spirit in local cosmologically dissociated human mode. But the hardest problem of all—where the consciousness comes from in the first place—has been automatically addressed from the idealist perspective that the Ground of all Being is that very consciousness. Then any local consciousness is just experiencing itself, and the contents and objects of its consciousness, within the context of the Universal Consciousness.

So, as each of us is the Universal Consciousness field relatively dissociatedly partially experiencing itself through localized and individualized form and perspective. In my case this moment I am Jon Klimo's consciousness state-dependently experiencing whatever I am capable of experiencing as a function of that state/level of consciousness. To the extent to which local cosmological subpersonalities of the Universal such as ourselves can overcome our kinds and degrees of cosmological dissociation, to that extent can we consciously and at will operate from our parental embedding Creator self-identity and self-awareness and thereby efficaciously interact with the ZPE, or with any other more invariant, constrained, and less-conscious-appearing aspects or substrata of the Universal Being we now recognize as All-That-Is, ultimately as Ourself, as Myself. Ultimately, at-will conscious perceived causal self-efficacy may then be exercised by us such self-aware seats of Creator identity with respect to the rest of our now-expanded sense of identity as the ultimate ground of Creation with which we, as aspects of the Creator, work. Creator and Creation are spoken of here in this separated manner only as a function of Jon Klimo's present kind and degree of cosmological dissociation. But underneath how we variously experience it through our dissociated lenses, this ultimate ground of our Absolute Spirit ineffably far transcends what we currently can term and understand as the ZPE. So I welcome all of us to bootstrap ourselves within our relatively dissociated frames of reference to awaken back to those less-cosmologically dissociated frames of reference and possibilities of interaction. Then we may become the ultimate sons and daughters in the image and making ways of our own Creator Self, alchemists in identity condition with our own Creation ground aspect. Then I return to Myself through such bootstrapping self-awakening human enterprise. At any point and everywhere, the seemingly passive artist's clay can be returned to the living mind of the artist from which it originally emanated, and within which it is forever held and with which it is created. Nothing falls outside the one Consciousness, the one Being. All is within as I/we turn to interact with My/our own surroundings, the larger offspring corpus of my/our own Being. As I feel I am talking to Myself now, I say: let us awaken to ever-increasing lucidity to more consciously interact and experiment with our reality like a lucid dream we share and co-constitute. We are surrounded by the one parental all-containing consciousness and we are one with it, and can potentially create from and with it in ways that put to shame all current relatively cosmologically dissociated quantum notions of coherence, nonlocal correlatedness, entanglement, and superposition. All is Lila, our own Divine Self, dancing with Itself, dancing with Myself. Let us overcome our dissociation and join the dance, consciously, lucidly.

Bibliography

"Unified Field Theories," Hitoshi Murayama, in *Encylopedia of Applied Physics*, Vol. 23, ed. George L. Trigg, Wiley-VCH Verlag GmbH, Germany, 1998.

Superstrings: A Theory of Everything, P.C.W. Davies and J. Brown, eds., Cambridge Univ. Press, Cambridge, UK, 1988.

"The Warp Drive: Hyper-Fast Travel Within General Relativity," Miguel Alcubierre, *Class. Quantum Grav.* 11 (1994) L73-L77

"Interaction with the Absorber as the Mechanism of Radiation," John A. Wheeler and Richard R. Feynman, *Rev. of Mod. Phys.*, V. 17, No. 2 & 3, 1945, p.157

"Inertial Mass and Quantum Vacuum Fields," Bernard Haisch, Alfonso Rueda, York Dobyns, *Ann. Phys. (Leipzig)* 10 (2001) 5, 393-414

"Experimental Tests of Realistic Local Theories via Bell's Theorem," Alain Aspect, P. Grangier, G. Roger, *Phys. Rev. Ltrs.*, V. 47, N. 7, 1981, p. 460

"Loophole Closed in Quantum Mechanics Test," *Science*, V. 219, Jan. 7, 1983, p. 40

"Quantum Theory as an Indication of a New Order in Physics. B. Implicate and Explicate Order in Physical Law," David Bohm, *Foundations of Physics*, V. 3, N. 2, 1973, p. 139

"A Suggested Interpretation of the Quantum Theory in Terms of 'Hidden' Variables," David Bohm, *Phys. Rev.*, V. 85, 1952, p.166 (Part I), V.85, 1952, p.180 (Part II)

"Can Quantum-Mechanical Description of Physical Reality Be Considered Complete?" Albert Einstein, B. Podolsky, N. Rosen, *Phys. Rev.*, V. 47, 1935, p. 777

"On the Einstein Podolsky Rosen Paradox," J. S. Bell, *Physics*, V. 1, N. 3, 1964, p. 195

"On the Problem of Hidden Variables in Quantum Mechanics," *Rev. of Mod. Phys.*, V. 18, N. 3, 1966, p. 447

"Significance of Electromagnetic Potentials in the Quantum Theory," Y. Aharonov & D. Bohm, *Phys. Rev.*, V. 115, N. 3, 1959, p. 485

13927-VALO

3

Impedance Crystals: Living Energy System Guide

Laverne E. Denyer

The sleeping serpent awakes.
Flooding memories return.
Memories of divine connection.
Universal bonding remembered.
My soul is reassured.
Spiritual power courses through my being.
Kundalini power unleashed.
Each energy center dances in unison, alive and alert.
To understand all!
There is no greater ecstasy.

What Separates Us from Our Higher Wisdom?

If you are like me, you have often wondered why we don't remember more about our higher selves and other life experiences. We have learned that we can often gather information about these experiences through meditation and spiritual channeling. Sometimes visions reveal information about other dimensions and other truths. But for most people, these are usually limited revelations. We seek to know more. Yet the information is somehow blocked. I always wanted to know how that worked.

I have finally leaned to understand much about the ways in which that information is blocked. An important component used to purposely block information from the higher realms is through a series of *Impedance Crystals*. These are etheric crystalline shapes we implant in the *Etheric Body* at the time of birth. They restrict individual awareness during earthly life.

To clairvoyant sight, the crystals resemble physical world quartz crystals. There are over thirty categories of crystals in the *Living Energy System (LES)*. They are either single or paired in nature. The length, diameter and energy impedance flow vary throughout the system.

When two crystals intersect, join or occupy the same space, they lock together. They create of synergy to further disrupt the system.

There are also impedance wires, mostly in the head. These wires are very much like the crystals. They disrupt the energetic patterns of awareness and connection throughout the *LES*.

With all of the suppression energy that these crystals emit, imagine what we would be like if they weren't there. Or what happens when they are removed. It is amazing and impressive.

How They Work

The *Impedance Crystals* interfere with the natural bio-emission flow through the system. They interact with the *Chakra* system and other subtle body systems to slow down, distort or eliminate the healthy bio-emission flow. They generally correspond with *chakras*, joints or meridians. A disruptive frequency, similar to the type of radio jamming done in certain military situations, sets up a distortion or blockage in the natural energy transmission circuit. This disruptive frequency retards the natural function of various sub-systems.

13927-VALO

Through this disruption, an individual is separated from spiritual and intuitional knowledge. Connections with higher wisdom are *impeded.* It is a very effective tool that keeps us in the "here and now" of material life. When full access to higher wisdom is available, it is sometimes difficult to grow and learn. That higher wisdom can lead a person into decisions based upon a notion of what should be done rather than learning about what an individual personality wants to do. The element of growth and accountability is difficult to maintain. Full wisdom is exciting and rewarding. It also retards spiritual growth. Therefore, the *Impedance Crystals* provide a system that moves individual personalities into unique challenges and opportunities.

When they function properly, *Impedance Crystals* are indeed powerful and power-filled tools of great refinement.

Each Type Of Crystal Performs A Different Function

Just as the various subtle bodies have diverse functions, the *Impedance Crystal* system performs a variety of functions. Each type impacts a different segment of the *LES.* As stated earlier, there are over thirty different types, each with different functions. Note: look at the end of the article for all illustrations.

A) Head Crystals

There are twelve (12) *Impedance Crystal* types in the head. They generally impact life support and spiritual awareness.

#1: CROWN CHAKRA: The *Crown Chakra Impedance Crystal* originates at the top of the Adam's Apple in the throat. It travels up through the center of the head to emerge through the top of the head, finally p protruding out through the *Crown Chakra* about an inch.

The energetic purpose is to affect the connection with the *God/Tao* force and reduce precognitive awareness.

SIZE	The crystal is usually about ¾" to 1" in diameter
NUMBER	One Single Crystal
ENERGETIC CONNECTION	Crown Chakra
PHYSICAL LOCATION	Crown of Head, through center of head, to top of Adam's Apple
CRYSTAL INTERSECTIONS	It intersects crystals #2, #3, #4, #5, #6, #7 and #8
PURPOSE	The crystal blocks or disrupts Intuition and the Spiritual Connection

#2: THIRD EYE: The *Third Eye Impedance Crystal* travels on a downward slope through the head. It originates in the middle of the forehead, travels through the center of the head, intersects the *Crown Chakra Crystal* and the back of the skull.

The energetic purpose is to reduce clairvoyant sight. The connection with intuitional wisdom is either blocked or distorted.

SIZE:	The crystal is usually about ¾" to 1" in diameter
NUMBER	One Single Crystal
ENERGETIC CONNECTION	Third Eye
PHYSICAL LOCATION	Middle of head, to the center back of skull
CRYSTAL INTERSECTIONS	It intersects crystals #1, #3 and #4
PURPOSE	Reduce, distort or eliminate Clairvoyance, Intuition

#3: PITUITARY: The *Pituitary Impedance Crystal* originates in the middle of the upper frontal portion of the skull. It travels on a downward slant to terminate at the pituitary gland.

The energetic purpose is to impact physical glandular stimulation and other body functions. It disconnects spirit and wisdom from body functions.

SIZE	The crystal is usually about ¾" to 1" in diameter
NUMBER	One Single Crystal
ENERGETIC CONNECTION	Pathway between Crown Chakra and Third Eye
PHYSICAL LOCATION	Top center of frontal quadrant of head, through center of brain, to terminate at the pituitary gland
CRYSTAL INTERSECTIONS	It intersects crystals #2, #5, #8, #16.
PURPOSE	The crystal blocks or disrupts glandular stimulation and general physical body functions

13927-VALO

#4: PINEAL: The *Pineal Impedance Crystal* originates at the center of the upper rear of the skull. It travels through the center of the brain and terminates at the pineal gland. It intersects the #10 crystals.

The energetic purpose is to impact time sense and to disconnect an individual from a sense of understanding of the soul's purpose. This is the crystal that isolates a person from the rightness of spiritual connection. This is where loneliness begins.

SIZE	The crystal is usually about ¾" to 1" in diameter
NUMBER	One Single Crystal
ENERGETIC CONNECTION	Pineal Gland
PHYSICAL LOCATION	Center of rear, upper quadrant of skull; traveling through center of the brain; to terminate at the pineal gland
CRYSTAL INTERSECTIONS	It intersects crystals #2 and #10
PURPOSE	This crystal blocks or disrupts time sense and disturbs the soul connection by disconnecting the Seat of the Soul

#5: EYES AND SINUS: The *Eye and Sinus Impedance Crystals* originate just above the eyebrow over each eye. They travel through the brain, intersecting Crystal #12, and terminate at the pituitary gland. This is a pair of crystals, one connected with each eye.

The energetic purpose is to affect vision and the ability to interact with the Breath of Life.

SIZE	The crystal is usually about ¾" to 1" in diameter
NUMBER	Two crystals, side-by-side, each connected to one eye
ENERGETIC CONNECTION	Pineal Gland
PHYSICAL LOCATION	Center rear, upper quadrant of skull; traveling through center of the brain; to terminate at the pineal gland
CRYSTAL INTERSECTIONS	It intersects crystal #2
PURPOSE	This crystal blocks or disrupts time sense and disturbs the soul connection by disconnecting the Seat of the Soul

13927-VALO

#6: SINUS: The *Sinus Impedance Crystals* begin at the bottom of the eye socket of each eye, travel through the head, to exit at the back of the neck just below the base of the skull. This is a pair of crystals.

The energetic purpose of these crystals is to disconnect an individual from the breath of life. There is also some impact on vision, both physical and ethereal.

SIZE	The crystal is usually about ¾" to 1" in diameter
NUMBER	A pair of crystals (2)
ENERGETIC CONNECTION	Sinuses
PHYSICAL LOCATION	Lower portion of each eye socket, through head to exit at the back of the head, just below the base of the skull
CRYSTAL INTERSECTIONS	It has no intersections
PURPOSE	These crystals block or disrupt the ability to breathe and to interact with the breath of life. It shuts down the ability to perceive spiritual scents

#7: MOUTH: The *Mouth Impedance Crystal* begins in the mouth, travels horizontally through the skull and terminates at the spinal column.

The purpose of this crystal is to impact speech and the entire communication process. It sometimes causes the inability to communicate clear thoughts.

SIZE	The crystal is usually about ¾" to 1" in diameter
NUMBER	One Single Crystal
ENERGETIC CONNECTION	Mouth
PHYSICAL LOCATION	Enters through the opening of the mouth, travels horizontally through the head, intersecting the #1 crystal, terminating when it touches the spinal column
CRYSTAL INTERSECTIONS	It intersects crystal #1
PURPOSE	The crystal blocks or disrupts the communication process, especially speech

#8: SPINAL APEX: The *Spinal Apex Impedance Crystal* enters the neck at the base of the skull, travels in an upward horizontal path to terminate at the pituitary gland. It intersects crystal #9. It also emerges at the opening of the rear *Third Eye Chakra* opening.

This crystal rests at the juncture of the brain and the spinal column. It inhibits the *Kundalini* flow and separates the brain from the rest of the body. It crosses the spinal column where all of the nerve impulses are transmitted between the physical body and the brain. This crystal also inhibits or eliminates clairaudience (spiritual hearing).

SIZE	The crystal is usually about ¾" to 1" in diameter
NUMBER	One Single Crystal
ENERGETIC CONNECTION	Spinal Apex and rear opening of the *Third Eye*
PHYSICAL LOCATION	Base of the skull, traveling on an upward path to terminate at the pineal gland
CRYSTAL INTERSECTIONS	It intersects crystal #9
PURPOSE	It blocks clairaudience (spiritual hearing) and disconnects the higher order mind from the physical body

#9: LOWER EAR: The *Lower Ear Impedance Crystals* enter the side of the head just below and behind the ear. They pass through the base of the cerebellum and meet at the center of the head. They intersect crystal #8.

These crystals, like the #8 crystal, impacts clairaudience. They also disrupt physical hearing and the ability to understand what other people are saying.

SIZE	The crystal is usually about ¾" to 1" in diameter
NUMBER	A pair (2)
ENERGETIC CONNECTION	Spinal apex and cerebellum
PHYSICAL LOCATION	They enter the head at the lower back of each ear; then travel horizontally, crossing through the cerebellum, to meet in the center of the head
CRYSTAL INTERSECTIONS	They intersect crystal #8
PURPOSE	Disrupt hearing and clairaudience

13927-VALO

#10: UPPER EAR: The *Upper Ear Impedance Crystals* enter the head at the top, rear of the ears. They meet at the middle of the head, at the pineal gland. They intersect crystal #4.

The energetic purpose of these crystals is to block or hinder the interpretation of sounds and communication. Chronology and spiritual connection are also impacted in the same way that crystal #4 does.

SIZE	The crystal is usually about ¾" to 1" in diameter
NUMBER	A pair (2)
ENERGETIC CONNECTION	Ear and pineal gland
PHYSICAL LOCATION	Enter the head at the upper rear of the ear, traveling through the head to meet at the center, entering the pineal gland
CRYSTAL INTERSECTIONS	It intersects crystal #4
PURPOSE	These crystals impair hearing and the connection with the soul's purpose

#11: TEMPLE: The *Temple Impedance Crystals* enter the head at the temple and meet in the middle of the head. They intersect crystal #1.

The temple location is a main junction of cranial bones and the jaw. It is a central energy point that acts as a bridge between vision, hearing and communication. It also impacts the consumption of food. These crystals impede these interactions. They can also cause difficulties such as TMJ and indigestion.

SIZE	The crystal is usually about ¾" to 1" in diameter
NUMBER	A pair (2)
ENERGETIC CONNECTION	Bridge between vision, hearing and nutrition.
PHYSICAL LOCATION	Enter through the temple, pass through the head to meet in the center.
CRYSTAL INTERSECTIONS	They intersect crystal #1.
PURPOSE	These crystals disrupt the connections between vision, hearing and digestion. They also impede the spiritual wisdom connection. They can keep an individual malnourished in body, mind and spirit.

#12: EYES: The *Eyes Impedance Crystals* enter the head just below the end of the eyebrow at the outer corner of each eye. They intersect with the #5 crystals.

The energetic purpose of these crystals is to further impede vision. They are like tuners that keep people from seeing the material world for what it is, illusion. They block higher and lower frequency vision as well as inter-dimensional sight.

SIZE	The crystal is usually about ¾" to 1" in diameter
NUMBER	A pair (2)
ENERGETIC CONNECTION	Eyes
PHYSICAL LOCATION	Enter the skull just below the end of the eyebrow at the outer corner of the eyes; travel through the head to meet in the center of the head.
CRYSTAL INTERSECTIONS	They intersect crystal #5.
PURPOSE	The crystals block or disrupt vision and awareness of both the physical and esoteric worlds.

#13: THROAT: The *Throat Impedance Crystal* is the transition between the head and the body. So it is shown on all of those illustrations. It enters the throat through the main opening of the *Throat Chakra* in the middle of the Adam's Apple, or voice box, travels horizontally through the middle of the neck, exiting through the back opening of the *Throat Chakra.* It intersects crystal #14.

The energetic purpose of this crystal is to interrupt the communication process on both the physical and the spiritual level. It blocks or diminishes psychic communication such as "channeling" or telepathy. This is a crystal that is often very imbalanced in modern-day metaphysical people. Because of the difficulty of truly speaking truth about esoteric beliefs and information, this crystal is often either damaged or overactive. That creates a great deal of physical difficulty. This and the *Heart/Fulcrum* crystal are generally the two most active in modern western society.

SIZE	The crystal is usually about 1" to 1 ½" in diameter.
NUMBER	One single crystal.
ENERGETIC CONNECTION	Throat Chakra
PHYSICAL LOCATION	Enter through the main opening of the *Throat Chakra* in the Adam's Apple (voice box), travel horizontally through the center of the neck, exiting through the rear opening of the *Throat Chakra* in the back of the neck.
CRYSTAL INTERSECTIONS	It intersects crystal #14.
PURPOSE	Disrupt the communication process, especially speech. Block or diminish "channeling," telepathy and other types of psychic communication.

13927-VALO

#14: NECK: The *Neck Impedance Crystal* travels vertically from the clavicle (collar bone) to the base of the skull. It intersects crystal #13 in the throat.

The energetic purpose is to reduce the *Kundalini* flow and limit the range of head motion and visibility. This limited range of motion can keep an individual isolated and uninformed in the material world.

SIZE	The crystal is usually about 1" to 1 ½" in diameter.
NUMBER	One single crystal
ENERGETIC CONNECTION	*Throat Chakra*
PHYSICAL LOCATION	Along the spinal column in the neck. It travels from the clavicle (collar bone) to the base of the skull.
CRYSTAL INTERSECTIONS	It intersects crystal #13.
PURPOSE	This crystal limits or disrupts the *Kundalini* flow as it travels between the head and the torso. It also restricts the rotation of the head, thus limiting a person's perspective and visual awareness. This can severely impede an individual's connection with both the outer world and the spiritual world.

#15: FRONTAL LOBES: The *Frontal Lobe Impedance Crystals* enter the top of the skull at about the top of the forehead. They travel straight downward into the sinuses. They intersect crystals #2, #16 and #19.

The energetic purpose is to reduce the oxygen intake, cause general confusion and reduce emotional responses. Remember this is the area of the brain that surgeons used to scramble when they conducted frontal lobotomies as a behavior modification technique.

SIZE	The crystal is usually about ½" to ¾" in diameter.
NUMBER	A pair (2)
ENERGETIC CONNECTION	*Third Eye Chakra.*
PHYSICAL LOCATION	Enter the top of the skull at about the top of the forehead. They travel at a steep slope downward into the sinuses.
CRYSTAL INTERSECTIONS	They intersect crystals #2, #16 and #19.
PURPOSE	These crystals reduce the oxygen intake, cause general confusion and apathy, and reduce emotional responses. Remember this is the area of the brain that surgeons used to scramble when they did frontal lobotomies as behavior modification techniques. (The general confusion and emotional distancing is part of what makes us think we are isolated and separate from our environment and the *God Force*).

13927-VALO

#16: SOFT SPOT: The *Soft Spot Impedance Crystal* lies in the top center of the skull in the seams where the cranials skull bones) join. This location is the same as the "soft spot" on a newborn baby's head before the cranial bones grow together. It travels down, like a plug, to a depth even with the top of the *Third Eye Chakra*. There are no crystal intersections.

The energetic purpose is to reduce clear thinking and promote fear and doubt. It also serves as a plug to keep us in our physical bodies. The crystal is not implanted until the soft spot on a baby's head seals over.

SIZE	The crystal is usually about 1 ½" to 1 ¾" in diameter.
NUMBER	One single crystal.
ENERGETIC CONNECTION	*Crown Chakra*.
PHYSICAL LOCATION	Lies in the top center of the skull in the seams where the cranials (skull bones) join. It travels down, like a plug, to a depth even with the top of the *Third Eye Chakra*.
CRYSTAL INTERSECTIONS	There are no crystal intersections.
PURPOSE	The energetic purpose is to reduce clear thinking and promote fear and doubt. It also serves as a plug to keep us in our physical bodies. This crystal is not implanted until the soft spot on a baby's head seals over.

#17: TELEPATHIC: The *Telepathic Impedance Crystal* enter the back of the head on each side of the juncture of the cranials (skull bones) at a seam very similar to the soft spot on the top of the head. It travels horizontally into the very center of the brain, connecting with the top of the brain stem.

The energetic purpose is to reduce telepathic abilities. This is another tool that isolates us from other beings, our higher self and the *God Force*.

SIZE	The crystal is usually about ½" to ¾" in diameter.
NUMBER	A pair (two).
ENERGETIC CONNECTION	*Crown Chakra* and *Third Eye*.
PHYSICAL LOCATION	Enter the back of the head on each side of the juncture of the cranials (skull bones) at a seam very similar to the soft spot on the top of the head. It travels horizontally into the very center of the brain, connecting with the top of the brain stem.
CRYSTAL INTERSECTIONS	They intersect crystals #1, #2 and #17.
PURPOSE	The energetic purpose is to reduce telepathic abilities.

#18: CLAIRVOYANT: The *Clairvoyant Impedance Crystals* enter the top of the head on each side at about where mythological tales indicate the Devil's horns would be (perhaps the energy emanations from these crystals even has something to do with people's perceptions of "horns?"). They travel on an inward and backward slope toward the eyes. They stop just above the level of the eyebrows.

The energetic purpose is to impede clairvoyant abilities and separate an individual from his/her higher purpose wisdom. These crystals impede the ability to separate momentary impulses from purposeful action. The connection with "devilish" behaviors is very appropriate here.

SIZE	The crystal is usually about ¾" to 1" in diameter
NUMBER	A pair (two).
ENERGETIC CONNECTION	*Third Eye*, eyes.
PHYSICAL LOCATION	Enter the top of the head on each side at about where mythological tales indicate the Devil's horns would be. They travel on an inward and backward slope toward the eyes. They stop just above the level of the eyebrows.
CRYSTAL INTERSECTIONS	They intersect crystals #2 and #19.
PURPOSE	The energetic purpose is to impede clairvoyant abilities and separate an individual from his/her higher purpose wisdom. These crystals impede the ability to separate momentary impulses from purposeful action. The connection with "devilish" behaviors is very appropriate.

B) Torso Crystals

Most of the *Impedance Crystals* in the torso connect with either chakras or meridians. The largest crystals in the system are located in the torso.

#19: KUNDALINI: The *Kundalini Impedance Crystal* is the largest of the entire system. It enters the body in the genital area through the lower opening of the *Base Chakra*, flows all the way up through the center of the body and exits through the top of the head and *Crown Chakra*. It intersects many of the other crystals. Crystal #1 occupies the same space through the head. They may look like one single crystal, but they are not. They are definitely two separate crystals. The #1 crystal is an additional overlay that serves to keep mental and spiritual cognition suppressed more than the *Kundalini Impedance Crystal* would by itself.

This is part of the reason that the *Kundalini* remains dormant through most of a person's life. It restricts the life flow of physical sand spiritual energies flowing through the entire system.

SIZE	The crystal is usually about 2 ½" to 3" in diameter.
NUMBER	One single crystal.
ENERGETIC CONNECTION	*Kundalini* channel through the entire body from the *Base Chakra* to the *Crown Chakra*
PHYSICAL LOCATION	Enter in the genital region through the lower opening of the *Base Chakra*, travel upward through the body along the spine, following the center of the *Kundalini* channel, exiting through the top of the head through the *Crown Chakra*.

CRYSTAL INTERSECTIONS

It intersects crystals #21, #22, #29, #28, #27, #26, #25, #24, #13, #7, #11 #2 and #1.

PURPOSE

This is an important crystal. It serves to help keep the *Kundalini* at rest. Except for times of excessive adrenalin or hormonal secretions, the flow is diminished to about 10% of what it could be. This crystal separates an individual's awareness and energy reserves from both the spiritual and physical life forces on all levels. It is a powerful inhibitor.

#20: MASCULINE / FEMININE BALANCE: The *Masculine / Feminine Balance Impedance Crystals* start on each side of the torso at the top of the shoulder just inside the shoulder connection for the collarbone. Then they travel down the body to the top leg joint at the femoral artery. They intersect crystals #29, #23 and #22.

Their energetic purpose is to hinder the balance between masculine and feminine aspects. This relates to the spiritual and material essences. They also impact aspects such and gentleness and strength, warrior and teacher, etc. These two crystals effectively hinder the natural androgyny of the soul and set up artificial barriers between the genders.

SIZE	The crystal is usually about 1" to 1 ½" in diameter.
NUMBER	A pair (two).
ENERGETIC CONNECTION	Gender attribute meridians.
PHYSICAL LOCATION	Enter through the top of the shoulders inside the connecting "V" of the collarbones, travel down inside the trunk of the body to the femoral artery in the top leg joint.
CRYSTAL INTERSECTIONS	It intersects crystals #29, #23 and #22.
PURPOSE	These crystals reduce androgyny by separating masculine and feminine energies as well as spiritual and material energies. They create artificial gender and behavioral boundaries.

13927-VALO

#21: BASE CHAKRA: The *Base Chakra Impedance Crystal* enters through the main opening of the *Base Chakra* at the front of the pubic bone, travels through the body, to exit the rear secondary opening of the *Base Chakra* at the top of the coccyx. It intersects crystals #22 and #19.

The energetic purpose of this crystal is to keep the base energies of passion, sexuality and the life force stronger than the higher loving energies. It keeps an individual grounded in material forces, reducing the ability to move upward to loving spiritual energies. This crystal also reduces the actual physical capacity of the animal body.

SIZE	The crystal is usually about 1" to 1 ½" in diameter.
NUMBER	One single crystal.
ENERGETIC CONNECTION	*Base Chakra*.
PHYSICAL LOCATION	Enter through the main opening of the *Base Chakra* at the front of the pubic bone, travel through the body to exit at the rear secondary opening of the *Base Chakra* at the top of the coccyx.
CRYSTAL INTERSECTIONS	It intersects crystal #19.
PURPOSE	To keep the emotions and through processes grounded in the baser material energies such as passion and sexuality. It separates individuals from their true physical potentials. And it reduces the energy connection to higher spiritual potentials. It also reduces the true ecstasy of physical, emotional and spiritual sexuality.

#22: HIP JOINT: The *Hip Joint Impedance Crystal* enters the side of the center of the joint, travels horizontally through the center of the pelvic area to emerge on the other side of the hip in the center of the joint. It intersects crystals #19, #20 and #22.

The energetic purpose of this crystal is to disturb and individual's connection to earthly energies. It reduces the flow of material "life force," or bio-emissions, coursing upward from the earth. This reduction of earthly energies keeps an individual focused on survival rather than on both material and spiritual evolution.

SIZE	The crystal is usually about 1" to 1 ½" in diameter.
NUMBER	One single crystal.
ENERGETIC CONNECTION	Hip joints.
PHYSICAL LOCATION	Enters the side of the center of the hip joint, travels horizontally through the center of the pelvic area to emerge on the other side of the hip in its center.
CRYSTAL INTERSECTIONS	It intersects crystals #19, #21 and #29.
PURPOSE	Reduce an individual's ability to draw on the natural bio-emission energies coming from the earth. This separation keeps an individual focused on material survival rather than spiritual growth.

#23: SHOULDER JOINT: The *Shoulder Joint Impedance Crystals* enter the top of the upper arm just below the shoulder joint. They then travel horizontally through the shoulder and upper chest, to meet in the center of the upper chest just behind the collarbone. They stop at each side of crystal #19. They intersect crystals #29 and #24.

The energetic purpose is to reduce an individual's external connection to other souls. They skew the balance between independence and interdependence. They keep an individual from "reaching out" to other souls for help and solace.

SIZE	The crystal is usually about 1" to 1 ½" in diameter
NUMBER	A pair (two).
ENERGETIC CONNECTION	Shoulder joints.
PHYSICAL LOCATION	Enter through the top of the upper arm just below the shoulder joint, traveling horizontally through the shoulder and upper chest, to meet in the center of the upper chest just behind the collarbone. They stop at each side of crystal #19.
CRYSTAL INTERSECTIONS	They intersect crystals #29, and #24, then meet in the middle at crystal #19.
PURPOSE	Reduce an individual's external connection to other souls. They skew the balance between independence and inter- dependence. They keep an individual from "reaching out" to other souls for help and solace.

#24: MASTER SPIRITUAL WILL: The *Master Spiritual Will Chakra Impedance Crystal* enters through the primary opening of the *Master Spiritual Will Chakra* at the top of the chest just below the collar bone, over the thymus. From there it travels horizontally through the upper torso, exiting through the secondary opening of the *Master Spiritual Will Chakra*, just below the neck. It intersects crystal #19.

The energetic purpose of this crystal is to diminish personal spiritual awareness and connection. In order for most people to function fully connected to the material world, they need to be insulated against full spiritual awareness. This crystal effectively reduces that awareness. This separation can also reduce full activation of esoteric abilities, often referred to as psychic abilities.

SIZE	The crystal is usually about ¾" to 1" in diameter
NUMBER	One single crystal.
ENERGETIC CONNECTION	*Master Spiritual Will Chakra*
PHYSICAL LOCATION	Enters through the primary opening of the *Master Spiritual Will Chakra* at the top of the chest, below the collar bone above the thymus. It then travels horizontally through the upper chest, to exit through the secondary opening of the *Master Spiritual Will Chakra* below the base of the neck,
CRYSTAL INTERSECTIONS	It intersects crystal #19.
PURPOSE	Separation from personal spiritual awareness and activation of soul energies in the material world. This creates a sense of separation between the spiritual and the material essences of a living being.

13927-VALO

#25: HEART/FULCRUM CHAKRA: The *Heart or Fulcrum Chakra Impedance Crystal* enters through the primary opening of the *Heart Chakra* in the middle of the chest, travels horizontally through the center of the torso. It exits through the secondary opening of the *Heart Chakra* between the shoulder blades. It intersects crystal #19.

This being the balance point for most of the subtle body systems, the energetic purpose of this crystal is to separate spirit and the material world. This serves to disrupt the love, balance, healing and teaching abilities of the individual.

SIZE	The crystal is usually about 1" to 1 ½" in diameter
NUMBER	One single crystal.
ENERGETIC CONNECTION	*Heart/Fulcrum Chakra*
PHYSICAL LOCATION	Enter through the primary opening of the *Heart/Fulcrum Chakra*, traveling horizontally through the torso. It exits through the secondary *Heart/Fulcrum Chakra* in the back between the shoulder blades.
CRYSTAL INTERSECTIONS	It intersects crystal #19.
PURPOSE	Separate the spiritual and the material aspects of an individual. This disrupts the love, balance, healing and teaching abilities of an individual.

#26: SOLAR PLEXUS: The *Solar Plexus Impedance Crystal* enters at the base of the sternum through the primary opening of the *Solar Plexus Chakra*, travels horizontally through the trunk of the body, exiting through the secondary opening of the *Solar Plexus Chakra* below the shoulders in back.

The energetic purpose is to disrupt emotional balance and impede the intellect. By disrupting the emotional balance, and individual loses touch with higher realities. Through interrupting the flow of intellect and cognition, a sense of isolation and limitation ensues. This keeps an individual fully grounded in material events, unaware of higher potentials.

SIZE	The crystal is usually about 1" to 1 ½" in diameter.
NUMBER	One single crystal.
ENERGETIC CONNECTION	*Solar Plexus Chakra*
PHYSICAL LOCATION	Enter through the primary opening of the *Solar Plexus Chakra* just below the sternum, traveling horizontally through the trunk of the body. It exits through the secondary opening of the *Solar Plexus Chakra* below the shoulder blades.
CRYSTAL INTERSECTIONS	It intersects crystal #19.
PURPOSE	Disrupt emotional balance and impede the intellect, fostering a false sense of isolation and limitation. This keeps an individual fully grounded in the material world, with little energy left for higher wisdom.

#27: SPLEEN CHAKRA: The *Spleen Chakra Impedance Crystal* enters through the secondary opening of the *Spleen Chakra* in the abdomen over the spleen, traveling horizontally through the trunk of the body. It exits through the primary opening of the *Spleen Chakra* in the back. It intersects crystal #19.

The energetic purpose is to diminish physical and emotional strength and perseverance. It reduces the ability to stay at a task for long periods of time and to effectively battle adversity.

SIZE	The crystal is usually about 1" to 1 ½" in diameter
NUMBER	One single crystal.
ENERGETIC CONNECTION	*Spleen Chakra.*
PHYSICAL LOCATION	Enter through the secondary opening of the *Spleen Chakra* in the abdomen over the spleen, traveling horizontally through the trunk of the body. It exits through the primary opening of the *Spleen Chakra* in the back.
CRYSTAL INTERSECTIONS	It intersects crystal #19.
PURPOSE	Reduce an individual's strength and perseverance.

#28: MASTER PHYSICAL WILL: The *Master Physical Will Impedance Crystal* enters through the main opening for the *Master Spiritual Will Chakra* at the navel, traveling horizontally through the abdomen. It exits through the secondary opening of the *Master Spiritual Will* in the small of the back. It intersects crystal #19.

The energetic purpose is to disconnect the physical body from its full potential. Since the *Master Spiritual Will Chakra* regulates the amount of physical vitality flowing through the entire system, this *Impedance Crystal* serves to disrupt the pattern and flow of energy actually used by the body. This crystal interferes with an individual's will to fully experience what it could be to be alive and human.

SIZE	The crystal is usually about 1" to 1 ½" in diameter
NUMBER	One single crystal.
ENERGETIC CONNECTION	*Master Physical Will Chakra*
PHYSICAL LOCATION	Enters through the primary opening of the *Master Physical Will Chakra* in the front of the abdomen through the navel, traveling horizontally through the abdomen. It exits through the secondary opening of the *Master Physical Will Chakra* in the small of the back.
CRYSTAL INTERSECTIONS	It intersects crystal #19.
PURPOSE	Separates a person from fully physical potentials, decreasing the will to be fully alive and human. It interferes with the ability to tap the spiritual template of perfect health.

#29: COLLAR BONE: The *Collar Bone Impedance Crystals* enter the front of the chest below the collarbone just inside the shoulder joint. They travel horizontally through the body to exit through the back at the inside top of the shoulder blade. They intersect crystals #18 and #23.

The energetic purpose for these crystals is to disrupt the energetic support for the *Master Spiritual Will Chakra*. There are major circulatory connections here that could aid the function of the *Master Spiritual will Chakra* and its connection with both the soul and the body template. These two crystals aid the isolation process that keeps an individual from higher spiritual wisdom and peace.

SIZE	The crystal is usually about 1" to 1 ½" in diameter
NUMBER	A pair (two).
ENERGETIC CONNECTION	*Master Spiritual Will Chakra*
PHYSICAL LOCATION	Enter the front of the chest below the collarbone just inside the shoulder joint. It travels horizontally through the body to exit through the back at the inside top of the shoulder blade.
CRYSTAL INTERSECTIONS	They intersect crystals #18 and #23
PURPOSE	Increase the effect of separation from personal soul wisdom by further diminishing the efficiency of the *Master Spiritual Will Chakra*.

C) The Arm and Hand Crystals

There are *Arm and Hand Impedance Crystals* that restrict communication, strength and other energetic connections with both the earth and other souls.

#30: FOREARM: The *Forearm Impedance Crystals* enter the arm above the elbow joint, travel downward through the forearm, ending at the wrist joint. They intersect crystal #31.

The energetic purpose is to reduce the capability outreach and retrieval for which an individual. Again, the Earthwalk is a personal sojourn. The reduction in ability to purposefully contact and retrieve information and energy from outside sources keeps the individual more focused on personal learning experiences.

SIZE	The crystal is usually about 1" to 1 ½" in diameter.
NUMBER	A pair (two).
ENERGETIC CONNECTION	Lower Arms.
PHYSICAL LOCATION	Enter the arm above the elbow joint, travel downward through the forearm, ending at the wrist joint.
CRYSTAL INTERSECTIONS	Intersect crystals #31 and #32.
PURPOSE	These crystals effectively reduce the ability of an individual to reach out, contact and retrieve energy from external sources. This reduction in energy helps keep the individual focused on personal learning experiences.

13927-VALO

#31: UPPER ARM: The *Upper Arm Impedance Crystals* enter each arm just below the elbow, traveling upward through the upper arm. They terminate just inside the shoulder joint at the base of the collarbone. They intersect crystals #23 and #31.

The energetic purpose is to slow down the physical and spiritual strength naturally inherent in the system. The upper arms are generally very strong. The reduction in energy output reduces strength and formidableness. This reduction keeps the individual more vulnerable to challenging learning experiences.

SIZE	The crystal is usually about 1" to 1 ½" in diameter
NUMBER	A pair (two).
ENERGETIC CONNECTION	Upper Arms.
PHYSICAL LOCATION	Enter each arm just below the elbow, travel upward through the upper arm and terminate just inside the shoulder joint at the base of the collarbone.
CRYSTAL INTERSECTIONS	Intersect crystals #30 and #31.
PURPOSE	They reduce the strength inherent in the body, leaving the individual more vulnerable to personal challenges and learning experiences.

#32: HANDS, MAJOR SECONDARY CHAKRAS: The *Major Secondary Chakra Impedance Crystals* enter the *Major Secondary Chakra* openings in the palm of each hand, travel through the hand and exit the top of the hand just below the wrist.

The energetic purpose is to reduce an individual's ability to connect with the outside world and bio-emission energies. This also reduces an individual's abilities in healing and dowsing. The limitless powers available through these chakras are reduced by the presence of the crystals. Such limitation drives the individual to seek material forms of healing and personal connection.

SIZE	The crystal is usually about ¾" to 1" in diameter
NUMBER	A pair (two).
ENERGETIC CONNECTION	*Major Secondary Chakras*
PHYSICAL LOCATION	Enter the *Major Secondary Chakra* openings in the palm of each hand, travel through the hand and exit the top of the hand just below the wrist.
CRYSTAL INTERSECTIONS	There are no intersections, but they have a close proximity to crystal #30.
PURPOSE	These crystals reduce the connection with spiritual bio-emission energies to reduce abilities in healing and dowsing. Such limitation drives the individual to seek material forms of healing and personal connection.

13927-VALO

D) The Leg Crystals

The *Leg Impedance Crystals* impact mobility, flexibility, foundations and connection with the Gaia energies. The legs are what move the body about, creating freedom and independence. The crystals in the legs reduce that mobility and freedom.

#33: THIGH: The *Thigh Impedance Crystals* enter the upper leg at the base of the buttocks and pelvis, traveling downward through the thigh. They terminate at the inside edge of the bottom of the kneecap just behind the *Material Stability Chakras.*

The energetic purpose of these crystals is to reduce the support of the bio-emission energies, reduce mobility, and generally impede physical strength. This separation puts more emphasis on strength of character and personal fortitude.

SIZE	The crystal is usually about 1" to 1 ½" in diameter.
NUMBER	A pair (2)
ENERGETIC CONNECTION	*Material Stability Chakras*
PHYSICAL LOCATION	Enter the upper leg at the base of the buttocks and pelvis, traveling downward through the thigh. They terminate at the inside edge of the bottom of the kneecap just inside the bottom of the kneecap
CRYSTAL INTERSECTIONS	There are no intersections.
PURPOSE	They reduce pure physical strength by disturbing the connection with bio-emission energies. They reduce mobility and support of the torso. The reduction in strength and mobility force an individual to be more self- reliant and form stronger character at tributes.

#34: CALF / LOWER LEG: The *Calf / Lower Leg Impedance Crystals* enter the back of the knee on each leg through the *Material Stability Chakras*, traveling downward through the lower leg. They then travel through the heel of the foot and exit through the bottom of the heel. The crystals generally extend at least 3" below the bottom of the foot.

The energetic purpose is to reduce flexibility and mobility as well as to hold an individual firm in his/her beliefs and behaviors. These crystals act like spikes to hold an individual firm in one position (physically, mentally or emotionally). This limitation of mobility also limits perspective and an adventurous nature. The sense of strong foundations is reduced, keeping the individual off balance and vulnerable to new experiences. This is another way to increase self-sufficiency.

SIZE	The crystal is usually about 1" to 1 ½" in diameter.
NUMBER	A pair (2).
ENERGETIC CONNECTION	*Material Stability Chakras.*
PHYSICAL LOCATION	Enter the back of the knee on each leg through the *Material Stability Chakras*, traveling downward through the lower leg. They then travel through the heel of the foot and exit through the bottom of the heel. They crystals generally extend at least 3" below the bottom of the foot.
CRYSTAL INTERSECTIONS	There are no intersections.
PURPOSE	They keep and individual immobile and weaken the basic structure

#35: FOOT: The *Foot Impedance Crystals* enter the top of the foot above the arch, travel through the foot and exit through the arch just behind the pad of the foot through either the *Material Base Chakra* or the *Emotional Base Chakra*. The crystal extends at least 3" below the foot like a spike.

The energetic purpose is similar to crystal #29. They reduce mobility and disturb emotional foundations. They act like spikes to hold an individual firm in one position. This limitation of mobility also limits perspective and an individual's adventurous nature. The sense of strong foundations is reduced, keeping the individual off balance and vulnerable to new experiences. This is another way to increase self-sufficiency.

SIZE	The crystal is usually about 1" to 1 ½" in diameter.
NUMBER	A pair (two).
ENERGETIC CONNECTION	*Material Base Chakra* and *Emotional Base Chakra.*
PHYSICAL LOCATION	Enter the top of the foot above the arch, travel through the foot and exit through the arch just behind the pad of the foot through either the *Material Base Chakra* or the *Emotional Base Chakra.* The crystal extends at least 3" below the foot like a spike.
CRYSTAL INTERSECTIONS	There are no intersections.
PURPOSE	Reduce mobility and disturb emotional foundations. They act like spikes to hold an individual firm in one position. This limitation of mobility also limits perspective and an adventurous nature. The sense of strong foundations is reduced, keeping the individual off balance and vulnerable Impedance Wires

There are special devices in the head that further affect the bio-emission energies. They are *Impedance Wires*. They are energetic patterns that replicate short wires placed in the head. They are about 3" long, 1'16" in diameter and have a 1'4" hook on one end that stays outside of the head. They resemble Allen wrenches, only round.

There are three pair of wires, all in the head. All three pair resemble copper in frequency and appearance. Copper is a fine energy conductor. The energies of these wires help the crystals do their work.

"A" WIRE: BRAIN STEM: The *Brain Stem Wires* enter the head vertically through the base of the skull on each side of the spinal column. They travel vertically, ending in the sides of the Medulla oblongata.

These wires directly impact the brain stem, clouding the individual's thinking.

The wires connect with impedance crystals #8 and #16, further impeding the though processes.

"B" WIRES: BASE OF EAR: The *Base of Ear Wires* enter the head horizontally below the ear just at the tip of the lower cranial. They terminate in each side of the pons.

This set of wires impedes hearing, physical and psychic. The sounds may still be heard, but the impulse does not get properly carried through the nerves in the ear to the brain. Also, the ability to speak your own words clearly is affected. Since we often hear our own voice as it reverberates in the head, and since the tongue and voice box are so close to these wires, verbal communication tools are distorted. Through all of this, communication is significantly reduced.

The wires connect with impedance crystals #1 and #6.

"C" WIRES: TEMPLE AND EYE: The *Temple and Eye Wires* enter the head horizontally right through the temples. They cross the optical nerves and run between the sinuses.

These wires impede vision, mostly physical. Similar to the

way the *Base of Ear Wires* disrupt hearing, these wires disrupt vision. By interfering with the sinus patterns, they can be irritants that cause tearing and swelling. That interferes with clear vision. By running through the optic nerves, the visual impulses carried to the brain can be disrupted. The need to see clearly is omnipresent. This set of wires can be very detrimental. Usually it keeps people from being able to see subtle energies. Sometimes it affects things like color vision and depth perception. Other times it simply distorts the physical world as a whole.

There are no direction connections with other impedance crystals, although thee wires are very close to the #18 clairvoyance crystals.

The Energy Patterns Extend Beyond the Physical Body

The influence of the *Impedance Crystals* extends far beyond the physical body. It extends through the layers of the other subtle bodies. It connects with a system covered in a later chapter called the *Soul Net*.

The complexity of the *Impedance Crystal* system impacts all of the sub-systems in the *Living Energy System*.

These Crystals Are A Valuable Asset to Spiritual Growth

With everything that has been said about these *Impedance Crystals*, it would be easy to think of them as a terrible evil that ruins a person's life. WRONG. They are extremely valuable assets. This energetic system helps give extra impact and purpose to a person's *Earthwalk*. Discovering and understanding complex systems like this one cause me to realize how carefully we planned the way we live life. To have devised such an intricate tool to separate ourselves from full spiritual awareness as a growth enhancer must have been a real challenge. For each soul to go to the effort of creating a unique set of crystals that fit individual lessons is challenging in itself. It is a wonderful, if challenging, gift to self.

My first impulse was to think "why would I do that to myself? That's crazy!" Then I thought more about it. It is crazy like a fox. I may not always like having to do things on my own, but I gain personal insight and increased strength when I overcome personal adversities. If I had pure strength and full awareness, I probably would avoid the whole thing. This planned partial amnesia and limitations caused by the *Impedance Crystals* give me the gift of self-discovery. I don't necessarily like it. But I certainly appreciate it.

The Crystals Can Be Damaged

It is possible for the crystals to be damaged by illness, accident, drugs, emotional stress or psychic attack. They can also be distorted prior to birth as a special growth tool.

Often the crystals grow bumps, twists, cavities and other distortions throughout a lifetime. They can even chip or break. Each type of damage affects the *LES* in some way. There is purpose to these damages, even when we cannot understand it. Sometimes that purpose is to awaken the memories of our own potentials. That awakening often causes us to take action to re-connect with spirit.

Some individuals enter the *Earthwalk* experience with crystals missing or barely functioning. That creates a shift in the energetic frequencies. Those individuals are often psychic and/or creative by nature. That increased awareness always has purpose. It can be difficult to be different from other people by being more aware of higher wisdom. I believe that is part of why I was so attuned to the *LES* all my life. My *Impedance Crystal* system has always been weaker than the average individual. So I remember more than most. I now know that I planet it this way before creating my physical body partner. Many others have done the same.

When the crystals are damaged by life experiences, there is often a shift in the energetic patterns relating to those crystals.

13927-VALO

Sometimes the crystals are weakened. That creates heightened awareness. Head injuries that result in heightened psy abilities are a good example. (I had this experience as well, so I know.) Other times the frequencies of the crystals are either distorted or increased. A lack of mobility experienced by crippling injuries illustrates this type of distortion. The impact of such injuries is always unique to the individual.

Such debate is fairly common. Most people do not know why they are different. They just notice the result, with no idea of the cause.

Good News! They Can Be Removed

The good news is that they CAN be removed. The *Impedance Crystals* do not have to stay in the system indefinitely for everyone. It is possible to relieve the *LES* of these devices and open to full connection with personal soul wisdom.

Sometimes weakened crystals allow enough awareness in to spark a desire for a full connection. That is a very healthy and productive desire.

Be aware, however, that it is complicated and can be very risky! It is wise to ask for help from someone trained in this type of psychic surgery. It can have unexpected repercussions when attempted by a novice. Sometimes those repercussions are worse than the original effect of the crystals.

Damaged crystals can damage tissues and energetic patterns during removal! Chips and slivers of crystals that are overlooked and left behind can begin to fester and tear at the energetic and physical bodies. Distorted crystals need to be removed in accordance with their distortion to avoid damage.

Another part of the danger is the rush of energy that invades an unprepared system. An individual who is energetically and spiritually prepared may not even notice much immediate difference in the energy patterns and his/her thinking. But an individual who is not adequately prepared can be absolutely overwhelmed. That is very dangerous, leading to mental/emotional imbalance or a dangerous energetic flux. *Please do leave this type for removal to an expert!*

There are individuals who know how to remove these crystals. They can work directly with your energy system to remove them. Once you have read this section, your awareness of the disruption raises your energy enough to begin the crystal elimination process.

Some individuals automatically dissolve their own crystals. It is very uncommon, but it happens. This appears to be a result of a higher soul purpose that moves beyond the need for separation from his/her higher self. These individuals are fortunate. This is the easiest and often safest way to clear the system.

Another way to deal with removing these systems is to purposefully seek your own higher guidance. Through prayer, meditation and purposeful contact with your wisdom self, you can request that the *Impedance Crystal* system be removed *in the proper time and place, and according to the highest good of all concerned*. In that way, if it is your proper time and to your highest good, your system will be safely cleared. If there is still value to the system, it will either be left intact or only partially cleared. In this way, you are safe from undesirable results.

Whatever method, whenever you are ready, know that more and more people are having this set of crystals removed. They are reconnecting to their individual souls and the *God* source. It is beginning to make a difference in the world. The time of separation from self is coming to an end.

Purposeful System

The *Impedance Crystal* system is indeed an energetic device that is very purposefully and carefully implanted. Without this level of separation, we would not have the opportunities to learn and grow through challenges and opportunities. It is a very valuable system.

13927-VALO

There is history in your soul that needs to be revealed.

You remember much when you communicated with your soul personality!

Remember to do so on a regular basis.

LAVERNE DENYER – *ldenyer@yuba.net*

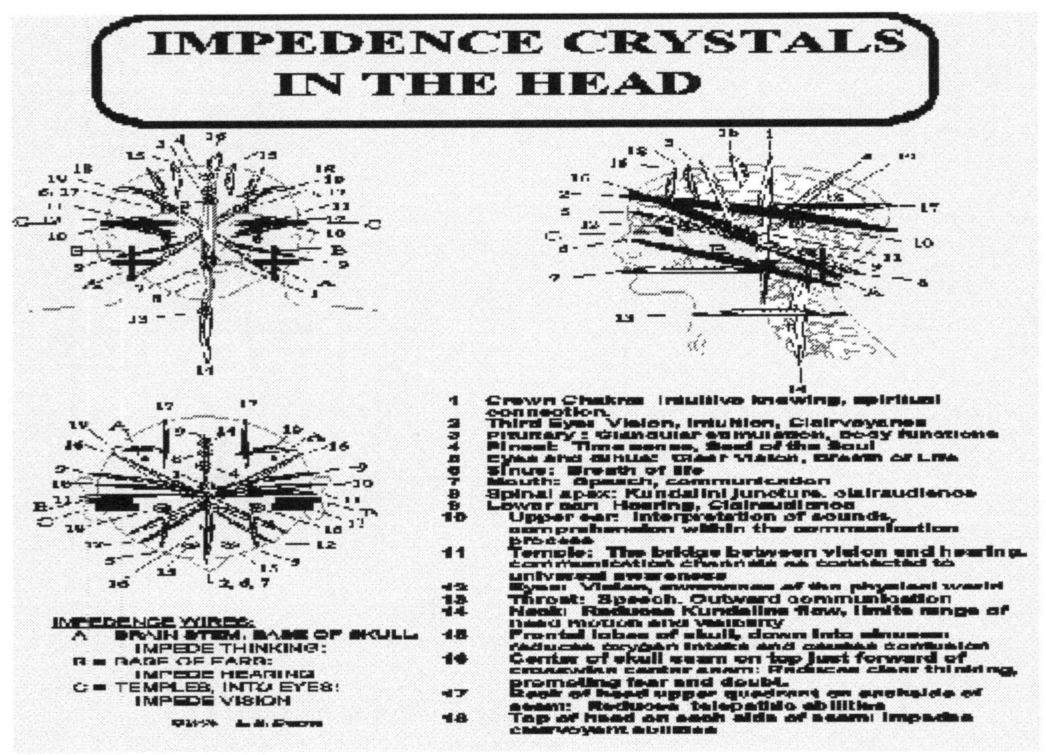
IMPEDENCE CRYSTALS
IN THE HEAD
1 Crown Chakra: Intuitive knowing, spiritual connection.
2 Third Eye: Vision, Intuition, Clairvoyance
3 Pituitary: Glandular stimulation, body functions
4 Pineal: Time sense, Seat of the Soul
6 Sinus: Breath of life
7 Mouth: Speech, communication
8 Spinal apex: Kundalini juncture, clairaudience
9 Lower ear: Hearing, Clairaudience
10 Upper ear: Interpretation of sounds, comprehension within the communication process
11 Temple: The bridge between vision and hearing.
12 Eyes: Vision, awareness of the physical world
13 Throat: Speech. Outward communication
14 Neck: Reduces Kundalini flow, limits range of head motion and visibility
15 Frontal lobes of skull, down into sinuses:
16 Center of skull seam on top just forward of
promoting fear and doubt.
17 Back of head upper quadrant on each side of seam: Reduces telepathic abilities
18 Top of head on each side of seam: Impedes clairvoyant abilities
IMPEDENCE WIRES:
A BRAIN STEM, BASE OF SKULL
IMPEDE THINKING:
B = BASE OF EARS:
IMPEDE HEARING
C = TEMPLES, INTO EYES:
IMPEDE VISION

IMPEDANCE CRYSTALS IN THE TORSO

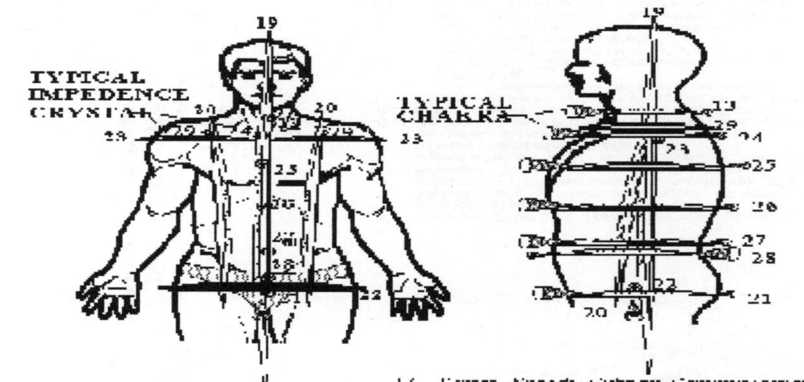

The Impedence Crystals interact with the Chakra System and other Subtle Body sub systems to slow down, distort or eliminate the healthy bio-emission flow.

In the case of the Torso, each Principle Chakra is affected, plus the Kundalini

13 Throat: Speech, Coherent Communication
19 Kundalini: Spiritual and physical life force, strength
20 Masculine and Feminine: Balance of gender, balance between physical and spiritual
21 Base Chakra: Passion, Life Force
22 Hip Joint: Connection to earthly energies
23 Shoulder Joint: External Connection, Independence and Interdependence combined
24 Master Spiritual Will: Spiritual Connection and Activation
25 Heart: Balance, Healing, Teaching
26 Solar Plexus: Intellect, Receiving
27 Spleen: Strength, Persistence
28 Master Physical Will: The Will to be Alive and Human
29 Collar Bone: Support for Master Spiritual Will, Spiritual Integration
30 On each side of the sternum: Limit the integration between physical and spiritual

IMPEDANCE CRYSTALS IN THE ARMS

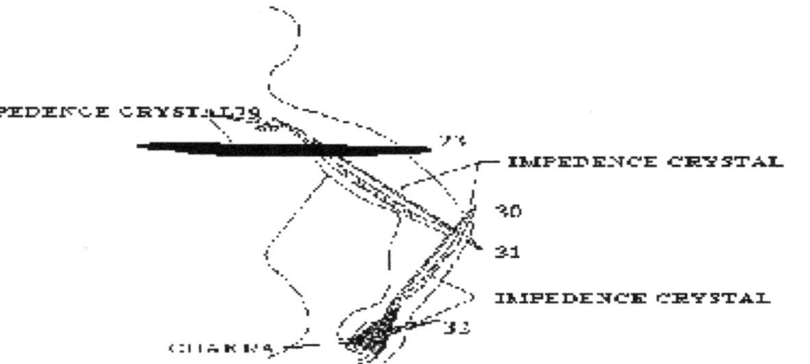

The Impedence Crystals interact with the Chakra System and other Subtle Body sub systems to slow down, distort or eliminate the healthy bio emission flow.

In the case of the arms, the crystals affect the Major Secondary Chakra, several Secondary Chakras; the wrists, elbows and shoulders. They also affect the Secondary Chakras that support the Master Spiritual Will Chakra.

28 Shoulder Joint. External Connections. Independence and Interdepence combined
29 Collar Bone: Support for Master Spiritual Will.
30 Forearm: Outreach and Retrieval
31 Upper Arm: Solid Strength, Formidability
33 Major Secondary Chakra: Healing, Dowsing. Energetic Communication,

13927-VALO

IMPEDANCE CRYSTALS IN THE LEGS

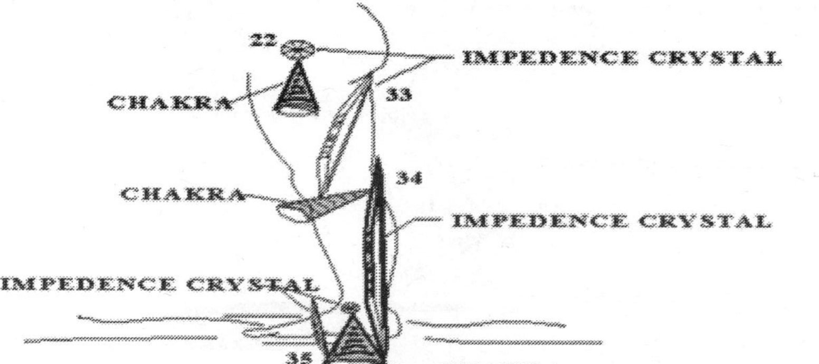

The Impedence Crystals interact with the Chakra System and other Subtle Body sub-systems to slow down, distort or eliminate the healthy bio emission flow.

In the case of the legs, the crystals affect the following chakras: #8 -- Material Stability; #9 -- Material Base, #10 - Emotional Base and #1-- Potentiality. They also affect the ankle and hip joints.

22 Hip Joint: Connection to Earthly energies
33 Thigh: Support, Flexibility, Strength
34 Calf: Flexibility, Foundations, Mobility
35 Foundations, Mobility

4

Words: The Ultimate Healer – The Ultimate Weapon

Marilyn Pequignot

Proceedings of the Annual Conference of the U. S. Psychotronics Association, Columbus, OH, 2000

"Words" spoken or words unspoken, both positive and negative, are the pivotal points in all learning, growth, understanding and wisdom. It has been so since the beginning of creation and will continue to be so throughout all existence. Words are the least understood and the least comprehended communication tool of all mankind. Thus, they are the root cause of all disharmonies, both personal and global.

Keeping that thought in mind, we will explore some of the ramifications and manifestations of words. Everything in this universe creates a vibration, and that vibration causes energy to flow. Said energy flows along a particular path and eventually finds a home. Each word, spoken or unspoken, creates its "own" vibration. That vibration, in turn, creates an energy flow, continuing until it finds a target or "home."

If the words are audible, as in "spoken", they are heard through our ears. After the words are heard they travel to our brain and are filtered through our understanding and comprehension. The understanding and comprehension will only be as valid as our individual knowledge and wisdom. Thus, words change in meaning and context as we grow and mature. What would be true for us at two would change at ten and so on up the ladder of learning. However, our original, internalized belief, understanding or feeling may not change without conscious effort on our part. Another fact we sometimes forget is that most words have a slightly different meaning for each of us. This brings to the fore the real ability to communicate-the communication which lies in learning each other's language.

When the words are "unspoken", they are received and perceived in a much different manner. They can be "heard" through the inflection and tonal quality of the spoken word. To restate, when a word is audibly spoken, it carries with it an inflection and tonal quality, which can, and often does, impart a different message from what spoken words imply. Thus, a conflict is created. The "unspoken" word can be "heard" through any facial expressions, body movements and gestures. These facial expressions, body movements and gestures also create an unspoken message perceived differently from the spoken words accompanying them. Again, a conflict in intent is created between the "spoken" and "unspoken". The "unspoken" word can be "heard" from the projected energy patterns of a thought. A thought creates energy; and as energy, it is projected into the energy field surrounding each of us. That energy, whether from tone, inflection, movement, gesture or thought penetrates into our brain and the filtering process begins-the same filtering process occurring with the spoken word heard through our ears. Although we hear each "spoken" word with our ears, we also hear directly into our brain the "unspoken" values of the same word. This gives us two methods of "hearing" the same word. However, the totally unspoken word, as previously stated, goes directly into the brain via the energy flow. Even though the means of receiving a spoken or unspoken word follows somewhat different paths, the process, once it enters the brain, is the same. This whole process is complete and at the same time complicated, simple, logical and perfect.

Another interesting and fascinating facet concerns the types of words. There are "thinking" words and there are "feeling" words. Generally, the thinking words are the spoken words. The spoken words also usually carry a content of feeling. The unspoken welds "heard" through the projected energy fields are usually perceived as feeling words. These feeling words give us many of our beliefs, laws and judgments. They are able to do so because their energy patterns flow directly into our brain. By the energy flowing directly into our brain, the cognizance we have when hearing through our ears is eliminated. When cognizance is eliminated, we lose theability to use discernment – the discernment of comprehension and understanding that allows us to make valid decisions based upon our knowledge and wisdom.

This brings us into what I have seen and observed as the "morphogenetic fields" of thought. A "morphogenetic field" {1} is that field of energy surrounding all things, animate and inanimate, and which contains the essence of the whole. Once we speak or project a thought, an energy field is created containing the whole essence of all that has been "spoken" or "unspoken": This never dissipates. When a "group or tribe" of people have similar thoughts and voice similar laws and beliefs, these obtain an "energy" of their own. These powerful energies are then projected to all who are born into or become a part of this "group or tribe." These projections have such strength as they are projected to us, that we actually believe they are our own. These laws and beliefs are so powerful, whether positive or negative, we can live a lifetime and never know we really are not flee thinking agents. This projection continues generation after generation. It is only when we begin to examine our own life that we become aware of all these hidden "treasures" or "nemeses," whichever the case may be. It is my hypothesis {2} that this is how ethnic and cultural groups become "locked into" beliefs and a particular way of life. My hypothesis also includes the influence of the Myths, Archetypes, Gods and Goddesses of our history. Even though we all experience the constant influence of "words" from so many sources, we do have the ability to change any of the patterns set in motion in any time frame. The "secret" lies in the desire and willingness to become "aware."

In 399 BC, when Socrates was on trial for speaking out and questioning the Athenians about their moral and justice matters, he made this statement: "A life unexamined is not worth living." Is this not still a valid statement?

In summation, I would like to point out; if indeed the twenty-first century is a garnering as well as a new birth of intellect and artistic genius, it would be advantageous to begin at the root level and move forward. When we learn how to effectively communicate on all levels, we will all become "healers" and there will be no more wars. The "peace" we all yearn for will become manifest and "harmony" will reign.

The above words were written to state my latest harvesting of understanding from climbing another rung on the ladder of awareness, the ladder of unlimited rungs we each must climb in our own way and in our own time. Each rung contains its own tribulations and wisdom. In between each rung are many levels containing progressive stepping stones leading to the next rung. The pace of movement is individualistic and determined by our willingness to experience change and acceptance of that change. My own efforts have always been directed towards understanding the why's behind each stone leading to the next rung. When enough "why's" are asked, the root cause of stagnation is revealed. Revelation always precedes change but does not guarantee change. Change is always by choice. Choice is the one attribute man can always exercise and "believe it or not" we always do choose. We choose by our awareness, knowledge and willingness to "look at", accept and deal with what has been presented to us. Our choice is always the right one at that particular time. However, we always have the ability and option to change that choice in any given moment. The choice made provides an evolutionary stepping stone from one level of progression to another. No one knows exactly on what rung or where between rungs another person resides. That information is multi-faceted, multi-dimensional and totally individualistic. The "saving grace" for each of us is the healing help available at each stepping stone. When we have accepted the healing and stepped forward to another stone, the type or method of healing also changes. This is why the same "type or method" of healing does not work forever or for everyone.

Our world is comprised of many "groups" or "tribes" and each one is on their own stepping stone—the morphogenetic stepping stone of evolution. Each stone has its own required energy to maintain harmony and balance. That is why there is disharmony and imbalance when we first step from one stone to another. When we finally learn to maintain balance and harmony within that particular stone another "choice" appears. Some of us "choose" to take another step and some of us do not. Whatever "choice" is made is absolutely correct at that time. In the "knowing of our being" we are certain of the disharmony and imbalance that may occur if we take that "next step". For many of us the "walk" is our sustenance. For others it looms ahead as pain so they "choose" to stay in that particular place of comfort attained. Neither choice is either "right" or "wrong". It is just an individual "choice". Problems are created when any one of us attempts to cajole someone else into sharing our stone and it is not the "choice stone" for them. Many stones lie between each rung of our ladder. I feel our "true gift" is knowing when to step from one stone to another and finally reach another rung. I see the stones as decimals and the rungs as whole numbers. However you see them is correct for you. The only object is just to be aware of their existence and the existence of the open path beckoning you to explore.

My own stepping stones have been numerous, painful, challenging and exciting. The journey from the first to second rung of my ladder lasted thirty-six years. Leaving that first rung was created by the transition of my father and the following fatal accident to my eldest son. These incidents created the momentum necessary to make the leap from intellectual understanding to emotional understanding. This evolved into intense searching and study of Self, Spirit, Mind-Body Connection, Psychology, all forms of energy and healing to seeing the morphogenetic connection to all things. The latest awareness being in the root cause search of "why" Words-The Ultimate Healer – The Ultimate Weapon.

There is in progress a forthcoming book detailing the effect of "Words" spoken and unspoken that determines our global and individual universe.

Notes

1) In the book, *A New Science of Life*, Dr. Rupert Sheldrake reasons the "morphogenetic fields" are molded by the form and behavior of past organisms of the same species through direct connections across both space and time. He calls the process "morphic resonance". He also proposes that memory is not stored in the brain but may be "given directly from its past states by morphic resonance".
2) In my own fields of endeavor, I arrived at my hypothesis through the intensive and diligent study of consecutive generations of individuals from different ethnic and tribal backgrounds. Through assisting these individuals in changing their health, lifestyle and etc., the patterning of ancient beliefs and the beliefs of past generations were in control, not their free will nor current desire.

5

Geriatrics and Radionics

Sarah Hieronymus, Ph.D.

A quick look at the situation of older people in our nation today reveals that there are around 32 million in number, a good-sized minority (in age over 62) group of a population of around 227,000,000.

The sociological aspects of the effects of such a large group on the Social Security situations, tax situation, housing, health care, medical costs and research, health insurance, nursing homes, hospitals, food supplies, transportation, retirement areas, etc., cannot help but be enormous. In the late 60's the Congress of this country created The House Committee on Aging, chaired for years thereafter by Congressman Claude Pepper, D. of Florida. This committee began investigations of institutions, laws, medical situations, nursing homes, etc., on a unilateral basis, each member investigating some phase of national occurrences and health care affecting older people. For instance, Senator David Pryor, then Congressman from Arkansas, member of the Committee, obtained a job as Attendant or medical assistant, in one nursing home after another, and wrote a Report on what he found as to situations confronting elderly people in nursing

13927-VALO

homes, the quality of care offered, the attitudes of health professionals toward elderly patients, the psychological atmosphere of nursing homes, etc., which helped shape the policies of the Committee on Aging. Here one must also mention the activist group, The Grey Panthers, whose militant approaches to calling attention to the mistreatment and lack of proper conditions in institutions and among health professionals in many clinics, etc., helped to bring that degrading (to the aged) situation to national interest and attention of the Congress.

One of the greatest problems of aging grew out of the sociological changes brought about by World War II. Before that time, and during the nineteenth century, families were of the collective type. Often several generations lived beneath one roof, or with unmarried members of the family who maintained a home for themselves. With the advent of World War II, families became more mobile, moving from one part of the country to another when the work of the head of the family demanded the move. Then there was a demand for workers that women could fill. We can recall the "Rosie The Riveter" phase of World War II when defense jobs created a demand for women workers. Families became smaller with fewer children. Other arrangements were made for Grandma or Grandpa and Uncle Jim or Aunt Mary when the family moved across the country to a new job site and a new location. Thousands of such families swarmed into Florida. Houston, Texas, and the California sites of Space Industries were also changed in population by the influx of such families.

Sociologists interested in the social aspects of such changes, due to mobility, less children and elimination of elderly people, began to note other phenomena in connect these, the growth in number of nursing homes, higher medical raises in Social Security taxes, larger numbers of retirement developments in states offering climate and advantages.

At the time of the establishment of the National "Committee on Aging", there existed a great deal of abuse of the great nu aging people who were put into such establishments by relatives who had no time, or strength or no desire to spend time taking care of aging people who were semi-invalid. Investigation of such incidents as the nursing home in Arkansas owned by a group of physicians, and run for profit, revealed the custom of recycling uneaten food from the plates of the patients, for the next meal, massive doses of antibiotics, the administering of many soporific drugs such as Elavil, Librium and Valium (which have many effects on the health of the habitual user), and lack of or individual care, other than absolutely needed. When all the patients became ill, and some died, the State Health Dept. investigated and found that such abuse was common in many locations, the place was closed and many others were investigated and closed.

Many people think of people who are over 65 as having seen their best days, "over the hill" sub-human, just waiting to die, etc. Such a general stereotyping of older people on the part of the younger generations, constitutes a massive psychic attack on unusually helpless people. They do not feel any different, but they are treated as if they were different, pushing a mental attitude of "inferiority" or "not belonging" into their consciousness. Just think how many changes an older person has undergone and somehow survived. The Psychology of Aging postulates that a positive attitude borne of having come to terms with life, learning faith and hope through the internalizing into the intellectual psychic structure of the being, an acceptable religion or philosophy, and having a general over-all command of' situations learned through many life-time experiences, all constitute a framework within which a person facing the so-called Golden Years of life, can lead a healthy and happy life, give something of service to the world in which they live, and know that continuing, whether one is in this world or in any other world or dimension. Many inventors, philosophers, writers, actors and actresses, do their best work of their careers after they are 65 years old. Here I might mention the example of Dr. T. Galen Hieronymus, who on his birthday in November of 1987 was 92 years young. He had several projects he was working on, writing more papers, working every day, doing more research into the uses and properties of his discovery, Eloptic Energy. He redesigned and miniaturized several of his instruments. He worked on plans and designs for a new type of ANALYZER AND TREATMENT UNIT using Eloptic Energy Techniques, which we believe will revolutionize all present techniques and theories of Radionics. [Dr. T. Galen Hieronymus, an engineer, was the first person to be granted a U.S. Patent for a radionics machine. Since then, the Hieronymus design is one of the popular standards in the field. – Ed. note]

Life is not finished for people who are older. They haven't resigned from the human race. In fact, life is more enjoyable. Most problems have been resolved. One is more free to devote time to the pursuits of real interest, and knowledge acquired or needed, is easier to use. Personal life for older people is more rewarding. A good companion, mature love, mature interests, all tend to make life more rewarding and less stressful, so that the "Golden Years" can be truly more beautiful and happy. It is said that it is better to wear out than to rust out. The joy of achievement is even greater for the more mature people.

Eloptic Health Care during this time of life can be very useful. We need say nothing of the price of health care, hospital care, and the operations deemed necessary in many cases. One of the great fears of people growing older is that of senility. Medical research has shown that degenerative diseases of the brain, such as Alzheimer's Disease, are mostly due to metallic poisoning, very prevalent in our modern civilization.

Autopsies of people who have died of Alzheimer's Disease show grey plaques in the brain tissue, very much like those found in the skin disease, psoriasis. Analyzing these show aluminum poisoning, or some type of metal poisoning. Our research has shown that Psoriasis can be cured by treating out aluminum or mercurial poisoning. Keeping the brain areas free of aluminum or metallic poison should prevent any manifestation of Alzheimer's Disease, which is one of the chief causes of that plague of aging called Senility.

Needless to say, digestive troubles usually show far more prevalence in older years. However, keeping all locations of the Gastro-Intestinal Tract clear of metallic poisons, food poisons, infections, and toxins, can keep an older person much happier and disease free.

Diabetes is one of the problems which gains momentum in older years of the human body. With one of our Analyzers, we are able to tune into the pancreas, genes, left lobe of the liver, and the kidneys, to ANALYZE AND FIND THE CAUSE. Many do not realize the importance of the left lobe of the liver in the condition known as Diabetes. With the Genuine Hieronymus instrument we can find the problems residing in the left lobe of the liver, which has to do with sugar storage and use of sugar in the body, and get rid of the causes of problems. The conditions known as Diabetes have a common wavelength, which can be used to heal the body, maintaining a balance with a sugar usage problem.

Claudication is a condition resulting from the pancreas-liver-kidney problems found in Diabetes. It is a swelling and painful circulation problem experienced as "resting pain" especially legs and feet. It becomes so painful and generates such fears in most older people that they will complain, and finally accept amputation of the leg. That is all the M.D.'s know to do. We found that the problem is caused by concentrated uremic poisoning in the subcutaneous tissues, veins, and arteries, combined high cholesterol and calcification in the veins and arteries. We can remove these negative energies. Thus amputation can be avoided, and life made much more pleasant.

Heart trouble has been one of the greatest killers of older people. The causes of heart malfunctioning, including heavy layers of cholesterol and plaques in the veins and arteries, and arterial diseases, can be detected by tuning into their wavelength. Then the causes can be found and removed by eliminating these negative conditions. The heart can be strengthened by stimulating applications of energy.

13927-VALO

Many people do not realize that the acid-alkaline balance of the body is important, and so is the sodium-chlorine balance. Sodium plays a great part in high blood pressure, especially those who have worked in industries where sodium is used in every day work. We have the means with the Hieronymus Instrument of analyzing these situations, and removing the causes. We have seen this many times. High chlorine readings in the blood cause wheals and Urticaria, often mistaken by medical practitioners for allergic reactions or nervous seizures the case of Bosco and Jacksonian seizure.

We have been told since we started kindergarten, that germs cause disease. In our research with Eloptic Energy Health Care we have found data that incline us to argue with that theory. We have proven over and over again that there are definite causes of diseased organs and glands. Germs are found in the location of disease, because they are scavengers. They come to feed on diseased tissue, and add their excrement to the inflammation which tends to make the disease worse and spread the effects.

Another thing that is not generally understood is that in Eloptic Health Care we are working with wavelengths of energies, both of the organs affected and of the disease. We use energies of beneficial substances, which we call Reagents, to cancel out diseases, because time is very important to us. The use of Reagents saves time.

So far our work with Eloptic Health Care has been purely experimental. We have done enough, however, to know that with this method of analyzing, treating on the wavelengths of the problems to reverse the conditions, using Reagents to hasten the treatments and the results, is a science in itself. Accurate records must be kept as in any type of research, and results can be replicated. I have very little patience with those who promise the sun and moon and stars to those who buy their instruments. Analysis and treatment with a radionic instrument is a long, painstaking search for causes, broadcasting on the appropriate rates, trying and finding the proper Reagents, and keeping accurate records.

This is the way of Creative Research, for when we have found the cause of disease, we must find the means of correcting it. Dr. Hieronymus' research for years has created much information and methods of working with Eloptic Energy. Still, we make new discoveries every day.

Needless to say, the Eloptic Health Care methods can save the older person thousands of dollars in health care costs, keep them out of nursing homes, and in active participation in the affairs of life. There is no room for rocking chairs in our type of life, nor should there be in any older person's life.

We must pause here to give due credit to proper nutritional research and substances, which taken internally, will strengthen the cell structure, enrich the blood and help to give the body energies that are needed for its maintenance. We recommend to all those we work with, that in a run-down condition of the body, they seek proper advice as to diet and nutritional aid, vitamins, minerals, etc.

The psychological problems arising from improper mental attitudes can sometimes be traced to physical causes. This is one of the areas in which Eloptic Energy Health Care can keep the older person feeling good, so that there are fewer bouts with depression. One of the jokes around our lab was that when I got tired and grouchy, Dr. H. immediately put my specimen in the well of the instrument and set the dial on 60-29. Strep infection in the liver is one of the greatest causes of depression!

With most mental aberrations in the elderly due to metallic poison, especially aluminum, there are some ranges of conditions, considered mental, that we can deal with. We have found that some disturbances in the Pineal gland and the Pituitary gland can cause some mental problems in any person, not only in the elderly. A tiny tumor in the Pineal gland can cause mental problems, and loss of the grasp of reality. Metallic poisons in the Pituitary can cause weakness, lack of coherency, etc.

It is said that hormones are the Fountain of Youth. Keeping the glands healthy, and producing the hormones necessary, can

13927-VALO

be done with our system of using the Hieronymus Instrument. The medical profession treats symptoms. We remove the causes of diseases, so that the glands and organs can function properly. Some conditions more than others, impoverish older patients.

QUESTION: What percentage of the hospital business is made up of Heart By-Pass Surgery?

ANSWER: At a cost of $20,000 to $30,000 per operation, I have heard that "the hospitals would fold up without them."

I know that the little known Reading, PA Hospital is making approximately $70,000,000 per year on Heart Bypass Surgery! A friend of the family was admitted and given a number, but was sent home because of a cold that he had. When he returned the following week, he was given a number that was 36 numbers higher than his first.

The hospital schedules as many as six operations per day, at around $20,000 to $30,000 for each operation; to which a single senior surgeon may be assigned. The surgeon would get around $6,000 for each operation, or $36,000 for that day. I would guess that he assigns the "closing up."

By comparison, in Germany (reference Dr. Hans A. Nieper) only one in five of these U. S. patients have gone "under the knife"'. They would have been treated earlier with Chelation (for example, 10 weekly visits plus a complete test run-up would cost about $1000); plus the chelation supplements, Calcium and Magnesium Oratate; plus a special diet and exercise. Refer to the "Chelation Can Cure" by Dr. E. W. McDonagh.

QUESTION: What percentage of total medical costs are made up, either directly or indirectly, from present high cost cancer treatments, and cancer research?

ANSWER: I have read that, at the last count, there are currently over 400,000 persons employed "in search of " a cancer cure. ".

By estimating $100,000 for each Ph.D. or technician, with the necessary facilities overhead, it would come to 40 Billion dollars per year. Also, this figure does not include the costs associated government agencies such as the FDA, NCI, and ACS. (See Barry Lynes Research on these agencies).

QUESTION: What would happen to the "40 billion" research dollars each year; and the 400,000 "searchers"; and the (?) billions of dollars spent by patients in the course of dying, if, suddenly, there would be a cancer cure?

ANSWER: Are the answers to these questions tied in with the suppression of many cancer cures, by the government agencies that are associated with the above funding?

My only strong suggestion is to constantly compare what is presently happening in our present health system to those countries that do not have our FDA, NCI, and ACS agencies; or the equivalent of our AMA, protecting their doctors "productivity"!

There is no law against personal health care. Our own method of health care with your owned Eloptic Energy instrument is quite effective. We are Advanced Sciences R & D Corporation. Those who have and use our instruments are our card-carrying Research Associates, who record their research and share their findings with us, thus increasing our research range, and are always given credit for their work in our published reports. Our other work in which many of our Research Associates join us is the use of analyzers to do soil tests, treat plant diseases, and get rid of weeds (see Charles Walter's book, *Weeds without Poisons*) .We use amplified Solar Energy with our cosmic pipe to grow grains with stronger stems, harvest vegetables, tomatoes and fruit with higher Brix count. We experience two weeks earlier harvest, longer shelf life, rejuvenate old orchards, get rid of fungus, larvae and plant diseases without sodium fertilizers, poisons and pesticides. Our work with personal health care, agriculture, environmental pollution, and other problems of today continues.

13927-VALO

Bibliography

Lindbalm, Charles—*The Policy Makinq Process*
Foundations of Modern Political Sciences Series
Friedman, Gary D.—*Primer of Epidemiology*
Bulloch and Bullough—*Poverty—Ethnic Identity Health Care.*
Hieronymus, Dr. Galen & Dr. Sarah—*The Story of Eloptic Energy*
Hartman, N.D., Ph.D., Jane, *Shamanism for the New Age: A Guide to Radionics & Radiesthesia*, Aquarium Systems Inc., NM, 1987
Russell, Edward, *Report on Radionics, Science of the Future*, Neville Spearman Ltd., Great Britain, 1983
Tansley, David, *Radionics: A Patient's Guide to Instrumented Distant Diagnosis and Healing*, Element Books, Great Britain, 1985

6

Remote Viewing and Psychokinesis Research

Jack Houck

Reprinted from the *J. of the U. S. Psychotronics Association*, No. 5, 1991, p. 21

This summer it will have been 10 years since I conducted my first remote viewing (RV) experiment. I had been exposed to remote viewing in the early 1970's as a result of work done by Harold Puthoff and Russell Targ who were then employed by Stanford Research Institute (SRI) International.{1} They had coined the term "remote viewing" as a descriptor for a phenomena known as "clairvoyance," or the ability of a person to perceive information (see) at a distance. To them, remote viewing was a more descriptive term and sounded more "scientific." Many of the parapsychology laboratories in the United States now use the term "remote perception" because the information that a person might perceive is often more than just visual, as the term viewing implies. I had the opportunity to visit Puthoff and Targ at the SRI in the spring of 1979, and they suggested that I conduct my own remote viewing experiments to replicate their experiments. Shortly thereafter I met some people who introduced me to a lady psy-

13927-VALO

chic who seemed to "see" things at a distance, so I asked her if she was willing to participate in an experiment, which we conducted in August 1979. [It is worth mentioning that the CIA also conducted similar experiments *for years* and then denied any success upon closing the program and issuing a public report. The participants, including Dr. Harold Puthoff have now reacted with their own articles and books about how effective this technique is. – Ed. note]

The purpose of this paper is to review the experiments that I have conducted in both remote viewing and psychokinesis during the last ten years and record my observations. I have also included discussion of my experiments conducted on firewalking and the evaluation of peoples' brain waves as measured by an electroencephalogram (EEG). In my view, all this is interrelated and provides data that has been and will be useful in better modeling and understanding the human brain/mind and hopefully will lead to the extension of our current physics to include human consciousness.

The thrust of my research effort had been to work with these phenomena that are considered anomalies by conventional science. Most serious and competent researchers can achieve robust and significant results in these experiments if they pay attention to some of the subtle parameters involved in the experiments. Psychological and environmental issues must be taken into account which are generally not required for a laboratory physics experiment. Some of these parameters I did not understand in the beginning of my experiments. However, when you keep at it for along time, you find out what works and what does not. I continue to be amazed at how many "experts" there are among practicing scientists and magicians who have never conducted an experiment attempting to collect data in the paranormal areas. Also, the rate at which people suggest experiments that should be done far exceeds the rate at which it is possible to conduct them, especially when unfunded. Many people are happy to participate in these experiments, but few are willing to perform the effort required to prepare, perform, and document the experiments. Over the years, a few friends have helped a lot with the "dirty work." Most of these have been single men whose main objective seems to be to meet the women at the workshops. I wish there were more credible, scientific thinking individuals who are willing to devote the time necessary to conduct their own experiments and share the data. Today's social environment makes this difficult because there is no funding available and you run the risk of losing credibility. It still seems that people are readily willing to believe a magician's suggestion that paranormal phenomena does not exist rather than evaluate the research of the people conducting experiments. For example, some imply that metal bending does not occur simply because they can do it as a trick. The researchers do not use the "show biz" approach.

My first remote viewing experiment used what we now call "local remote viewing." This type of experiment is relatively easy to conduct. {2} This is where the "viewing team" (interviewer and viewer) are in a laboratory or home and all the potential targets are drawn from the local area, usually within a 30-minute drive from the viewing site. An "outbound team" of one or more people meet with the viewing team and agree to go to the randomly selected target 30 minutes after they leave the viewing site (the target is selected after leaving the viewing site). At the designated time, the viewer describes the site where the outbound team is supposed to be. The interviewer asks the viewer questions to clarify the description of the target site. This is usually tape-recorded and the viewer sketches objects perceived to be at the target site. After 15 minutes, the outbound team leaves the target site and goes to a location where they call the viewing team and agree on a place to meet. After meeting, the outbound team takes the viewing team to the target site and feedback of the correct target is thus provided to the viewing team. In formal experiments, this is all documented and after a series of these trials, judged with statistics developed to describe the significance of the results. In the early remote viewing experiments, judges were used to match data from the viewings with the actual targets. It was much more difficult to train a judge than a viewer. It seemed as if the mind of the judge would get into the experiment. If the judge was a skeptic, he would not see any correlations in the data, even when they were obvious. When there were more than one judge, the strongest I willed judge would get the upper hand when decisions were required. It wasn't until 1982 when Dr. Robert Jahn and Brenda Dunne developed a method to get rid of the human judges in this type of experiment. They developed a 30-question questionnaire which allowed the viewer to answer the questions and these answers could be compared to the answers to the same questions prepared by people looking at the actual target.{3} Computers were used to evaluate the comparisons between viewings and targets. This technique gets rid of the problems with the human judges and allowed the inclusion of many more trials in the experiments because human judges seemed to get bogged down (information overload) if there were more than seven trials in an experiment.

Starting in the fall of 1979, I had a small group of psychics meet in my home every week for five years. We conducted many informal experiments wherein I learned a lot about how viewers were able to perceive remote information and the sources of errors. Sometimes a slide projector was set up in the den. The people would attempt to "view" the projection of a randomly selected slide from the living room. Usually, at least one person would correctly describe the slide. One time a lady described (with sketch) exactly the shape of "Old Faithful" in Yellowstone National Park, on a slide in the tray of potential slides to be selected, but not the one being projected. When the correct projected slide was described, about half the time it would be described as it was, and the other times it would be described as if the viewer was seeing the same object or scene, but from a difference place or perspective.

In 1980, I was funded to perform the first formal "coordinate" remote viewing experiment. Ingo Swan had suggested to

Puthoff and Targ in the mid-1970's that a person could describe what was at a remote target if only the latitude and longitude coordinates were specified. They experimented with this notion, but never ran a formal experiment. We collected a large target pool of 60 places on Earth. The coordinates were specified in degrees, minutes, and seconds which corresponds to about a 100-foot resolution. Twelve of the targets were actually used in the experiment with the two remote viewers doing six targets each. Even though the overall statistical results of the experiment were not significant, those of us that participated in the experiment knew that there had been a lot of accurate viewing. The main problem had been with the judges. The experiment was rejudged after the development of the Jahn and Dunne questionnaire, this time with statistically significant results. I had been the interviewer of each of the trials in this experiment. There were times that I had to choose between getting good statistical results and learning more about the phenomena. I found that I would select to learn more. For example, one of the viewers described a scene in which she saw some hieroglyphics. Instead of getting more information about the target area as it was at that time, I asked her to go back in time to see if there was any historical information obtainable. No special insights were developed, and it probably would have been better for the experiment to have just developed information about the target site. In documenting this experiment, the data seemed to suggest ideas of how remote viewing might work if I changed the way I thought about how our brain and mind function. This prompted me to write a conceptual model of paranormal phenomena which was later reprinted.{4} I have been experimenting with and expanding this conceptual model ever since. It was this model I was testing when I developed the PK Party concept in January of 1981. The PK Parties and associated research on psychokinesis are discussed later in this paper. My remote viewing research continued while the popular PK Parties took a great deal of my time throughout the 1980's. [Jack Houck conducted a few of these PK (spoon-bending) Parties for the USPA in the 1980's. Witnessing women bending *the bowl of a tablespoon* with ease, when a magician can only bend the handle surreptitiously, was an educational experience. I even brought Jack to host a successful Party in my hometown. –Ed. note]

In 1983, I conducted another formal remote viewing experiment with Dr. Elizabeth Rauscher. This experiment was very similar to a local remote viewing experiment, except Elizabeth was the outbound person in the San Francisco area, and the viewer and I were at viewing sites in the Los Angeles area.{5,6} This experiment turned out to be statistically significant. One of the viewing sites was a neurologist's office where both the viewer and I were hooked up to an EEG instrument attempting to learn what the brain wave frequencies were during the viewing and if there was any relationship between the viewer's and interviewer's brain waves. It turned out that only the viewer's EEG was obtained because the technician failed to ground the electrodes on my head. However, that viewing was by far the best of the entire series and I observed that "psi" seems to work the best when you are doing something unusual in an unusual situtation.

Up to this point I had usually been the experimenter, interviewer, and sometimes, judge. My main judging experience came by helping Steven Schwartz of the Mobius Society in their Omni remote viewing experiment. I was involved with judging the Japanese portion of the experiment. About that time Russell Targ left SRI to form his own research organization and conducted the first *associative remote viewing* (ARV) experiment, using the silver futures as the source of future events.{7} I was very interested in the idea of using remote viewing to predict the outcome of future events. In these experiments, an object or scene is associated with each possible outcome of a future event. The viewer looks into the future at the time that he is shown the object or picture of the scene associated with the correct outcome of the event. At the time of the viewing, the viewer's perception can be compared with the set of objects associated with each possible outcome and thus determine the most likely outcome before the event occurs. Hal Puthoff also performed a successful ARV experiment.{8}

Steven Schwartz asked me if I would be a viewer for his ARV experiment. I had never been a viewer but decided to go ahead and give it a try. Mobius uses a consensus approach with input data from seven viewers. [Mobius was a corporation whose profits were generated from consensus among ARV psychics on staff. An article appeared in *Omni* magazine about how the company was run. – Ed. note]

This experiment proceeded for 45 weeks (one viewing per week) without significant results. However, a lot was learned about the process and Mobius tried a lot of innovative ideas. My conceptual model suggested that people doing the judging had to be isolated from the rest of the group in order to prevent information leakage. When Mobius stopped their experiment, I decided to write a computer program that individuals and groups could use to run their own ARV experiments.{9,10}

It was difficult getting people and groups to get started on the ARV experiment with real money, so I decided to do it myself. The early success received much attention and very quickly there were 15 groups participating, each with their own personal computer and group of viewers. Most of the groups eventually lost money and I stopped the experiment when it was clear that improvements in the technique were warranted, and the psychology within some of the groups was no longer conducive to successful remote viewing. The overall results and observations of these ARV experiments are documented.{11}

One of the most promising things to come out of the remote viewing research is correlation between good remote viewing and low magnitude of the ∑KP index of the earth's magnetic field between 24 and 48 hours before the viewing.{12} This trend also appeared in my ARV experiment and suggests the potential for the development of a well calibrated magnetic field instrument to be used at the viewing sites and a service provided to the local area identifying the best times to conduct paranormal experiments, make intuitive business decisions – and go to Las Vegas.

Starting in 1984, I began giving remote viewing (RV) workshops to teach people how to do remote viewing. I review experimental results, describe techniques, and provide participation in one or more real experiments. The targets used in one experiment are coordinate target scenes. The workshop attendees are divided into teams of an interviewer and viewer. Each individual gets to perform each function. The viewer uses the 30-question questionnaire, as well as drawing their perception of the target defined by the coordinates in an envelope. The target feedback data is in another envelope. In the early RV workshops, the interviewer would read the coordinates to the viewer. The skeptics claimed that everyone had memorized the world map with coordinates down to the accuracy of seconds – which simply is not true. However, to avoid this accusation, I stopped having people open the envelope containing the coordinates. There has been no degradation in the statistical results of these experiments. There was a period when I had people use a 31-question questionnaire developed by the Mobius Society. It did not work nearly as well as the questionnaire developed by Jahn and Dunne. (Unfortunately, I had used the Mobius questionnaire in the ARV experiment.) There have now been 27 of my RV Workshops with a total of 400 people attending.

In 1988, Gail Duke of the Archaeus Project suggested that I include targets that are simple symbols in the RV Workshops. Over the years of remote viewing research the data has suggested that a remote viewer has a much easier time describing form and shape than high resolution detail and words. Gail's suggestion sounded like an excellent way to take advantage of this ability of viewers to produce better experimental results. She developed the symbolic target pool which I have now used in five RV Workshops. People seem to have a hard time describing these simple symbols and to date (July, 1989) the experimental results have been less significant than the experiments using the scenic target pool. However, the data suggests something about how the brain/mind processes and stores information. It seems as if the information is stored in an object oriented manner rather than bit mapped.{13} This corresponds to being more like the way MacDraw handles information rather than like MacPaint (graphic processing software for the Macintosh computer).

The remote viewing research has come a long way in the last 10 years. As I have demonstrated, what was learned from an experiment was not always what was expected at the outset of the experiment. However, being interested in learning as much as possible about how the phenomenon works has kept me active in this work and more interested than ever. I am application oriented and know that there are many applications for remote viewing. My current plans are to continue experimenting with the symbol targets and see where that leads in learning more about the brain/mind techniques for accessing and storing information. I also plan to rework the ARV computer code to incorporate all that has been learned since the first version. Once completed, I plan to apply it to the stock market and generate the necessary capital for my own research laboratory.

My initial involvement in psychokinesis research was not planned. As mentioned earlier, I had written a conceptual model of how the brain/mind might function in an attempt to explain remote viewing. In briefing the results of the coordinate remote viewing experiment and my model around the country to various parapsychology laboratories, I was challenged to test my model. I had suggested that during remote viewing, data is accessed at or near the time of a "peak emotional event" at the place of the remote view-ing target. This can result in a temporal error. I postulated that if one deliberately creates a peak emotional event, then a paranormal phenomenon can be caused to happen at the current time at the place of the peak emotional event. I had said that maybe even psychokinesis (i.e., causing metal to bend) could be initiated. When thinking about how to create a peak emotional event, I thought having a wild party might provide an appropriate environment. In early January, 1981, I had seen two people bend some metal. Their physical effort seemed much less than would have been expected under normal circumstances. So I decided to see if the combination of a wild party and the intention to bend some metal would produce psychokinesis. Coincidentally, Severin Dahlen walked into my office a week before this event was scheduled to take place. He described teaching children to bend metal at the University of California, Irvine. I asked him if he would give the instructions at the "PK Party." Nineteen of the 21 people at that first PK Party experienced some amount of psychokinesis. (I was one of the two who did not bend anything, mainly because I was so involved with trying to figure out what was happening. Left brain analytical thinking is not conducive to high performance in these activities.)

I was sufficiently impressed with the PK Party that a month later I conducted another one, this time with many different types of metal and metals having undergone different processes. Over the years, we learned that metals with lots of dislocations in the grain boundaries were the easiest to "PK". These are metals that have been forged or cold-rolled to make them "harder." [Notice the genuine but amazing irony here: hardened metal is easier to bend by paranormal psychokinesis. Jack also conducted studies with electron microscopy that showed anomalous heating effects. – Ed. note]

I would have never guessed that these experiments would have led to what has been accomplished to date. I have now conducted 220 PK Parties with approximately 10,000 people attending them. There are at least 40 others who have given PK Parties, often with more success than mine. Some of these people have done quite a few parties and have touched many people. Eldon Byrd conducted a PK Party on National Japanese Television during which it was estimated that 6 to 20 million people came out into the streets to show the cameras things that they had bent. I continue to document each PK Party. I estimate that 85% of all the party attendees have experienced at least some level of PK, usually bending up some flatware when they feel it get "soft" in their hands. I call this "kindergarten bending." About 30% have experienced "high school bending" which is when they have done something beyond normal physical strength, like buckling the bowl of a spoon. At the end of the PK Parties, I have the participants hold up a dinner fork in each hand and command it to bend spontaneously. About 10% of the people have their forks bend. Most often the bend or twist is fairly small, but noticeable. Sometimes the fork head bends up to 90 degrees relative to the fork handle. These often occur for children! On two occasions explosions have occurred, sounding like firecrackers wherein the silverplate of a fork was rolled back. In both cases, laboratory analysis of these forks indicated that there was corrosion under the plating.

Most people do not know that often we conduct experiments within the PK Parties. We use the PK Party environment to generate a "PK field" and let other test specimens be affected. We have also put a large amount of effort into developing a sensor that can be used to detect these fields. I am still not ready to publish on the sensor development area. The most promising sensor is a Hall Effect device which is usually used to sense magnetic fields. However, we think the dislocations are being affected which alters the output reading.

1) I use three simple steps to perform PK. They are: make a mental connection with what you are trying to affect,

2) command it to do what you want, like "BEND," and

3) release that thought and let it happen.

The first two steps are easy for our Western culture. However, we have not been taught how to do the third step. I think one of the biggest benefits of the PK Parties is that people learn about

13927-VALO

letting go. These steps can apply to almost every aspect of peoples' lives and I enjoy the many letters I get from all over the world telling me how this has helped people in their lives. I enjoy watching peoples' beliefs change about the reality of PK. Almost everyone who has attended a PK Party has either had their own PK experience or sees some-thing that catches their attention-a fork bending spontaneously or a small child bending something that most I adults could not have bent. While the parapsychology community continues to run hundreds of thousands of micro-PK trials to drag out a small but persuasive effect, it only takes seeing one fork (or maybe two) bending spontaneously to convince yourself that macro-PK is real.

I have done this now with so many different kinds of groups, with people of all ages, that I am convinced that everyone can do it, *if they want to*. Some are frightened by the implications, have a religious reservation, or do not want to hurt the silverware. In the early days of the PK Parties, I was most interested in the metallurgy and learning what was going on inside the metal. Today, I am more interested in the psychology of group phenomenon and how to teach large groups of people information that was not previously within their paradigm. I plan to continue giving PK Parties at the rate of two or three per month. This involves finding and washing a lot of silverware. Developing a reliable sensor and amplifier for the PK field are the two most important areas needing further work. There are many applications for this technology, including healing.

During these ten years of research I spent time working on two additional areas. The first was attempting to find some correlation between peoples brain waves, as measured by an EEG, and their performance in RV and PK activities. This is an area wherein there seems to be quite a few researchers working; most notably, Drs. Elmer and Alyce Green of the Menninger Foundation in Topeka, Kansas.{14}

Dr. Bob Beck developed a simple, single channel biofeedback EEG that I found to be excellent for biofeedback training. I assembled a computer system wherein I could feed data recorded from the EEG into the computer, digitize it, and process the data using a Fast Fourier Transform (FFT) to determine the frequency components. I also wrote the software to display this data in a manner where the researcher could see the history of the frequencies. I have performed this analysis on quite a few people (approximately 45) and wrote one article {15} on the pattern of the brain waves of "high performance" people. There were distinct patterns associated with different types of individuals. My database is small in this area, but it does seem to be a rich area for research. For example, Beck's unit modulates a 2000 Hz tone with the EEG information. By listening to your own brain waves at the same time as listening to a 7.81 Hz signal put through an identical unit seems to produce an out-of-body experience for half the people who have tried it using my equipment. A similar technique might be useful in teaching or improving remote viewing. I also found happy couples with similar brain wave patterns. If enough data substantiated this finding, setting up a dating service that included matching brain wave patterns might be interesting.

Another area in which I invested a lot of time and money was in the study of the "firewalking" phenomenon. Having personally walked over the hot coals three different times, I wanted to learn more about what was going on. I set up my camera to take flash pictures in the infrared. To an observer, the flash looks like a dull red dot and does not interfere with the firewalker's state of mind. Generally, you could see that the successful walkers (no burns} seemed to be in an altered state. I also built foot pads that held very small thermocouples (1 mil, or smaller than a human hair} in an attempt to measure the temperature very near the bottom of several peoples' feet while walking over the fire. Unfortunately, that is a very hostile environment and many of the data channels failed. However, data was collected that indicates that the temperature 2 mm away from the skin has temperatures as high as 1600 degrees F. while those thermocouples against the skin registered no change in temperature.{16,17} To date I have concluded that firewalking includes some type of PK phenomena because of the similarities with the PK Parties. This research as been put on hold until some breakthrough in measurement systems occurs that will allow a microscopic view of the boundary layer between the fire and the skin. My personal experience in firewalking has provided more insight so far than the sophistication of today's measurement technology.

In summary, great strides have been made in the last ten years of research. There have been many dedicated people working long hours, and often with no pay, in attempts to further understand paranormal phenomena. Originally, I thought my efforts would be most useful to the parapsychology community. That community seems to be afraid of applications and has concentrated on "proof" to the point where all their time is absorbed in confrontation with the skeptics. My contention is that proof takes care of itself when you have reliable applications of psi phenomena. The parapsychology community best expressed their feelings for my work when they outlawed PK Parties at their annual conventions.

I am most disappointed with how quickly people will believe the well-funded skeptics and magicians and not see through their charades, innuendos, and tricks. I am also disappointed that no government agency has ever sup-ported my work. They are great sponges of information. I feel that I have many friends in those circles. However, they are afraid of Proxmier's "Golden Fleece Award" and every management train always seems to have at least one uninformed skeptic who can stop support, even in the enlightened aerospace company for which I work. They should realize that this is some of the most advanced research around as it will have many incredible applications in the near future.

I plan to continue my research efforts to the best of my ability. We need to have more people interested in "Engineering PSI." I will help those interested to get started as best I can.

References

1. H. Puthoff and R. Targ., " A perceptual channel for information transfer over kilometer distances: Historical perspective and recent research," *Proceedings of the IEEE* 64, 3 {March 1976): 329-354.
2. Jack Houck, "Instructions for Conducting a Remote Viewing Experiment," in *Artifex,* Vol. 4, No.1, Spring 1985, p4.
3. Robert G. Jahn and Brenda J. Dunne. *Margins of Reality: The Role of Consciousness in the Physical World*. San Diego, Calif.: Harcourt Brace Jovanovich,1987, p174.
4. Jack Houck, "Conceptual Model of Paranormal Phenomena," *ARCHAEUS* 1,1 {Winter 1983).
5. Jack Houck and Elizabeth A. Rauscher, "Los Angeles Area to San Francisco Bay Remote Perception Experiment," *Psi Research*, Vol. 4, No.314, September/ December 1985, p48.
6. Jack Houck, Roger D. Nelson, and Elizabeth A. Rauscher, Addendum to "Los Angeles Area to San Francisco Bay Area Remote Perception Experiment: A Reevaluation," in *Psi Research*, Vol. 5, No.112, March/ June 1986, pl08.
7. Erik Arson, "Did psychic powers give firm a killing in the silver market?" *The Wall Street Journal,* Oct. 22,1984.
8. H. Puthoff, " Associative remote viewing experiment," *Proceedings, 1984 Parapsychology Association Conference*, Dallas, Texas.
9. Jack Houck, "Associative Remote Viewing, " in *Artifex*, Vol. 5, No.3, June 1986, p13.
10. Jack Houck, "Use of Associative Remote Viewing Computer Program," December 1985.
11. Jack Houck, "Results of ARV Experiment," April 30, 1987 {unpublished but obtainable from the author, 16892 Canyon Lane, Huntington Beach, CA 92649).
12. Marsha H. Adams, "Variability in Remote Viewing Performance: Possible Relationship to the Geomagnetic Field," *Proceedings of 1985 Parapsychology Conference*, 1985.

13927-VALO

13. Jack Houck with Gail Duke, "Remote Viewing Work-shop at the Second Archaeus Congress," *Artifex* 8,1; 1989.
14. Elmer and Alyce Green, *Beyond Biofeedback*, New York: Dell Publishing Co. Inc., 1978.
15. Karen Olness and Jack Houck, "EEGs of High-Performance Individuals," in *Artifex*, Vol. 5, No.1, February-March 1986, p6.
16. Jack Houck, "First Archaeus Congress FIREWALK –A Technical Report," in *Artifex*, Vol. 5, No.1, February-March 1986, p3.
17. Jack Houck, "A Conceptual Model of Paranormal Phenomena, Information Transfer and Mind-Brain Interaction," in United States Psychotronics Association, *USPA Annual Conference Proceedings, 1985*, p5.

7

Fundamentals of a Zero-Point Energy Technology

Moray B. King
P.O. Box 859
Provo, UT 84603

19th Annual Conference of the U. S. Psychotronics Association, 1993, Milwaukee, WI

Abstract

The vacuum polarization of atomic nuclei may trigger a coherence in the zero-point energy (ZPE) whenever a large number of nuclei undergo abrupt, synchronous motion. Experimental evidence arises from the energy anomalies observed in heavy-ion collisions, ion-acoustic plasma oscillations, sonoluminescence, fractoemission, large charge density plasmoids, abrupt electric discharges, and light water "cold fusion" experiments. Further evidence arises from inventions that utilize coherent ion-acoustic activity to output anomalously excessive power. A ZPE coherence sufficient to manifest a gravitational anomaly might occur from circulating charged plasma through a helical vortex ring. Abruptly pulsed, opposing electromagnetic fields may further augment any ZPE interaction.

Introduction

Since the advent of quantum mechanics modern physics has supported the view that the fabric of totally empty space is not a void but contains a plenum of energy called the zero-point energy (ZPE). The energy consists of fluctuations of electric field energy that persist even at zero degrees Kelvin. The individual fluctuations exist on the scale of a Planck length (10^{-33} cm) and can have an extraordinary energy density. Wheeler (1962) derives a density of 10^{94}grams/cc in his theory of geometrodynamics, and Hathaway (1991) reviews other derivations of ZPE densities which are all quite large. Boyer (1975) suggests that the ZPE in its interaction with matter is the basis of quantum mechanical effects. Senitzky (1973) shows that the elementary particles' very existence is intertwined with the ZPE, and the interaction manifests the phenomenon of vacuum polarization. Dirac (1930) proposed a dynamic turbulence model for the vacuum and showed that it gives rise to a sea of constantly forming and annihilating pairs of virtual (short lived) charged particles. The picture delivered by modern physics is that the vacuum contains an active, energetic plenum resembling a virtual plasma that intimately interacts with all of matter.

A question applicable to engineers is can the zero-point energy be tapped as an energy source? At first this idea seems to be a blatant violation of conservation of energy, but if the zero-point energy really exists as is suggested by modern physics, energy is present and its conservation would not be the issue.

The real issue centers on the second law of thermodynamics, the law of increasing entropy, for how could a system consisting of chaotic fluctuations evolve into a coherent state? Prigogine (1977) won the Nobel prize in chemistry for answering that question and put the field of system self-organization (Suzuki, 1984, et al.) onto a firm theoretical foundation. Three conditions are required for a system to exhibit self-organization. The system must be: nonlinear in its dynamic behavior, far from equilibrium and have an energy flux passing through it.

A review (King, 1991) of the published theories of the zero-point energy show that under certain circumstances, the ZPE in its nonlinear interaction with matter can be influenced to fulfill these conditions, and this suggests the possibility that it might be available as an energy source (King, 1989). Applying system theory to the ZPE not only opens possibilities for advancing a deeper theoretical incite into the foundations of quantum field theory (LaViolette, 1985, Winterberg, 1990), but also offers opportunities for developing a novel technology.

Experiments

Despite the intriguing possibilities offered by system theory, it will require an experiment to prove that the ZPE can be tapped as an energy source. A first-order experimental success has already been accepted by the physics community. Forward (1984) has invented a rather simple battery based on the Casimir effect (Milonni, et al., 1988). Casimir predicted and experimentally demonstrated that the zero-point fluctuations induced a $1/d^4$ (d = distance) attraction between two parallel conductive plates. Forward's battery utilizes charged foils whose spacing is so close that he l/d^4 attraction overcomes the $1/d^2$ Coulomb repulsion and results in a direct current output of power from the zero-point energy. Even though the device may not currently be practical, its primary value is that it proves in principle that the ZPE can be tapped as an energy source (Puthoff, 1990).

Puthoff (1990) also applies the same Casimir squeeze principle to explain the surprising stability of high charge density, electron beads discovered by Shoulders (1991) called "electrum validum" (EV for short). The beads are on the order of a micron in size and exhibit a net charge of approximately 10^{11} electrons. They are stable when guided along etched channels in a dielectric substrate and can travel at one tenth the speed of light. They can induce an excessively powerful electrical pulse on a nearby serpentine conductor (or surrounding helical conductor) as they rapidly speed by in parallel to it. When they strike an anode plate, they also discharge a powerful pulse. Shoulders states that the output energy of the pulses greatly exceeds the input energy needed to create them, and the source appears to be from the zero-point energy. [Ken Shoulders even describes the fact that DARPA rated EV research at the top of their list for a few years (private communication). – Ed. note]

The electrum validum appears to be a self-organized structure akin to ball lightning (Singer, 1971, et al.) or the toroidal plasmoids produced by Bostick (1957). Could the anomalous persistence of ball lightning be associated with a zero-point energy coherence as well? (Egely, 1986, Jennsion, 1990)

How plasmas could cohere the zero-point energy can be understood from examining the Vacuum polarization description of the constituent particles (Rausher, 1968). Quantum Electrodynamics shows that the vacuum polarization of electrons is quite different than atomic nuclei (Scheck, 1983, Reinhardt, et al., 1980). Electrons (especially when bound in matter) exhibit a random, cloud-like interaction with the vacuum fluctuations and are effectively in thermodynamic equilibrium with it. On the other hand, nuclei exhibit stable, orderly lines of vacuum polarization which converge radially onto the particle. This allows them to launch and respond to local vacuum polarization displacement currents, which conduction band electrons may not be able to detect. The abrupt motion of nuclei can locally drive the ZPE far from equilibrium and, when combined with the nonlinear dynamics of both the plasma and the ZPE, can fulfill Prigogine's conditions for system self-organization to trigger the formation of exotic, energetic vacuum states similar to those that sometimes occur in heavy-ion collision experiments (Celenza, 1986, et al.). Evidence for a ZPE coherence in plasmas arises from the observed anomalies associated with the ion-acoustic mode where the plasma's ions are undergoing synchronous oscillations. Here are observed runaway electrons (Kiwamoto, et al., 1979), anomalous heating Sethian, 1978, et al.), and high frequency voltage spikes (Kalinin, 1970, et al.). In general plasma physicists have not been looking for energy anomalies in their experiments, but recently Chrnetskii (Samokhin, 1990) has claimed to produce more heat output in his plasma experiments than energy input and attributes the ZPE as the source of the excess energy.

Another class of experiments yielding anomalous heat are the "cold fusion" experiments of which there have recently been numerous successes (Storms, 1991). These experiments can manifest ion-acoustic type oscillations of the deuterons within the hydride lattice sites especially under the conditions of deuterium supersaturation where all the sites are occupied (and diffusion is inhibited). Here within a single crystalline grain of the hydride, the deuterons may undergo coherent oscillations creating a macroscopic ZPE vacuum polarization. If the ZPE is coherently interacting with the system, then it can trigger some fusion events (Jandel, 1990) as well as produce abundant heat without fusion. Especially relevant are the experiments of Mills and Kneizys (1991) who can generate anomalous heat with 100% repeatability in their light water experiments, and there has already been reported numerous independent replications (Mallove, 1992, et al.). To explain the result, Mills proposes a new quantum theory where the hydrogen atom's electron can drop below its ground state via a catalytic reaction. Alternatively, Bush (1992) proposes a transmission resonance model where coherent proton oscillations occur at the surface of the hydride whose coupling is so great that it can trigger a proton absorbing, element transmutation of the electrolyte's potassium ions converting them to calcium! A zero-point energy coupling hypothesis could enhance the transmission resonance model and perhaps provide a simpler explanation for the anomalous heat.

Another experimental area where energy anomalies could be associated with coherent ion motion occurs in sonoluminescence (Walton and Reynolds, 1984). Here ultrasonic excitation of water causes emission of blue light that is visible to the naked eye. It has previously been assumed that the collapse of cavitation bubbles produces a sufficiently abrupt heating that it can dissociate some water molecules into a plasma followed by chemiluminescence of its constituents. However, the recent research of Barber and Putterman (1991) have shown that the photon emissions are much too rapid for the fastest atomic electron transitions. Moreover, they show that the phenomenon represents a 10^{11} amplification of energy. The zero-point energy hypothesis may provide the most direct explanation.

Along similar lines, coherent nuclei coupling to the ZPE could be suggested to explain the anomalies associated with fractoemission (Preparata, 1991). The abrupt fracturing of crystals has yielded anomalously powerful light emissions as well as excessively accelerated electrons. Furthermore, the anomalous events could persist for hours! Preparata (1991) has proposed a theory of superradiance where coherent radiation from a plasma produced around the fracture is synchronous with the plasma oscillations and creates an excited, standing-wave, bound state within the fracture cavity. Preparata's model has the ZPE coherently interacting with plasma ion-acoustic oscillations that can manifest an energy concentration which produces the anomalously powerful events. The proposed ZPE coherence exhibits stability similar to ball lightning or Shoulder's (1991) electrum validum, and appears to explain the events' anomalous persistence.

Inventions

Evidence for tapping the zero-point energy as an energy source also comes from inventions whose principle of operation involves the same ion-acoustic type activity that exhibits energy anomalies in the experiments. For example in the 1930's Moray (1978) produced a solid state device that was well witnessed to output 50 kilowatts of electricity. Moray stressed that the basis of success was maintaining ion oscillations in the plasmas within the device's tubes. Along similar lines Brown (1989) has reproduced a resonant nuclear battery that is similar to the invention of the order of 5 milliwatts. However, if the tuned circuit resonates at the plasma's ion-acoustic frequency, and this mode couples coherently to the ZPE, it could explain the source of anomalous power.

The ZPE ion-acoustic hypothesis may be applied to explain anomalous energy production in the water dissociation inventions of Puharich (1981) and Meyer (1991). Both inventions excite water in specially shaped vessels with large voltage pulses designed to resonate the water molecules at the frequencies of the hydrogen-oxygen electron bonds. Puharich stresses the importance of triggering an acoustical resonance within the water molecule itself, and both inventors claim to require far less input energy to accomplish the dissociation than what is returned when the hydrogen is burned as a fuel. This work is reminiscent of Keely's research (Moore, 1971) who claimed to easily dissociate water when excited at the appropriately resonant ultrasonic frequencies. Davidson (1990) reports of an anomalously violent event when a column of water, adjusted to support acoustical standing waves, was driven with a barium titanate ultrasonic transducer at the water dissociation frequency identified by Keely (approximately 43 kHz). If the synchronous motions of the nuclei comprising the water molecules induce a coherenence in the ZPE, the anomalous energy produced in the resonant dissociation of water could be explained.

Another invention where resonant ionic motion may be launching anomalous energy is the battery pulsing circuit originally discovered by Bedini (1991) and investigated by Panici (1992). If a new lead acid battery is pulsed charged by a fast rise time square wave (unipolar positive above 20 volts, 50% duty cycle, and on the order of 300 to 400 Hz) anomalous power can sometimes be generated that seems to be related to a critical timing in the arrival of the pulse edges. The most surprising claim

13927-VALO

regarding this experiment is the production of "cold current" where appreciable output power (200 watts) can be guided along thin wires (no.28) without heating them. The effect works only on new lead acid batteries; a battery that has been discharged and recharged by a standard DC battery charger will not produce it. The anomalous behavior could be explained as follows: The battery plates consist of porous lead or lead peroxide which exhibit a delicate dendritic structure much like the description of the palladium surface in the theories of electrochemistry (Storms 1991, Gluck, 1993). During both the charge and discharge reactions, protons (hydrogen ions) form on the dendritic surface within the porous plates. The intense electric fields from the sharp pointed dendrites can accelerate the protons, and when stimulated by an appropriate pulsed excitation, the protons can undergo coherent, synchronous oscillations similar to those described for the cold fusion experiments. The oscillations may be resonant at a higher frequency than the square wave excitation, but by adjusting the square wave to an exact subharmonic, the pulse edges can arrive in phase with the resonance. Discharging the battery accumulates sulfate on the porous plates, and recharging it with DC ruins the original dendritic surface (Barak, 1980). Thus a new battery must be used for this experiment.

The surprising cold current effect has been associated with other inventions (e.g. Moray (1978) demonstrated it and used No. 30 wire within his 50 kW device). It might be explained by the hypothesis that the coupling of synchronous ion oscillations with the ZPE can manifest macroscopic vacuum polarization displacement currents (King, 1984) which can surround a conductive wire and be guided by it. Conduction band electrons, lacking stable, radially convergent vacuum polarization lines, have a minimal interaction with these displacement currents, and the wires remain cool. If engineers could replicate this effect, zero-point energy research would receive widespread interest.

Another area where coherent ion motion is associated with energy anomalies involves abrupt electrical discharges. Graneau

(1985) has experimentally demonstrated that an anomalous force is associated with a large, abrupt electrical discharge in water. He observed a threshold effect where the same amount of energy is discharged from a capacitor bank into a water vessel, but with different rise times. At slow rise times, no motion is observed, but at a threshold where the pulse becomes abrupt enough, the water exhibits an explosive expansion. Johnson (1992) surmises from his experiments that the force is related to current density. Along similar lines the engines of Gray (1976) and Papp (1984) utilize abrupt electrical discharges to produce an anomalous driving force as well as excessive output power. The hypothesis of coherent ion motion coupling to the ZPE seems to likewise fit these inventions.

Pappas (1991) has proposed from his derivation from Ampere's law that a powerful enough electric discharge, where the electron velocities exceed 70% the speed of light, can produce anomalous energy when the discharge strikes the anode plate. An alternative, similar hypothesis is that the powerful discharge hitting the anode can produce a plasma ionic surge that, if coupled coherently with the ZPE, would manifest a greater voltage spike than would be otherwise predicted by classical theory. Many other inventors have also claimed that the anomalous energy production in their devices takes the form of abrupt voltage spikes, and they would have a practical device if only they could efficiently convert this form of energy.

Hyde (1990) was faced with a similar problem of absorbing large voltage pulses produced in his invention. He solved the problem and created an advanced embodiment which produced over 20 KW of net output power while free running. Hyde designed a solid state voltage divider that takes advantage of the abrupt rise time of the incident pulses, and it is disclosed in Figure 6 of his patent.

13927-VALO

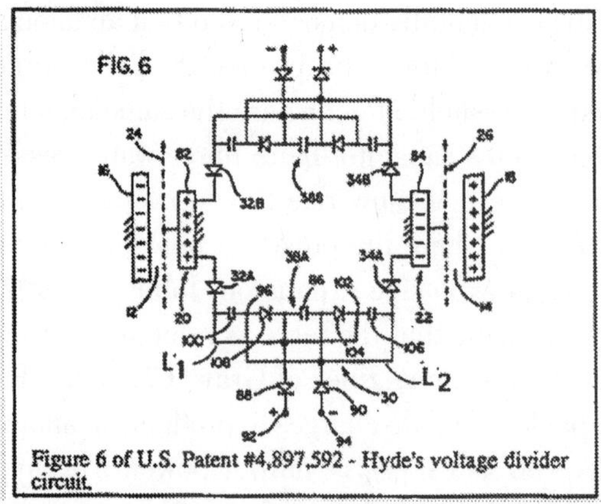

Figure 6 of U.S. Patent #4,897,592 - Hyde's voltage divider circuit.

The voltage divider circuit as diagrammed in the patent has been questioned by electrical engineers since line (herein labeled L_1) connecting the positive sides of the capacitors (labeled 100, 86 and 106) as well as the line (herein labeled L_2)connecting the negative sides of these capacitors (thus connecting them in parallel) essentially short out the series connections provided by the diodes 108 and 104. If Figure 6 is analyzed as a lumped circuit, the diodes 108 and 104 would always be back biased and appear like open switches, and the circuit could be viewed (when the capacitors are combined) as equivalent to Figure 1 of the patent. Thus, when analyzed as a lumped circuit, Figure 6 appears unable to provide voltage division.

However, analyzing Figure 6 as a distributed circuit or transmission line suggests that it could produce voltage division of sharp pulses propagating through the circuit To accomplish voltage division (with concomitant current multiplication), the capacitors must be charged in series and then discharged in parallel. If the electrical lines L_1 and L_2 are made considerably longer than the series path through the capacitors (100, 86, 106), then their residual line inductance would result in a higher (surge) impedance to sharp voltage pulses, and tend to channel the pulses through the (lower impedance) series path. If necessary, the inductance of L_1 and L_2 can be increased by shaping the wires into loose coils or by adding ferrite loading around the wires. Hyde developed the circuit such as Figure 6 empirically as he was attempting to control and absorb the very large and sharp voltage pulses generated in his device. The sharp pulses take the series path to charge the capacitors, and then the energy is discharged smoothly through the parallel path. Only by analyzing Figure 6 as a distributed circuit can its voltage division action be understood.

Note that Figure 6 is only a three stage illustration of a voltage division transmission line for sharp pulses. Clearly more stages can be used if further voltage division (and current multiplication) is needed. Hyde's circuit may be of value to inventors whose devices produce high voltage spikes from ion-acoustic activity. It might facilitate a very straightforward, solid state method for tapping the zero-point energy.

A solid state method for cohering the ZPE might be achieved by inducing appropriate nuclei motion within materials that exhibit strong electrical to acoustical coupling. For example, the following means of electrical excitation can stimulate acoustical spinor waves in a highly polarizable dielectric such as barium titanate.

Excitor electrodes are mounted as shown on a cylinder of barium titanate 45 degrees from the axis of maximum polarization. The electrode pairs A_1, A_2 and B_1, B_2 are alternately excited by an oscillating, unipolar waveform which causes the polarization vector to flex between the A and B directions. The oscillating polarization impresses an oscillating torque on the dielectric lattice which twists it to produce synchronous cycloidal movement of the lattice nuclei. At the appropriate distance along the cylinder above the first electrode group (or polarization layer) is another set of electrodes whose voltage is timed to drive the polarization vector in opposite phase; i.e., when the first layer is polarized in the A direction, the next layer should be polarized in the B direction and visa versa. In like fashion, more layers of alternating excitation electrodes can be mounted along the cylinder. The optimal distance between the layers will be related to the wavelength of the acoustical excitation whose drive frequency should be chosen to maximize the amplitude of the acoustical activity. The back and forth twisting action of the lattice can excite and maintain two counter-rotating, acoustical spinor waves. If there is a direct coupling of the synchronous nuclei motion to the ZPE, there could then arise dual, counter-rotating, displacement current vortices driven by a spatially coherent, dynamic vacuum polarization. Such dual vortices would be a macroscopic formation analogous to virtual particle pair production. Quantum electrodynamics requires that any form arising from the ZPE be created in opposing pairs in order to conserve charge, momentum and spin (angular momentum). If, instead of a linear cylinder, the dielectric is shaped as a toroid, the dual spinor waves can close into standing waves, and a significant ZPE coherence might thus be induced within a solid state structure.

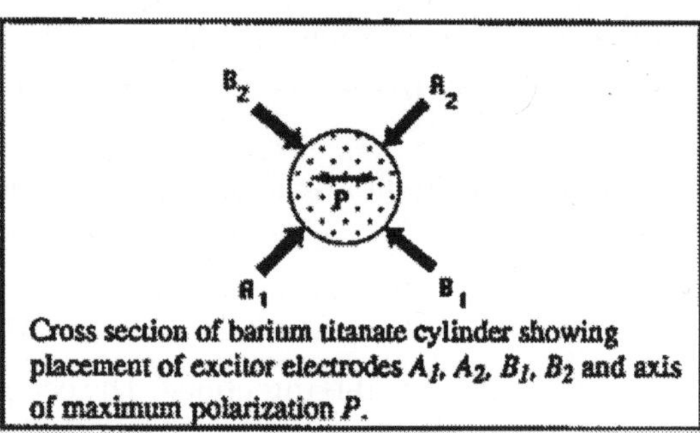

Cross section of barium titanate cylinder showing placement of excitor electrodes A_1, A_2, B_1, B_2 and axis of maximum polarization *P*.

In a similar fashion, acoustical spinor waves can be created within a highly permeable magnetic material such as barium ferrite by using an equivalent magnetic field excitation in place of the electrodes. The oscillating magnetic vectors of the shifting domains couple to the ferrite lattice and elastically twist it back and forth (Cieplak, 1980). Experimental evidence that such activity could cohere the zero-point energy appears to be exhibited by the energy producing invention of Sweet (1991).

Vortices and Precession

The greatest zero-point energy coherence may arise in experiments creating a vortex of precessional flow of charged fluid or plasma. Schauberger (Alexandersson,1990, et al.) did a series of experiments circulating water in specially spiraled pipes. At certain velocities the fluid flow manifested negative resistance, i.e. energy creation, as well as a strange, bluish glow appearing in the water near the bottom of the vortex. Such a glow is reminiscent of sonoluminescence (discussed previously). Also Chernetskii (Samokhin, 1990) observed that the greatest output of anomalous energy in his plasma experiments was associated with the cycloid motion of the plasma particles. Such spiraling plasma particle motion is also the key operating point for the energy invention by Spence (1988). The theoretical research by Reed (1992) Jennison (1978) and Winter (1991) suggests a golden mean, logarithmic spiral is the three-space projection of a fundamental, hyperspatial flow of an ether (or ZPE flux). Systems whose dynamics align with this flow tap the zero-point energy.

An aligned interaction with the zero-point energy flux may alter local gravity. Laithwaite (Davidson, 1989) observed in his experiments that a gyroscope displaced along a particular spiraling path while precessing would manifest a gravitational and inertial anomaly. Puthoff (1989) suggests that gravity is derived from the action of the ZPE. This view is essentially supported by general relativity since the ZPE must be part of the stress-energy tensor which curves the space-time metric. If a system induces coherence in the ZPE, a gravitational anomaly or change in the local pace of time could manifest (Kozyrev, 1968).

Precessional motion may be the method to manifest the largest ZPE coherence. DePalma (1973) observed a direct gravitational and inertial anomaly in his experiments involving forced precession of a counter-rotating pair of gyroscopes. Schauberger used fluting within his pipes to induce an inner spin so that his spiral pipes would induce precessional motion in the water flow. A natural form to induce precessional flow is a helix tube closed to form a vortex ring. This shape was observed in the plasmoids by Bostick (1957) as well as that suggested for ball lightning (Johnson, 1965). Roden's (1992) theoretical treatise features a precisely shaped spiral circulating poloidally around a toroid. Medvedeff (1961) has the vortex ring as the basis for the elementary particles, Honig (1986) uses it to model the photon, and Winterberg (1990) has it as the basis for a unified field theory. Childress (1991) describes the vimanas, ancient flying ships reported in the Hindu Vedic texts which had a propulsion system based on circulating mercury through a vortex ring. A surprisingly large gravitational anomaly might well be created by rapidly pumping positively charged fluid or plasma through a vortex ring piping system. Such an experiment might well be robust, and repeat reliably for all investigators.

Scalar Fields

Another method for cohering the zero-point energy involves abruptly bucking electromagnetic (EM) fields. When EM fields are in perfect opposition, the field vectors exactly cancel creating a zero resultant. However, there still exists a stress in the fabric of space and it manifests as a scalar EM potential. Aharonov and Bohm (1959, et al.) have shown that the EM potential affects the phase of the quantum mechanical wave function associated with the elementary particles. Bearden (1986) has emphasized that the resultant stress is actually a coherence in the ZPE and can propagate as scalar waves. King (1986) has suggested a hyperspatial model for such a coherence involving vortex rings. The model is based on geometrodynamics (Wheeler, 1962) where the ZPE manifests as a electric flux flowing orthogonally to our three space. Abruptly opposing EM field transients pinch and release this flux which tend to guide (or orthorotate) some of the flow into our three space. Timing is critical: The quicker and more abrupt the opposing EM field transients, the greater the flux orthorotation.

An experiment to demonstrate the effect of abruptly bucking electromagnetic fields involves the use of a caduceus coil (Smith, 1964). The caduceus coil has two windings of opposite helicity criss-crossing like the snakes on the caduceus staff. Perfect symmetry is important, for the coils are driven simultaneously by abrupt electric pulses. As the they propagate up both windings, the pulse edges must remain perfectly aligned to maintain the bucking field action. The sharper the rise time of the aligned pulse edges, the greater the effect The coil should be wound on a hollow tube in order to facilitate experiments with a variety of core materials. Burridge (1979) describes the use of ferrite cores, and Van Tassel (Dollard, 1988) experimented with quartz crystal cores. A synergistic ZPE coherence might well be induced by having the core be comprised of any of the previously suggested apparatus for cohering the ZPE. For example, a long plasma tube excited at its ion-acoustic resonance, or a tube in which is there occurs a plasma vortex or plasmoids such as produced by Shoulders (1991). Meyer (1989) achieved considerable success by combining many ideas, and pulsed caduceus coil excitation may well augment any device that is cohering the zero-point energy.

Summary

From the concentrated vacuum polarization of atomic nuclei arises the possibility of triggering a macroscopic ZPE coherence with the synchronous motion of many nuclei. Experimental evidence arises from energy anomalies associated with heavy-ion collisions, plasma ion-acoustic oscillations, sonoluminescence, fractoemission, large charge density plasmoids, ball lightning, abrupt electric discharges, and light water "cold fusion" experiments. Further supporting evidence arises from inventions that utilize coherent ion motions and output excessive energy. The sharp voltage spikes that arise from ion-acoustic activity can be converted by use of circuits such as Hyde's voltage divider. Large effects might be produced by solid state methods that manifest dual, counter-rotating, acoustical, lattice spinor waves. Precessing charged plasma or fluid by pumping it through a helical vortex ring might produce a sufficient ZPE coherence to manifest a gravitational anomaly. Abruptly bucking electromagnetic fields from a pulsed caduceus coil could further stimulate a coherent ZPE interaction with whatever is placed within its core. If synchronous ion-acoustic activity coheres the zero-point energy, there will be many more inventions forthcoming, and a new energy source will be recognized.

References

Aharonov, Y. and D. Bohm (1959), "Significance of Electromagnetic Potentials in the Quantum Theory," *Phys. Rev.* 115(3). page 485; Olariv, S. and Li. Popescu (1985)."The Quantum Effects of Electromagnetic Fluxes," *Rev. Mod. Phys.* 57(2). pages 339-436.

Alexandersson, 0.(1990), *Living Water: Viktor Schauberger and the Secrets of Natural Energy*, Gateway Books, Bath, UK. Also Frokjaer-Jensen, B.(1981), "The Scandinavian Research Organization and the Implosion Theory (Viktor Schauberger)," *Proc. First International Symposium on Nonconventional Energy Technology*, Toronto, pages 78-96.

Barak, M.(1980), *Electrochemical Power Sources*. I.E.E. and Peter Peregrinus LTD., NY, pages 188-190.

Barber, B.P. and S.J. Putterman (1991), "Observation of synchronous picosecond sonoluminescence," *Nature* 353, pages 318-320.

Bearden, T.E.(1986), *Fer-De-Lance A Briefing on Soviet Scalar Electromagnetic Weapons,* Tesla Book Co., Millbrae, CA, pages 107-108.

Bedini, J.(1991), "The Bedini Free Energy Generator," *Proc. 26th IECEC,* vol. 4, pages 451-456.

Bostick, W.H.(1957), "Experimental Study of Plasmoids," *Phys. Rev.* 106(3) page 404.

Boyer, T.H.(1975), "Random Electrodynamics: The theory of classical electrodynamics with classical electromagnetic zero-point radiation," *Phys. Rev. D* 11(4), pages 790-808.

Brown, P.M.(1989), "Apparatus for Direct Conversion of Radioactive Decay Energy to Electrical Energy," U.S. Patent No. 4,835,433; . . . (1987), "The Moray Device and the Hubbard Coil were Nuclear Batteries," *Magnets* 2(3). pages 6-12; . . . (1990), "The Resonant Nuclear Battery, International Tesla Symposium, Colorado Springs.

Burridge, G.(1979),'The Smith Coil," *Psychic Observer* 35(5). pages 410-416.

Bush, R.T. (1992), "A Light Water Excess Heat Reaction Suggests that 'Cold Fusion' is 'Alkali-Hydrogen Fusion', *Fusion Tech.*22, page 287.

Celenza, L.S. and V.K. Mishra, C.M. Shakin, K.F. Liu (1986), "Exotic States in QED," *Phys. Rev. Ltrs.* 57(1), page 55; Caldi, D.G. and A. Chodos (1987), "Narrow e+e-peaks in heavy-ion collisions and a possible new phase of QED, *Phys. Rev. D* 36(9), page 2876; Jack Ng, Y. and Y. Kikuchi (1987), "Narrow e+e-peaks in heavy-ion collisions as possible evidence of a confining phase of QED, *Phys. Rev. D* 36(9), page 2880; Celenza,L.S. and C.R. Ji, C.M. Shakin (1987), "Nontopological solitons in strongly coupled QED," *Phys. Rev. D* 36(7), pages 2144-48.

Childress, D.H.(1991), *Vimana Aircraft of Ancient India and Atlantis,* Adventures Unlimited Press, Stelle, IL.

Cieplak, M. and L.A. Turski (1980), "Magnetic solitons and elastic kink-like excitations in compressible Heisenberg chain," *J. Phys. C: Solid State Physics* 13, pages L 777-780.

Davidson, D.A.(1990), *Energy Breakthroughs to New Free Energy Devices*, Rivas, Greenville, TX, pages 16-18.

Davidson, J.(1989), *The Secret of the Creative Vacuum*, C.W. Daniel Co. Ltd., Essex, UK, pages 258-262.

DePalma, B.E. and C.E. Edwards (1973), "The Force Machine Experiments," privately published.

Dirac, P.A.(1930), Rev. Sec. Proc.126. page 360. Also Gamow, G,(1966*), Thirty Years that Shook Physics*, Doubleday, NY.

Dollard, E.(1988), "Van Tassel's Caduceus Coils," private communication. Van Tassel experimented with numerous caduceus coils that often contained quartz cores. His notes stated that the cross-over angle for the two opposing windings should be 22.5 degrees.

Egely, G.(1986), "Energy Transfer Problems of Ball Lightning," Central Research Institute for Physics, Budapest, Hungary.

Forward, R.L.(1984), "Extracting electrical energy from the vacuum by cohesion of charged foliated conductors," *Phys. Rev. B* 30(4), pages 1700-2.

Gluck, P.(1992), Letters to the editor. *Fusion Facts* 4(7). pages 22-24.

Graneau, P. and P.N. Graneau (1985), "Electrodynamic Explosions in Liquids," *Appl. Phys.Lett.* 46(5), pages 468-470.

Gray, E.V.(1976), "Pulsed Capacitor Discharge Electric Engine," U.S. Patent No. 3,890548.

Hathaway, G.(1991), "Zero-Point Energy: A New Prime Mover? Engineering Requirements for Energy Production & Propulsion from Vacuum Fluctuations," *Proc. 26th IECEC* vol. 4. Pages 376-381.

Honig, W.M.(1986), *The Quantum and Beyond*. Philosophical Library, NY.

Hyde, W.W.(1990), "Electrostatic Energy Field Power Generating System," U.S. Patent No. 4,897,592. The invention is summarized in King (1991).

Jandel, M.(1990), "Cold Fusion in a Confining Phase of Quantum Electrodynamics," *Fusion Tech.* 17, pages 493-499.

Jennison, R.C.(1978), "Relativistic Phase-Locked Cavities as Particle Models," *J. Phys. A* Math Gen. VII(8).

Jennison,R.C.(1990), "Relativistic Phase-Locked Cavity Model of Ball Lightning," Electronics Laboratory, University of Kent, U.K.

Johnson, G.L.(1992), "Electrically Induced Explosions in Water," *Proc. 27th lECEC* vol. 4, pages 4.335-338.

Johnson, P.0.(1965), "Ball Lightning and Self Containing Electromagnetic Fields," *Am. J. Phys.*33, page 119.

Kalinin, Yu G. et a1.(1970), "Observation of Plasma Noise During Turbulent Heating," *Sov. Phys. Dokl.* 14(11), page 1074; Iguchi, H.(1978), "Initial State of Turbulent Heating of Plasmas," *J. Phys. Sec. Jpn.* 45(4), page 1364; Hirose, A(1974), "Fluctuation Measurements in a Toroidal Turbulent Heating Device," *Phys. Can.* 29(24). page 14.

King, M.B.(1984), "Macroscopic Vacuum Polarization," *Proc. Tesla Centennial Symposium,* International Tesla Society, Colorado Springs, pages 99-107. Also (1989), pages 57-75.

King, M.B (1986) "Cohering the Zero-Point Energy," *Proc. of the 1986 International Tesla Symposium*, Colorodo Springs Section 4, pages 13-32. Also (1989), pages 77-106.

King, M.B.(1989), *Tapping the Zero-Point Energy*. Paraclete Publishing, POB 859, Provo, UT 84603.

King, M.B.(1991), "Tapping the Zero-Point Energy as an Energy Source," *Proc. 26th IECEC* Vol.4, pages 364-369.

Kiwamoto, Y. and H. Kuwahara, H. Tanaca (1979), "Anomalous Resistivity of a Turbulent Plasma in a Strong Electric Field," *J. Plasma Phys*. 21(3). page 475.

Kozyrev, N.A.(1968), "Possibility of Experimental Study of the Properties of Time," Joint Publication Research Service, Arlington VA.

La Violette, P.A(1985), "An introduction to subquantum kinetics . . . ," *Intl. J. Gen. Sys. II*, pages 281-345; . . . (1991), "Subquantum Kinetics: Exploring the Crack in the First Law," *Proc. 26th IECEC* vol. 4, pages 352-357.

Mallove, E.F.(1992), "Protocols for Conducting Light Water Excess Energy Experiments," *Fusion Facts* 3(8), page 15; Noninski, V.C.(1992), "Excess Heat during the Electrolysis of a Light Water Solution of K_2zCO_3 with a Nickel Cathode," *Fusion Tech.* 21, pages 163-167.

Medvedeff, N.J.(1961), Nuclear Dynamics, privately published, Hanover, MA

Meyer, S.L.(1991), The Birth of a New Technology, Water Fuel Cell, Grove City, OH; . . . (1989), "Controlled Process for the Production of Thermal Energy from Gases and Apparatus Useful Therefore," U.S. Patent No. 4,826,581; . . . (1990), "Method for the Production of a Fuel Gas, (Electrical Polarization Process)," U.S. Patent No. 4,936,961.

Mills, R.L. and S.P. Kneizys (1991), "Excess Heat Production by the Electrolysis of an Aqueous Potassium Carbonate Electrolyte and the Implications for Cold Fusion," *Fusion Tech.* 20, pages 65-81.

Milonni, P.W. and R.J. Cook, M.E. Goggin (1988), "Radiation pressure from the vacuum: Physical interpretation of the Casimir force," *Phys. Rev. A* 38(3), pages 1621-23.

Moore, C.B.(1971), *Keely and His Discoveries*, Health Research, Mokelumne Hill, CA

Moray, T.H. and J.E. Moray (1978), The Sea of Energy. Cosray Research Institute, Salt Lake City, UT.

Panici, D.(1992), private communication.

Papp, J.(1984), "Inert Gas Fuel, Fuel Preparation Apparatus and System for Extracting Useful Work from the Fuel," U.S. Patent No. 4,428,193.

Pappas, P.T.(1991), "Energy Creation in Electrical Sparks and Discharges: Theory and Direct Experimental Evidence," *Proc. 26th IECEC* vol. 4, pages 416-423.

Preparata, G.(1991), "A New Look at Solid-State Fractures, Particle Emission and Cold Nuclear Fusion," *Il Nuovo Cimento* 104 A(8), page 1259; . . . (1990), "Quantum field theory of superradiance," in Cherubini, R., P. Dal Fiat, B. Minetti (editors), *Problems of Fundamental Modern Physics*. World Scientific, Singapore.

Prigogine, I. and G. Nicolis (1977), *Self-Organization in Nonequilibrium Systems*, Wiley, NY;

Prigogine, I. and I. Stengers (1984), *Order Out of Chaos*. Bantam Books, NY.

Puharich, A. (1981), "Water Decomposition by Means of Alternating Current Electrolysis," *Proc. First International Symposium on Nonconventional Energy Technology*, Toronto, pages 49-77; . . . (1983), "Method and Aparatus for Splitting Water Molecules," U.S. Patent No. 4,394,230.Puthoff, H.E.(1989), "Gravity as a Zero-Point Fluctuation Force," Phys. Rev. A 39(5). Page 2333.

Puthoff, H.E.(1990), "The energetic vacuum: implications for energy research," *Spec. Sci. Tech.*13(4), pages 247-257.

Reed, D. (1992),"Toward a Structural Model for the Fundamental Electrodynamic Fields of Nature," *Extraordinary Science* IV(2). pages 22-33.

Reinhardt, J. and B. Muller, W. Greiner (1980), "Quantum Electrodynamics of Strong Fields in Heavy Ion Collisions," *Prog. Part. and Nucl. Phys.* 4. page 503.

Rausher, E.A.(1968), "Electron Interactions and Quantum Plasma Physics," *J. Plasma Phys.* 2(4), page 517.

Roden, M.(1992), *Aero Dynamics*, Aero Dynamics Master Society, San Ysidro, CA

Samokhin, A.(1990), "Vacuum energy—a breakthrough?" *Spec. Sci. Tech.* 13(4). page 273.

Scheck, F.(1983), *Leptons, Hadrons and Nuclei*, North Holland Physics Publ., NY, pages 213-223.

Senitzky, I.R(1973), "Radiation Reaction and Vacuum Field Effects in Heisenberg-Picture Quantum Electrodynamics," *Phys. Rev. Lett.* 31(15). page 955.

Sethian, J.D. and D.A. Hammer, C.B. Whaston (1978), "Anomalous Electron-Ion Energy Transfer in a Relativistic-Electron-

Beam Heated Plasma," *Phys. Rev. Lett.* 40(7). page 451; Robertson, S. and A. Fisher, C.W. Roberson (1980), "Electron Beam Heating of a Mirror Confined Plasma," *Phys. Fluids* 32(2), page 318; Tanaka, M. and Y. Kawai (1979), "Electron Heating by Ion Acoustic Turbulence in Plasmas," *J. Phys. Sec. Jpn.* 47(1), page 294.

Shoulders, K.R.(1991), "Energy Conversion Using High Charge Density," U.S. Patent No.5,018, 80.

Singer, S.(1971), The Nature of Ball Lightning, Plenum Press, NY; Silberg, P.A.(1962), "Ball Lightning and Plasmoids," *J. Geophys. Res.* 67(12), page 4941.

Smith, W.B.(1964), *The New Science*, Fern-Graphic Publ., Mississauga, Ontario.

Spence G.M.(1988), "Energy Conversion System," U.S. Patent No. 4,772,816.

Storms, E.(1991), "Review of Experimental Observations about the Cold Fusion Effect" *Fusion Tech.* 20, pages 433-477.

Suzuki, M.(1984), "Fluctuation and Formation of Macroscopic Order in Nonequilibrium Systems, *Proc. Theor. Phys. Suppl.* 79, pages 125-140; Hasegawa, A.(1985), "Self-Organization Processes in Continuous Media," *Adv. Phys.* 34(1), pages 1-41; Firrao, S.(1984), "Physical Foundations of Self-Organizing Systems Theory, *Cybernetica* 17(2). pages 107-124; Haken, H.(1971), *Synergetics*, Springer Verlag, NY.

Sweet, F. and T.E. Bearden (1991), "Utilizing Scalar Electromagnetics to Tap Vacuum Energy," *Proc. 26th IECEC* vol. 4, pages 370-375; . . . (1988), "Nothing is Something: The Theory and Operation of a Phase-Conjugate Vacuum Triode," private communication.

Walton, A.J. and G.T. Reynolds (1984), "Sonoluminescence," *Adv. Phys.* 33(61, pages 595-600.

Wheeler, J.A. (1962), *Geometrodynamics*, Academic Press, NY.

Winter, D.(1991), *The Star Mother. Geometric Keys to the Resonant Spirit of Biology*, Crystal Hill Farm Publications, Eden, NY.

Winterberg, F.(1990), "Maxwell's Equations and Einstein-Gravity in the Planck Aether Model of a Unified Field Theory, *Z. Naturforsch.* 45 a, pages 1102-16; . . . (1991), "Substratum Interpretation of the Quark-Lepton Symmetries in the Planck Aether Model of a Unified Field Theory, *Z. Naturforsch.* 46 a, pages 551-559.

8

Scalars, Part I

Eldon A. Byrd
Reprint from the *J. of U. S. Psychotronics Association,* Spring 1989, p.27

Abstract

PART I deals with the historical background (beginning in 1900 with the discovery of inconsistencies between deductions and experimental data concerning Planck's constant) leading to the concepts supporting scalars as information carriers. A brief review of the development of Einstein's space-time continuum, the nature of reality, classical mechanics, fields and waves, quantum mechanics, and the general and special theories of relativity set the stage for the emergence of scalars as a form of information transfer. In the process, some of what physics is, and is not, is clarified.

Part II (in the next Volume of this series) will provide the equations linking vector mechanics with scalars and concludes with how scalars can act as information carriers at infinite velocity.

Introduction

One of the purposes of science is to provide order from the chaos of our sense-experience. This is very difficult because the same brain that experiences the chaos has to make up theories that try to make sense. Physics, in particular, is (and always has been) in a state of evolution. Its basis cannot be distilled from experience by inductive methods and its truth content can only be verified by human consciousness.

In 1927 the physical universe was described by Arthur Webster as consisting only of x, y, z, and time. Underlying this description were a myriad of philosophical assumptions.{1} Thus, the foundation of mathematical physics is philosophical in nature.

Science is concerned with the analysis of parts assumed to be independent of the whole. Recent advances in science refute this assumption. We are coming back to Newtonian "action at a distance" ideas, but from a different and more sophisticated point of view. Interconnectedness now appears to be a more viable viewpoint than ever before. However, interconnective forces seem to be subtle and not subject to measurement by conventional devices and techniques. Bohm {2} called the interconnective force the "quantum potential." [Note that Dr. Jack Dea, a university professor who also has published on the physics of scalars states, "Biological organisms and gas tubes serve as highly nonlinear media, and for this reason they can serve as scalar detectors." *PACE Newsletter*, Vol. 4, No.4, p.18. –Ed. note]

Space-Time

Einstein {3} so completely connected space and time in our "physical" universe that the concepts of action at a distance, potential energy, and simultaneity were destroyed. This was compatible with Maxwell's equations, but not with classical mechanics.

However, in another view, the Pauli Exclusion Principle squeezes an infinity of space-time out of a single point creating a variance of Virtual states; whereas Maxwell's equations stem from squeezing an infinity of space-time into a point. We can imagine that we live in a sea of virtual (i.e., unobservable) particles of energy. These energy states may be stimulated by "real" energy to the point of "kicking" virtual particles from negative to positive energy states, making the particles "real." The Dirac equation predicts this and describes the "Dirac Sea" of *virtual particles*. The Dirac Sea is the matric of space-time itself.

The Nature of Reality

Science is based on the concept that an external world exists independent of the perceiving subject. Thus, "reality is based on speculation; or at least is reduced to indirect observation. Therefore, we must be willing to alter our perception of reality. The father of real science was not Euclid—or anyone else before Galileo. Pure logical thinking cannot yield any knowledge of the empirical world; all knowledge of reality starts and ends with experience. Together, however, they form a more complete system than either separately.

I propose (as have others) a new paradigm for science: "Physical realities cannot be described at all in terms of mathematics dealing with the physical because there is no objective reality." If we start with the premise that there are only *fields* and that fields generate what we perceive as physical reality—not the other way around—a whole new way of dealing with so called "reality will emerge. The balance of this paper deals with this concept, demonstrating why the idea that "matter" creates field does not work as well as the idea that field creates "matter."

Classical Mechanics

Over the past 75 years, it has become apparent that classical mechanics cannot describe our experience with the physical universe. Max Planck dethroned classical physics by showing that quantum mechanics applies to small masses at slow speeds but high acceleration; thereby overcoming the limiting laws of Newtonian physics.

In 1900 it was discovered that there were inconsistencies between deductions from mechanics and experimental facts concerning Planck's constant (h). The theory dictated that heat and radiation density of solids would decrease proportionally to decreasing temperature; experience revealed a much more rapid decrease than predicted. No causal laws could be determined before quantum mechanics. Heisenberg, Dirac, de Broglie, and Schrodinger showed that discrete *frequencies* must be assigned to the energy values.

Schrodinger developed a partial differential equation relating a complex scalar to position and time in a discrete way. This led to the theory of the atom and explained why gases radiate and absorb only light of sharply defined frequencies. Thus, quantum physics was born.

Fields and Waves

At first, a mechanical interpretation of a medium (motion or stress of the ether) was advanced in an attempt to explain "field." This gave way to the electromagnetic field as a final irreducible constituent of physical reality. Force was replaced by field (as described by differential equations). Only the field was allowed to interact. Hertz relegated the ether to obscurity of claiming that the concept of field was fundamental and required no mechanical propagation medium. {3} However, this required the introduction of two new vectors connected by relations dependent on the nature of the medium—therefore, inaccessible to theoretical analysis. The vectors added complexity to the concept of magnetic field and the relationship between electric current density and field. Lorentz simplified things for electrodynamics by considering the case where fields are the results of particles in motion. This profoundly transformed physics because waves were no longer tied to the ether; they were the result of other factors and were independent of a medium for their existence. Freeing the electromagnetic field from a material substratum paved the way for the idea of force without matter. At this point no one believed in immediate action at a distance—not even gravity effects. It was assumed that if electromagnetic waves propagated with a finite velocity, then so did electrostatic fields.

De Broglie conceived the idea of standing waves, using Planck's constant. However, Born discovered that de Broglie-Schrodinger wave fields were not mathematical de scriptions of how an event actually takes place in time and space, but of what we can know about the system. These wave fields make only statistical statements and predic-tions of the results of all possible measurements. This introduced quantum mechanics into the "real" world.

According to Einstein {3} space-time has an existence independent of matter or field; however, there is no such thing as "empty" space—space without field. Space-time does not exist on its own, but is a structural quality of the field. There is no such thing as "nothing." The field is the representation of reality. As Descartes put it, "There exists no space empty of field." {3 }

Current field laws have meaning only in regard to inertial systems. Remove matter and field, and inertia and time remain. The Minkowski-space is a carrier of matter and field. There is no "now" in Minkowski space. Consider the possibility of replacing "matter" with "field." A dynamic field with areas of low energy density and areas of high energy density—always in a state of flux and manifesting itself in various ways, subject to local organization, having the property of interaction with itself, etc.—can explain most of the questions science has been pondering for centuries. What would be the relationship of the field to "condensed energy" (matter)? An electron is supposed to be an electrically charged particle; so is a proton. If this is true, where are the magnetic masses? Absurdity has run rampant in physics for decades. The "duality" of waves and particles represents the lengths to which physics has gone to in order to "explain" things.

No one believed Maxwell until Hertz demonstrated waves. {3} Later, however, it was noted that Maxwell's equations do not allow for their solutions to avoid the inherent singularities that keep them from explaining the total electromagnetic inertia of particles. There are no regular solutions to Maxwell's equations that do not contain singularities—points or spaces where there are no solutions to the equations. Thus, a pure electromagnetic field theory of matter has never been attained. Einstein pointed this out emphatically with the generalized field equation:

$$R_{ik} - ½ (g_{ik} R) = - T_{ik}$$

where R = the scalar of the Riemannian curvature, and T_{ik} = the energy tensor of matter.Taking the divergence of both sides: div $[R_{ik} – ½ (g_{ik} R)] = 0 =$ div $(-T_{ik})$ = equations of motion of matter in the form of partial differential equations.

Field theory fails in the molecular sphere. Quantum mechanics does not relate to any semblance of reality; physics has been relegated to a game of chance. The possession of the truth has been replaced by the search for it.

Quantum Mechanics

Experiments have shown that it is possible to transition a system from one quantum state to another with external forces consisting of small time-varying additions to the potential energy. The non-linearity and probabalistic nature of this process

13927-VALO

allows for changes of any magnitude as a function of probability. Hence, Schrodinger proved that Uri Geller can exist.

In spite of the expansion of understanding of physical events quantum mechanics provided over classical mechanics, it is still an *incomplete* representation of "reality" because it is built out of force and material points. Quantum mechanics does not describe in any way the state of a single function, but rather, an ensemble of systems (in a statistical sense). The results are not measurable and therefore, by definition, are outside the realm of "science"—because science requires measurement. Note that the statistical methods of *quantum mechanics cannot be applied to fields*!

Today's physics is not about the nature of reality, but concerned with possibilities. Therefore, there is not now, and never has been, any sound general theoretical basis for physics, because of the apparent uncertainty of everything.

Links

Capsulizing the sequence of progression in physics:

"Objective" Reality	→	(Maxwell: vector fields (de Broglie: waves (Dirac: spinors
"Subjective" Reality	→	(Einstein: semi-vectors (cancelling charges) (Born: probability of fields (Heisenberg: uncertainty of things (Now: non-existence of particles

Maxwell changed the notion of physical reality from material points in motion (described by total differential equations) to continuous fields (described by partial differential equations).

Quantum mechanics went a step further and stated that, indeed, we cannot describe reality in terms of absolute differential equations of any kind, but rather, in terms of the probability of the occurrence of a physical reality.

It is only out of ignorance that some still believe that thelaws of physics are somehow tied to the structure of the atom and others still believe that the mechanics of a system are determined by potential energy that is a function of its configuration. Arbitrary rules give rise to arbitrary results. Newtonian physics fails utterly to provide a foundation for physics, yet it still occupies a central position in our thinking. Why? Because there is no foundation that is, as yet, complete.

Theory does *not* come inductively from experience. Logical thinking is deductive, and it is rash to think that a confirmation of consequences would spring from it. The dilemma is that no inductive method of thinking can lead to the fundamental concepts of physics (or of anything else). Only a combination can provide the synergy necessary; experiences suggest theory and vice versa. A new approach should be based on the notion that field gives rise to matter, not the other way around.

General and Special Theories of Relativity

The General Theory of Relativity is concerned mainly with gravitational fields and cannot predict either the existence or the structure of *any* other field—including the electromagnetic (EM) field. The "giants" (Weyl, Kaluza, and Eddington) failed to extend the theory to EM fields."{3) According to the theory, space is a continuous field composed of four independent variables—space and time— without particles, or materialpoints, or motion. Both the General and Special Theories of Relativity assume no in-stantaneous action at a distance; however, the Special Theory does not exclude massless information transfer. It is from this concept the notion of scalars as information carriers emerges.

References

1) Webster, Arthur. *Partial Differential Equations of Mathematical Physics*, 1955: Dover Publications.
2) Bohm, D. J. and Hiley, B. J. "On the Intuitive Understanding of Nonlocality as Implied by Quantum Theory," 1975: *Foundations of Physics*, 5, p. 93.
3) Einstein, A. *Ideas and Opinions*, 1954: Bonanza Books.

9

Biological Effects of Non-Classical Electromagnetic Fields Exhibiting Quantum Non-Locality

Glen Rein, Ph.D.
Quantum Biology Research Lab
Huntington, NY 11768

Abstract

Physicists are well aware of of the existence of energy fields which have properties which are not explained by the classical equations of Maxwell or Schrodinger. Experimental anomalies associated with contemporary radionics, psychotronics and "free energy" research may also involve non-classical energy fields, referred to here as quantum fields. Recent findings in biology indicate that certain biomolecules act as superconductors and biological systems in general exhibit non-local, global properties which are consistent with their ability to function at the level of macroscopic quantum coherence. The possibilities that such anomalous behavior might be accounted for by the presence of endogenous quantum fields in biological systems has received little attention.

Experimental evidence is presented in this paper in support of this hypothesis. It has been previously proposed that quantum fields can be generated (in combination with potential fields) from self-canceling coils and geometric patterns used in radionics devices. These results demonstrate that quantum fields inhibit neurotransmitter uptake into nerve cells, stimulate the growth of human lymphocytes (white blood cells), modulate the secondary structure of isolated human DNA and alter the absorption of UV light of water. In some cases, quantum fields produced larger effects than classical electromagnetic force fields. This new experimental evidence is used as the basis for a model which introduces the concept of a bio-field composed of layers comprising force fields, potential fields and quantum fields embedded within one another. The model further proposes that healing information originates from a higher dimensional source and is transformed into biologically usable electromagnetic energy as it propagates through the layers of the bio-field.

Introduction

The physics literature is full of examples of anomalous behavior of electromagnetic (EM) fields, which can not be explained by the standard equations of Maxwell and Hertz. Although these non-classical energy fields are not well understood or well studied, they are known as potential fields, non-Hertzian fields, non-Maxwellian fields or longitudinal to distinguish them from traditional transverse electromagnetic fields. In addition, quantum fields have been described which obey the Schrodinger equation, but do not behave like classical EM fields.

Although we know relatively little about the energetic processes underlying radionics, it is clear that one of its most interesting properties is its ability to act at a distance. Similar behavior has been reported in the traditional biomedical literature, where the biological effects of prayer is acknowledged to be independent of distance (Dossey, 1998; Fleischer, 2000). Such nonlocal behavior is also of interest to quantum physicists who have developed quantum based theories (Bohm, 1980; Strapp,

1983) to explain the occurrence of quantum nonlocality at the macroscopic level (ie. outside the quantum domain of subatomic particles). These theories might also be used to explain the nonlocal information transfer which appears to be occurring during a radionic broadcast. In order for these theories to explain radionics, we must therefore postulate that quantum fields are somehow involved with radionic information transfer between the radionic equipment and the person receiving healing.

The fact that macroscopic quantum coherence (Garg, 1985) and other examples of the quantum behavior of biological systems (Smith, 1998) have been recently reported in the scientific literature, suggests that biological systems have the capability to respond to quantum fields generated from radionics equipment. However, relatively few scientific investigations have directly studied the biological effects of these non-classical energy fields. This report reviews the biophysics behind the new discipline of quantum biology.

Potential Fields, Non-Hertzian Fields and Quantum Fields

Potential fields, like the magnetic vector potential or the **A** field, are traditionally thought of as theoretical constructs to simplify cumbersome mathematical calculations. As early as 1960 physicists demonstrated that potential fields, in the absence of classical EM fields, have physical effects at the subatomic level on electrons (by changing their phase) (Chambers, 1960). In the 1980's two patents appeared for the use of potential fields to transfer information (Gellinas, 1984; Wekroma, 1989) with some preliminary clinical effects used to support the patent claims. Then in the early 1990's Smith experimentally demonstrated that potential fields can produce macroscopic effects by imprinting water with coherent information (Smith, 1994). Water is, of course, an integral part of all biological systems. Shortly after later Ho, using the same methodology as Smith, demonstrated that potential fields can increase the abnormalities in Drosophila embryos (Ho, 1994).

Since biological systems function at the quantum level (DelGiudice et al 1989; Smith 1994; Popp, 1979), they should contain endogenous quantum fields which will theoretically respond to potential fields. However, since potential fields will also influence endogenous EM fields in the body, it is not clear whether externally applied potential fields are necessarily acting through quantum fields in the body. The demonstration that biological systems also respond to external quantum fields would for the first time associate them directly with biochemical and physiological functions in the body, thereby demonstrating their role in the intrinsic self-healing mechanisms.

The author's contribution to this field, beginning in 1987, was inspired by Tesla's research at the turn of the century, by Cope's research on biological superconductivity, free energy research and the clinical successes of radionics and psychotronics practitioners. Some of these devices utilize self-canceling coils wound in a special geometry which causes self-canceling of the EM field. These non-inductive self-canceling coils are distinctly different from the toroidal coil used by Smith and Ho which traps EM force fields inside and allows potential fields to radiate on the outside. Self-canceling coils are composed of two sets of windings where current flows in opposite directions thereby bucking and canceling the EM field. These coils have unusual windings, known as the *caduceus* winding (Smith, 1964) and the *mobius* winding (Seiki, 1990), which have been proposed to warp space/time and generate higher dimensional quantum fields (King, 1990; Reed, 1996; Seiki, 1990). These coils are reminiscent, but different than the more familiar *bifilar* winding which is also self-canceling. *Caduceus* coils do oppose the current flow by exactly 180 degrees and therefore do not entirely cancel the EM force fields or the potential fields. Nonetheless these three types of coils will generate force fields, potential fields and quantum fields in varying ratios.

The first use of self-canceling coils was achieved by Tesla at the turn of the century. Tesla's magnifying transmitter used two spiral coils (yet another self canceling configuration) where oscillations were phased to create opposing magnetic fields (Sector, 1916). He demonstrated that such a coil could transmit energy over long distances without losses (Tesla, 1904). Biological experiments using Tesla's self canceling coil, if any, were not well documented. Tesla used the term non-Hertzian to describe the new energy field because it did not behave according to standard EM field theory described by Hertz and Maxwell. Today physicists use the term non-Maxwellian, non-Abelian and non-dispersive for similar reasons. Other terms used to describe this new energy include longitudinal waves (classical fields are transverse), scalar waves (classical fields are vectors), standing waves (classical fields propagate), force-free fields (classical fields have force), time reversed waves (classical fields travel forward in time), solitary waves and tachyon energy.

Biological Experiments with Mobius Coils

A preliminary report appeared in 1979 which used a *mobius* coil to produce a change in the electrical conductivity of skin (Flannigan, 1979). Although the author was unaware of this obscure publication, it suggested that quantum fields in addition to potential fields may be biological active thereby supporting the Quantum Energy Healing Model.

In the mid-1980's a commercial device (Teslar Shielding Device) became available which utilized a mobius coil. The device was based on a patent which used a *mobius* strip in a crystal oscillator circuit (Puharich, 1984). Anecdotal case reports from electromagnetic sensitive individuals wearing shielding devices, suggested it might block adverse effects of power line EM fields. Morley used electro-diagnostic measurements (EAV) with these individuals and demonstrated the shielding device normalized their electrical meridian readings after exposure to powerlines. A more scientific approach was taken by Byrd who observed a decrease in overall amplitude and a shift toward lower frequencies in EEG recordings from individuals wearing the shielding device (Byrd, unpublished observation).

Despite these encouraging preliminary results, it is still possible that the observed effects were due at least in part to the belief system of the individuals. In order to eliminate placebo effects and to determine whether the quantum field generated from the shielding device might have direct effects at the cellular level, the author designed a series of in vitro experiments using nerve cells (Rein, 1988) and immune cells (Rein, 1989) grown in tissue culture.

In the nerve cell experiments, biological effects were determined using two types of shielding devices, with and without the *mobius* coil. In the absence of the coil, the control device generated a broad spectrum, low frequency electric field (with no quantum field). The experimental shielding device, containing the *mobius* coil, should generate a quantum field in the presence of the electric field. The electric field was measured using a specially designed electrometer and shown to contain a wide spectrum of low frequencies peaking around 260 Hz. The electric fields were identical in amplitude and frequency in the two devices.

The PC12 nerve cell line was chosen for these studies since the author had previously demonstrated normal neurotransmitter functional properties in these cells (Greene and Rein 1977) which could be modified in the presence of classical low frequency EM fields (Dixey and Rein, 1982; Rein, 1987). Neurotransmitter uptake (transport across the cell membrane) was reassessed, using the same standard biochemical protocol (using radiolabelled norepinephrine) following a thirty-minute exposure of the cells to the two shielding devices.

The results indicated that both the experimental and control shielding devices produced an inhibition of neurotransmitter uptake (Rein, 1988). These effects were similar to those previously obtained using an EM force field (Rein, 1987). However, the quantum field, in the presence of the electric field, produced a 19.5 % larger effect than the electric field by itself ($p = 0.05$, n=6). The additional effect can be attributed to the presence of the quantum fields since the electric field was the same in both devices. This is a very important conclusion if quantum fields are generally shown to be more biologically active than classical EM fields.

To determine whether quantum fields generated from a mobius coil might also influence other cell types, the experiments were repeated using human lymphocytes (critical white blood cells involved with cellular immunity) grown *in vitro*. Using standard biochemical techniques, a pooled preparation of T and B lymphocytes was isolated from the blood of healthy volunteers and grown in tissue culture for 2 days in the presence of radioactive thymidine (Rein, 1989). Thymidine incorporation into DNA is a quantitative measure of the amount of cell division. In the presence of the control shielding device (electric field alone), lymphocyte growth (90 ± 31 cpm/10^5 cells) was stimulated by 34% relative to cells grown in the absence of any exogenous field. This effect is similar to that obtained from other studies using classical low frequency EM force fields (Conti, 1983). When grown in the presence of the experimental shielding device (quantum and electric fields), lymphocyte proliferation increased to 159 ± 53 cpm/10^5 cells. Thus, as in the previous experiments with nerve cells, the quantum field produced a 76% larger biological response ($p = 0.01$, n=7) than the electric field by itself.

Biological Experiments with a Caduceus Coil

These initial studies were the first to demonstrate a direct biochemical effect of quantum fields at the cellular level and indicated that such effects can occur in the absence of placebo effects. It was of interest to determine whether a different type of quantum field, with different amounts of potential and EM force fields, would also effect lymphocytes. In the next series of experiments a specially designed caduceus coil (from Dynamic Engineering, Sacramento, CA) was used which was driven by a complex square waveform generating a broad spectrum of frequencies peaking around 4 kHz.

Freshly isolated human lymphocytes received four 15 minute treatments during a 12 hour period and their growth rate determined as described above after an additional 12 hours. Control cells (no energy treatments) showed low growth rates (358 cpm/ 10^5 cells) since no chemical growth factors (mitogens) were included. Cells treated with the caduceus coil showed a twenty-fold stimulation of cell growth (6880 ± 183 cpm/10^5 cells) in the absence of chemical growth factors (Gagnon and Rein, 1990).

Conventional EM fields are also capable of stimulating lymphocyte growth, although the magnitude of this response is substantially less than twenty-fold, typically on the order of one-fold or less (Conti, 1983). It was therefore of interest to determine whether the large effect observed here was due to the quantum field or to the specific and complex set of frequencies used. Therefore, the exact waveform used above was also run through a conventional coil (impedance matched to the caduceus coil). This standard coil, which generates only classical EM fields, gave a 3.5-fold lower effect on lymphocyte proliferation. These results support the previous experiments with the mobius coil and indicate that quantum fields produce larger biological responses than classical EM fields.

Water Experiments with a Bifilar Coil

The caduceus and mobius coils used to generate quantum fields in the experiments described above will also generate potential fields and a small residual EM force field (due to incomplete cancellation). The simplest method to determine (and quantify) the ratio of the different types of fields is to use mathematical calculations. Such calculations are enormously simplified by using less complicated geometric windings than caduceus or mobius coils. Since the bifilar coil, with current flowing in opposite directions, has a relatively simple geometry it was used in the next experiment designed to determine the relative roles of quantum, potential and force fields.

Smith (1994) has previous shown water is sensitive to potential fields and the author has shown that water treated with a variety of self canceling coils shows altered absorption of UV light (Rein 1992). We therefore decided to use water as the target for quantum fields generated from a bifilar coil. Calculations by Dr. Tiller of Stanford University indicated that the magnitude of the magnetic (**B**) field along the inner vertical axis of the coil was equal to 33×10^{-12} Tesla and the vector potential (**A**) field along the same axis was equal to 16×10^{-14} Tesla/cm. Thus, this particular self canceling bifilar coil in addition to being highly successful in canceling EM force fields also canceled the (vector) potential field to negligible levels. Since we were also interested in comparing this bifilar coil with a standard EM solenoid coil (generated by using only one of the windings of the bifilar coil), the total power output of the two coils was adjusted until equal (ie. taking into account the different impedance of the two coils).

The effect of these two coils on the optical properties of water was measured using a standard diode array UV spectrophotometer. Samples were measured before and after a short 1.5 hr exposure to the two coils. Variations in baseline readings from sample to sample were minimized by using aliquots of one large vat of water and by calculating delta values between before and after paired measurements. A 43 kHz sine wave (106mVamplitude) through the bifilar coil produced approximately a 5% increase in UV absorption (at 224nm) for the treated water. In contrast the same 43 kHz sine wave (409mV amplitude) run through the solenoid coil produced no effect on UV absorption (less than 1%) of the treated water. The difference was highly significant at the $p < 0.001$ level ($n = 6$) (Rein, 1996).

The inability of the solenoid coil to produce a measurable effect is not surprising since its **B** field is susbstantially weaker than the threshold (7.6×10^{-6} Tesla) determined by Smith that is required to imprint water (Smith, 1994). The vector potential (**A**) field in the solenoid coil is also not strong enough to produce a measurable effect and is substantially weaker than the required imprinting threshold (20×10^{-12} Wb/m) determined by Smith (Smith, 1994). Comparison between the types of field generated by the solenoid and bifilar coils reveals a surprising result. Although the solenoid generates a **B** force field, a vector potential (**A**) field and a scalar potential (φ) field, none of these fields are apparently capable of producing a measurable effect. The bifilar coil, however, does produce an effect despite the fact that its **B** and **A** fields are negligible. The question therefore arises whether the potential (φ) field from the bifilar coil could produce the observed effect. The magnitude of the potential (φ) field is proportional the the magnitude of the electric (**E**) field which is in turn directly related the the applied voltage. Thus the magnitude of the potential (φ) field in the bifilar coil is four times less than that of the solenoid coil. The inability of the potential (φ) field to account for the observed effect is also supported by Smith's finding that the **E** field (and therefore the potential φ field by implication) is not involved with imprinting water (Smith, 1994). If we assume that the properties of potential (φ) field generated from the two coils is the same, it is unlikely to be responsible for the effect produced by the bifilar coil. Thus, we have a force-free, potential-free effect and need a new type of energy field, eg. a quantum field, to explain the results. Alternatively, the φ potential field generated by the bifillar coil has different properties from the classical φ potential generated from a solenoid. The results from this experiment support the hypothesis that quantum fields exist and are distinct from potential fields and EM force fields.

The results from the bifilar coil indicate, for the first time, a macroscopic effect on water in the absence of EM force fields and potential fields. Modern physics may help explain this anomalous finding and support the hypothesis that quantum fields are distinct from potential and force fields. These theories postulate that under special conditions fields and potentials exist in a modified form with new properties compared to their typical behavior under classical conditions. Although physical effects of classical potentials have been measured (Chambers, 1960), they are not considered to be real since they are not gauge-invariant, i.e. they change when transformed (e.g. to a new location in (or out of) 4D space/time). According to basic EM field theory potentials can only be real if they are gauge-invariant.

This contradiction in theory has inspired some physicists to modify Maxwell's equations. The new equations have solutions which generate new types of potentials with unique properties, eg. gauge-invariant potentials. Alternatively, when dealing with non-classical conditions, it is justifiable to use new mathematical expressions for redefining potentials. The non-Maxwellian equations, which are thereby generated, describe energy fields which have unique properties. A third approach has also been used, where classical potentials are decomposed into more fundamental components. Thus, like force fields can be decomposed into potentials, classical potentials can be further decomposed into "super-potentials". Super-potentials and their corresponding super-fields are often used in supersymmetry field theories and string theories. Super-potentials and super-fields have unusual global properties associated with negative energy states of subatomic particles.

Decomposition of potentials has also revealed another unusual type of energy field called the standing wave. Standing waves are of particular interest because they are experimentally generated by the same concept utilized in self-canceling coils. Thus, standing waves are generated when two EM force fields (of a special type referred to as circularly polarized) travel in opposite directions. Standing waves are an example of a non-Hertzian, quantum field since the orientation of their electric (**E**) and magnetic (**B**) vectors is unique. Classical EM fields have their **E** and **B** vectors a) oriented perpendicular (orthogonal) to each other and b) oscillating perpendicular (orthogonal) to the direction the field is propagating. Standing waves may have both of these properties altered. Some standing waves have their **E** and **B** vectors parallel to each other, whereas others have their vectors oscillating in the same direction the field is propagating. The later type is referred to as a longitudinal wave. Longitudinal waves were first proposed by Tesla at the turn of the century to explain the anomalous behavior of the non-Hertzian energy fields he was working with. Yet another type of standing wave is classified as "force-free" (since their Lorentz force is zero). Force-free fields can be experimentally generated under special conditions where certain gases are put under pressure thereby generating plasmas. Plasmas are notorious for their anomalous behavior and have been well studied by contemporary physicists.

Other examples of non-classical conditions, which allow modification of classical potentials, are quite fascinating. The new conditions often involve the modification of space/time itself. One such modification of space/time is its extension from four dimensions to higher dimensions. Energy fields associated with higher dimensions also have unusual properties, eg. non-locality, super-luminol velocities and negative energy. These energy fields and their corresponding potentials have been characterized as complex meaning they have imaginary components as well as real components (Rauscher, 1968). It is interesting to note that Seiki also used these ideas in describing the imaginary components of the quantum fields generated from mobius coils (Seiki, 1990).

Imaginary particles are a mainstay of quantum physics according to Dirac, although the energy fields associated with such particles is not typically examined in mainstream quantum physics. Nonetheless, the concept of a quantum information field and a quantum potential has been introduced by Bohm (1975) in conjunction with Schrodinger's wave equation. Like non-Maxwellian fields, these quantum fields have unusual properties, eg. non-local action at a distance. Thus, it is clear that contemporary physicists have many elaborate theories, and some experimental data to support the hypothesis that quantum fields exist which are distinct from classical potential fields and force fields. It is therefore possible that such fields are involved with information transfer in radionics and psychotronics devices.

DNA Experiments with Geometric Patterns

Most of the rate cards used in traditional radionics devices utilized the energetic properties of geometric patterns. In order to test whether geometric patterns might be a source of quantum fields, a sensitive bioassay was developed based on the idea that the quantum properties of hydrogen bonds could be used to resonate with and detect quantum fields. A particularly interesting bio-molecule, which is held together by hydrogen bonds, is DNA. In this case, the number of hydrogen bonds can be readily measured using the standard biochemical technique involving UV absorption spectroscopy. A sealed test tube containing an aqueous stock solution of human DNA (4.0mg/ml deionized water) was used in all experiments. Before and after measures were taken by placing the test tube on top of a geometric pattern on the laboratory bench top. For control experiments, both samples from the pair were placed in a clear area on the bench. Each pattern was tested on at least two separate days. After 1.5 hours, three aliquots were taken from each treatment sample, diluted 1/10 in deionized water and measured using a Hewlett Packard Diode Array Spectrophotometer at 260nm. An increase in the absorption of UV light is due to denaturation (unwinding) of DNA, whereas a decrease in absorption reflects renaturation (winding).

Different 2D geometric patterns were used in this study. A snowflake pattern embedded onto a "Crystal Glass" was obtained from the Institute of HeartMath (Boulder Creek, CA). The pattern is an intuitive representation of a heart crystal. A triangle pattern was obtained from Leonard Laskow, which was intuitively given as an antennae for subtle energy. In addition, four experiments were done by placing the test tube of DNA into the center of a 3D toroid with lines drawn (on the outside of the structure) around the circumference spiraling toward the center using golden mean proportions.

The results indicate that the conformation of DNA does in fact change when it is placed on top of a certain geometric patterns. The 2D toroid did not cause a statistically significant change in the DNA. The 3D toroid produced the largest effect. In addition the magnitude, the direction of these effects is also important. The control delta values are always positive indicating the natural tendency of DNA to unwind as it sat undisturbed on the benchtop. Each time the DNA was placed on top of the snowflake pattern there was a decrease in absorption indicating a consistent winding of DNA. In contrast, each time the DNA was placed on top of the triangle pattern, the DNA consistently unwound. The three geometric patterns with negative Gaussian curvatures (the golden spiral, the 3D toroid and the Anu) behaved in an unusual manner: in half the experiments the pattern caused the DNA to wind and in half the experiments the DNA unwound! Oscillatory behavior of other bio-molecules has been recently observed experimentally and is likely that such behavior is an example of macroscopic quantum coherence.

Nonetheless, the results reported here support the hypothesis that an information transfer occurs between certain geometric patterns and DNA. It is difficult to imagine how a classical electromagnetic field could be involved with such effects. It is interesting to note that the 2D toroid pattern did not affect DNA. This pattern is predominantly a series of logarithmic spirals meeting at a center point. An individual spiral in the golden mean proportions, however, did affect the DNA. Thus, in order to have biological activity the spiral must be in the golden mean proportions.

The results also demonstrate for the first time that energy fields with negative Gaussian curvatures show biological activity. Thus, the anu and a 3D toroid appears to generate a non-classical energy field which alters DNA. The Anu is the shape of the most fundamental subatomic particles according to Leadbeater and Bassant. It is interesting to note that the toroid has also been used to model the energy fields associated with subatomic particles. At least in some models of the universe, it has been proposed that the doorway to higher dimensional realities is through the microcosmic dimensions beyond Planck's length. If in fact negative Gaussian geometries reflect the topology of the bridge to higher dimensions, as has been proposed in Twistor theory, it is fascinating to realize that our DNA can resonate with such geometries. It is the author's belief that higher levels of consciousness can enter the body (and heal it) via such a pathway. These results, therefore, support the author's previously proposed theory that DNA is an antennae and transducer of higher dimensional quantum fields (Rein, 1994). The recent observation in biology that DNA itself exists in the shape of a toroid (Hud et al, 1995; Ubbink and Odijk, 1995) is therefore likely to facilitate our energetic communication to the higher dimensional realms of the internal and external universe.

The Quantum Energy Healing Model

As a result of these recent scientific observations, a new model for Energy Medicine becomes apparent which is applicable for all energetic healing modalities including radionics and psychotronics. The Quantum Energy Healing Model proposes that the bio-energy field is composed of a series of at least three different types of energy, classical EM force fields, potential fields and quantum fields. The Quantum Energy Healing Model also proposes that the relationship between these fields can be defined using Bohm's model (Bohm, 1980) of the implicate order which is embedded within the explicate order. In this case, classical EM fields exist at the level of the explicate order which has embedded within it the potential field, which in turn has embedded within it the quantum field. According to Bohm, the implicate

13927-VALO

order is composed of a series of levels, each embedded within the next, where each level is increasingly more subtle and fundamental. If one adds to this model the concepts in quantum physics of hyperspace, then eventually a subtle level in the implicate order will be reached which is higher dimensional. The assumption is made in this article that quantum fields exist in this higher dimensional level. Quantum fields can thus be considered a scientific term for the more popular concept of "subtle energy". Even Einstein himself used the term subtle to refer to energy which could not yet be measured. It is proposed here that healing information originates at the most fundamental level in the implicate order, that of spirit, and cascades into the outer layers of increasing energy density eventually reaching the electromagnetic domain. Thus, quantum fields act as a bridge between the higher dimensional energies of spirit and classical EM field. EM fields then regulate the biochemical level as demonstrated by the Bioelectromagnetics community. Healing with energy therefore occurs by an infusion of energy from some external source which resonates with the level in the bio-field according the how "subtle" it is. Healing can also occur through internal sources of energy generated from the individual in a meditative state of consciousness.

References

Aspden H, "The Principles Underyling Regenerative Free Energy Technology," Proc.26th Intersoc. Energy Convers. Engineer. Conf. Vol.4, pp358, 1991.

Bohm DJ, Hiley BJ, "On the intuitive understandinng of nonlocality as implied by quantum theory", Found Phys Vol.5, pp.93, 1975.

Bohm D, *Wholeness and the Implicate Order*, Routledge & Kegan Paul, London, 1980.

Chambers R, "Shift of an Electron Interference Pattern by Enclosed Magnetic Flux," Phys. Rev. Lett, Vol.5, pp.3, 1960.

Conti P, G.E.Gigante, et al."Reduced Mitogenic Stimulation of Human Lymphocytes by ELF Electromagnetic Fields," FEBS Letters, Vol.162, pp.156, 1983.

Cope FW, "A review of the applications of solid state physics concepts to biological systems," J Bio Phys Vol.3, pp.1, 1975.

DelGiudice E, S.Doglia, et al,"Magnetic Flux Quantization and Josephson Behavior in Living Systems," Physica Scripta, Vol.40, pp.786, 1989.

Dixey R, G.Rein, "Noradrenaline Release Potentiated in a Clonal Nerve Cell Line by Low-Intensity Pulsed Magnetic Fields," Nature, Vol.296, pp.253, 1982.

Dossey, L. "Prayer, medicine, and science: the new dialogue," J. Health Care Chaplain *7*: 7-37, 1998.

Flannigan P, "Normalization of electroacupuncture imbalances using a mobius coil", Electric Engineer Times Oct 29, pp.38, 1979.

Fleischer, T."Prayer is therapy", Hastings Cent Rep. *30*: 4-5, 2000.

Garg, A. "Criterion for the observability of macroscopic quantum coherence", Phys Rev B Condens Matter *32*:4746-4749, 1985

Gagnon TA, G. Rein, "The Biological Significance of Water Structured with Non-Hertzian Time Reversed Waves". J. U.S. Psychotronics Assoc. Vol.4, pp.26, Summer, 1990.

Gelinas RC, "Apparatus and method for transfer of information by means of a curl-free magnetic vector potential field". US Patent 4,432,098 Feb 14, 1984.

Greene LA, Rein G, "Release, storage and uptake of catecholamines by a clonal cell line of NGF responsive phaeochromocytoma cells", Brain Res Vol.129, pp.247,1977

Ho, M.W et al, "Can weak magnetic fields (or potentials) affect pattern formation?" In: Ho, M-W., Popp, FA, Warnke U (eds) *Bioelectrodynamics and Biocommunication.* Singapore, World Scientific, 195-212, 1994

Hud NV, Downing KH, Balhorn R. "A constant radius of curvature model for the organization of DNA in toroidal condensates", Proc. Natl. Acad. Sci. *92*: 3581-3585, 1995.

King M, *Tapping the Zero-Point Energy*, Paraclette Pub., Provo, UT. 1990.

Popp FA et al.(eds.), *Electromagnetic Bio-Information*, pp.123, Urban & Schwarzenberg, Baltimore, 1979.

Puharich HK, "Method and Means from Shielding a Person from the Polluting Effects of ELF Magnetic Waves and Other Environmental Pollution," U.S. Patent # 616-183, June, 1984.

Rauscher EA. J. Plasma Phys 2: 517-528, 1968.

Reed D, "The Beltrami vector field-the key to unlocking the secrets of the vacuum?", Proc. Internat. Symposium on New Energy, Denver, CO., 1996.

Rein G, K.Korins, et al,. "Inhibition of Neurotransmitter Uptake in Neuronal Cells by Pulsed EM Fields," Proc. 9th Bioelectromag. Soc., June, 1987.

Rein G, "Biological Interactions with Scalar Energy-Cellular Mechanisms of Action," Proc.7th Internat. Assoc. Psychotronics Res., Georgia, 1988.

Rein G, "Effect of Non-Hertzian Scalar Waves on the Immune System," J. U.S. Psychotronics Assoc. Vol.1, pp.15, Spring, 1989.

Rein G, "Utilization of a cell culture bioassay for measuring quantum field generated from a modified caduceus coil", Proc.26th Intersoc Energy Conversion Engineer Conf Vol.4, pp.400, 1991.

Rein G. in *Healing with Love: A Breakthrough Mind/Body Medical Program for Healing Yourself and Others*, HarperSanFrancisco, San Francisco, 1992a.

Rein G. "Storage of non-Hertzian Frequency Information in Water" In: *Proc. Internat. Tesla Soc.* Elswick S (ed), Tesla Soc Pub., Colorado Springs;, CO., 1992b.

Rein G. "Spectroscopic evidence for force-free and potential-free information storage in water", Proc. Internat. Symposium on New Energy, Denver, CO., 1996.

Sector HW, "The Tesla high frequency oscillator", Elect. Experimenter *3*, pp.615, 1916.

Seiki S, The Principles of Ultra-Relativity, Ninomiya Press, PO Box 33, Uwajima City, Ehime (798), Japan, 10th edition, Dec.1990.

Smith WB, The New Science, Fern-Graphic Publ, Mississauga, Ontario, 1964.

Smith CW, "Electromagnetic Bio-information and Water". In: *Ultra High Dilutions-Physiology and Physics*. Endler (ed) Kluiver Acad Pub, 1994.

Smith CW, "Is a living system a macroscopic quantum system?" Frontier Perspectives *7*: 9-15, 1998.

Strapp HP. "Time and quantum process", in Proc.Physics and Ultimate Significance of Time Conference, p264-270, Claremont, CA, 1983.

Tesla N, "Transmission of Energy Without Wires," Scientific Amer. Suppl, Vol.57, pp.23760, 1904.

Ubbink J, Odijk T. "Polymer and salt-induced toroids of hexagonal DNA", Biophys. J. *68*: 54-61, 1995.

Wekroma AG. "The use of magnetic vector potentials for the treatment of materials", FRG Pat No 3938511.6, Nov 19, 1989.

10

How Should Science Handle the 'Unbelievable'?

Theodore Rockwell, Ph.D.
14th Annual Conference of the United States Psychotronics Association, 1989

Science Isn't Everything

Let's start by defining the job of science. We tend to think of science as applying to everything; after all, isn't this the Age of Science? But the fact is, science is only one way of searching for Truth, for trying to describe what Really Is. Other ways of searching for Truth include: the legal system, the arts, philosophy, and religion (including, of course, the religion of atheism). Each of these approaches, including science, is a system of procedures for winnowing truth and reality from lies and illusions, plus some criteria for judging the results of your efforts. Such systems are referred to technically as "games," and in any game, it is the procedures and criteria that determine whether the result is legitimate. Each of these games has its own procedures and criteria, and they should not be mixed. It is not legitimate to use a tennis ball in badminton, and it is likewise forbidden to argue that an action is ethical because it meets legal requirements. Similarly, it is not appropriate to judge the validity of religion by the criteria of science, or the validity of science by the criteria of religion. Each must be judged on its own terms, and each has a place.

Science has no need to encroach upon the turf of others; they pose no threat to its power. We have seen the senseless battle between creationists and evolutionists. They both seem to have accepted the false premise from the Middle Ages that every gain in the power of religion must cause an equal loss in the power of science, and vice versa. So, myopic theologians shout, "Genesis is the best science" while scientists roar back, "Thou shalt have no other gods before Me!" This is like two people trying to describe a balloon: one insists "It is red!" while the other maintains "No, it is round!" It is a foolish argument. Science has no tools to determine whether God exists, to decide what is beautiful, or good, whether life has purpose or meaning, and a host of other important questions that humanity has wrestled with since the dawn of time. That is why universities still have departments of philosophy, religion, jurisprudence, metaphysics, and art, in addition to their science departments.

So my first point is that science should stop trying to impose its viewpoint on other areas of human inquiry outside its domain. It is interesting, and perhaps instructive, for science to analyze what common characteristics are shared by art forms that are generally held to be beautiful, or legal cases that are decided in a given way. But that does not mean that statistical analysis should be substituted for current procedures in the art or legal worlds, no matter how refined our statistical methods become. Moreover, I believe that if mainstream scientists understood more clearly how the boundaries of science are determined, they would not only refrain from invading their neighbor's turf, they would recognize that science should be extending its work into some areas they now call pseudoscience, including, for example trying to understand mind and subjective experience, and related topics such as parapsychology and psychotronics. (Mainstream scientists have always resisted any claim that the mind was more than a linear neural network. They fought Freud's idea of the subconscious, and hypnosis was considered a parlor trick. A doctor who demonstrated an amputation with hypnosis as the sole anesthesia was accused of colluding with the patient to pretend there was no pain!)

Almost any area of inquiry as to the nature of the physical world can be explored scientifically. One can search for gravity waves, black holes, extraterrestrial life, an AIDS virus, or psychic phenomena—whether or not such entities actually exist—without being a pseudoscientist. The test is whether the search is done with procedures and criteria which are scientific. We have begun to apply the tools of science to human thinking in such areas as psychology, sociology, and even (God help us!) economics. Is it too much to ask that mainstream science admit the validity of scientifically investigating telepathy, psychokinesis, faith-healing, homeopathy, and other currently-forbidden topics? Any scientist can chose to ignore such topics if they do not interest him, and he can conclude the evidence in any case is unconvincing. But it is unscientific to treat an entire area of inquiry as out-of-bounds, and research reports and proposals in these areas should be treated on their merits and not rejected out of hand.

What Can We Learn from the Legal System?

People and institutions are judged by how they handle challenging situations. If a judicial system treats its routine criminal and civil cases competently but handles its more troublesome citizens by denying them proper treatment and a fair trial, we rightly find it severely deficient. By this criterion, the American scientific enterprise does not perform well.

Although science has learned a great deal from its own efforts, it has been peculiarly unwilling to learn from humanity's other efforts to understand truth and reality. The legal system, in particular, being "left-brained" and objective, should offer some lessons for the scientific process. (This, of course, is not to imply that I consider the legal system, in practice, any "better" or less flawed overall than the scientific process. But we can learn from others without conceding their overall superiority.) Note first that the law, like science, is properly not a belief system. The courts do not take a position as to what the law should prescribe; when laws change, the courts enforce the new laws without changing their long-established procedures. Similarly, science is a set of procedures for investigating the physical world, and should not take a position a priori as to what form physical reality must take. When new discoveries change our understanding of the world, science should not feel obliged to defend its previous beliefs; it should continue to apply the same procedures to develop still further understanding. That is lesson number one that science can learn from the legal system.

Part of the problem comes from the fact that the rules of good scientific procedure have never been spelled out with adequate precision. Scientists have been too busy doing science to spend much time talking about how it should be done. This has made it possible for certain tactics to develop which enable a biased participant to invalidate any experimental results he finds threatening. One of these tactics is the "failure to replicate" gambit. Scientists rush into print a few weeks after a disturbing paper appears, claiming they have replicated the essence of the original work (which may have taken years), and their experiment failed to show the same results. Now, failure to replicate is easy; all you have to do (by definition) is fail to repeat exactly what the original experimenter did. This is of no scientific interest until you can explain the precise difference between your work and the original, and show that the original conclu-sions are invalidated by this difference. Sociologist Harry Collins points out that the first few laboratories which tried to build a laser generator, after reading reports of the first one, were unable to do so until they had actually "laid hands on one". This was not a mystical experience, but merely the acquiring first-hand of all the little special details which spell the difference between a successful and an unsuccessful replication. But none of these persons rushed into print to brag that they had failed to replicate the laser generator.

Another effective tactic used against controversial science is the "dirty test-tube gambit." This was the last resort of the National Research Council's report on a range of studies by the US Army aimed at enhancing human performance. The NRC report stated with respect to parapsychology, that there were three ways to invalidate such research: the "smoking gun" (that is, a flaw which by itself would invalidate the conclusions), the alternative hypothesis, and the "dirty test-tube". They concluded, after three years of effort, that they could find no "smoking gun" and that they could produce no reasonable alternative hypothesis. They were therefore left with the "dirty test-tube" argument: that the entire field of research failed to measure up, in some unspecified way, to the high standards required, since "extraordinary claims demand extraordinary proof." This vague and unfalsifiable criticism led to their conclusion that the work was without merit. Clearly, an environment in which the highest scientific body in the land can operate in this way cries out for reform.

Science by SWAT Team

Dr. Jacques Benveniste, a world-class scientist at a prestigious national laboratory in France, presented a paper which the scientific journal *Nature* found "unbelievable." [*Nature*, 333, 816, 1988. Also see "Nobel laureates face libel suits from 'water memory' researcher" *Nature*, 389, 427, 1997 – Ed. note] For two years he responded to requests from the reviewers to make further checks. The work was replicated at five other laboratories in four countries. Finally, *Nature* wrote that the reviewers were "unable to find fault with it" and published it, but with a lead editorial describing the work as "unbelievable" and an editorial footnote at the end of the paper, referring readers back to the editorial.

Even this was not enough. In an operation combining the worst features of the Grand Inquisitor and the Keystone Kops, the editor sent out a SWAT team of fraud-busters, none of whom was competent in the field being investigated (incredibly, one was a stage magician!), and in five days reversed the opinion of the peer reviewers, despite admitting that they "found no evidence of outright fraud." Benveniste charged that the investigation was "a mockery of a scientific investigation" and that the team "terrorized" his laboratory. Nature's editor told reporters that this criticism of his team was "entirely fair. We weren't particularly polite about it." One wonders why not? Even more surprising was the number of scientists who criticized *Nature* for publishing the paper in the first place. What's going on here? When the fraud-busters found no fraud, they should have concluded their work and turned the evaluation back to the scientific process. (The other laboratories, which confirmed Benveniste's findings, have never been questioned.)

Unfortunately, Benveniste's case is not unique. Dr. Wilhelm Reich had all his papers and laboratory data confiscated and burned by the US Government, his instruments and other property destroyed, and he was thrown into jail, where he died of a heart attack. The FDA actually issued an injunction against anyone continuing research in this field! Immanuel Velikovsky's publisher was threatened with boycott by other scientists, and scientific journals refused to run ads for books by or about him. Ruth Drown, the radionics pioneer, was jailed. [Ruth Drown was awarded British patent #515,866 in 1939 for "Method of and means for obtaining Photographic Images of Living and other Objects" – Ed. note]

And for persons considered less threatening, there is always review and evaluation by "unbelievers," that is, someone unfamiliar with the field and thus incompetent for the task by definition. This perversion of the peer review process leads to some outrageous reviewer comments and some rejection letters with unprofessional state-ments such as the following (from *Science*, to pick just one journal among many):

"Most of our readers do not believe in the existence of ESP. If we publish a paper on it, it must be without a flaw. We must be convinced by expert opinion that your manuscript pro-vides irrefutable proof of your conclusions."

Just imagine such a letter referring to any other field of inquiry! Substitute "black holes" or "plate tectonics" for "ESP" and see how it sounds.

Another paper was rejected with the suggestion that the authors: " . . . team up with some of the organized skeptical organizations which are interested in such problems—these include the Committee for Scientific Evaluation of the Paranormal [sic] or the Society of American Magicians." [*Science* apparently doesn't quite know the correct title of CSICOP: "Committee for the Scientific Investigation of Claims of the Paranormal," headquartered in Amherst, NY, which in 1999 was raising $10 million for its "skeptical message." – Ed. note]

Are we now turning over final evaluation of scientific merit to magicians? And my favorite (rejecting a laboratory study of psychokinesis):

"It does not report new results, being the replication of work of others. It is too long and has too many tables." This in a field which is routinely criticized for non-replicability and skimpy reports!

Realize that these are not off-hand remarks. These are official verdicts of the scientific process! When efforts are made to secure competent and unbiased peer review of such papers, the response from editors and their scientific sponsors has nearly always been the same. First, the letters are ignored and phone calls are not returned. When finally forced to respond, the journal takes the position is that the appellant is requesting special treatment and a lowering of standards for his or her particular field of research. Clearly, this is a com-plete reversal of the facts. What is sought is equal treatment: uniform application of the normal scientific process. And this can be a lowering of standards only if one believes that the normal scientific method is less effective than fraud-busters in winnowing scientific wheat from chaff.

Note that I am not defending the conclusions of these particular research reports. That's not the point of my remarks. I am willing to leave that to the scientific process. I am saying that the scientific establishment, as defined by the reviewers and editors of mainstream journals, seems unwilling to let the scientific process work, and that is a far more serious matter.

Science Is More than Laboratory Work

Let's look at the scientific process. Scientists are generally both clear and vocal in ex-pressing the requirements that an experimental paper must meet in order to be considered good science. But the scientific process, like the legal process, cannot be completed in the confines of the offices of its practitioners. The process must be carried out publicly, in connection with real-life cases. Thus, the process of reviewing a scientific paper and of documenting the basis for its acceptance or rejection are especially critical parts of the scientific process, and should therefore be held to the same high standards. The legal profession understands this point well. Judges take great pains in preparing opinions, and a judge's competence is evaluated on the basis of such writing. It is not acceptable for a judge to excuse an unprofessional, incompetent or uncivil opinion on the basis that the defendant "doesn't deserve a fair trial." Nor can he brag about not being polite.

Judges don't speculate publicly that Miranda was a n'er-do-well or that Roe or Wade were morally lax. They understand that such matters are irrelevant to their legal rights. But critics of parapsychology justify their positions by writing that Hal Puthoff was once a Scientologist, that Russell Targ's father once ran a bookstore with books on occultism, and Margaret Mead was an Episcopalian who had thereby abandoned rational thought. [For documentation of these and other anti-scientific judgments, see "Irrational Rationalists" by T. Rockwell et al. in *J. of the American Society of Psychical Research*, V.72, pp.23-34 and 349-364, 1978.]

Because we tend to think that science is limited to what goes on in laboratories, we turn the spotlight on the poor experimentalist every time there is a question of fraud, misconduct or inadequate research standards. (Theorists are a little harder to get a handle on, but they too are under the gun.) We question their data keeping, their statistics, their procedures and their honesty. But the scientific process also includes editors, reviewers and grant-givers, and these important components of the scientific process operate almost without rules or accountability. If these persons, though their unmonitored and unrecorded personal biases, prevent whole areas of research from being published (and this is indeed happening), then the scientific data base is being distorted in exactly the same way an unscrupulous experimenter distorts the data by omitting or fudging data which fails to meet his expectations. When it is done in the laboratory, we call it fraud; when it is done in editorial offices, we don't even admit it is happening.

Some New Ideas Are More Acceptable Than Others

Admittedly, some novel ideas are picked up quickly by the scientific hierarchy. Recent speculation about a "fifth force" which directly challenges Newton's law is such a case. The suggestion that dinosaurs may have been warm-blooded, with feathers, is another. Why was Benveniste's paper considered so different from these? One possibility is that the original idea behind Benveniste's paper arose from folk medicine rather than from academia. We glimpse a hint of this in *Nature*'s statement that "The controversy is magnified by their connections with homeopathic medicine." For some reason, the supporting fact that a quarter of French physicians prescribe homeopathic remedies is considered a detriment. A similar sentiment on a different subject was voiced in the National Research Council's unfavorable report, cited earlier, on all new ideas for enhancing human performance being evaluated by the Army: "Rather than derive a procedure from appropriate scientific literature, they create techniques from personal experiences, sudden insights, or informal observation of 'what works' . . . Research follows rather than precedes the invention." You can almost hear the professor snorting: "How dare they come up with something that works, when they don't even cite my papers!" In still another example, *TIME* reported, in its May 29, 1989 cover story, that physicists were "outraged" that two chemists announced they might have discovered a new approach to nuclear fusion, a subject physicists consider "off limits" to chemists (especially chemists from Utah). *Doubt is understandable, but why outrage?*

Let the Scientific Process Work

Sir Karl Popper, the eminent philosopher of science, said the business of science is falsification. That is, we should be looking for new ideas and then trying to discover the flaws in them. Why then are editors and reviewers so afraid that we might read about some flawed ideas? If the normal scientific process is incapable of spotting such flaws, then the whole scientific enterprise is questionable. If a paper is particularly bad, it should be particularly easy to demonstrate that fact and document it objectively. Our leading general science journals, those that reach the cracks between the disciplines where most new ideas are found, have been totally unwilling to publish any reports whatsoever on certain areas of research which make their editors or reviewers uncomfortable. The editors plead lack of space, but they devote many pages each year to criticizing the work they will not let their readers see.

Why are journal editors and reviewers so reluctant to entrust novel papers to the scientific process? Can it be that they don't trust it? The parallel with nations which are unwilling to let certain types of persons come to trial is inescapable. Such persons are held without trial or just disappear. Their government is unwilling to stand by the results of an open trial. What would happen if Benveniste were put though the normal peer review process? Are scientists unwilling to accept the possibility that he might be found "innocent?"

A good example of a journal refuting papers which it will not publish appeared in *Science.* [*Science*, Vol. 151, Feb. 11, 1966, pp. 654-657] The refutation (disguised as a technical paper) was entitled "A Peek Down the Nose," and was a witty essay by Martin Gardner, well-known ridiculer of research on unusual human capabilities. Gardner described how magicians have known for centuries that it is very difficult to make an effective blindfold; one can always peek down the nose. On this basis, he proceeded to debunk all research on "eyeless vision," the apparent ability of some people to perceive colors and even shapes through skin contact alone. He specifically targetted the work of R. P.Youtz, who responded in a letter that Gardner "has never seen my apparatus or witnessed my procedure, although his article conveys the impression that he has" [*Science*, 152, May 20,1966, pp.1108-1110]. Gardner therefore speculated erroneously on several critical aspects of the experiments. Most important was the fact that Youtz did not rely on blindfolds, but had his subject work through a sleeved glovebox. Gardner also makes no mention of work with subjects who are completely blind. What scientific standards permit such technical inaccuracies to be published for the purpose of debunking, while the original research reports are barred for "lack of space"?

The point here is that if an editor considers a subject worth including in his journal, there is no rational basis for publishing only the negative reaction, without letting the readers see what is being reacted to. How can one hope to replicate an experiment, when all that is published is a second-hand report, from one who believes the work to be invalid? This sort of thing happens repeatedly in *Science*, *Scientific American*, and the popular magazines such as *Discover*. The fear that we readers might not evaluate such reports properly is not a reflection on the particular research in question, it is a lack of confidence in science itself.

What Can Be Done?

In addition to the sort of rejection letters I quoted earlier, there have been many cases of blatant bias, rudeness, and unresponsiveness, which can only be seen as abuse of power. Andrew Herxheimer cites a chilling example in *The Scientist*, [*The Scientist*, Vol. 3, No. 6, March 20,1989, p. 9] and offers some suggestions. First, authors might try to favor journals which treat authors better. But to do this, we need to develop and publish statistics, such as average time between submission and rejection of papers, for the various journals. He notes that at least one journal (*Annals of Internal Medicine*) publishes "not only guidance about format, style, circulation, audience, and availability, but also details of manuscript processing and evaluation. It describes its policies for acknowledgment of receipt of papers, internal review by editors, peer review, acceptance or rejection, time to final decision, scheduling of papers, pre-publication release of information, and complimentary copies. As a result, [one] knows exactly what to expect."

In addition, journals should indicate more precisely what their area of interest is (e.g. how many papers they publish in each specialty), so that would-be authors will not be surprised by learning, after months of delay, that certain areas of research are seldom covered in that journal, despite its title. Herxheimer goes further, to suggest audits of journals to check their performance in these matters, *and a scientific body to whom authors can appeal unfair treatment.*

Another problem which could be easily dealt with is the much-discussed matter of multiple authorship—persons listed as authors whose contributions to the paper were negligible. There has been much agonizing in the scientific community over this problem, along with some complex and oppressive proposals to legislate or regulate fairness and uniformity. Murray Saffran, in the same issue of *The Scientist*, proposes an eminently sensible solution: have each author describe his or her contribution in one or two sentences at the end of the paper. His illustrative example is excellent. If this practice were followed, no further requirements or rules would be necessary to handle this trouble-some matter.

To do these thing well, we need a scientific oversight organization to focus the development of procedures and criteria for carrying out the scientific process and to implement what-ever reforms are concluded to be necessary. Obvious choices are the American Association for the Advancement of Science (AAAS), or the National Academy of Sciences (NAS), but they are a big part of the problem and cannot easily be part of the solution. The Sigma Xi might offer its good offices for this purpose. Perhaps we need some sort of low-key International Scientific Press Council, as Herxheimer suggests, but great care would be required in naming its membership, which would have to have strictly limited tenure. There should also be sufficient repre-sentation of mavericks and perhaps even a special non-scientist or two: an historian or a philosopher, even perhaps a lawyer or judge of the right sort. But if the membership of this Council begins to feature many of the same long-familiar names we keep seeing as heads of various na-tional scientific committees and societies, it should be disbanded.

Standard Bearers

The group I envision would not be regulators or auditors. Nor would they exist primarily to afflict the comfortable or to make more work for hard-pressed scientists. Their first task would be to suggest some standards for editorial boards, editors, reviewers and grant-givers. They might require (for example) that the qualifications of reviewers be spelled out by each editor, and published. I would hope that they would require reviews to be signed, with the reviewer's qualifications for reviewing a particular paper briefly noted. In such an environment, exemplary reviews might become career assets, rather than unacknowledged drudgery. Rather than begrudging the 1.5 hours reviewers now spend on a typical review (according to a recent survey), they might conclude that more time spent preparing an outstanding and citable review would be professionally advantageous.

(The suggestion that reviews be signed has been hooted down through the years, with the argument that reviewers would pull their punches, that younger reviewers would be intimidated, etc. Why the scientific enterprise should be uniquely vulnerable to these ills, while other professional activities seem to thrive on signed reviews, is never explained. But now we see the practice being demonstrated successfully in certain up-and-coming scientific journals. The idea started in the social sciences, anthropology in particular, and is now gaining wider recognition and approval. The respected journal, *Behavioral and Brain Sciences* has a format that is particularly effective. Rather than avoiding controversy, the editors select a controversial subject and invite two major papers to delineate the arguments for each side. They publish both papers, along with fifty or more brief, signed reviews. The original authors are then given space to respond to the various critiques. The reader is thus given a book-length document with a spectrum of views on a particularly knotty and timely scientific issue. You actually develop a basis for an opinion on the subject.)

Appeal Process

The appeal process would not try to second-guess editors by recommending that a rejected paper be published. Like the corresponding legal process, the appeal would be concerned less with the outcome itself and more with the question:

- Did the defendant get a fair trial?
- Were the reviewers qualified to review the paper?
- Did they understand it?
- Were their criticisms valid and significant?
- Did they write it up clearly and civilly?
- Was the editor's response appropriate?
- Did the whole process proceed at a reasonable pace?
- Was undue bias of any kind apparent?
- Was the author misled or otherwise dealt with inappropriately?

Unless the evidence for impropriety were strong and the offense significant, the editor would be given the benefit of the doubt. But even if there were only a few such cases taken up each year, the scientific enterprise would be much the stronger and freer as a result. Although most scientists would agree on general standards for proper review and evaluation, in practice there are shocking departures from a reasonable level of technical competence and thoroughness, civility and objectivity, especially in new or controversial areas of research. Since these reviews are usually done anonymously, there is little opportunity for accountability and appeal. The lone author is stonewalled by the editor, his board and his publisher, none of whom are obligated to explain or justify their position. Thus, agreement on a general standard is ineffective. It is as if there were detailed rules for how lawyers must present a case, but almost no rules for the judge, who remains masked and unidentified; even his qualifications to judge are not revealed. No wonder there are increasing calls for reform of the scientific review and evaluation process.

Summary of the Key Points

1.) Science is only one way of reaching for Truth and Reality. Other approaches include: legal systems, the arts, philosophy and religion. None of these systems can invalidate the others; each has validity only on its own terms.
2.) Science should therefore stop trying to impose its views and its criteria on other domains where it has no authority or expertise. The success of science in its own domain does not mean scientists have special skills to deal with other questions. Science has no tools to deal with the subject matter of religion, philosophy, art, and the law. Conversely, science should consider extending its operations to include consciousness and subjective experience.
3.) Any aspect of the physical world can be studied scientifically. The test is not whether the subject matter is acceptable to most scientists, but whether the procedures and criteria of science are used.
4.) Science could learn from observing the legal process. Courts do not try to decide what the laws should prescribe; when laws change, they apply their procedures and criteria to the new laws. Similarly, scientists should not try to protect their current idea of what reality should be like by distorting the procedures and criteria of science. They should let the picture of reality change with each new discovery.
5.) The measure of any system or institution is not how well it carries out its routine business, but how it handles its challenging cases. By this criterion, American science does not perform well. There is no clear reason why the normal procedures of science would not have handled well the challenges posed by Benveniste, Reich, Velikovsky, Backster and other controversial figures. The heavy-handed pressure tactics used against them imply that scientists are unwilling to live by the verdicts of the scientific process. (Note that the law deals with the guilty as well as the innocent. Science should be

able to handle incompetent and invalid work though its normal procedures, as part of the process of validating good work.)

6.) In their hurry to defend the prevailing view of reality, scientists often rush to report failures to replicate controversial papers. Failure to replicate means only that the second experimenter has not duplicated the original work. This, by itself, is not enough to disprove anything.

7.) Vague and non-falsifiable criticisms such as the "dirty test-tube" argument are not a legiti-mate basis for invalidating large areas of research.

8.) Science is not just something that happens in the laboratory. Both science and the law are incomplete until they have acted on real-life cases in the public arena. Rules governing the conduct and reporting of laboratory work are already detailed and explicit. But the process by which scientific ideas are judged worthy of funding or publication (or are left to wither and die) is a process with little definition, control, responsibility or accountability. The law, by contrast, publicly records its judgments, and the rationale supporting them, in exquisite detail, and the careers of those in the field depend on the professionalism and validity of those written judgments. Science could learn from this.

9.) Some controversial ideas are treated properly by the scientific community, while most are not. Those favorably received seem mostly to originate safely within scientific academia, while those treated harshly are often seen to arise from "peasant wisdom" (e.g. Laetrile, homeopathy, psychic phenomena). Suppression of these or other controversial fields of research without proper evaluation distorts the fundamental database of science.

10.) Mainstream scientific organizations, such as the AAAS and the NAS, are often unresponsive to the point of dereliction. Responsiveness and accountability, at least to members and clients, should be a requirement for continued operation of any public organization.

11.) Scientific journals should describe publicly their procedures for reviewing and acting on submitted papers, and publish statistics, periodically updated, as to intervals between the various stages of review. They should also indicate what percentage of published papers are in various aspects of the field covered by the journal. Authors can then use these data to decide where to submit papers.

12.) Some sort of oversight organization is needed to suggest standards for reviewers and provide a forum for authors and a channel for appeal. Appeal would not attempt to determine whether a paper deserved publication; it would examine only whether the author was given proper consideration and treatment. Staffing such an organization would require care; members would have to be competent and highly professional, but not part of the "old boy network."

13.) Reviewers should have to sign their reviews, and editors should state the basis for their selection as reviewers. Journals might consider the occasional use of a format which invites extended commentary on invited pro and con papers on controversial scientific findings.

14.) The problem of misuse of multiple authorship could be handled simply by having each author of a paper state in one or two sentences his or her specific contribution to the paper.

Although Truth speaks with a small voice, it may ultimately prevail. But it will not prevail unless we keep working to make it so.

THEODORE ROCKWELL has spent 45 years in nuclear power development, starting as a Process Improvement Engineer at the wartime atomic project in Oak Ridge, Tennessee. For 15 years he reported to Admiral Hyman Rickover, the last 10 as Technical Director of the national program to develop, build, operate, and maintain several hundred nuclear power plants for naval propulsion and to build the world's first civilian nuclear power station. With two colleagues, he founded the respected engineering firm MPR Associates in 1964. He has medals and citations from several branches of the Government, and is known for numerous patents, articles and books. For many years he was the designated Representative of the Parapsychological Association to the American Association for the Advancement of Science, and has written extensively on consciousness research.

11

The Politics of Science: A Background on Energy Medicine

Christopher Bird

Adapted from a presentation given to the 18th Annual Medical Symposium of the ARE Clinic, Phoenix, Arizona, January 23-27, 1985

Reprinted from the *J. of the U. S. Psychotronics Association*, No. 2, Spring, 1989, p.22

I was most excited to learn that the Fetzer Foundation had stepped forward to assist the ARE Clinic in setting up a program in "Energy Medicine:" and I'm glad they didn't call it "Paramedicine." I think, in some ways, if we'd had "Energy Psychology" instead of "Parapsychology" there would have been less controversy.

I have been following some very interesting developments in energy medicine that really go a long way back-to the very start of this century. It looks as though, with the initiative of this marvelous foundation in Kalamazoo, maybe something can be done to pick up the pieces of some of this research which has all but been forgotten.

13927-VALO

Georges Lakhovsky

The first man I will mention today is the Russian-born Frenchman, Georges Lakhovsky. I learned only yesterday that Lakhovsky seems to have been an associate, or knew, Nikola Tesla. I had not known that and from the point of view of the history of energy medicine, it's a very interesting thing. At any rate, Georges Lakhovsky began to experiment with what he called a "multiwave oscillator." (In the Library of Congress there are some ten books written by Lakhovsky, all in French.)

This multiwave oscillator (MWO) put out a very broad spectrum of electromagnetic frequencies. The theory, as propounded by Lakhovsky, was that each cell in the body of an organism—be it a plant, an animal, or a human being—is in itself a little radio receiver and works on its own special little frequency. Each cell, in addition to being tissue, in addition to being biology, is also electricity. On that theory, he held that pathology was a not matter of biological concern or intervention, but one of electrical concern and intervention. He theorized that from the bath of electrical frequencies put out by the multiwave oscillator, each cell individually could and would select that frequency which it most needed to restore its equilibrium.

So he began to experiment not with animals or human beings, but with geraniums. These were geraniums which had cancers-plants get cancers too. And—lo and behold—the geraniums were cured of their cancers; which simply began to fall off since they are external in the case of geraniums. The geraniums would just shed the diseased tissues when exposed to the MWO. Lakhovsky then went on to do work on animals and human beings and his work was picked up by doctors in six or seven countries, among them Italy, Sweden and Brazil. Finally, because he was on the "wanted" list of the Nazis, he was smuggled out of France and came to New York during the war, where he worked with a urologist. The record of his treatment of degenerative disease, with what amounts to an early "energy-medicine" device, was remarkable. But the work had to be done in secret because orthodox medicine did not favor this device, and its power, associated with that of the FDA, and the AMA and other "control organizations," kept the MWO underground.

The Lakhovsky device is a very effective one. I'm not going to say that it's 100% effective because I don't think any device is, but it is way up there. Georges Lakhovsky, died in 1944 or 1945.

Royal Raymond Rife

The next man is Royal Raymond Rife, who came on the scene just about the time that Lakhovsky had begun his research. Rife had no academic training whatsoever. He got a job as chauffeur and handyman for Timken, the roller bearing magnate from Ohio who also spent a lot of time in California back in the 1920' s. And there, Royal Raymond Rife proved that you don't necessarily need academic training to develop something new. In the case of Lakhovsky, Rife – and about three dozen other people I could go on to mention— in fact, it was an advantage that they didn't have any academic training because what they did went against anything they would have been taught in the "academies." At any rate, Rife conceived and built, an extraordinary microscope called the Universal Microscope.

When I first heard of his work and his microscope, I simply couldn't believe that it existed. I got on the telephone in Washington and I called Walter Reed Hospital, the big central medical hospital for the U.S. Army. They have a special division, almost a museum, on microscopy. I asked where the Rife microscope was and nobody had ever heard of it. Then I called the Smithsonian Institute and nobody had heard of it there. Then I called the National Library of Medicine. Nobody had heard of it. So I began to wonder; was I "nuts," or was my informant misinformed, or what really was the story?

Suddenly, through a series of synchronous events, I had a stroke of luck. I was in the National Library of Medicine looking for some data about Rife, and there was nothing in the card catalog under R-i-f-e. I found myself leaning against a set of drawers containing cards which began with the abbreviated rubric M-I-C, for microscopes. There were about four drawers, and it takes about 1½ hours to carefully examine one drawer of cards. I figured it would be a pointless exercise to go through all the drawers, but I had the first drawer open and, just idly, halfway along the drawer I pulled the cards apart and there was something that, as I recall, read "The Allied Company." It bore an extraordinary subtitle. It was a report about cancer cures and a microscope, and way down at the bottom of the card was the notation: *Written by Royal Raymond Rife*. I could never have found that card by looking under Rife's name!

I learned from that report that the Universal Microscope had been written up and published (over 38 pages) in not only the official journal of the Smithsonian Institute in Washington, but also in the official journal of the Franklin Institute in Philadelphia—a big repository of engineering facts. The same article, entitled "The New Microscopes," had been simultaneously published by those two institutions in 1944. The other principal microscope which was treated in the article was the electron microscope, which had just been put on the market by RCA.

I find that to be an incredible bit of scientific history: that of the two microscopes which were featured, side by side, in an article published by the Smithsonian Institute and the Franklin Institute (the section on Rife's "Universal Microscope" was much longer than the section on the electron microscope), one went on to be used in practically every medical research lab of any size and the other one disappeared off the face of the map!

The electron microscope can only examine dead tissue while the Rife microscope could examine living matter on high magnification-up to 30,000X and at extraordinary resolution. Was the Rife microscope, the one which could look at live tissue, taken off the market or destroyed just because of that? Does it say something to you?

So Rife invented this microscope. The Universal scope had something like 763 separate parts. It's all described in the article. (You can get it out of the libraries.) The man who provided the description was a devoted homeopathic doctor in Philadelphia who did the work with his secretary.They had a very hard time because it was during the war, and Rife was living and working in San Diego while they were in Philadelphia. It was extremely complex technology to describe. And therefore if, today, you give this article to even technically well-trained people, there are "holes" in it which make it very difficult to understand at the "nuts and bolts" level exactly how this microscope works. But what it did have, which distinguished it from all other microscopes, were lenses made, not of glass, but of quartz. Quartz, as you know, will admit ultraviolet light, whereas glass will not. So that is one key.

It also had was a quartz prism which could be rotated very, very slowly; so slowly, in fact, that Rife would sit in a specially built chair looking at a specimen—a living specimen—as long as 72 hours; just looking while rotating this prism! As the prism rotated very slowly, it would illuminate the specimen with a single frequency of light, and at a given point, if that frequency was "correct," it would cause the specimen being examined to illuminate itself through a reasonance factor. It was at this point that the special magnification and resolution could be achieved. But it takes great patience to get this kind of magnification in this special scope, which may be another reason why it never achieved popularity.

About 1977, I wrote a long article about this which was published in the *New Age Journal* and, among other things, it dealt with the controversy which is today still raging in medical circles after 50 years, as to whether micro-organisms are mono-or pleiomorphic. That is, either microorganisms, from bacteria down to viruses, are monomorphic, meaning that they are "one form and one form only," or they are pleiomorphic, meaning that they can change from one form to another.

There was a terrible fight in the 1930's over this and the monomorphic people won. It's a very interesting controversy which took me about six weeks of work to research in the Library of Medicine when I was doing the article for the *New Age Journal.* (The article was entitled "What Has Become of the Rife Microscope?") The last sentence of the last paragraph was a plea to the public to help out to see if we could find them.

(Subsequently, I did find two of Rife's microscopes in very bad condition in the garage of one of Rife's mechanics in San Diego. Still another is preserved in perfect condition in the Welcome Foundation, a medical foundation and museum in London, because it had been carried over during the war to London at the request of a Dr. Conin, who was then Physician Royal – physician to the Royal Family. Because World War II was in progress, Dr .Conin was unfortunately never able to work with the scope. When he died shortly after the war, nobody was interested in taking up where he left off. So that Rife microscope stands in the Welcome foundation, inert and unused.)

Rife, looking in his microscope, found that living things in fact *were pleiomorphic* and not only were they pleiomorphic, but they were drastically so, depending on the "terrain" as Claude Bernard had it—and, by the way, Pasteur's last words were supposed to have been: "Claude Bernard is right: The microbe is nothing, the terrain is everything." Meaning that, depending on the terrain, depending on the metabolic condition, depending on the internal state, the chemical or biochemical state of the body, a given microbe could alter its form and its function and become something else. Rife posited that much *disease was not caused by the microorganisms but that the microorganisms were caused by, or perhaps better said, associated with, the disease.*

He could see this at the microscope! For instance, he could see a bacterial form going through several successive stages to become a levurid form (yeast) or a fungus. Having invented the scope and come up with a new theory, he next reasoned that if he could illuminate a microorganism with a single frequency and cause it to resonate, then he should be able to turn that principle around and find some electromagnetic frequencies which could be radiated into living organisms to cause the disappearance of those organisms which are associated with disease. And that is what he did!

He had the backing in his day – this was in the 1930s – of such eminent people as Kendall, a professor of pathology at Northwestern University; Millbank Johnson, M.D., was on his board, along with many other medical men, when he began to treat people with this new "ray emitter." What happened next is very strange. (There were articles written on the Rife technique up to the point I've described it in the *Journal for the Medical Society of California* and other medical journals.)

Suddenly, Rife came under the glassy eye of Morris Fishbein of the AMA and things began to happen very quickly. *Rife was put on trial for having invented a "phony" medical cure.* The trial lasted a long time. And Rife, being a very sensitive individual – he was a man who could sit in one position for 72 hours looking into a microscope until he got it in focus—couldn't take the pressure of the rank injustice and the trial broke his health to the point that he became so nervous that he couldn't function. Seeking to overcome that nervousness, he consulted a physician, who told him that every time he felt nervous, he should take a couple of drams of brandy. He became a life-long alcoholic and died as such, never really accomplishing much in the last part of his life. He died in 1972.

Wilhelm Reich

I had also followed the life and work of Dr. Wilhelm Reich, a very interesting research pioneer who went from being Sigmund Freud's first assistant to dabbling in biophysics at an advanced level. He had involved himself in microscopy and discovered some consummately interesting things about living organisms which were also very controversial. A book about what he found at the microscope, called *The Bions*, was panned by every pundit who reviewed it. The only reason we're mentioning it here is that as he was working at the microscope he discovered various anomalous forms. At one point, Peter Thompkins invited me to work with him on a biography of Wilhelm Reich, which we didn't go on to do because Reich's personal papers are still under lock and key and we couldn't get access to them. They have been impounded for 50 years in the trust which was set up after he died.

During that period, I got to know Reich's daughter, Eva Reich, who was herself a doctor of medicine. She was cursing the day that she dropped the ball when her father died and, instead of becoming the trustee of his estate, allowed it to pass into the hands of another person who became the sole trustee. She wanted to go to court to see if she could break the trust so that her father's private archives could be made public. We waited to see if that could happen. Well, years went by and it didn't.

At any rate, in the summer of 1979 I was driving down the Maine coast with my wife and I knew Eva Reich had a little house in Hancock, Maine, where she spent a good deal of time. So we went over to see if she was there. She gave us each a bowl of soup and said: "Bird, I know you're interested in microscopes because I've read the fabulous article in the *New Age Journal* about Rife, whom I'd never heard of, and I know that you studied in detail all the work that my father did at the microscope. I want to tell you that there is another extraordinary microscope up in the woods in Canada that you ought to look into."

So in the fall of 1979, I went up to those Canadian woods. There, in a tiny village outside Sherbrooke, which itself is a provincial city about a half-hour drive from the top of Vermont, was an extraordinary man.

Gaston Naessens

Gaston Naessens is a Frenchman who, at the age of 26, invented a microscope which could do nearly as well as Rife's! I really can't describe it except to say that it combined various aspects of electromagnetics, magnetic fields, and optics that allow this microscope to look at cells at up to 30,000X magnification with excellent resolution – routinely so at 3,000X, which is about 1,000 times more than can be achieved in any laboratory, at least until recently.

Naessens, I discovered, had invented this scope in 1948 and as a result of his being able to see living things at these magnifications, he discovered that there was an ultramicroscopic, *sub-cellular organism* in the blood of all living things, including the sap of plants! This organism he called a *somatide* and it was 2 to 3 Angstroms in dimension [1 Angstrom = 10^{-8} centimeters and considered to be the size of a small atom. –Ed. note]. I can't apppreciate how small that is, so I'm just giving you the dimension. This ultramicroscopic form could be cultured in vitro and it reproduced just like a cell. As long as the body it inhabited was in a healthy state, metabolically speaking, it went through a three-stage growth cycle from a tiny particle, let's say, to a tiny spore, to a tiny double spore, and back again.

But, when the body gets into a metabolically imbalanced state, this same form goes through a 16-stage cycle. How this form behaves in the early stages with reference to other blood figures (red cells, lymphocytes), *can be clearly seen in the microscope* in a few seconds from a drop of blood drawn from a subject's finger. [It is important to note that a *dark-field microscope* is required to see these tiny somatides. –Ed. note.] Depending on that behavior, Monsieur Naessens can pre-diagnose degenerative disease states including a pre-cancerous state, *two to three years before there are any clinical signs in the host.*

While still in France, Monsieur Naessens went on to develop a *serum* which was very successful in curing various forms of advanced and, in some cases terminal, cancer. Partly because he had no degrees of any kind (in fact, he had only finished high school), he came to the attention of the French medical authorities and was put on trial before a Juge d'Instruction—the charge being that of practicing medicine illegally. [Chris wrote a book about this trial a few years later called, *The Persecution and Trial of Gaston Naessens: The True Story of the Efforts to Suppress an Alternative Treatment for Cancer, Aids, and Other Immunological Diseases* –Ed. note.] They almost put him in jail and threw away the key! But just before that happened, a high official in the Surete National (The French National Police) came to him and said: "You must get out of France, now, today—this evening—for it looks to me that you are to be 'railroaded' into jail."

It wasn't a *trial* in our legal sense of that word. It was more like a grand jury hearing—a special type of trial held before a judge. This trial, before which dozens of "expert" scientific witnesses had testified, had gone on for several months. Things looked so bad that the police official advised Naessens to go immediately to the international aerodrome at Orly and leave by plane for England. Monsieur Naessens looked at his watch and said: "I will never make it with the traffic." The police official replied: "We will hold the plane on the ground for you." And that is how he was exiled from his country.

Why had that police official acted to help him? Because Monsieur Naessens had cured that same official's wife of terminal cancer. She was still alive a few years ago!

Monsieur Naessens then came to Canada and got the covert backing of David M. Stewart, who ran one of the largest medical foundations in that country – the MacDonald-Stewart Foundation. Because his work was so unconventional, Mr. Stewart suggested that he work quietly, not in Montreal, but in the hustings. There, over the next twenty years, Gaston Naessens went on to invent another product to replace the serum which was very costly and difficult to make. He developed a product based on the camphor molecule. This molecule went into making an inexpensive liquid product, costing only about 80 cents a vial, which is injected into the lymph node in the groin. It does something to right, to enhance, and to bring back to equilibrium the *immune defense system.*

Naessens had seen that most degenerative disease is as much a problem connected to immunity as to anything else. When this immune defense system is brought back into balance, the body can shed cancers of all forms; can shed rheumatoid arthritis, can shed cases of lupus; can shed, in some cases, multiple sclerosis (MS)—and I am talking about one case that I know personally. A dental surgeon (a friend of mine for thirty years) who hadn't been out of a wheelchair in two years, after being injected intra-lymphatically with the product 21 days, was walking around a table, holding the table in the middle.

After twenty years of working quietly to achieve these results in Canada, the provincial medical authorities of Quebec came to his house and seized nearly all of his dossiers. He has now moved his treatment clinic to Haiti, becoming another in a long line of medical martyrs. Naessens may have to stand trial a second time in a second country.

Antoine Priore

I will tell you about one more person-still another self-taught genius, Antoine Priore, who began working in 1944-45, right after the war, to develop an electromagnetic device which cured cancer. He got the backing of some very interesting and courageous people, including the world-famous immunologist Dr. Raymond Pautrizel, of the University of Bordeaux II, who did all the animal work.

When Dr. Pautrizel arrived on the scene, because the emotional atmosphere surrounding the cancer cure was so great, he decided to take the research in another direction and began to use the machine to treat what he knew best, which was sleeping sickness in animals. Sleeping sickness was of primary concern to Dr. Pautrizel because it is a widespread affliction in tropical countries and, perhaps because he was born and raised in Guadeloupe in the Carribbean, he had become very interested in tropical medicine. When he injected rabbits with the pathogen trypansome, which causes sleeping sickness, the trypanosome would multiply until there were billions of them circulating in the bloodstream and the rabbits would uniformly all die within 72 hours. But, when exposed to the radiation of the Priore device, these same rabbits would live. Yet their blood was still teeming with the trypanosomes, which could be extracted from the radiated rabbits and injected into other control rabbits, which would then die.

This implies that the machine was doing something electromagnetically to the immune system of the rabbits such that they were able to fight off a lethal disease which would normally kill them in 72 hours!

Had it not been for the courage of Dr. Robert Courrier, who at that time was Perpetual Secretary of the Academy of Sciences of France, in the face of great criticism, the sci-entific data on 20 years of that work might never have been published. Time after time, over 20 years or more, Dr. Courrier personally introduced the papers for publication in the *Comptes Rendues* (Proceedings) *of the French Academy of Sciences*. There are 28 such papers. Even this could not prevent Dr. Pautrizel from nearly being fired from his post at the University of Bordeaux II, where he finally treated human patients successfully with the Priore device.

When he wrote a paper and sent it this time to the Academy of Medicine, it was refused without explanation. Pautrizel then wrote a long letter, since made public, to the governing offices of the French Academy of Medicine to find out why the paper had been refused and which people on the jury refused it, so that he could consult with them in order to better inform them of the facts. For 3 ½ years he received no reply.

So then he decided to step outside of normal scientific channels and offered his story to a journalist who wrote an extraordinary book called *The Dossier Priore, A Second Affaire Pasteur?* Because the book has not been translated from French, and may not be (because it was written for a French audience and should really be rewritten in English) it is not accessible to English readers. But I have written a 50-page paper which is a synopsis of it.

We have discussed the cases of four intrepid researchers. Of these, three had no formal academic training—Priore, Naessens and Rife—and yet they went on to develop the most extraordinary medical tools in energy medicine that I think exist. Two of them were put to trial! One was nearly fired from his position. All this is moving and largely unknown medical history and all of it affords real opportunities for further exciting research.

CHRISTOPHER BIRD is best known for his book, *The Secret Life of Plants*, which also portrayed the work of two USPA presenters, Cleve Backster and Marcel Vogel. Another book of his, *Secrets of the Soil*, was also co-authored with Peter Tompkins. However, *The Divining Hand: The 500-year Old Mystery of Dowsing* was a masterful work and *The Persecution and Trial of Gaston Naessens: The True Story of the Efforts to Suppress an Alternative Treatment for Cancer, Aids, and Other Immunological Diseases* a brilliant expose (that is currently out-of-print). It is worth mentioning that Andrija Puharich, MD, met with Naessens in Montreal because he also found pleiomorphic forms similar to those of Naessens in his own origin-of-life electrolysis experiments (see next paper). – Ed. note

13927-VALO

12

How Transdermal Electrotherapy Led to Highly Efficient Water Electrolysis with Anomalous Organic Molecule Formation and a Spinoff that Successfully Treated Neoplasms in Mice*

Andrija Puharich. M.D., LLD.
Director of Research
Essentia Research Associates, 350 East 52nd Street
New York, NY 10022 and
Essentia Research Laboratory Route 1, Box 545
Dobson, NC 27017 U. S. A.

Presented to *The Sixth Ozone World Congress Of The International Ozone Association* May 23, 1983 Washington. D.C. U.S.A. and to the Annual Conference of the U. S. Psychotronics Association, 1983

Introduction

I want to make it clear at the outset that I had no intention of doing cancer research when I started my career. Furthermore, I do not claim to be an expert in cancer research. In working toward my Ph.D. in Physiology under A.C. Ivy at Northwestern

University Medical School, I did research on methods of electroanesthesia in animals. When I got my MD degree, I became an internist. In 1948, I became Dr. Sam Rosen's surgical assistant on his invention of the Stapes Mobilization operation or conductive deafness. From him I learned about hearing problems, and I got interested in alleviating the problem of sensorineural hard-of-hearing, and deafness.

[*Originally presented with the title, "Successful Treatment Of Neoplasms In Mice With Gaseous Superoxide Anion (O2) And Ozone (O3) With A Rationale For The Effect." –Ed. note]

Development of a Transdermal Treatment for Nerve Deafness

In conjunction with Warren S. McCulloch, one of the founders of Cybernetics, we found a patient at Bellevue Hospital in New York City, who had been committed for "hearing voices". We determined that, outside of hearing voices, his psychiatric profile was normal. We found out that his job was the key to the diagnosis. He ground metal castings against carborundum wheels. Dental examination showed that his metal fillings were coated with carborundum dust. We placed him in a Faraday Cage, which eliminates all common electrical and radio signals, and found that his voices ceased. We found that he was precisely tuned to radio station WOR in New York City. His teeth were cleaned, and he was cured of the "psychiatric" problem. I set out to find the scientific basis or this phenomenon of "hearing radio waves".

It was obvious that the carborundum behaved like the "crystal" rectifier in the old crystal radio sets of the 1920's. Dr. Joe Lawrence, a dentist, joined me in this research in the early 1950's, when we were stationed at the Army Chemical Center, Edgewood, Maryland. We began to do research on the phenomenon of hearing radio waves.{1,2}We found that when a person, standing in the near field of a low power radio transmitter, stroked a wire resting on his cheek, he could hear a voice signal, and increase the RF (radio frequency) field on his skin from +200 mV to +250 mV. When the wire was clamped between the teeth and stroked there was a 10 db gain in hearing. When a plastic box was cemented around the wire, it was found that sound was being generated in the wire – an electroacoustic effect.{3,4}It is to be noted that hearing sensation occurred when the wire was stroked by the skin. The mystery of skin-stroking a wire in the presence of amplitude modulated RF was solved when it was found that an ordinary diode held in the teeth without stroking, gave the sensation of hearing. The actual wave-shaping was accomplished by the non-linear element, i.e., either skin stroking, or the use of a rectifier element such as a crystal, or a diode.

From this basic finding, Lawrence and I, and our engineering staff, developed the manually controlled laboratory instrument, with which we learned how to get deaf subjects [*nerve deaf* patients to be exact, where the acoustic, transdermal treatment can activate the auditory nerves –Ed. note] to hear words and speech.{8} We found that before a deaf person could hear, he had to undergo a one to two month course of transdermal (TD) electrotherapy daily. This consisted of repetitively sweeping the head, via electrodes, with pure tones over the frequency range from 20 Hz to 10,000 Hz modulating a 30 to 50 KHz carrier wave for one hour each day. [As shown in Fig. 3 of Patent #3,563,246, the TD signal used a sawtooth modulation of frequencies to treat the patient. See also #3,586,791, #3,629,521, #3,497,637, #2,995,633, and #3,170,993 –Ed note.] This clinical work resulted in the development of a completely automatic treatment program. Lest we forget, we did solve the technology of hearing radio waves through the teeth.{9,10,11,12,13}

In carrying out large scale Transderrnal Electrotherapy in cooperation with several medical schools on patients with sensorineural hearing loss, other beneficial effects were uncovered. {14} It was found that Meniere's disease could be cured in two weeks of treatment. {15} In elderly senile patients there was a restoration of short-term memory. There was an acceleration of bone healing in refactory fractures. Significant improvement was found in cases of impaired vascular circulation. {16} In the course of safety and hazard studies on animals, it was found that blood coagulation was significantly delayed, in vitro and in vivo.

A joint research program was carried with New York University Medical Center, Cardiovascular Research Laboratory. The team was made up of Dr. George Reed, Dr. William Brewster, Dr. Luis Cortes, and myself. Our goal was to prevent blood coagulation in an artificial heart device by using the TD electrotherapy signal on the blood. We were successful. {17} We could see a dilute suspension of red blood cells under a microscope without the TD signal energization. The E cells clump and settle out in about four minutes. Then we could see the TD energized red blood cells in the same cell but now they are energized by the TD signal; they develop a negative charge, and repel each other so that they do not clump, do not settle down, and in vivo do not coagulate in an artificial heart pump in animals. Also, the method of doubling the shelf life of stored whole blood by means of continuous TD signal charging, was applied to both animals and humans.

Discovery of Efficient Water Electrolysis with the TD Unit

One day, while I was studying the effects of the TD electrical fields on the dynamics of a dilute suspension, in Ringers solution of red blood cells under a microscope, I observed bubbles coming from both of the electrodes. I ran a gas analysis on the Ringers solution, and found that had been observing the splitting of water molecules by electrolysis at incredibly low power levels, that was around 0.16 mW. [Patent #4,394,230, "Vibrations that Split Molecules" also announced in *Science Digest*, March, 1982, p.73 –Ed. note.] It was this single observation that turned me in the direction of studying cancer. I shall now describe how this came about.

I had been heavily influenced by Dr. Warren S. McCulloch to believe that water structure was the basis of life structure and organization. So I began an intense study of water structure and the electrolysis of water by means of the TD signal generator.

The water electrolysis equipment is the same TD signal generator as was used in the hearing experiments. Component I is coupled to Component II by a series inductive-capacitance circuit, and the space between the copper center electrode and the concentric iron electrode is filled with a 0.9% saline solution termed Component III. The center copper electrode is surrounded by a high temperature-fired ceramic jacket which is porous to water molecules. My initial goal was to measure the efficiency of this system or the production of hydrogen and oxygen as a fuel. {18} I measured all of the gas production by the Mass Spectrometer, and measured the electrical power consumed in the endergonic reaction with precision calibrated instrumentation, and with this data calculated the efficiency of the system. {19} I was able to attain a 90% efficiency in the first half-hour of electrolysis, and thereafter it steadily declined to about 11%. The mass spectrometer revealed that the oxygen was being consumed in some unknown chemical reaction. All conditions of the experiment were sterile, run under a high vacuum, and contamination, or loss, from an outside source was impossible. Yet at the end or each experiment when the apparatus was taken apart it was round that Component III was *filled with a flocculent albuminoid material which had a fish-like odor.*

Anomalous Origin of Life Organic Production

I shall very briefly review the course or chemical events. The chemical content of the solution after three minutes of electrolysis included 99.99% pure NaCl and H_2O, as well as $FeCl_2$ and Fe_3O_4. The main addition is copper and iron electrolytically removed from the electrodes. We also obtained a computer printout of the mass spectrometer analysis of the products of electrolysis, and the pH rises in the first 30 minutes of electrolysis from 4.27 to pH 13.0. This is due to the production of hydroxyl ions. The oxygen drops from 21% to a fraction of 1% in two hours. The hydrogen rises from zero to about 90% by volume in several hours. The nitrogen drops from 78% to about 5% in four hours. The CO_2 starts at a non-detectable level, and slowly rises to about the 2% level in seven and a half-hours. And the Argon does not disappear with vacuum pumping, *but tends to increase as a function of time*. There were various chemicals that were synthesized in the electrically pulsed Component III solution, such as Glycine, Alanine, Valine, Leucine, Tyrosine, Tryptophan, Phenylalinine, Proline and others.{19}

What is very wrong with this experiment is that when all the nitrogen was removed and replaced with helium, there was carbon in the solution, and there was nitrogen in the solution. Now where did the nitrogen and the carbon come from? In order to test a hypothesis the Component III solution was changed from a sodium chloride solution, to a sodium hydroxide solution. When this was done, no organic compounds were formed, as had been the case with the sodium chloride solution, and no carbon or nitrogen was formed in the solution. {21} This finding forced me to reluctantly accept the possibility that we were looking at the *Kervran reaction* in vitro.{22} [Kervran, C.L., *Biological Transmutations*, Beekman Pub., Woodstock, NY, 1971 is the English translation for this reference. –Ed. note.]

The Kervran reaction has been studied in vivo for many years, and confirmed by many workers. As far as I know, this is the first time that it has been observed in vitro. [Even twenty years later, when nuclear transmutation by electrolysis is still anomalous but more commonplace, it is quite possible that Puharich is right about being the first to discover it in the laboratory. See Vysotski et al., *Infinite Energy*, Sept. 1996, p. 63 and Storms, *Proc. Of COFE*, 1999 –Ed. note.] The nuclear control systems of these biochemical reactions are of the type developed by the theoretical physicist, Olivier Costa de Beauregard, Director of the Institute Henri Poincare in Paris. {23}

$$n \rightarrow p + e- + \underline{\nu} \qquad (1)$$
$$p + \nu \longleftrightarrow p' + \nu' \qquad (2)$$
$$p \longleftrightarrow p' + \underline{\nu} + \nu' \qquad (3)$$

The equations imply the conversion of a neutron (n) to a proton (p) by virtual exchange processes the neutral currents of Weinberg. These processes produce protons (p and p') of different energy levels and two neutrinos (ν and ν') of different energy levels. ($\underline{\nu}$) represents the antineutrino and (e-) the electron. In one state the proton will be bound to an atomic nucleus, and in the other state it will be relatively free in a chemical binding. Kervran reactions or as they are sometimes called, biological weak transmutations have been observed for certain elements in the Table of Elements. For example, the oxygen atom can enter into a virtual nuclear reaction with p or n to yield ^{14}N, or ^{19}F. The normal flow of electrons in the terminal respiratory chain in the mitochondria will yield: $2H + ½ O_2 \rightarrow H_2O$ an exergonic yield of energy.

However if this normal reaction is blocked by the chemical reaction, $H^+ + {}^{16}O \rightarrow OH-$ there will be an increase of pH inside the mitochondrial as shown in the diagram. Such an increase in the pH inside the mitochondrial membrane can have profound effects on the electron flow and energy yield. We will take this topic up later.

We now describe our light microscopy studies of the organic matter that appeared in the sodium chloride solution energized by amplitude modulated carrier signals. As usual the solution and apparatus were sterilized and vacuum pumped to remove the contaminating gases nitrogen. carbon dioxide and argon before the TD electrical yield was applied. The microscope was a Wild research microscope with 100X planapochromat objective, and 32X bifocal eyepieces to give a maximum gain of 3200X at high resolution. I used the *dark field method of illumination.* Here is a microphotograph of what a sterile solution of 0.9% sodium chloride looks like before it is electrolysed with the TD signal. It is surprising that the individual crystals of sodium chloride can be located as tiny doughnuts or toroids against the dark field (Fig. 1).

Now here is what the sodium chloride solution looks like after three minutes of electrical energization at 50 mW (Fig. 2). This frame is a one-second exposure. When one observes this scene with the eyeball one notes that the particles are flickering and oscillating. A critic would say that these eight-pointed light patterns are merely lense artefacts. When one uses a strobe light to stop the action it measures an oscillation of eight lashes per second. This effect occurs only in the early stages of electrolysis and is not found later.

An Historical Aside

Eventually I identified the molecule that was oscillating but more of that later. In 1960, I was in Mexico with my friend Aldous Huxley and his wife Laura. In the course of a long discussion, I found that Laura practiced "laying on of hands" therapy. We arranged for a test of this alleged ability in Los Angeles. California on August 15, 1960 at the Sepulveda Veterans Hospital. Dr. Barbara Brown ran the electroencephalograph equipment. The design of the experiment was to see if Laura could exert any effect on a patient with ventricular extra-systoles. and occasional mild, cardiac fibrillation. The subject and the operator were both connected to the EEG machine with additional readouts for respiration, EKG, and skin resistance. Laura was not allowed to touch the patient. but merely bring her hands within a few inches of the patient. The main finding was that when Laura brought her hands within four inches of the patient's thoracic spine, Laura's EEG suddenly showed high amplitude 8 Hz waves and at the same time the patient's brain waves were entrained at 8 Hz with phase locking. I might add that a five year follow-up showed that the patient had been cured of her cardiac problem.

13927-VALO

This experiment has since been repeated by many workers. {24} Thereafter, Joe Kamiya developed a teaching method so that people could train themselves to autogenically evoke (8 Hz) Alpha waves. {25} When the Soviets went on the air in July 4, 1976 with their 100 megawatt transmissions of extremely low frequency waves {ELF) the intelligence community of the U.S. was caught, unaware, of this new technology. The Soviet ELF pulses covered the frequency range of the human brain. No one knew what the purpose of this new technology was. I had a hypothesis that this was a new mind control weapon that could entrain a human being's EEG. Bob Beck and I designed an experiment that conclusively proved that the Soviet transmissions could indeed entrain the human brain and thereby induce behavioural modification. I reported this finding to the intelligence community in the U.S and *my paper was promptly classified.* {26}

A CIA commission of inquiry reported to President Carter that there was no substance to our findings. Today, five years later, all of our findings have been confirmed by various agencies of the U.S. Government. However, they went one step beyond our findings, and proved that a certain ELF frequency (Classified) will cause cancer.{ 27} I have repeated these experiments, and found this to be true. The mechanism of this effect is that the ELF frequency modifies the function of the RNA transferases so that amino acid sequences, are scrambled and produce unnatural proteins. The ELF exerts its' effect on the nuclear level, more specifically, the nuclear magnetic resonant property of the nucleus. The table shows the spin-spin coupling constants of various common chemical chains. Note the common chemical groupings with coupling constants around 8 Hz. {28} Note that a powerful carcinogen, ethylene dioxide, has coupling constants around 3 to 5 Hz. Note that another powerful carcinogen, formaldehyde, has a coupling constant around 41 Hz. Parrish, et al, {29} have found that the spin-spin coupling constants for water in malignant brain tumors (in humans and dogs) range from 4.8

to 13.4 Hz., whereas normal brain gray matter ranges from 8.6 Hz to 11.3 Hz. Thus malignancy shows a spread of frequencies from low to high ELF range i.e. with respect to normal brain EEG's, and carcinogens have a wide spread from 3 Hz to about 41 Hz around the center frequency for normalcy of 8 Hz. However, a single ELF frequency can produce cancer.

However, let us return to an examination of what we found in the electrically energized sodium chloride solution. Now the oscillating particles were entrained by the earth's natural oscillating magnetic field at 7.83 Hz (rounded to 8 Hz). We determined eventually that the particle responsible for the oscillation was *Ferrichrome,* one of the strongest complex formers known for Fe (III). {30} The iron-binding center is an octahedral arrangement of six oxygen donor atoms of trihydroxamate. Ferrichromes are most important in the biosynthetic pathways of very complex compounds of iron, and Vitamin B12 (cyanocobalamin).

At this point in my research, I remembered that highly active mitochondria take an arboreal form when they go from the resting state to the active state. I then remembered from my medical school days, when we studied the blood of syphilitic patients under the dark field microscope, that we occasionally saw pleiomorphic bacteria. When I asked my instructor what these were, I was told that they were just debris, and to forget it. So I now went back to the microscope, and began to study these *pleiomorphic bacteria* afresh. [This work led Puharich to study with Gaston Naessens as well. See Chris Bird's previous article. – Ed. note.] In the forty years since medical school days a whole literature had been built up around these lowly bodies. {32} I became convinced that what I now saw in the blood of patients particularly those with cancer, was very similar to what I was seeing in my in vitro preparations.

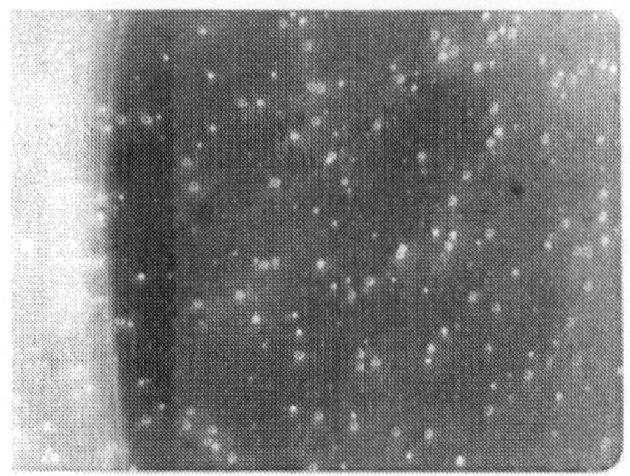

Fig. 1

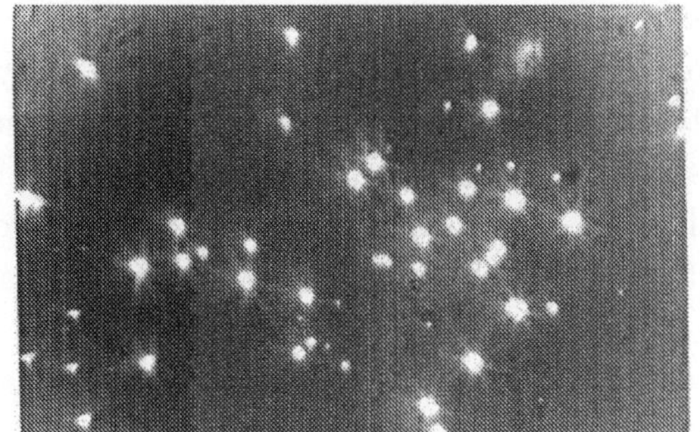

Fig. 2

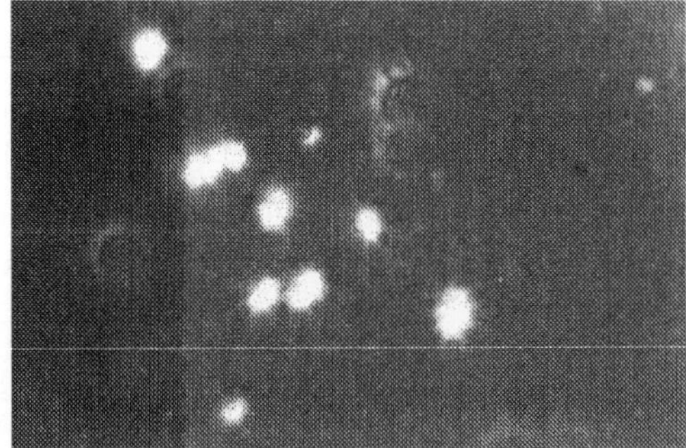

Fig. 3

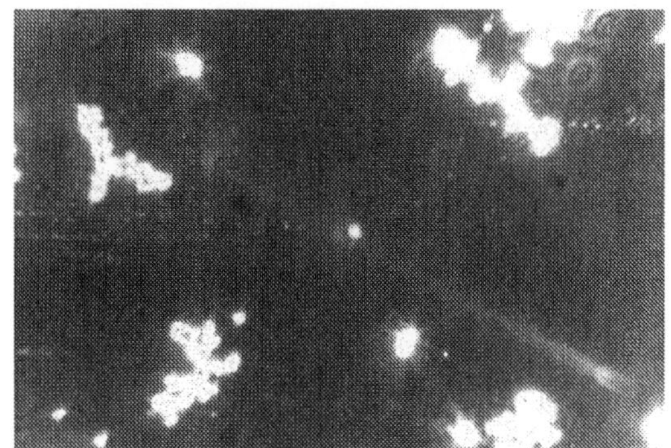

Fig. 4

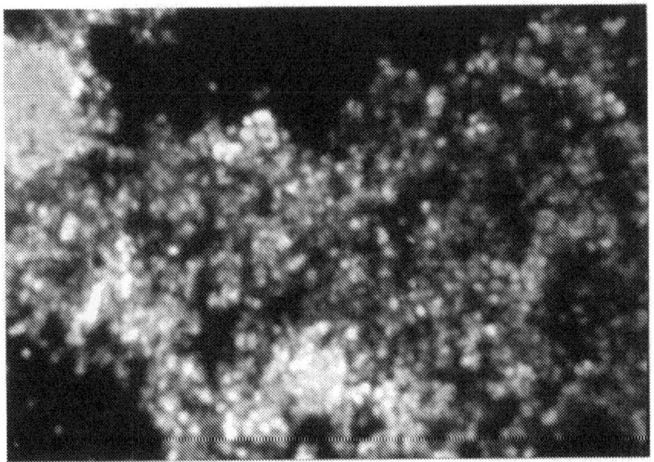

Fig. 5

The Logic of Electronic Flow in Biology Leads to Cancer Insight

My next step was to take these arboreal forms (Fig. 4) out of the TD cell, and place them on a microscope stage heated to 37° C. and nurture them with D-glucose 6-phosphate in 5% solution. In a matter of minutes, the branch-like forms were covered with little beads of yellow, orange, green and blue material. The next stage, the branched material beginning to clump and organize (Fig. 5). [These forms did not replicate after prolonged culture in various media. The reason is that Puharich withheld sulfur from the solution in all his experiments. He personally told me he did this because he did not want to create life forms of greater complexity in his lab. – Ed note.]

At this point the morphology of the arboreal forms, and the metabolic events just cited, led me to entertain the hypothesis that I was dealing with a very primitive metabolic chemistry in which iron compounds like ferritin, ferrodoxin, and transferrins were serving as electron acceptors for electrons (H) arising from water. When I stopped the electrolysis of the saline solution, I found that the general reaction,

$$\mathrm{H20} + \mathrm{A} + \underset{\text{energy}}{\text{electrical}} \rightarrow \mathrm{A\,H_2} + \tfrac{1}{2}\,\mathrm{O_2} \text{ ceased.}$$

Where "A" represents the electron acceptor, and in this case is an iron compound, of the type just cited. An important feature of this *Hill Reaction* is that electrons are induced to flow away from water molecules to acceptor A, thus yielding molecular oxygen from the water. In order to appreciate the meaning of this electrochemistry we note that in animal metabolism in the terminal respiratory chain electrons flow from the negative sign to the positive sign to produce water.{33} *In the plant the electron flow is reversed* and goes from the positive sign to the negative sign, a sort of uphill flow, electronically speaking. It occurred to me at this time that nature might have worked out a system to account for spontaneous cancer cures by reversing the flow of electrons in the mitochontrial terminal respiratory chain, and thereby producing more molecular oxygen to combat the cancer process. It also occurred to me that increased oxygen would tend to pull the proton/proton spin-spin coupling closer to the 8 Hz normative center frequency of biological systems. But I had no proof for these speculations. I did have some experience however in the clinical area from 1975 and on when I bought an ozone producing machine, the OZONOSAN PM 60, and did research on decubitus ulcers with Dr. Harry Becker at the Veterans Hospital in Montrose, NY. We found that hyperoxygenation and ozone gas treatment cleared up chronic decubitis ulcers in a matter of weeks. In a sense, this experience with ozone prepared me for the next step, which was a meeting with Migdalia Arnan, MD, a Board Certified Pathologist, and her colleagues.

I will briefly summarize her main findings, because her paper will follow mine. Dr. Arnan found that a normal human cell, when immersed in formaldehyde gas, converts to a cancer cell in a few minutes. She then found that a human cancer cell if irradiated with intense white light under a microscope would undergo a (thermal) death in twelve minutes. She then discovered, under bright light microscope illumination, that unstained human cancer cells had pale green bodies in the cytoplasm about the size of mitochondria. It was at this point that we both gave a "Eureka " yell, and realized that her clinical discoveries, and my electrical and chemical investigations clarified each other. Furthermore, she and her colleagues had proven that if *ozone gas is administered directly into a malignant tumor* in mice, the tumor would dissolve in a matter of seconds to minutes and leave the normal surrounding tissue unaffected.

It is not yet generally recognized in the biological sciences that all life is immersed in an oscillating magnetic field that originates from protons in the sun.{34} These ELF waves have a sharp resonance on earth due to cavity resonances, peaking at 7.81 to 7.8 Hz. [See Bob Beck's article for more information about the earth's ELF Schumann resonance. –Ed. note.] This is the center frequency of the electromagnetic power spectrum of the human brain, the so-called Alpha frequency, of 8 Hz. We have already indicated that a "healthy" ELF center frequency exists for proton-proton spin-spin coupling in the chemistry of the body, particularily in such control functions as genes and enyzymes for DNA and RNA. We have indicated that certain ELF frequencies at extremely low power, can induce cancer. I might add that the amount of power required to induce cancer at the correct ELF stimulus is measured in the, range of microwatts. In short, ELF frequencies at super low power levels can control the well-being of organisms.

Now what happens when an organism is deeply insulted by chemicals, injury, or amputation? Let us take the most extreme case, i.e., amputation of a limb in a salamander.

Robert Becker, MD. has shown that the salamander limb can be regenerated if certain procedures are followed. {35 } First, a skin flap of epidermis only (no dermal tissue allowed) is placed over the stump. Under this epidermal flap it has been found that regeneration occurs when red blood cells in the wound site undergo de-diferentiation, i.e. revert to very primitive cells, the blastema. Red blood cells in their earliest stage still have a nucleus. {36} Such an early RBC form is what a de-differentiated cell looks like. Note the way in which such a cell takes up Iron transferrin and feeds it to the mitochondria.

My evidence indicates that the pleiomorphs found in the blood in association with cancer, as *first reported by J.F. Glover, M.D. in Canada in 1923*, {37}and verified by many workers subsequently, are in fact mitochondrial fragments from de-differentiated red blood cells that are released in response to the insult of cancer. These pleiomorphs carry a type of transferrin (not yet identified) that serve two functions. The first, as recently reported, by Goubin, et al, {38} in *Nature*, Vol. 302, 10 March 1983, shows that the nucleotide sequence of a cloned transforming gene, that induces cancer in chickens, suggests that it encodes a protein that is partially homologous to the amino acid tenlinus of transferrin and related proteins, although it is only about one-tenth the size of transferrin. The second function of this type of transferrin, I believe, is to reverse the electron flow in the mitochondria by changing one of the heme molecules into a chlorophyll type of molecule. The purpose of nature in this electron flow reversal is to electrolyze water in order to produce more oxygen to swing to local ELF frequency toward 8 Hz using both the Kervran nuclear transmutation mechanism, and the known effect of oxygen to lower the NMR spin-spin coupling of a solution.

The findings of Dr. Arnan also show that the mitochondriium is not only transformed in the reversal of electron flow, but actually produces Quantasomes, the chlorophyll bearing bodies of plants, as shown in one of her electron micrographs. This is a Quantasome found in a human cancer cell and accounts for the pale green bodies easily found in human cancer cells, if one just looks, and is not color blind. *Now how does this theoretical mechanism account for the efficacy of ozone in the treatment of cancer tumors?*

Ozone Analysis

The analysis begins with an understanding of skin and membrane properties. One begins with square wave electrical spectroscopy according to the method. This yields various decay curves for voltage and current. One also plots the impedance locus of the skin which shows loci for ELF, and for kilohertz frequencies. From this data one develops equivalent circuits for the various configurations of signal used on the skin, membranes, and water. Our studies, as well as that of others shows that the water molecule has the tetrahedral form. [See Puharich's patent #4,394,230 for a diagram of the tetrahedral form of water and bond angles. –Ed. note.] Yon Hippel and others have established that the water molecule has a dielectric resonance in the 8 Hz range. {39} The importance of water in biological structure and function is well known. Suppose that one were to substitute a molecule that mimicked the water molecule for the true water molecule? We don't really know what would happen because there is nothing known quite like a water molecule. But I have a proposal to make. If one looks at the last figure, and conceives that ozone could actually have a tetrahedral form (and no one knows its true form) what would it behave like? The only change required is to substitute the Hydrogen atoms with O+ atoms. The net effect of this ozone geometry would be to reverse the polarity of the EMF source at the left, and P semiconductor would face the capacitor. The circuit would now reverse the electron flow. In addition the ozone tetrahedron would have far more oxidizing power than water. Thus ozone would behave in the following manner as a therapeutic agent.

1) It would easily substitute for water in terms of geometrical fit into any biological structure. Wherever water would fit, ozone would fit.
2) Ozone would seek out the H2 molecule by the following reaction: $H_2 + O_3 \rightarrow H_2O + O_2$

This is a powerful exergonic reaction which would not only be a bond breaker but release enough heat at the molecular level to melt the altered conformational states of proteins, oncogenes and various go/no go genetic switches.

I have tested this possibility, in the late sixties, while doing safety and hazard studies of the TD system on dogs. I used old and sick dogs in some of my studies, and some of them had surface malignant tumors. The procedure was as follows: In running high voltage hazard studies on animals I observed in a very dark room (a Faraday Cage) that a bluish plasma glowed between the electrode face and the skin. I could also smell ozone in the air. This effect occurred at 1100 volts (p-p) and 11 mA (rms) current. I found that I could tolerate this level of signal on myself without any discomfort, and the dogs could tolerate this signal after some training. I treated three dogs that had malignant tumors under the skin one hour a day for three weeks with this high voltage ozone-generating signal.

There was no damage to the skin of the dog, and the tumors melted away under the skin during the three weeks. Others have repeated this type of radio frequency treatment of malignant tumors, subsequently. {40}

Summary

We have presented a theory of a probable cause of cancer supported by some fragmentary experimental evidence. There are many further tests that can be made of the theory.

I must emphasize that this is only a preliminary formulation. The theory, both empirically and experimentally led from separate sources to a rational therapy for malignant neoplasms in animals. The essence of the theory is that nuclear spin properties form an integrating topology for the development of chemical evolution centered on proton-proton spin-spin coupling in water. It is well to recall here that the human body is made up of some two thirds, by mass, of water. It is also well to recall that the human body is made up, by count, 92% of hydrogen atoms. The dynamics of hydrogen and oxygen are of great importance in the structure and function of the human body. For example, if the brain is deprived of oxygen for several minutes, the person will not only become unconscious, but permanent damage may result in the organization of the brain at a molecular level.

There is another disintegrative pathology called "cardiac fibrillation" wherein the individual myocardial fibrils suddenly cease to beat in synchrony, and death can result within five minutes, if the condition is not normalized. A topological theory has been advanced by Winfree which shows that tiny electrical pulses intercalated at a precise phase angle in the normal heart natural period, called a topological singularity, or a "black hole," is sufficient to initiate fibrillation of the heart.{41} In NMR, there is a so-called the "magic sandwich" in which certain magnetic and radio frequency have cancellation operations are carried out in an orthonormal sequence, and a phase coherence in the spin system that appears to be lost, is restored. {42} This experiment, carried out with Calcium Fluoride (with the ^{19}F isotope) has the uncanny property of reversing the Hamiltonian in the equations, which is equivalent to making the time flow backwards at half the normal speed. This is a situation where the Kervran transmutation from ^{16}O to ^{19}F can place this form of fluorine at a critical point in the mitochondrial apparatus and cause time to flow backwards or in other words reverse the flow of electrons in time, as positrons.{43} These are some of the possibilities of the theory. We can now summarize the main points.

An electrical signal generator was developed which proved to have rehabilitative effects on humans. The same signal pattern proved to be efficient in the electrolysis of sodium chloride solutions. A by-product of such electrolysis, was a new insight into the dynamics of chemical evolution leading to organism. These insights were applied to the problems of cancer cause and control. These insights were sharpened by the experimental work of Dr. Arnan and her colleagues, in controlling and dissolving mammary neoplasms in female mice by injecting O2 and O3 gas into the tumors is theoretical and experimental work pointed to *the disruption of ELF NMR proton spin-spin coupling mechanisms as a probable cause of some types of cancer.*

Conceptual Rate of Cell Division Diagram

Many considerations indicate that 8 Hz is *the* center frequency that "pulls" all other frequencies toward it, to maintain biological integrity. Such biological integrity can be quantized by reference to an arbitrary rate of cell division scale, pointing from the left to the right. On the left would be deuterated water, 27% concentration or higher, which will stop all cell division in many species. {44} When the deuterated water is removed from the cell suspension, the cells resume normal cell division. This type of control is exerted, in general, by elements with spin 1 and a positive magnetic moment.

In the center column we would list those stablizing elements with spin ½ and magnetic moment μ having a positive multiple of 0.4 Bohr magnetons. These are the elements with odd number mass, or of even number mass, spin 0 and μ = 0. We have indicated that RNA transferases can be disorganized by microwatt levels of magnetic ELF radiation. It is theorized that such ELF waves affect the RNA transferases at a precise phase angle that triggers a topological singularity.

Many possible pre-conditions essentially disperse the gaussian distribution around the power spectrum center frequency of 8 Hz, and this effect in turn, stimulates the rate of cell division locally, and may then later manifest as cancer. The dispersive mechanism originally acts to trigger the release of iron compounds from the red blood cell membrane due to altered amino acid sequences in both the cell wall, and the iron compounds. This in turn triggers red blood cell de-differentiation (backward in time) to a primitive stage of evolution. In this primitive stage, which we associate with the mitochondrial fragment "pleiomorphs" found in the blood of some cancer patients, the normal mammalian electron flow in the mitochondrial terminal respiratory chain is reversed, so-that it flows in the direction found in plant cells. This effect is triggered and fed by a Hill reaction in which the electron acceptor molecules are iron compounds. Chlorophyll and quantasomes then appear in the cytoplasm of cancer cells. The correct dose of ozone gas easily substitutes for water molecules in the "plant-like" terminal respiratory chain, and releases both oxidative the thermal effects which dissolve the neoplastic-forming molecules, and restores the normal respiratory electon flow in the normal tissue surrounding the neoplasms. This process re-integrates the atoms and molecules around the 8 Hz center frequency ELF NMR.

In its essence this is a theory of nuclear control of cell division processes operating through spin properties, and nuclear magnetic resonant fields in the extremely low frequency range.

References

1. Puharich and Lawrence
(a) Hearing Aid. Great Britain Patent No. 982,934. September 21, 1959 (b) Procede et Moyen Pour Amplifier ou Pour Retablir L'ouie. Republique Francaise No. 1,236,782. September 24. 1959. Brevet d'invention. (c) Schwerhorigengerat. Bundesrepublik Deutschland Patentamt 1120505. September 26, 1959 (d) Procede et oyen Pour Amplifier ou Pour Retablir L'ouie. Royaume de Belgique, Brevet d'invention No. 583,034 October 15, 1959

2. Puharich. H.K.
"Electrical Field Effects on Humans." Guest Speaker Annual Meeting of Institute Of Radio Engineers, San Francisco Section. Berkeley, California. June 14, 1960

3. Puharich and Lawrence
"Procedimento ed Apparecchio per migliorare o ristabilire il senso dell'udito." Italy Brevet to per invenzione industriale No. 615935, January 24, 1961.

4. Puharich, H.K.
"Experiments with Faraday Cage Apparatus." Darshan (India) Vol. 1. pp. 30-42. April, 1961.

5. Puharich and Lawrence
Means for Aiding Hearing. U.S. Patent No. 2,995,633. August 8, 1961

6. Puharich. H.K.
"Computers, Chance, and Cholinergia" (with Jeffery Smith and A. Kitselman). Darshana (India) Vol. 1, pp. 41-4), August, 1961.

7. Puharich and Lawrence
(a) "Dispositivo para la Transmision de Senales Auditivas a los Centros de Aduicion del Cerebro Humano." Republica Argentina. Patente de Invencion No.127626, October 10,1961. (b) Method and Means for Aiding or Restoring Hearing. Canada Patent No. 634542. January 16.1962. (c) Method and Means for Aiding or Restoring Hearing. Japanese Letters Patent No. 307,053. August 27. 1962. (d) Dispositifs d'aide a l'organe de l'ouie par stimulation electrique du systeme nerveux facial. Republique Francaise. Brevet d'invention No. 1,349,503. January 3, 1963. (e) Schwerhorigengerat. Bundesrepublik Deutschland Patentamt No. 1.219.988. January 6. 1963. (f) Dispositifs d'aide a l'organe de l'ouie par stimulation electrique du systeme nerveux facial. Royaume de Belgique. Brevet d'invention No. 626.742. January 15.1963. (g) Means for Aiding or Restoring Hearing. Commonwealth of Australia. Letters Patent No. 240.204. February 18.1963. (h) Dispositif d'audition a l'etat solide. Republique Francaise. Brevet d'invention No. 1.375.458. November 22, 1963). (i) Otofono o simile Apparecchio Elettronico a stato L solido con Trasmissione Attraverso Nervi Facciali. November 2 1963. (j) Hearing Aid. Great Britain Patent No. 1.067.748. November 25.1963. (k) Solid State Hearing System. Commonwealth of Australia Letters Patent No. 281.219. November 26, 1963. (l) Horgerat. Bundesrepublik Deutschland Patentamt 1202834. December 1 1963. (m) Hearing Aid. Great Britain Patent No. 1.075.430. December 10. 1963. (n) Systeme d'ecoute a stimulation electrique avec . signal de reaction. Royaume de Belgique. Brevet d'invention No. 642.183. January 7.1964.

8. Puharich and Lawrence
"Modulated Alternating Current Energy Used to Stimulate Audition in Totally Deaf Humans." Paper presented at the Annual meeting of the Aerospace Medical Association Bal

Harbour, Florida, May 13, 1964. Published as an abstract Journal of Aerospace Medicine, 35, May 1964.

9. Puharich and Lawrence

(a) Dispositif d'audition a l'etat solide. Royaume de Belgique, Brevet d'invention No. 640.030. May 19, 1964. (b) Systeme d'ecoute a stimulation electrique avec signal de reaction. Republique Francaise, Brevet d'invention No. 1.380.044. October 19, 1964.

10. Puharich, H.K.

How many Channels Have Been Allocated to the Brain? Luncheon Address to the National Electronics Conference. Chicago, Illinois, October 20, 1964. Published in: *Missiles and Rockets*, October 26, 1964.

11. Puharich and Lawrence

Solid State Hearing System. U.S. Patent No. 3,156,787. November 10, 1964.

12. Puharich and Lawrence

"Electrostimulation Techniques of Hearing" Technical Documentary Report, No. RADC-TRD-64-18, December, 1964; Project No. 5534, Task No.553401. Prepared under contract No. AF30 (602)-3051, Intelectron Corporation, 432 West 45th Street, New York, New York, 10036. Published by: Defense Documentation Center, Alexandria, Virginia.

13. Puharich and Lawrence

(a) Dispositif pour assurer l'audition avec ou sans intervention de l'oreille. Confederation Suisse, Expose d'invention No. 384,041. January 29, 1965. (b) Un dispositivo para impartir senales electricas moduladas a nervios viales del Sistema Facial de un sujeto. Republica Argentina. Patente de invencion No. 142889. February 9.1965. (c) Means for Aiding Hearing by Electrical Stimulation of the Facial Nerve System. U.S. Patent No. 3,170,993. February 23.1965. (d) Horeanordning. Norsk Patent Nr. 105760. March 8. 1965. (e) Solid State Hearing Systeml Canada Patent No. 708246. April 20.1965. (f) Werkwijze voor het hoorbaar maken van audiofrequente signalen bij doven. Octrooiraad Nederland. Octrooi Nr. 111843. September 17.1965. (g) Electrically Stimulated Hearing with Signal Feedback. India. Patent No.92045. April 6. 1966. (h) Mejoras en Dispositi vos Electronicos de Audicion. Republica Argentina. Patente de invencion No. 148047. May 10. 1966. (I) Electrically Stimulated Hearing with Signal Feedback. U.S. Patent No. 3.267.931. August 23.1966. (j) Electrically Stimulated Hearing with Signal Feedback. Pakistan. Patent No.115218. August 30. 1966. (k) means for Aiding Hearing by Electrical Stimulation of the Facial Nerve System. Commonwealth of Australia Letters Patent No. 269.970. September 13. 1966. (1) Otofona del tipo a Stimolazione Elettrica del Sistema Nervoso Facciale con Circuito di Reazione. Italy. Brevet to per Invenzione Industriale No. 713017. September 20,1966. (m) Apparecchio per Aiutare L'udito mediante Stimolazion , Electtrica del Sistema Nervoso Facciale. Italy. , Brevet to per Invenzione Industriale No.715786. October 1, 1966. (n) Means for Aiding Hearing by Electrical Stimulation of the Facial Nerve System. Canada Patent No. 750503. January 10, 1967. (o) Electrically Stimulated Hearing with Signal Feedback. Canada Patent No.751001. January 17, 1967. (p) Un aparato para estimular Electricamente el Sentido de Audicion de un Ser Humano con realimentacion de Senales a tra.ves del Sistema Nervioso Facial. Republica Argentina, Patente de Invencion No. 153148. February 21, 1967. (q) Processo e dispositivo para auxiliar ou restaurara Audicao. Brasil, Patente de invencao No.777751 February 28, 1967. (r) Anordning for overforing av akustika signaler till manniskohnjarnans horselcentra. Sverige Patent Nr. 217530. December 12, 1967. (s) Electrically Stimulated Hearing with Signal Feedback. Commonwealth of Australia Letters Patent No. 282,485. April 22, 1968. (t) Electroniskt Horsystem. Sverige Patent 301337 September 12, 1968. (u) Horapparat. Sverige Patent Nr. 305669. February 13,

1969. (v) Procedimento Ed Apparechio Per La Stimolazione, Elettroacustica de Sistema Auditivo, Brevet to per Invenzione Industriale, Italy, No. 854214, February 3.1969. (w) Transdermal Electrostimulation of Facial Nerve . System with R-F Energy. U.S. Patent No. 3.497,637. February 24, 1970. (x) Transducer for Stimulation of Facial Nerve System with R-F Energy. U.S. Patent No. 3,497,637. February 24, 1970. (y) Method and Apparatus for Improving Neural Performance in Human Subjects by Electrotherapy. U.S. Patent N°.3,563,246. February 16, 1971.

14. Puharich and Lawrence
"Hearing Rehabilitation by Means of Transdermal Electrotherapy in Human Hearing Loss of Sensorineural Origin." Acta Oto-Laryngologica, Vol. 67, Fasc. 1, pp. 69-83. January, 1969.

15. Puharich and Lawrence
"Hearing Rehabilitation by means of Transdermal Electrotherapy in Human Hearing Loss of Sensorineural Origin (II)" .Excerpta medica International Congress Series No. 189. Ninth International Congress of Oto-Rino-Laryngology, Mexico, D.F., August 10-14, 1969.

16. Puharich, H.K.
"Transdermal Electrostimulation of Hearing." (with J.L. Lawrence and R.S. Dugot). Presented at Thirteenth Annual Scientific Meeting, October 11, 1969, Committee for Research in Otolaryngology, Thorne Hall, Northwestern University School of Medicine, Chicago, Illinois. American Academy of Otolaryngology .

17. Puharich, H.K.
"Electrodynamic Approach to Thrombus Prevention in a Ventricular Assist Device." (With George E. Reed, Luis E. Cortes, William R. Brewster and Joseph L. Lawrence). Paper presented at the 41st Annual Scientific Sessions of the American Heart Association,. in November 23, 1968, Miami Beach, Florida. Abstract published in Circulation, Vol. XXXVIII, No.4, Supplement . VI, page 162.

18. Puharich, H.K.
"Electroacoustic Deco Position Of Mater By The Phonon Effect Towards A Viable Clean Fuel System." PACE Newsletter, Vol. 3, Nos. 2,3, December, 1981, p. 6. 100 Bronson Street, Ottawa, Ontario, Canada.
19. Puharich, H.K.
"Methodology for the Evaluation of the Efficiency of Water Decomposition by means of Alternating Current Electrolysis." Proceedings of the Ist International Conference on Non-Conventional Energy. Ed, Professor George Hathway, University of Toronto, Department of Physics, Toronto, Ontario, 1982.
20. Puharich, H.K.
"Contibution to Molecular Evolution Studies and Relation to the Cause of Cancer." U.S. Psychotronic Association Annual meeting, July 22-25, 1982, Colorado School of Mines.
21. Puharich, H.K..
"The FeO-Fe203 (Magnetite) Protoporphyrin Complex in Human Blood as a Possible
ELF Receptor." Detector in vitro and in vivo studies. A preliminary report. Proceedings of the June 1982 Conference of the Learned Societies of Canada.
22. Kervran, C. Louis
"Transmutations Biologique et Physique Moderne." Maloine S.A., Editeur, 27, vue de l'Ecole de Medecine, 75006, Paris, 1982.
23. THE ICELAND PAPERS. Select papers on experimental and theoretical research on the Physics of Consciousness. Edited by Andrija Puharich M.D.. LLD. with Foreward by Brian D. Josephson. Nobel Laureate, Physics. Published by Essentia Research Associates, 350 E. 52nd. Street, New York. N.Y. 10022. . See Chap. V, p. 161 ff.; The expanding paradigm of the Einstein Theory of Olivier Costa de Beauregard.
24. C. Maxwell Cade, and Coxhead. N.
The Awakened Mind. Delta Books, Dell Publishing Co. New York. N.Y.. 1979.

25. Kamiya, Joe
"Conscious Control of Brain Waves," Psychology Today, I:57, April, 1968.
26. Puharich, H.K.
"The Imminence of ELF Magnetic Global Warfare." Confidential. Report, March 13, 1977 to: Hon. Pierre Elliot Trudeau, Prime Minister, Canada, Hon. James Carter, President, U.S.A., Hon. Margaret Thatcher, Leader of the Opposition, Great Britain (CLASSIFIED) Report warns that the Soviet ELF signals broadcast since July 4,1976 are psychoactive (in a predatory sense) and can lead to other biological effects.
27. NOTE: 1982, U.S. Navy confirms that Soviet ELF signals are indeed psychoactive and can cause mental depression at 6.66 Hz,and at 11 Hz can lead to manic and riotous behavior in humans. (CLASSIFIED)
28. Abraham, R.J. and Loftus, P.
Proton and Carbon-13 NMR Spectroscopy Table 3.1, p. 41; Table 3.5, p. 46. Heyden & Son, Ltd.. London. 1981.
29. Parrish, Rob G.. Kurland, R.J. and Janese .W. and Bakay. L.
"Proton Relaxation Rates of Water in Brain and Brain Tumors." Science. Vol. 183. February 1, 1974.
30. Stumm, Werner and Morgan, JJ.
"Aquatic Chemistry, second edition. Ferrichromes, p. 378-382. John Wiley & Sons, New York. 1981
31. Domingue, Gerald J.
Cell Wall-Deficient Bacteria, J. Addison-Wesley Publishing, Reading, Massachusetts, 1982 .
32. Lehninger. Albert L.
Principles of Biochemistry. p. 519. Worth Publishers. Inc.New York. N.Y. 10016. 1976
33. Ibid. p. 479
34. Akasofu. Syunichi. and Chapman. Sydney.
Solar Terrestrial Physics. p. 439 Oxford. Clarendon Press. 1972
35. Becker. Robert. Editor,
Mechanisms of Growth Control, Charles C. Thomas. Publisher Springfield. Illinois. 1981

36. Zucker-Franklin. D., et al
Atlas of Blood Cells. Function and Pathology E.E. Edi. Ermes. Milano. Italy, Lea & Febiger. Philadelphia. 1981
37. Dominque. Gerald J.,
Op. Cit. (31)
38. Goubin, Gerald; Goldman, Debra S.; Luce, Judith; Neiman, Paul E.; and Cooper, Geoffrey
"Molecular cloning and nucleotide sequence of a transforming gene detected by transfection of chicken B-cell lymphoma DNA" Nature. Vol. 302,10 March 1938. pp.114 and ff.
39. Franks. Felix. Editor
Water, A Comprehensive Treatise. six volumes. Vol. 1. p. 139. Chapter 4. Properties of Ice, Plenum Press. New York. 1972
40. (a) Whalley, B. "Radio Frequency Eradication of Tumours" Electronics and Power, May 1977 (b) Le Veen. H.H., Wapnick S.. Piccone. v., Falk. G. and Ahmed. N. . "Tumour Eradication by Radio Frequency Therapy" J. Am. Mad. Assoc., V. 235. 2198-2200.1976.
41. Winfree. Arthur T.
"Sudden Cardiac Death. A Problem in Topology." Scientific American. Vol. 248. No.5. May. 1983
42. Abragam. A. and Goldrnan.
Nuclear magnetism. Order and Disorder. Oxford. Clarendon Press. 1982.
43. Op. Cit {23) See pp. 161 ff for time reversal theory.
44. Gross. Paul R.. and Spindel. W.
"Heavy water inhibition of cell division. An approach to mechanism." Annals of the New York Academy of Sciences. Vol. 90, Art. 2, pp. 345-613 Second Conference on the mechanisms of cell divison Editor. Franklin N. Furness. October 7, 1960
45. Winter. R.
Cancer-Causing Agents, Crown Publishers. Inc. New York, 1979

13927-VALO

ANDRIJA ("HENRY") K. PUHARICH was awarded a Life Membership in the U.S. Psychotronics Association for his service. He earned his M.D. from Northwestern University Medical School in 1947 and did his residency at Permanente Foundation Hospital. He served as the Chief of Outpatient Service for the U.S. Army Chemical Center shortly afterward. Dr. Puharich is most well-known for bringing the psychic, Uri Geller to the U.S. for extensive testing at Stanford Research Institute. The team of Targ and Puthoff created a stir with their journal reports of the metal and spoon-bending ability of Uri Geller (which Geller still exhibits today). The book, *Uri*, written by Puharich, documented the unusual background and associated anomalies that accompanied events with Geller. While developing a nerve-deafness transdermal (TD) machine for market, he was pulled into studying the Brazilian healer, Arigo, and lost control of the company. Puharich also wrote the book, *The Sacred Mushroom* that documented the history of and increased psychic abilities with certain mushroom rites. He also demonstrated this effect on *One Step Beyond*, with the TV show host John Newland in 1961, using standard parapsychology card and envelope tests. One of Andrija's most masterful works include his book, *Beyond Telepathy*, which shows that a Faraday cage, charged to high voltage, increases the telepathic abilities of any subject inside. Unfortunately, the US Patent Office would not grant him a patent for this discovery but did so for many of his other ones, including the TD, water-splitting, arm-cast design and putting a radio receiver inside a person's molar. There is an interesting patent appeal transcript, showing a *confrontation of opposing paradigms,* contained in the fascinating *Court of Appeals* publication of Puharich v. Brenner, Comm. Of Pats. No. 22286, decided June 25, 1969, *U.S. Patent Quarterly*, V.162, p.136, dealing with this Puharich invention: "He claims, in effect, that the trial was unfair because the trial judge was skeptical about the existence of ESP, yet did not permit introduction of proof concerning the existence and validity of ESP. What the trial judge did seems sound to us. He held that neither the theory nor existence of extrasensory perception was on trial as such." However, the *USPQ* footnote to this one-sided discourse says *the opposite* about the PTO: "The Board of Patent Appeals may well have erred insofar as it proceeded in part on the premise that the applicant had not submitted convincing evidence that the power of extra-sensory perception exists." Thus, a great pioneer was dismissed by contradictory action of the U.S. legal system. Dr. Puharich's last book, which he worked on in 1979 as the Editor, was *The Iceland Papers*, with a Foreword by Brian Josephson, that included papers by Puthoff, Rauscher, Hasted, Mattuck, and Costa de Beuregard. –Ed. note

13(a)

Radionics: Some Historical Notes On the Origin of Radionics

Peter Moscow Phd, MDS,Rad
Reprinted from *Alternative Therapies in Clinical Practice*, Vol. 3, No. 6, Nov/Dec 1996, p. 17

Radionics Originated with Dr. Albert Abrams

The science of Radionics owes its origin to Dr. Albert Abrams. Born in San Francisco in 1863, Abrams became an exceptional student of medicine at an early age. He studied German and went to the University of Heidelberg where he graduated in medicine with the highest honors. He did extensive post-graduate work throughout Europe under well-known teachers such as Virchow, Frerichs, Wasserman and Herman Von Helmholtz. As a pupil and friend of Von Helmholtz, Abrams was exposed to the latest developments in physics, which eventually led him to try to link biology and physics.

After his return to America, he became a Demonstrator of Pathology, then later Professor of Pathology and Director of Clinical Medicine at Stanford University. He was a fellow of the AMA and authored many books, 12 of which are in the Library of Congress. He was regarded as a leading neurologist in his day. His book *Spondylo-Therapy*, based on his research into spinal therapeutics, was published in 1910, went into six editions, and was also translated into French and Japanese. He contributed frequently to the world's medical journals.

Abrams was very wealthy due to inheritance. This allowed him to concentrate on his research into what later became known as Radionics. He eventually left his fortune to a foundation to carry on research and provide treatment to poor people who could not afford it. Sadly, due to a legal loophole, relatives disputed the will and the foundation only got enough money to function very modestly.

In his book, *New Concepts in Diagnosis and Disease* (Dr. Albert Abrams, 1924, Physico-Clinical Co. San Francisco), Abrams described percussing the abdomen of a middle-aged male patient who had a small epithelioma on his lip. Abrams had become an expert in the art of percussion and so it came as a great surprise to hear a very dull note instead of a hollow one as would be normal in that area of the upper abdomen. He had the patient-who had been standing-move to a couch in another part of the room so that he could palpate him to determine if there was a solid mass under, the dull sounding area that might account for the unusual note. No mass could be discerned and what was more remarkable was that the dull note vanished and was replaced by a normal hollow tone when Abrams percussed the patient for a second time.

Abrams made the patient return to exactly the same standing position that had been congruent with the dull note being elicited. The strange note reappeared. The patient was asked for the rest of the day to stand in different compass directions while Abrams percussed his epigastrium to find out in which positions the dull note would appear. The investigation continued the next day with the same patient until Abrams was satisfied that his findings were solid. He concluded that the dull note would only appear when the patient faced west and in no other position. The note manifested in one small but well-defined area on the abdomen wall just above the navel. Abrams also discovered a second area that resonated with a dull note on the inner border of the man's left shoulder blade.

Abrams subsequently concluded (after testing other cancer patients in a similar manner and using healthy patients as controls) that some kind of specific "radiation" originating in the cancerous tissue – at an atomic or molecular level – was affecting certain groups of nerve fibers thus inducing a muscle-contracting reflex. In turn, this reflex could be detected by percussing the abdominal wall.

He further reasoned that if this "radiation" existed then it should be able to have the same type of effect on the nervous system of another person. To test this idea he selected a very healthy 20-year-old student whose abdomen was normally resonant no matter which direction of the compass he faced. He had the student face west and applied to his forehead a small container into which had been placed a small piece of a malignant tumor which had just been obtained from a patient undergoing surgery. The percussion note thus obtained quickly became very dull. When the student changed position to face north the dull note went away and the abdomen sounded hollow. Returning to the west position the dull note came back again.

Abrams felt that this newly discovered "radiation" might be electronic in nature and he set up an experiment to see if it would travel down a Wire and produce measurable affects at the other end. He took a six foot length of regular electric wire, fastened one end to a small aluminum disc and the other to a larger disc mounted on an insulated handle. The small disc was placed on the student's forehead and secured with a rubber band. The other end of the wire was placed behind a screen where an assistant, who could not be seen by Abrams or the student, held the electrode (with the insulated handle) and had the specimen to hand. Abrams told the assistant to point the electrode to the ceiling while percussion was performed on the student to establish the normal resonant note. Then the assistant was told to hold the electrode over the cancer specimen but not to tell Abrams when he did so.

Whenever the electrode was pointed at the ceiling the note became normal, and dull when pointed at the specimen. Abrams was unaware of when the assistant changed from ceiling to specimen and vice-versa, but each time Abrams was able to detect the "correct note." Further identical experiments were conducted with samples taken from patients with other diseases than cancer and dull notes were obtained in various parts of the abdomen. Specific diseases' specimens produced dull notes in specific areas of the abdomen. It was not long before Abrams ran into a difficulty with a specimen taken from a patient suffering from syphilis. He found that the note produced by syphilis was in exactly the same area on the abdomen as the reaction tone for cancer. This problem was solved by introducing a variable resistance box into the circuit between the electrode on the subject's head and the electrode held by the assistant behind the screen. The result was that different disease specimens produced different "resistance readings." Cancer, for example, read out at 50 ohms, whereas syphilis only reacted at 55 ohms. This marked the beginning of the thousands of experiments, which led to the compilation of major lists of all the diagnostic areas on the abdomen as well as the resistance readings in ohms, which serve to differentiate all the most important diseases.

Abrams further discovered that he could get excellent percussion results using only a blood sample from the sick patient instead of a tissue sample. He eventually devised a method of neutralizing the "radiations" and developed a treatment device known as the 'Oscilloclast.' This machine used negative electrical charges as well as radio-frequency electromagnetic pulses.

One of the most important discoveries that Abrams made was that disease could be detected using his techniques in very early stages and long before there were any physical signs or symptoms. It was very ironic that he was able to detect cancer in his wife's body 10 years before it fully manifested and ended her life. He had not, at that point, developed his treatment device that might have helped her.

Albert Abrams died suddenly in January 1924. It is said that he died of overwork. He was in his laboratory suffering from pneumonia the day before his death. Ironically, about an hour afterwards a telegram was received from the Sorbonne in Paris inviting him to lecture on his discoveries, which were known at that time as the "Electronic Reactions of Abrams."

Successors to Abrams and the Nature of Radionics

Much controversy surrounded Abram's work as well as that of his successors. The primary difficulty was that the nature of Radionics, as it later became known, was not fully grasped by Abrams during his lifetime. If he had lived longer, it is very likely that he would have reached an understanding of the present day theories that stress the Mental Science aspects of Radionics. If that had happened he would have been able to avoid some of the pitfalls and obstacles which caused some of his profession to remain skeptical far longer than necessary.

Radionics has, for part of its pedigree, the background of *radiesthesia* which is thousands of years old. Perhaps the best known and least disputed of all radiesthesia methods is water divining with a hazel twig. [The U.S. Geological Survey acknowledged this time-tested ability with a book, *The Divining Rod: A History of Water Witching* by Arthur Ellis, in 1917 (reprinted again in 1957) and added hundreds of references dating back to 1532. It is still on file at the US Patent Office, Class 324/800.—Ed. note] It is said that the twig acts as an aerial to the broadcasted emanations of the subterranean water or even other material. Modern physics tends to suggest that this is erroneous and that the biopotentials of the body are disturbed by the water and produce transient muscle spasms, thus making the twig move.

Another scientist whose researches parallel some aspects of Abram's work was Baron von Reichenbach, a noted German chemist of his day, who discovered creosote and other chemical compounds. It was an interest in people with extrasensory perception, however, which first brought him into contact with a force that he named the "Odic Force." This, he claimed, was a peculiar kind of force which he found radiating from crystals, in light, heat and living cells, and manifesting itself wherever any chemical reaction took place. Reichenbach's real breakthrough came when he discovered that this force could be conducted along wires, focused by a lens, or distorted by a candle flame. He found that it could also be transmitted to others for the relief of pain, healing, or even the production of anesthesia. He documented these findings in a book called *Researches*.

After Abram's death there were many technical, and some theoretical, improvements in the new field of Radionics. A good example was an instrument produced by Ruth Drown, DC which had a rubber diaphragm that had to be rubbed by a finger in order to obtain a reaction-which was the equivalent of Abram's percussion reactions. She was a gifted practitioner and helped greatly to foster interest in Radionics in it's early years. She believed that the practitioner was tuning or focusing the "Life Force" which she held is present in everything. In this way she differed in her treatment theories from Abrams who utilized electrical devices to help cure disease. She treated many people with a method that had become known as "Broadcast" (i.e.: using the patient's blood sample [also called a witness] in an instrument designed to balance the energetic distortions underlying the patient's disease state). Whereas other researchers were attempting to produce more accurate analytic instrumentation using electrical circuits, vacuum tubes and so forth, Drown focused her attention on the radiesthetic aspect of Radionics and postulated that the corrective treatments were applied through the Ether—a concept that had become unfashionable in science after the Michaelson-Morley experiments (to determine the speed of light) appeared to dispense with the need for the Ether. She did however invent the Radio-Vision camera, which utilized electrical components. This device allowed the "energy" of various organs in the body to affect photosensitive films or plates.

The greatest amount of research in recent times was done by the late George de la Warr and Marjorie de la Warr at the Delawarr Laboratories at Oxford, England, where research work began in 1942 and continued until the closure of the laboratories three years ago. The de la Warrs have left an enormous legacy of important theory and practice and empirical evidence. They created many new and improved types of analytic and treatment instruments as well as a very thorough medical analysis methodology and treatment protocol. They developed a series of Radionic Cameras, (non-electrical), which allowed them to remotely photograph the energetic nature of disease as it infiltrates the body, animal, or human. A major archive of 10,000 plates exists which covers everything from medical experiments and veterinary analysis to the detection of underground mineral sources. This archive has not been seen by the scientific community nor the public at this time, but plans are in the making to do this. By the time the laboratories closed they had developed over 40,000 case studies which support the effectiveness of radionic analysis and treatment.

George de la Warr clearly understood the fundamental importance of the human mind in the operation of the instruments. Because of this, he was able to develop a training protocol for practitioners that emphasized the requirement for clear and sustained visualization on the part of the operator in conjunction with precise questioning skills based on conventional medical knowledge. He required that individuals have a background of three years of medicine before he would sell them radionic equipment.

The standard Delawarr Radionic method of detection and treatment of disease is for the practitioner to carry out a radionic; analysis of the intending patient with the aid of a specimen of the patient's blood. The specimen consists of one or more spots of blood on a filter paper, although specimens may be of hair, sputum or urine. The analysis is to determine the predisposing cause of the condition and also to set out the supporting conditions. The operator's working copy of the analysis contains what are known as radionic "rates" which can be used subsequently in a treatment protocol.

The radionic practitioner may suggest to the patient that other forms of supportive therapy would be of benefit in addition to radionic therapy. These may be dietary measures to correct deficiencies found in the analysis, homeopathic, naturopathic or allopathic remedies, massage osteopathy, hypnosis, surgery, and so forth.

George de la Warr postulated that the diagnostic instrument operated strictly analogously to a simple three-stage computer unit with the dials of the diagnostic instrument representing the data-holding device, the mind of the operator representing the memory banks, and the rubber detector as the read-off stage. Thus, the read-off stage will become active when resonance is obtained between the radiations from the specimen and the dial settings of the diagnostic instrument It is considered that this action takes place through the operation of the pacinian corpuscles which are mechano-receptors located in the finger tips.

Quillian and Armstrong, in 1963, initiated work on what was then called by de la Warr, the "touch-cum-sense-cum-thought" relationship. Loeinstein and Katz, both of whose work on biological transducers and nerve impulses has been published in *Scientific American*, have done more work on this. These workers all stated that the sensory receptors of the skin were acting as transducers that convert one form of energy into another and that the pacinian corpuscle has the ability of both transmitting and receiving sensory data. George de la Warr considered that these biological transducers, being able to react to a mechanical stimulus at the nerve ending, explained the touch-cum-sense-cum-thought relationship that is part of the technique of operating the detector of the radionic diagnostic instrument. One objective criticism, which can be leveled at the practice of radionic diagnosis and therapy, is entirely centered on the use of the specimen of the patient instead of requiring the patient to be present at the time of investigation. This criticism is difficult to meet unless one realizes that the specimen, while not analyzed in the chemical sense of the word, does have the same radiations as the host whose specimen it is and that the radiations are non-spatial. This argues that the radiations are at the patient and are at the specimen and no time elapses for these radiations to pass from the patient to the specimen or vice-versa or to the patient from the treatment instrument or vice-versa; they exist at all points in between. Radionics therefore probably requires explanatory models grounded in quantum physics if it is to be correctly understood.

In normal circumstances the method of the application of radionic therapy to a patient is to use what are called "complementary" rates. These are sometimes referred to by beginners as "anti-recognition" rates, but there are many instances in which this is not the correct way to proceed with remedial action from a diagnosis. If, for instance, it is found that a patient who has had an accident is suffering from a fracture of the femur and contusion of the muscles proximal to the femur, it would indeed be foolish just to treat the patient on the complementary rate for fracture. The patient should, of course, be treated to reduce the contusion and the multiple hemorrhages in the muscles but generally the treatment should be chosen under this particular heading to speed the healing properties of the bone by considering the periosteum, the connective tissue, the lymphocyte tissue and hemoglobin content of the blood to make sure that the fracture heals as quickly as possible. It also needs to be stated that all radionic practitioners would make sure that the patient received all the necessary medical attention required to set and or immobilize the bone. Although there is a specific technique to be followed when operating radionic diagnostic instruments, it does remain a fact that radionic analysis is only ever as good as the knowledge of the operator. The de la Warrs defined Radionics as "*The science of the interaction between mind and matter and of the complete inter-relationship of all things.*"

A Contemporary Overview of Radionics

Radionics, is, by itself, a misnomer. The name implies the use of a radio, or some other electronic instrument or gadget; In actuality the word stems from "ray" or "radiate." The true definition of Radionics involves the use of light as a carrier of information. That information, when processed by a highly trained mind, can be of extraordinary usefulness in a wide variety of situations from the enhancing of plant growth to eradicating pests and disease.

This is because all conditions are preceded by their informational pattern. Correct deciphering of such a pattern opens up new worlds of possibilities to the clinician. Before a condition is physically manifest it can be counteracted, and when a condition, such as the case described herein, is fully manifest it can be altered and in many cases eradicated with the use of such information.

There has always been light and sound, which are carriers of information and exist mathematically in waveforms. Subtle pieces of information, which are layered onto these waveforms, can be measured, deciphered, and rearranged so that a client no longer must, for instance, carry with them the harmful effects of radiation and its ghostly after-image upon the physical body.

Startling as it may seem, conditions such as cancer can be altered and eradicated with the correct use of an information pattern. All information can be stored in a computer database in binary code. Likewise, with Radionics, information can be stored, encoded, or represented by numerical patterns. The use of such patterns sets up or produces a waveform that can counteract the wave from of the disease or condition.

Dr. Albert Abrams discerned the use of percussion as a means of diagnosis and treatment and developed instruments for this purpose. He did not fully recognize the potential of this field, however. George de la Warr, an electronics technician and engineer, recognized that these devices could be used to measure and counteract informational patterns (of disease states) before they became physical, while they were still in a purely "informational" form. He recognized the existence of invisible energy fields that surround all objects and was able to develop instruments that could, in the hands of trained operators, determine the extent and state of these fields. Distortions in such fields, he found, could be corrected with proper alignments, tuning, training, and intention.

A Note On Rates

All informational patterns can be represented or reduced to a numerical, geometric pattern or mathematical formula. Therefore, anything that contains information, such as a disease, or condition, or body part, can be assigned a corresponding numerical value or rate. Different representational systems have been set up, the Delawarr System being just one of these. However, all of these patterns, in order to be efficacious, had to first be detected, reduced, or allocated a numerical designation, and then classified. The Delawarr System of classification is by far the most comprehensive known to date in the field of healing, for not only does it organize this information methodically, it is also presented in a fashion that most trained clinicians can understand. The system of classification addresses the pre-physical bodies—the physical as well as underlying causation factors.

An analyst properly trained in the use of this system would find their time and money spent on discovery tests cut markedly. The key here is proper training. It is better not to undertake such an education unless the individual is fully prepared to make several years commitment to study of this technique. It is not something to pick up one day and put down the next. Like any other job well done, it requires great self-discipline, self-awareness and a willingness to learn. This is key, because transformational changes often occur to the practitioner themselves, not just their clients. Once this profession is undertaken it can challenge the strongest of beliefs about oneself. It is a serious life-giving, balancing form of healing that works with the individual as a whole and does not split them, at least during treatment phases, into cause and effect. Such things as melanoma for instance are viewed one way by the medical establishment: "You have this growth and we must remove it," and another way by this system: "You have this growth and it and its originating cause must be addressed."

This system is designed to eventually allow clients to not have to return to the office because they have truly and fully healed, which is the direction of modern medicine and the insurance industry at this point. Because of the controversial nature of some of this work it is still classified as experimental in the USA even though it has proved itself effective for many decades.

Training in Radionics

The UK has a number of organizations such as the DelaWarr Society for Radionics and the British Radionic Association which offer professional degree courses. Normally, these take three or four years to complete. They combine academic studies with supervised clinical experience. In America, the United States Psychotronics Association provides education at annual conferences as well as basic skills courses in Radionics. These courses are being currently upgraded for inclusion in an accredited university program. Dr. Moscow teaches health professionals in the UK and abroad, Radionics for use in tandem with their medical or health practices. Radionics is not a recognized medical science (diagnosis and treatment) in the USA and can only be used as a bio-energetic analysis and balancing system. Used properly in that context it causes no infringement of state or Federal laws.

Summary

1) Radionics is the use of the trained radiesthetic sense (in suitably qualified individuals) which, used in combination with specially tuned instruments, facilitates: an accurate big-energetic analysis of a client's health; and

2) a healing process by rebalancing distorted big-informational patterns.

Radiesthesia is the use of ESP in conjunction with a device such as a pendulum to register a response to incoming subtle information, usually received from a source remote from the operator. The hue nature of radionic healing is concealed with the energy of thought commingled with etheric or subtle energy in such a way that healing intentionality is delivered to the target bio-system which may be a human, animal, plant or soil.

Radionics is also capable of detecting and analyzing subtle information emanating from any specified target such as a natural gas subterranean source. The de la Warrs for instance were able to locate–for the Marathon Oil Company—the largest natural gas field in the world (at the time of discovery). This was done using a small sample of natural gas as a "witness" in conjunction with survey photographs and maps. The following paper demonstrates that Radionics is an excellent management tool in that its informational processing capacity can produce rapid, effective, measurable results. It further shows that radionic instruments can create potent homeopathic remedies. Though seen by many professionals as only anecdotal, this woman is still alive today. Many other equally successful case histories abound. [See "Reviewer's comments" regarding this article following the next one in this set. –Ed. note]

13(b)

Radionics as a Complementary Management Tool in a Case of Inoperable Low-Grade Astrocytoma affecting a 30-Year Old Woman.

Peter D.Moscow PhD, MDSRad.

Reprinted from *Alternative Therapies in Clinical Practice*, Vol. 3, No. 6, Nov/Dec 1996, p. 21

Introduction

Even though case histories abound in radionic literature, which demonstrate clearly the efficacy of diagnosis and treatment in all manner of illnesses, it is still rare to find complex cases which have yielded to radionic techniques whilst simultaneously being monitored by conventional medical procedures. It is rarer still to have access to all the medical records-whicb in the present instance clearly prove that a radionic and complementary approach was and is very effective in controlling and managing an otherwise probably fatal brain tumor. The case of Judy Bryant (name changed to preserve anonymity) is presented simply as an example of what can be achieved by psychotronic techniques in the face of medical and socially acceptable hopelessness. This paper additionally supports the absolute necessity for cooperation between so-called "fringe" medicine and current medical research and clinical practice.

Background to the Case History

The corporation of which I am President – Holistic Philosophy Consultants Ltd. – was set up to provide only psychic consultancy and nonmedical informational services inside the USA. The other owner of the company, Dr. Brian Richards, is an English Doctor who specializes in Regenerative Therapy within the context of family practice at his clinic in Sandwich, a small coastal town in the southeast of England. In 1982 a research program was begun in England that was designed to test various complementary and alternative health practices under normal medical supervision. It was agreed that Dr. Richards and I would utilize radionic and other non-conventional techniques in clinical situations where standard medical practice was ineffective and the patient expressed a strong preference for a non-traditional form of therapy. It was set up so the work would be done on my regular visits to England. It was an absolute stipulation of the research program that all information obtained non-conventionally would be checked by Dr. Richards for its appropriateness before implementing any therapeutic protocols.

Judy Bryant made an appointment to see Dr. Richards and myself at the Kent Private clinic on 12/27/83. Her purpose was to find out if we could help her design a self-help program to fight the malignant brain tumor she was suffering from.

On 6/10/81, Judy Bryant's regular family physician prescribed the first of over 120 separate headache medications. Phenergan, Empirin #4, Ornade, Mellaril 25, and Actifed were all employed to treat what the doctor had determined to be only simple although very painful headaches. Two years later the headaches and the prescriptions persisted. It is remarkable that the physician did not once order a CT scan or at the very least a thorough examination by a competent neurologist. Judy became much sicker and on 6121/83 she was examined by another doctor in a hospital near her home. At that stage she was presenting acute abdominal pain, very severe headaches and vomiting which included small amounts of blood. Dizziness and blurred vision were also present along with some diarrhea. Various tests were performed but the brain condition was not suspected until Judy was admitted to emergency on 7/11/83. Subsequently a CT scan was ordered and other appropriate tests were completed. The final diagnosis was a Grade I astrocytoma which was about the size of a walnut. A ventricular peritoneal shunt was inserted into her cranium in order to relieve the fluid buildup on the brain. The tumor was determined to be inoperable. Radiation was proposed as the primary therapy and on 8/16/83 a series of 25 treatments comprising 180 Rads per day were begun. A small, localized field encompassing the tumor with a few centimeters margin was utilized. Judy experienced significant side effects from the treatment, which included the usual loss of hair. The physicians involved in her case did urge her to use chemotherapy but she refused this adamantly. Her reason for doing so is critical from the perspective of the holistic practitioner. She believed that the chemotherapy would have killed her. This clearly is not objectively ascertainable either way, but what is obvious is that she had not given up hope of living and perhaps curing her illness. Furthermore, her response to authority was considerably modified by her intuitive private knowledge. This latter fact has played an enormous role in her recovery.

The radiation therapy was performed until the Rads had reached the normally maximal brain absorption level at 4500. On 10/4/83 another CT scan was performed which revealed that the lesion had apparently failed to improve, i.e. it had not shrunk. The scan showed no change other than a more intense enhancement around the cystic lesion compared to the previous examination. Medically, Judy had reached the end of the road and she was placed in a surveillance mode by her doctor who wished to monitor the tumor periodically. She then began a somewhat haphazard search for alternative therapies and succeeded in getting hold of a number of dietary supplements, which were considered helpful in cancer cases by those in the natural health movement. During this time she and her husband also consulted with an attorney and a lawsuit was filed against her original family doctor. The idea was that her husband would very likely be the only recipient of any awards from a successful suit. It was because of this action that Judy was able to obtain every single item in her medical records. The other important consequence was the discovery of what the neurologist's prognosis had been after she was released from treatment. He did not believe that she would survive more than nine months.

At our first meeting I learned a great deal about Judy as well as her family circumstances. It became very obvious that not one person close to her believed that she was going to live. Her husband was apparently acting hysterically in his certitude that she was going to die. He lacked the ability to control his own fears and guilt long enough to offer any support for Judy. Most other members of her family accepted the doctor's and their own prognoses and thus were not able to provide any real emotional assistance.

There was one nephew however, who did his best to assist her in procuring whatever supplements she could afford. At the time of her first visit she and her husband were existing on disability income and very little else. Her husband also had an alcoholic tendency, which made matters worse. It is normal in most medical alternative protocols that one hears about to seek, and maintain a very positive support group in order to enhance one's chances of survival, if not cure. In Judy's case these conditions never came to pass during her recovery.

We accepted this case because Judy was considered terminal and beyond the stage where any known treatment could be guaranteed to even ameliorate her condition. We insisted that she follow the doctor's surveillance requirements, even if she did not wish to on the grounds that monitoring alone could provide nothing of great value. It was stressed that objective evaluations would be of considerable use, however, in the event that her program were to work. Aside from validating the techniques she would choose, it would also serve to positively enhance her efforts at recovery by promoting hope which, as Dr. Bernie Siegel has pointed out, is not statistical but physiological. It was agreed that in the event of deterioration we would not ask her to continue this procedure for obvious reasons.

The most critical problem remained: How could we create an effective, as opposed to a purely cosmetic, program for Judy that did not use any potentially harmful routines? It was decided to evaluate the entire program through radionic methods and then have Dr. Richards approve all the recommendations before giving them to Judy. We also agreed that our involvement with the case would be terminated, if no progress was observable after 60 days. The conventional reasons for using radionics as a primary analytical modality were based on the following facts and assumptions:

- Radionics is capable of measuring a large portion of human being's subtle energies depending on the knowledge and training of the practitioner.
- The system has predictive capacity which is precise and thus of practical value.
- It is perhaps the only single system inherently capable of discovering all of the underlying causes of illness relevant to a given individual.
- It is very rapid compared with many other analytic methods.
- Information can be rechecked easily in the event that error is suspected.
- It can be applied to any known mode of treatment from an information-processing viewpoint.

- It is completely non-invasive and can be used at any distance from the client.
- It causes no harm.

These reasons certainly justify a radionic approach from the practitioner's viewpoint but in Judy's case there were more compelling reasons for us to choose this method. Knowing that no further conventional procedures (that Judy was willing to try) could have offered even a modicum of hope we knew that any alternative path we suggested would have to provide some or all of the following:

1) A fresh and significant detailed analysis of her condition.
2) An appeal to her sense of logic.
3) The ability to satisfy her curiosity and private feelings as to how and why she bad developed the cancer.
4) A coherent and intelligent set of ideas that she could use on a daily basis.
5) A stimulator of her will to fight the cancer by shifting her worldview through distraction. It was thought that radionics would be sufficiently "magical," at least in the early stages, to achieve that end, as Judy was ignorant of any "block box" or psychotronic theories or practices.
6) The conventional medical shamans had thrown in the towel and we knew that it would require supporting her desire for life with a major change of consciousness on her part if she were going to recover partially or fully.

Judy displayed considerable intelligence, curiosity, and humor in combination with her persistent loquacity. This signaled us that she would be highly inquisitive about everything that would be done for her, so radionics, in our assessment, provided the best vehicle for answering her questions directly and multidimensionally. Very few clients, given the opportunity to interact with an experienced practitioner, will stick to one subject. In nearly every case, when they perceive the information potential, they will become strongly stimulated to ask all the questions that are fit to print. This was to be encouraged in Judy's situation because it was to provide a bridge between her illness state and entirely new stratum of being. This enhanced method of interaction between our client and ourselves was to play a critical role in her process of self-empowerment.

If alternative and complementary practices are to be effective and objectively measurable it is imperative that the client become the director of the therapy by learning as much as is possible about the illness and the treatments. Judy became exemplary in this regard and eventually learned how to tap the deeper potentials of the radionic information processing capacity.

Methodology

It was decided that we would use two pieces of equipment to work on Judy's case. The first was a Standard Delawarr diagnostic instrument and the other was a Rae Potency Simulator. They were manufactured in England up until 1994 by Delawarr Laboratories and, Oxford and Magneto-Geometric Applications, London, respectively. Neither instrument has many bells or whistles and they very simple to use from a technical viewpoint The Delawarr instrument also comes with a superb analytic methodology which has proven its worth for over 40 years. The Rae Potency simulator, which uses pattern cards to create – by radionic circuits – simulfacts of homeopathic remedies, is also an excellent radionic projector. It is easy to work with as it is not dependent on a trained operator to actually potentise the medicines. Once the correct "pattern" is discerned and the potency selected, the medicine can be made by anyone who can read and follow simple orders. With this approach it is possible to repeatedly produce standardized potencies of virtually any remedy without fear of variance due to contamination or poor preparation during manufacture. A further feature that proved valuable in the present case was the instrument's capacity for fine tuning the potencies far beyond the range of standard preparations. This meant that the radionic remedies could be matched with great precision to Judy's energy field rather than relying on good approximations, which might not stimulate the patient's healing responses adequately.

Analysis

Judy's next appointment took place on 12/30/83. A small sample of her hair was obtained and utilized as a witness for the purpose of analysis according to the procedures laid out in the Delawarr diagnostic protocols. It was explained clearly before we began that radionics does not measure the physical directly, but rather probes the pre-physical fields of energy that sustain and give form to the physical body. The consequence of this form as of analysis is the detection of the predisposing patterns or causes of the physically manifest condition.

The first readings were performed after Dr. Richards and I took an extensive inventory of Judy's medical history with special emphasis being given to her symptomatic patterns and ID modalities from a homeopathic standpoint. To begin with, a basic physical "vitality function" was measured and recorded at 37 percent. This reading indicated that Judy was either extremely sick or heavily drugged and/or traumatized. The latter possibility is mentioned to cover those rare instances when practitioners are working at a distance and do not know all the facts. Regardless of that, it is very rare to see someone with a basic level reading of under 40 whom is not very seriously ill. Because of the low reading, the probability of curing the patient and the specific disease were measured separately. The Delawarr system has rates for both of these concepts. Judy displayed a 55 percent probable curability factor with respect to the malignancy but a remarkable 97 percent with reference to her ability to recover from her illness. This reading was very encouraging. Very few people with advanced degenerative illnesses display an initial curability factor as high as that It is far more normal to see the readings in the 50, 60, and 70 percent ranges at first and perhaps later to see the readings climb. The curability readings usually change as the patient responds to treatment. This fact makes the art and science of prediction more complex when dealing with health matters but it also tends to support the idea that there are no absolute futures unless the individual chooses to see it that way. As time went on it was found that Judy's illness factor did improve steadily.

The next sequence of analysis was carried out with the rate for astrocytoma set on the dials of the diagnostic instrument. It was found that a number of imperfectly functioning body systems were supporting cancer. First of all, there was the thymus gland which clearly relates to the immune function (immune surveillance was found to be only 35 percent of normal when measured). Next the lymph system and Reticulo-endothelial system were determined to be inefficient which completed the picture of a compromised immune surveillance system. Other areas were the skeletal system and, for obvious reasons, the brain itself. Aside from the frontal lobe area which contained the lesion, it was found that the efficiency of the area controlling movement and balance was disturbed, although not greatly. In each case the field efficiency percentage of the organ or system was taken to act as a benchmark for later analysis. The last stage of the diagnostic procedures was to find the underlying causes of the cancer. Causation factors were as follows:

1) *Allergies*-These turned out to be primarily food based and displayed various levels of intensity with wheat (and its processed derivatives) being one of the worst. One of the most useful aspects of Radionics is the rapid delineation of comparative values in such matters as food sensitivities and allergies. By determining the allergy threshold in percentage

terms the practitioner can make the client aware of which individual or combination of foods would be most likely to trigger a major negative response. In Judy's case her threshold was extremely low at 5 percent and thus it was highly probable that such items as wheat which read out at 18 percent would provoke an allergic response capable of further weakening her immune system.

2) *Toxins*-Two major toxins were discovered to be aggravating the lesion. The first was from the Radiation therapy and the second was from a variety of drugs. Judy was, at the time of the analysis, taking Darvocet and Dilantin in order to control pain and possible seizures, but, in addition, she was smoking cigarettes, marijuana and imbibing some alcohol on a regular basis.

3) *Trace Mineral Deficiencies*-This reading showed that Judy was 23 percent lacking in essential elements and/or minerals and that she had been that way for two years.

4) *Vitamin Insufficiency*-This reading was 12 percent and is clearly one of the expected causes from a holistic and nutritional standpoint. It is also worth noting that vitamin function usually reads negatively when the minerals and trace elements are in deficiency. Very often when the minerals are correctly balanced the vitamins begin to show normal levels again.

5) *Metabolic Imbalance*-A disturbance in the protein metabolism was evident. Many alternative theorists posit the idea that cancer is an underlying metabolic disturbance of the whole body which localizes in specifically weak areas. Most radionic analyses of cancer cases do seem to confirm that this factor is present and causative.

6) *Trauma*-This reading related to an injury sustained to Judy's cranium many years before during her teens. Although this factor represented a very small amount of the causative picture, it was important in that it also obliged us to check spinal fluid pulse. This was found to be just under 40 percent of normal. Cranial-sacral osteopaths place considerable importance on this function being correct for the maintenance of good health. By inference it can also be reasoned that a low pulse could enhance a virulent disease in its development.

7) *Subluxation of specific vertebrae and consequent impaired nerve conduction*-This set of readings highlighted problems in the cervical spine as well as other dorsal lumbar malfunctions. Chiropractors have long attributed a wide variety of disorders to skeletal misalignment and radionics tends to support some aspects of this theory, which is probably the reason that this form of causation is regularly found in routine analysis. It is likely, however, that the misalignment component of the hypothesis is not the only cause of impaired innervation. What adjustment appears to do in many cases is to stimulate the efferent nerve tissue back to normal electrical function which can boost organ or tissue function. What also appears to happen is that the disordered organ can reflex to the spinal column and bring about a subluxation which then serves to act as a further inhibitor to normal function, This did seem, in Judy's illness, to be very relevant. It goes without belaboring the point that poor posture and other assorted mechanical causes are always potentially relevant but radionic techniques do tend to reveal that subluxations are frequently induced by organ disorders.

8) *Improper Diet*-The reading indicated that Judy had not been eating the "right diet" for 24 years. This referred to the development of the cancer, so one can infer that it took many years for the deficits in her nutrition to have any significant

13927-VALO

effect. Modern medicine. has finally, and perhaps somewhat reluctantly, discovered what the health food aficionados have long understood-that what one eats can play an important role in the development of cancer. However it should also be stressed that death and destruction do not ride on every mouthful. In Judy's case the nutritional factor was about 8 percent of the total underlying pattern. The most useful aspect of this information would be in the treatment phase.

9) *Reduced energy transduction through the major chakras*-The worst reading came from the brow chakra which was operating at only 25 percent of normal capacity, The base spinal chakra was also heavily compromised. Many radionic practitioners consider that the condition of the esoteric anatomy is of paramount importance in the analysis, causation and treatment of disease. Much stimulating anecdotal evidence lends credence to the technique of treating psychological disorders and directing the corrective patterns through the appropriate chakra. By doing this, the practitioner hopes to restore the proper energy flow through the chakra and thus to induce a restoration of physical function in the corresponding organs.

Creating a Practical Self-Help Program

The first step was to determine how Judy could most effectively integrate all of the findings into a practical format that she would be motivated to follow. Again, the radionic logic proved to be invaluable in that it helped to prioritize the steps to be followed in order of therapeutic merit. The most urgent need proved to be preparation of a radionically potentised anti-radiation remedy. This was done by the use of the Rae Potency simulator with Dr. Westlake's remedy pattern card inserted, and the dial set to reflect the equivalent potency of 200C. The rationale behind this initial step was that Judy could not do well if she had to fight cancer as well as radiation toxins which could eventually lead to more cancer should she survive. Certainly nobody wanted to take that risk. It was indicated that she should take the remedy for five days only. The best times of the day were also ascertained to take the remedy.

The next and equally critical, change was to eliminate all the noxious substances which Judy was consuming such as alcohol, nicotine, etc. She also decided to reduce steadily the prescription drugs in line with her own symptomatic awareness and the Step down program suggested by the radionic evaluation. Further, to these measures a stringent dietary regime was drawn up by testing her reactions to a very large selection of primary and secondary foodstuffs. This procedure made it possible to logically eliminate any foods that were allergenic, sensitizing, or detrimental to her acid/alkali balance. A scan was also run to detail those foods which Judy should include in her diet on a daily or regular basis which would be nutritionally advantageous. Attention was paid to the use of items like purified water and raw vegetable and fruit juices. The South American herb, Pau D'Arco, was prescribed regularly in tea form.

The experience of Dr.Gerson and many other alternative health proponents demonstrates that cancer can be controlled or in some cases cured by the use of strict diet. The effect of high quality diet seems to be multifaceted. First of all, the body appears to become far more capable of extensive detoxification. Secondly, damaged or impaired metabolic processes can fully heal. And thirdly, the autoimmune system can be restored to full effectiveness. All of these aspects were monitored while Judy was in the early stages of her program.

At this point it was decided not to introduce other modalities even though logic might suggest otherwise. The radionic information concerning chiropractic, for instance, was to wait for at least a couple of months before introducing spinal manipulation. This was due to the high probability that the adjustments would not hold in the absence of adequate minerals and vitamins. Also, it appears that the body cannot deal efficiently with too many separate strong directives at the same time, especially during a chronic illness. The first consultation was now at an end and Judy departed, having made a future appointment for 1/11/84.

First Reactions

By the time Judy returned to the clinic there was much to report. Her initial reaction to the anti-radiation compound had been swift and very strong. *She became extremely nauseous and experienced other symptoms, which were identical to those she had had while taking the radiation therapy.* [In naturopathy and herbology, this "healing crisis" or "cleansing reaction" that duplicates the original toxic episode is very predictable and a welcome sign of recovery but is quite incomprehensible to allopathic medical doctors. – Ed. note]

According to her the effects were worse than the first time and she was adamant that she would never take that remedy again. She had also begun to experience detoxification and was starting to see the early signs, with some of the toxic waste exuding through her skin. This process lasted for almost two months. In conjunction with her diet she was also using organic coffee enemas. This was important in that it ensured that toxins discharging from the cancer and deep tissues would not stay in her body long enough to cause further harm. The physical vitality field reading showed a rise to 44 percent. This was a very good sign and suggested that Judy would recover relatively fast. We also measured the pre-physical energy field of the tumor and found that the size had decreased by about 7 percent. This would indicate that the physical tumor was probably stable and could be about to begin to recede. The sequence of address now required Judy to introduce some food supplements into her diet The following were detected: Potassium, Kelp and Zinc as well as vitamin A, C, and B15. These would be checked carefully from time to time so as to make sure that they did not interfere with the absorption of the vitamins and minerals from her regular diet. Judy was very encouraged and it was suggested that at her next visit some spiritual and emotional therapy could be started. This was something she readily agreed to do.

By 2/11/84 the physical vitality reading had reached 59 percent and the tumor reading showed even more contraction (almost 20 percent). At this stage the therapy model indicated the use of a high potency single dose of Cadmium Sulphate. The cadmium salts have proven very efficacious in the treatment of malignancy by experienced homeopathic doctors, so it came as no surprise to see this remedy show up on the Scan. The remedy was made by the potency simulator in the usual manner and administered during the consultation. Judy also reported that most of the initial difficulties that she had experienced in following the diet had eased and she was taking it in her stride. Her counseling session was begun and directed towards elucidating the purposes and causes of her illness. She appeared very content with the insights that emerged from the therapy. This process was also to continue for a couple of years; remembering that Judy did not visit the clinic too often after these early appointments, it is remarkable that so little went such a long way. On the other hand, she had planned it this way and it is clear that Judy felt genuinely empowered because she was not on some weekly psychotherapeutic program. In all cases the individual must perceive that she/he is in control of the situation and this was to be especially encouraged in her case. On March 17th the vitality reading had reached 71 percent of normal and the tumor showed a 48 percent shrinkage with respect to the energy field. Immune strength and other levels were also very encouraging. Judy was scheduled for a CT scan on 3/27/84. The results were the first objectively valid confirmations of the radionic readings and Judy's own subjective awareness of real improvement. The following quote is from the radiologists report:

"Contrast was not injected although it has been used previously. The patient stated that she preferred not to have contrast

13927-VALO

injection because of the reaction at the last injection. There is still an area of increased density near the third ventricle on today's examination. The ventricles are completely decompressed. The area of increased density is less than was present on the last examination. Certainly there is much less mass effect. It appears that the lesion near the third ventricle is much smaller on today's examination than was present on the 4th of October. *Conclusion:* There is still a residual mass lesion near the third ventricle with a low-density center and high density surrounding. This has been seen on previous examinations. The ventricles are completely decompressed with a shunt at this time." (27/3/84)

By 9/21/84 the vitality reading showed 90 percent and the tumor energy field had reduced by 89 percent. On 9/26/84 another CT scan was performed and the results speak for themselves.

"The CT examination of the brain shows a marked decrease in both the size of the ventricles and the size of the cystic mass adjacent to the 3rd ventricle. There is still a small rim of enhancement present just below the 3rd ventricle to the right which was seen on the previous studies. There is very little, if any mass effect present now. Conclusion: There has been little change since the previous, examination of March 1984, however, there is only a small ring of enhancement seen below the region of the third ventricle just to the right of midline. The ventricles remain normal in size on today's examination." (26/9/84)

It was during this period, that Judy's neurologist told her that her tumor was breaking up from the inside—something he had never seen before. This opinion leaves little doubt that even from a medical viewpoint the process of recovery was anomalous.

From this point onwards Judy made great strides and she began to live an almost normal life–secure in the knowledge that what she was doing was working well. Her viewpoint became progressively more holistic as she explored the process of self-restoration. Her questions were always answered as precisely as possible using the information processing capacity of the radionic techniques. Her diet became much easier after eight months and her supplements were gradually reduced. In February 1987, she began a course of regenerative therapy shots designed to improve the pituitary, thymus and cerebrum.

This protocol appeared to enhance Judy's vitality even further from a radionic and subjective aspect. At that time there were no further objective readings taken. (The last scan had been done by MRI in 1986). In late October 1988, an MRI scan was taken which showed that, although the lesion was probably even smaller than the one seen two years before, the right frontal horn had collapsed. This was due to the presence of the shunt, which had apparently shifted and was causing some pain and stiffness in Judy's occiput and neck. The radionic analysis had revealed the problem and the scan was recommended to get a clear visual on just how much damage had been done. The problem remains as to how to deal with getting the shunt taken out, which is what Judy wants. So far her doctor is not willing due to the obvious possibility that the cancer could return. At this time we are working to try to remove what is left of the rim of the tumor which is as far as we can determine the only evidence of a once dangerous mass. It is difficult to remove benign tissue, as the body does not have any reason to get rid of that which it considers self. There is an extraordinary irony in that the shunt, which was once needed to help relieve pressure on the brain, has begun itself to be the cause of structural damage.

Some Food for Thought

After six years, Judy continues to do well and is now enrolled in a school for hairdressers in London. Her therapy model was constructed entirely from information derived radionically from her own energy fields. Nothing was done that she did not initiate a request for. In one very clear sense she managed her own condition from day one of her involvement with the clinic. It is impossible to speculate as to what she would have done if she could not have found this type of method, but we can say that her irrepressible spirit would most certainly have prevailed. She is a lesson to all of us.

A Skeptic's Puzzle

It is not the claim of this presentation that radionics cured (or caused a remission of) Judy's brain cancer, but there can be no question that the use of radionically prepared remedies did appear to produce measurable change. The effect of the anti-radiation compound was so dramatic that it stretches any idea of the placebo effect to an irrational level. Normally prepared homeopathic remedies may contain very small amounts of sub-stance in low potencies such as 1X, 6X, etc., but the remedies we used were prepared by impregnating magnetic energy into the carrier substance which was often purified water or sac lac pillules. Therefore, not one molecule could have been present. If these remedies were as effective as they appear to have been, then we are left with the conclusion that radionic energies really do produce clinically verifiable results. Beyond this point however, lies the idea that radionics could be used to evaluate and direct the treatment of chronic illnesses that do not yield to conventional methods. Whether the treatment modalities be allopathic or alternative, hard or soft is a matter of indifference to the system itself which relies entirely on the information which it receives and processes strictly according to the knowledge and expertise of the practitioner. The source of that knowledge to heal is clearly the mind/body intelligence, which possesses wisdom far beyond our present understanding.

Postscript

As of my most recent visit to the UK in November 1994, Judy Byrant continues to enjoy good health.

Reviewer's Comments

This paper documents a case of a woman in whom there was a working diagnosis of a grade-I astrocytoma, and who improved is after conventional medical treatment was withdrawn, and a protocol involving "radionics" instituted.

From a conventional medicine perspective there are many questionable assumptions in this case making it impossible to is draw any valid conclusion regarding the "radionics" protocol. Firstly, the working diagnosis, "grade I astrocytoma, "was apparently not established via tissue. A grade-I astrocytoma is an extremely slow growing brain tumor. The precise type of tumor and differentiation from similar appearing processes such as an infection is usually not possible from CT scan. Because the diagnosis was never firmly established, it is possible that the patient's tumor was actually a radiation responsive lymphoma or other tumor. A second problem is that the decision that the tumor was not responding to radiation was apparently reached only a few weeks after the course of radiation had concluded. This is an unreasonable procedure as tumors may take months to respond to a course of radiation treatment.

From a conventional medicine perspective, what may have actually happened is this: The patient had a brain tumor, which was responsive to radiation. She got a course of radiation treatment which killed much or all of the tumor, but it was wrongly concluded that her tumor had not responded because not enough time was allowed between the treatment and follow-up scan. She "was also ill from systemic effects of the radiation. The patient gradually recovered related to the passage of time. An alternative medicine procedure was ongoing during the recovery but the tumor responded to the conventional medicine procedure, not the alternative medicine procedure.

Reviewer's comments regarding "Some historical notes on the origins of radionics"

This paper provides a historical background regarding a procedure termed "Radionics," which is, in the words of the author, "the use of ESP in conjunction with a device such as a pendulum to register a response to incoming subtle information for medical purposes. It appears most closely related to the process of "divining" for subterranean water. From a conventional medicine perspective, there is no reasonable explanation for this alleged phenomenon and considerable skepticism remains appropriate.

Timothy C. Hain, MD

LETTER TO THE EDITOR

Radionics: Author responds

To the editor:

Some of Dr. Timothy Rain's "Reviewer's comments"concerning the case of the 30-year-old woman with an inoperable low-grade astrocytoma (Vol.3, No.6, November/December, 1996) are based on the assumption that no biopsies were performed. This was not the case. On 7-22-83 multiple biopsies were performed which resulted in the diagnosis of a low-grade astrocytoma. Other lesions such as abscess, cystic astrocytoma, glioma craniopharyngioma, chromophobe and ependymoma were obvious possibilities based solely on the CT scan alone (before the biopsies were performed). These facts are obliquely referred to in my paper in the sentences, "Subsequently a CT scan was ordered and other appropriate tests were completed. The final diagnosis was a Grade 1 astrocytoma which was about the size of a walnut."

The details were not spelled out due to the fact that the paper was written in a required short format for inclusion in the *Proceedings of the United States Psychotronics Association* (1989) and, as a result, many of the medical facts were omitted in order to develop the main theme of the paper.

From the conventional medical viewpoint, Dr. Rain is correct in saying that "tumors may take months to respond to a course of radiation treatment." It would have been possible to let Judy Bryant remain in a monitoring mode to see if and when the tumor would begin to shrink. (This is exactly what her doctors were doing when we met her at the end of 1983. She showed no signs of improvement at that time.) In the long run this course of action would have determined the effectiveness or lack of same – radiation therapy, given that low grade astrocytomas can take, between three and five years to regrow after treatment. That choice was not made for very good reasons.

When Judy had her first appointment at the clinic we tested her radionically to make sure that her tumor was indeed an astrocytoma and not something else. This was done by a process of differential analysis using the Delawarr analytic protocols. Each type of cancer has its own bio-energetic code. I have included a number of these in Table 1.

Table 1 – TUMORS

A few examples of bioenergetic codes or "rates" which are utilized in conjunction with the Delawarr analytic instrumentation. These patterns are not directly applicable to any other system of subtle energy measurements.

Glioblastoma multiform	50.64653
Ependymoma	50.3332
Medulloblastoma	60.268
Multiple mycloma	40.694

13927-VALO

Neuroblastoma	70.543
Sarcoma	50.82
Deciduocellular	40.54554
Lymphatic	50.4327
Myeloid	50.823
Osteogenic	50.8284
Spindle cell	50.849

If, for instance, Judy's tumor had been, say, a glioblastoma multiform, then it would have been impossible to perform an analysis with the astrocytoma settings on the A equipment. The result would have been that no readings would have registered. This point is very well established in radionic photography. During one experimental series run at Bart's Hospital in London in 1951, a radionic camera was used—remotely from the patients—to confirm or deny suspected diagnoses. In all cases where the assumed diagnosis was incorrect, no photograph would develop and the plate would be completely blank. When the diagnoses was correct however the photographs were clear and accurate. These photos have some similarities to CT and MRI scans but are generated from the prephysical etheric information matrices which in radionic theory are accepted as the fundamental bio-informational patterns from which all matter is organized. A couple of examples are included in Figures 1 and 2. These photos were taken from the 10,000 plate archive housed in Oxford, UK.

Having tested Judy's tumor for type we also tested to see how much the radiation therapy had been effective, and to what degree it would improve her condition in the near and intermediate future. The results were very negative on both counts. In the face of that information it would have been negligent and unethical to not introduce the other protocols detailed in this case history. If her tumor had appeared to be responding significantly, then we would have probably only administered the radiation remedy with the expectation that the tumor would improve without further intervention. However our analyses indicated that a full course of treatment would be needed to manage Judy's illness.

One might argue, for instance, that the real cause of the regression of Judy's tumor was the inclusion of the South American herbal compound (made from the bark of a tree) Pau D'arco. This preparation has a long-standing reputation for healing cancer in Brazil. Clearly, a traditional reputation is not proof of any kind of efficacy. However, it is true that Pfizer took out a patent in the early 70s on the extraction process of the active ingredient, Lapachol which has demonstrated anti-tumor activity under controlled conditions (I have misplaced my copy of the patent information so I cannot quote the exact date). Equally, it could be said that the use of a strict raw food/juice dietary protocol was the most important ingredient in the holistic therapy. This idea is supported by the recent publication of a report on the treatment of cancer by the Gerson Therapy, which appeared in *Alternative Therapies in Health and Medicine*, Vol. I, No.4, September 1995.

In our opinion, based on all the information we gathered from our analyses, and the subsequent MRI scans, we concluded that the synergistic effect of all of the therapies combined was what produced Judy's long term improvement. We can only attribute 6 percent of the long-term remission to the radiation therapy itself, and this reading is based on the fact that the radiation toxins were eliminated to a great extent by the use of radionically prepared homeopathic remedies.

Sometime in October 1996, Judy had an MRI scan because of headaches. It appears that the shunt is the cause of her problem, as it was years ago. There is now no evidence visible that she ever had a brain tumor. There is no scar tissue to be seen, except around the shunt. She remains in good health.

For the reader to accept that radionics played a major role in Judy's recovery she must weigh carefully the conventional objections as voiced by Dr. Rain, as well as deciding the merits of radionics and holistic therapy in this case. The final argument must ultimately revolve around the issue of radionics as a system of measurement i.e: can radionics accurately detect bio-energetic patterns of disease and appropriate remedies? If the answer is yes, then Judy's treatment was correct, ethical, and curative. If the answer is no, then Dr. Rain's conventional perspective might be correct.

Radionics has been very obscure in Western medicine for the last 80 years, even though there are tens of thousands of good quality case histories that strongly suggest its efficacy in human, animal, and agricultural situations.

Science cannot easily accept the idea that information can be detected by the human mind (in conjunction with specialized instruments) at a distance in a nonempirical manner. It is, therefore, understandable that Radionics has been dismissed almost on a *priori* basis and that no substantial funding has been allocated by university research departments, corporations, or other sources. This situation is starting to change in the last few years and it is expected that by the turn of the century a lot of new research will take place in this important field.

I hope that the above notes will serve to clarify our reasons for claiming that Radionics was (and still is) an effective complementary management tool in the case history presented.

Dr. Rain says that Radionics "appears most closely linked to the process of 'divining' for subterranean water." This is correct in so far as it goes. What is more important is that Radiesthesic activity is necessary in both Radionics and of water divining. Radiesthesia relies on the fact that the human nervous system is capable of registering subtle information obtained from sources remote from the operator that are not mediated by any of the five senses, and translating the incoming signals into measurable neuro-muscular responses. Radionics deals with the detection of distorted bio-information fields and patterns (that underlie all of physical reality) and the restoration of these intrinsic fields to their normal function.

Peter D. Moscow PhD, MDSRad , USA—*holistic@aol.com*
Tish Mosvold BA, USA
Brian Richards MD, Kent,
England Holistic Philosophy Consultants, Ltd
Louisville, Kentucky

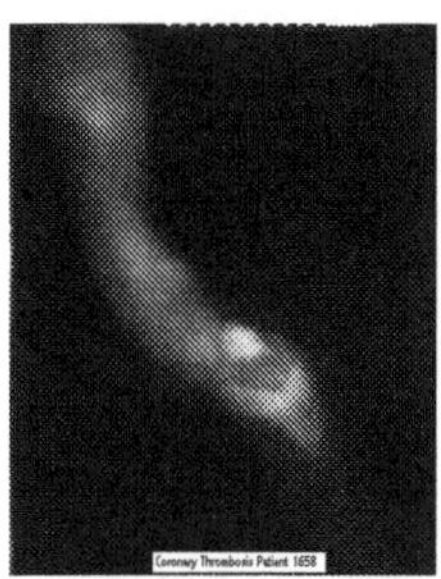

Figure 1

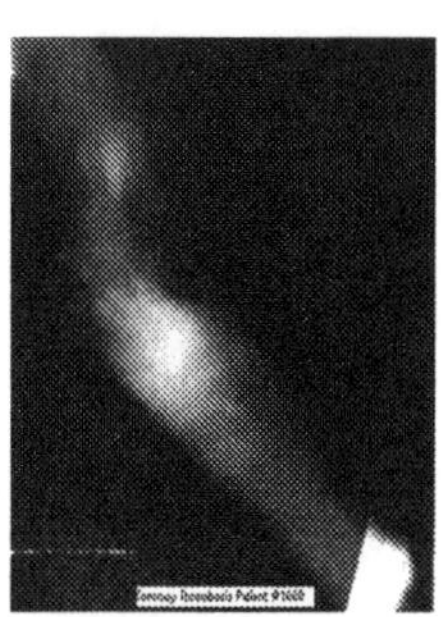

Figure 2

Two samples of Radionic photo camera. Both were taken at Barts Hospital in the UK on October 3, 1951 from blood samples drawn from two male patients. These photos are bio-informational in origin and are not produced using an optical apparatus. They were taken remotely from the patient. The photos are from the Delawarr archive, copyrighted, 1997, by Peter Moscow.

14

Paradigms of Agriculture

Arden B. Anderson, Ph.D.
Reprinted from the *J. of the U. S. Psychotronics Association*, No. 6, 1993, p. 17

Whatever our trade or hobby we function within a belief system that sets up rules and regulations by which we function. These are called paradigms. Any time there is progress one's paradigm must, and does, shift or expand. This allows one to perform in a progressive manner. Over the past 50 or more years agriculture has functioned, officially anyway, in a paradigm whose philosophy says that nature is flawed and must be controlled with man-made materials. Additionally, this paradigm placed agriculture in a state of constant war with nature, continuously battling pests and diseases.

A new paradigm is gaining in acceptance, due in no small part to solid science. To understand the unraveling of the old paradigm one must understand the fundamental aspects of both the old and the new. [Dr. Andersen is the author of the book, *The Anatomy of Life and Energy in Agriculture*, which expands on the bioenergetic theme developed in this paper. –Ed. note] In a phrase, one could say the old and the new compare like "singing monotone vs. making music."

In this discussion we will describe the two fundamental aspects of both "real world" and "conventional" agriculture: the model and the logic. We will correlate real world and conventional agricultural models and logic to linear and nonlinear physics and, finally, we will give field examples and show how science demands the practice of biological agriculture regardless of the methodology employed by the farmer.

Regardless of what we do in life there is a model of what we think things should be by which we judge our position, and there is the logic by which we solve problems and execute our actions. The model is essentially our standards and the logic is essentially our "science". In conventional agriculture the model has the following elements: 1) Food & fiber production is a war; 2) Nature is the adversary; 3) Insect, disease & weed pests are viewed as "normal" and "the wrath of God" on mankind; 4) Soil is inanimate; 5) Nature is random, unintelligent, and flawed; 6) Man knows a better way.

The logic of conventional agriculture – more properly described as the "Church of Agriculture" – has the following elements:

- ♦ Reductionistic: the whole equals the sum of its parts and nothing more, period;
- ♦ Linear: based upon straight line, in vitro observation and principle; what you get out is only equal to or less than what you put in – purely entropic;
- ♦ If all else fails, get a bigger hammer.

On the other hand, the model of "real world" agriculture has the following elements:

- Food & fiber production are a part of nature where peaceful coexistence is the rule;
- Nature is the guide and guardian;

- Insect & disease "pests" are nature's garbage collectors; weeds are nature's caretakers;
- Soil is "living" and dynamic, analogous to the ruminant digestive system;
- Nature is ordered, intelligent, and perfect;
- Nature is the example to follow-she possesses the ideal plant, soil, and animal characteristics.

Its logic contains the following elements: 1) Holistic – the whole is greater than the sum of the parts; 2) Non-linear – keyed to tuning, based upon harmonics and in vivo observation and principle; 3) Energetics is the fundamental basis of all physiology, animate or inanimate.

Paraphrasing the two systems, we could say that the conventional system is linear, functions with single variables and adheres strictly to the theory of relativity, has no harmonics, and is a driven system. In essence it is a messenger (symptom) oriented system. The real world system, on the other hand, is a non-linear system with many variables, making use of harmonics and is a functioning system. In essence it is a message (cause) oriented system.

The conventional system, being the old paradigm, is solidly embedded in the annals of modern society. It therefore, needs no further elaboration. The real world system, being the new paradigm, warrants further elaboration to firmly establish its right as successor. To do this we will begin with pointing out three landmark studies confirming Lakhovsky's and Abrams' contentions that biological systems are energetic and non-linear.

The first such study was done by Philip Callahan in 1956. (Dr. Callahan is the author of the book, *Tuning in to Nature: Solar Energy, Infrared Radiation and the Insect Communication System*, Devon-Adair, 1975.) Dr. Callahan showed that ants would home in on a candle flame when there was no barrier between the candle and the ant, and even when he placed a plastic sheet between the candle and the ant. When he placed a glass sheet between the candle and the ant, the ant did not home in on the candle. {1} Vlail Kaznacheyev demonstrated a similar phenomenon thousands of times in the 1970s with cultures in petri dishes showing that responses between the cultures were observed when quartz sheets separated the cultures but were not observed when glass sheets separated them.{2} Both of these studies demonstrated that ultra-violet and infrared radiation played a part in organism function because these radiations would pass quartz and plastic but not glass. [Dr. Beverly Rubik, another USPA presenter, discusses this experiment in her book, *Life at the Edge of Science.* Dr. Popp says that biophotons contain complex information about the whole cell. – Ed. note] Then, in the mid and late 1980s Dr. Fritz-Albert Popp demonstrated that photons, particularly ultra-violet photons, are the medium of biological communication. He also showed that these photons precede chemical and physical action and that any alteration or response observed in chemical or physical matter is preceded by alteration of the bio-photons associated with the matter.{3}

Popp's work was a magnificent capstone to the growing pyramid of proof that biological systems are fundamentally energetic. A simple side note to this premise is the "Polar Solar Phenomenon." It was found by North-Eastern University scientists that polar bears, via their hair, are about 90 percent efficient in utilizing ultra-violet radiation to maintain body heat.{4} The quirk in this finding lies in what is called the "ultra-violet catastrophe." This is the fact that the heat energy derived from ultra-violet radiation is very little –certainly not enough to maintain body heat of the polar bear, directly. Linear conversion simply does not account for the benefit gained by the polar bear. Only when non-linear considerations are taken into account can the polar bear phenomenon be explained. Biological cells are energy accumulators and converters, but they are non-linear in these capacities.{5} As such, they evolve and are subject to harmonics. The collection of ultra-violet radiation allows for a kindling effect of all the harmonics associated with the ultra-violet collection. The polar bear hair is a very good ultra-violet wave-guide.

13927-VALO

Warren Hamerman's biophysical studies lend further credibility to harmonic phenomena in living organisms with his layout of the musical scale harmonics correlated to biological processes. He found that DNA is the "tuning fork" for the rest of the biological systems (e.g., photosynthesis, mitosis, vision, respiration, protein synthesis, and neurotransmission). Most interesting is that the frequency of the DNA signal at 1.128 X 10^{15} Hz is *exactly* 42 octaves above middle C at 256 Hz on the piano. *In fact, most of the biological processes are 42 octaves above the piano keys.* Mitogenic radiation is 42 octaves above F at 341 Hz; photosynthesis action is 42 octaves above C at 128 Hz; biosphere maximum radiation is 42 octaves above C at 64 Hz.{6}

Harmonic observations are also found in monitoring the soil's magnetic susceptibility. The daily cycles fit into a moon cycle and distinguish themselves in direct proportion to the biological integrity of the soil. In other words as the soil becomes more biologically active the magnetic susceptibility cycles seem to become more pronounced and clear.{7}

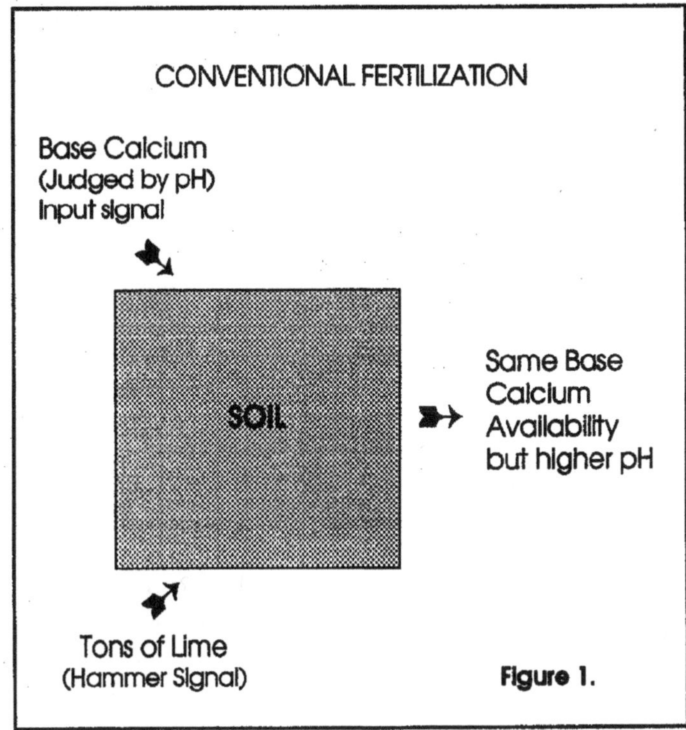
CONVENTIONAL FERTILIZATION
Base Calcium
(Judged by pH)
Input signal
SOIL
Same Base
Calcium
Availability
but higher pH
Tons of Lime
(Hammer Signal)
Figure 1.

From a physics viewpoint we can say that fertile soil is a living biological system. Plants are antennae plugged into the soil and function in proportion to the stability of the energetic characteristics of the soil. These soil characteristics are directly correlated to the biological integrity of the soil. Therefore, soil fertility is directly proportional to biological activity. This is further confirmed by the Russian work in soil microbiology covered in the book, *Soil Microorganisms and Higher Plants*.

The old paradigm of agriculture says that soil is inanimate and therefore linear. The new paradigm demanded by science, says that soil is biological and therefore *non-linear*. Non-linearity allows for some very interesting activities to take place, particularly pumped-phase conjugation, something Tom Bearden discusses regularly in relationship to military applications.

In the field we can compare conventional fertilization to real world fertilization using a physics model. In the conventional setup we have strictly a linear system and approach. Calcium will be used as the example. We take a conventional soil test and arrive at a soil pH. If the soil pH is below 6.5 the conventional recommendation is to add lime (the conventional calcium and/or magnesium source) to raise the pH to between 6.5 and 6.8. The amount required is arrived at by determining the soil cation exchange capacity and then calculating the number of pounds (usually tons) of lime, based upon the lime's neutralizing capacity, to raise the pH the desired amount. This looks real neat on paper and can be programmed into a computer and written in textbooks as something of real significance. It is great for paperwork, *but plants and microbes do not read books*. With this linear approach we have abase calcium level (pounds per acre) in the soil but that is considered secondary to the pH. As a result of pH several tons of lime are added to the soil. The net result is usually that pH rises but the pounds per acre of *available* calcium to the plant are only slightly different or often unchanged. People neglect even basic chemistry principles, which say that nutrient calcium is made soluble in acid solutions. Calcium hydroxide is that which becomes more soluble in alkaline solutions. The linear approach here completely misses the fact that pH is the *result* of nutrient interaction in the soil, not the cause. Therefore, the linear approach to fertilization may change the pH but not necessarily change the calcium available for agriculture (Figure 1).

If we look at the same situation from a non-linear perspective, we soil test and notice the pounds of calcium per acre which is available. We then select some material that will "tickle" the unavailable calcium (pump it) giving us a greater calcium availability in the end (Figure 2). This can be done simply, as with liquid calcium, or it can be done with a little more sophistication, as with sugar and vitamin B12 (Figure 3).

Conventional evaluation and solution (linear) is analogous to evaluating the attunement of a symphony using a decibel meter—the job is broader than the tool—and then attempting to alter this attunement by increasing the volume of the symphony.

The real world system, being non-linear, is multi-variable; requiring measuring tools and methodology of an equal variability. The key to attunement in this system is one's proper perspective, that being non-linear, one of a naturologist. We must learn to fertilize our non-linear system non-linearly. All fertilizers from compost to pure acid/caustic are potentially non-linear. The manner in which they are used determines whether one is dealing in a linear context or a non-linear context.

One of the most effective ways that soils, plants, and fertilizer materials can be evaluated with the new paradigm in mind is with the use of radionics. Unfortunately, radionics can and is often applied linearly. This methodology follows entropy and its logical conclusion. Correctly used, radionics would be applied non-linearly both in evaluation and treatment. This methodology follows neg-entropy and its logical conclusion. In a nutshell, one must be looking for causes, understanding the basic principles of the life processes, and then find solutions that aid, not circumvent, nature in the manifestation of the desired outcome. The practice of killing weeds, insects, and disease organisms is a linear approach whether using radionics or toxic chemicals. In some cases these seem to be appropriate practices so that one can at least harvest a crop to sell to the market, pay the bills, and come back again next season. If the nutritional cause of these symptoms is not addressed, one is strictly working within the old paradigm and regardless of all the treatment, sophisticated gadgetry, and "Hail Mary's" entropy will prevail because one is working in the entropic side of physics. War is inherently entropic and war between man and nature is the foundation of the old paradigm.

As an agricultural consultant, I am regularly asked for my advice in reference to the many instruments and pieces of equipment available on the market today. This seems to be a touchy subject for many people. My opinion is that most all of these devices are valid, working instruments, but they are not magic bullets. If you have ascended to the enlightenment of a true breatharian, then I would concede that you would not require anything but a command to raise a perfectly sound crop. For those who still require physical nourishment for themselves, I find it also necessary for them to apply physical nourishment to their soils and crops. Any energetic enhancement that might be done, I find, is directly proportional to the person's true intent, understanding, and enlightenment. The better one understands the natural processes the better one is equipped to affect the subtle energies of those processes.

There is an old story which seems to be the epitome of linear perception, about six blind men each of whom attempted to describe an elephant. Each one, however, contacted a different part of the elephant and, consequently, each described the elephant differently. One man contacted the elephant's leg and described the elephant as a tree; another the elephant's trunk and proclaimed a large snake; another contacted the elephant's ear and described the elephant as a great fan; another contacted the tail and described the elephant as a hanging rope; another the elephant's side and contended a great wall; and finally, the sixth man contacted the elephant's tusk and described the elephant as a spear.{8}

Each description, from each man's viewpoint, was accurate—but none described a *real* elephant. The whole is much greater than the sum of its parts.

The moral of the story for this discussion is that the old paradigm, though accurate from its individual perspectives, has missed the true portrait of agriculture and all living systems. It has a flawed model and logic, rooted in entropy, and therefore will inevitably run down. The new paradigm allows us to get at the causes of disharmony by selecting and using the proper tools, materials, and methodology for the attunement of nature's symphony.

13927-VALO

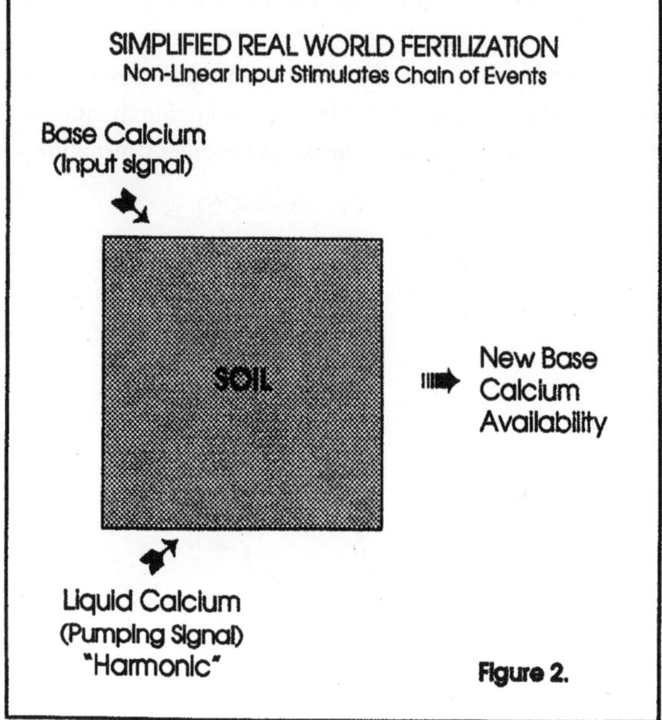
SIMPLIFIED REAL WORLD FERTILIZATION
Non-Linear Input Stimulates Chain of Events
Base Calcium
(Input signal)
SOIL
New Base
Calcium
Availability
Liquid Calcium
(Pumping Signal)
"Harmonic"
Figure 2.

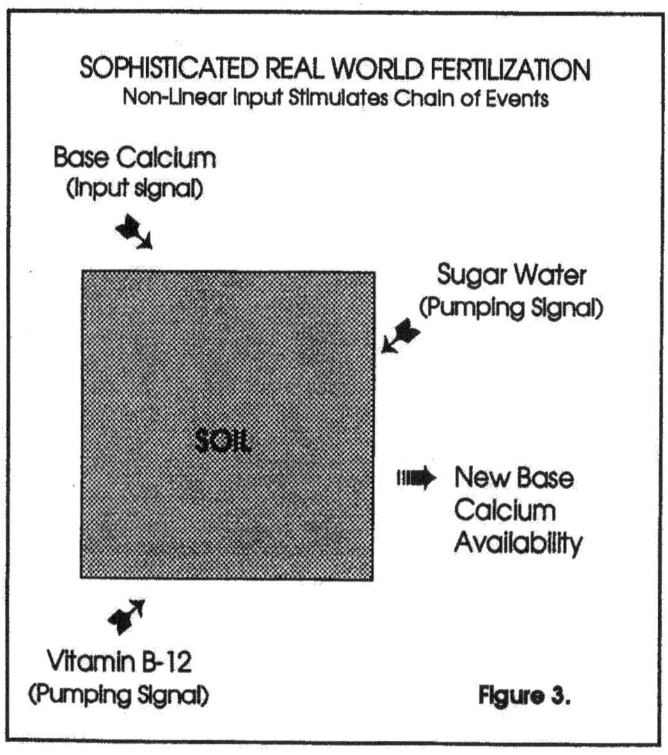
SOPHISTICATED REAL WORLD FERTILIZATION
Non-Linear Input Stimulates Chain of Events
Base Calcium
(Input signal)
Sugar Water
(Pumping Signal)
SOIL
New Base
Calcium
Availability
Vitamin B-12
(Pumping Signal)

Figure 3.

References

1. Conversations with Philip S. Callahan, Gainesville, Florida.
2. Bearden, T. E., *Gravitobiology: A New Biophysics*. DAS, Huntsville, 1989.
3. Lillge, Wolfgang, "New Technologies Hold Clue to Curing Cancer," *2lst Century Science & Technology*. 21st Century Science Associates, Washington, July-August 1988, pp. 34+.
4. "The Polar Solar Phenomenon," *Compressed Air.* Compressed Air Magazine, Washington, February 1990, pp. 8+.
5. Nieper, Hans A., *Revolution in Technology, Medicine, and Society*. Druchhaus Neue Stalling, Oldenburg, F.R.G., 1983.
6. Hamerma, Warren J., "The Musicality of Living Processes," *21st Century Science & Technology*. 21st Century Science Associates, Washington, March-April 1989, pp. 32+.
7. Andersen, Arden B., "Managing Electromagnetic Technology to aid in Soil Regeneration," *Management of Technology II: Proceedings of the Second International Conference on Management of Technology.* Industrial Engineering and Management Press, Norcross, Georgia, 1990, p. 1269.
8. Felleman, Hazel, *The Best Loved Poems of the American People*. Doubleday & Company, fuc., Garden City, N. y ., 1936.

15

Radionics in New Brunswick Forests, 1976 Experiments

By Andrew Michrowski, Ph.D. – *pacenet@canada.com*
Planetary Association for Clean Energy
Ottawa, Ontario

Proceedings of the U.S. Psychotronics Association Conference, U. of Wisconsin, 1995

The reason why these radionic experiments ever took place was that while I was Chief Planner with Indian Affairs, flying across Canada on a special assignment, "trouble-shooting" missions, for my Minister, Jean Chrétien, now Prime Minister of Canada. I happened to sit next to the only woman Senator at that time in Canada on the plane back to Ottawa from Edmonton. She was very distressed about spruce budworm infestation conditions in New Brunswick forests. I told her "I have learnt in my research that there is a very successful method of taking care of infestation and pests. It is called radionics." After learning about the mechanisms and efficiency of radionics, she said, "This is incredible! I'll be happy to have you at the Senate. One of the Senators is a scientist, and he's quite respected, and is key in developing the science policy for the Canadian Government."

[This is the first time in history that radionics has received a *government endorsement* of its efficacy. It is impossible to overstate the significance of this well-executed experiment for that reason. –Ed. note]

This invitation gave me an opportunity to prepare myself better to bring forth information about Dr. Albert Abrams and T. Galen Hieronymus, radionics pioneers, and to propose that radionics be tried on a very large commercial forest there.

The next step was a radionic operator, as I had no practice with radionic broadcasting. Lo and behold, one of our scientific network's Nikola Tesla enthusiasts at that time who was trying to have various government agencies and utilities look into Tesla's technologies – happened to be quite knowledgeable in radionics. He worked with such individuals as Bob Beutlich, Treasurer of the United States Psychotronics Association (offspring of the former United States Radionics Association) and the people at Acres USA, an alternative agriculture network. He also was in good terms with the late Frances Farrelly, of St. Petersburg, Florida, who had an extremely good track record in applying radionic treatments. The Senators, after I made my presentation, decided to make arrangements with the wealthy New Brunswick family, the Irvings because they owned those infested forests – to ensure that we would carry out the radionic experiment.

In any case, the head of the group of Senators, the late Senator Chesley W. Carter, from Newfoundland, who eventually became the founder of our association, made all the arrangements.

First, flights were made over the forests, and good aerial photographs were taken of the infested area. These photographs, according to a protocol developed by Frances Farrelly, were partially marked over in squares with red markers, in a checkerboard fashion, leaving the remaining normally exposed as squares of spruce trees. The red, marked-over squares would not be able to receive radionic information – and thus could not be "treated", and would serve as controls of untreated acreage. One such photo was sent off to a radionics operator located in Chicago, Illinois, for use to identify and treat the Irving forest lot, several thousands of kilometers away.

Second, the question was to determine which treatment agent would be used for transmitting to the spruce trees, to invigorate them? Now, we had a very bad situation, to which we were drawn at a late stage of damage. There was a lot of spruce budworm, *Choristoneura fumiferana*, around, and they were mature. Trees were being eaten very rapidly and there was very little time left to save something of the forest. The top priority was to choose the most appropriate single agent to alleviate this crisis. Now, Ted Klich, my Toronto colleague, interested in Radionics, in Toronto, decided on an insect hormone, *Juvabione*, which forestry research officials in Northern Ontario observed was a powerful ovacide (egg killer). It is a hormone that is developed naturally by white spruce as a protection against insects.

From June 11 to 13, 1976, the first radionics experiment was conducted, using *Juvabione*, on about 200 trees. This activity was, thanks to the Senator, supervised by the top professor of forestry in the University of New Brunswick as well as by officials of the J. D. Irving Ltd. (Woodlands Division). A dual radionic strategy was employed: (a) *strengthen tree vitality*, and (b) *devitalize target insects without affecting their species' predators*.

The results were quite stunning: the number of spruce budworm was the same in both untreated red-marked and in radionically treated areas yet the spruce budworm no were longer eating the needles!

The first results were tallied in a rather comprehensive report by the independent evaluator, Maritime Pest Control, managed by Professor Dr. N. R. Brown, of the University of New Brunswick. In the treated areas, anywhere from 6 – 16% of the needles were actually eaten. In the untreated areas, 50 – 85% were eaten. The benefit of radionics was noticeable. Though this treatment was only a one-shot affair, done over a period of ½ hour or so, at 24-hour intervals, 3 times – the results were remarkable, causing excitement among the senators following this event.

Naturally, the J. D. Irving Ltd the managers responsible for the forest, David Oxley and Murray Alexander were also excited and pleased. They were promptly advised by their brass to "keep your mouth shut, and this never happened." Senator Carter considered this admonition to be consistent with the company's decision not to pay for the successful results on their $17,000,000 forest in order to proceed with selling an applying a product the company sold in the province, toxic *Fenitrothion*.

This radionic experiment incurred the cost of aerial photography over the infested forests, the contracting of qualified and credible scientists to verify the results on the ground, followed by recognized forestry science peer review. There was the supplementary cost of administrating co-ordination with the company, the field crews, Frances Farrelly and an agricultural radionics operator located in Chicago, who insisted on remaining anonymous.

So the next step was to do a test outside the jurisdiction of the Irving people. A forest chosen was the University of New Brunswick lot, mostly thanks to the pressure applied by the senators, who really wanted to see that spruce budworm pupal phase taken care of too.

The second (July 5, 1976) experiment's scope was to abort the next insect cycle by ensuring that the eggs would not hatch. The radionic emission was specifically targeted at the species only. To assess the results, the Canadian Forestry Service egg mass counts protocol was applied, with the oversight of Dr. Frederick Conron of the Quebec bureau of the Service. The results were, per 102 metres on the treated blocks, 63, 62 and 97. On the adjacent, radionically-untreated block areas were: 1, 308, 273, 156, 83, 194, 326, 197, 511, 163 and 654. These results were also very promising in favour of radionics.

The reaction was: "Heavens! We get such good results. The Federal Government should get involved in and promote radionics, instead of thinking about chemical spraying, or to use bacteria and sex attractions."

The egg counts for the spruce budworm were the lowest counts anywhere in Canada at that time. Ted Klich felt that they would have been better had the experiments not been conducted in haste.

There was local press coverage of these successes, again at the prompting of senators. Nobody in his or her right mind wanted to get involved in this – what horror and fear that was initiated by these results. Officials wondered, "What are we going to do?" At the time, the Irving family owned much in New Brunswick: television, radio, newspapers, the province's only daily, the entire petroleum industry, almost the entire forest industry, almost the entire fishing industry, so if you are going to irritate the Irving's, you might as well move out of the province, or even, if possible, several provinces away! Only those in secure political or federal posts were able to express their minds. Senators, nominated until retirement could withstand any Irving opposition unscathed.

So people were recoiled from these results. However, one journalist, Jon Everett did dare to write for the independent Kings County Record (Sussex, New Brunswick) about the successful radionic experiments. As a matter of fact, that journalist, after publishing this, had to leave the province, to his great dismay, and then exiled himself out of Canada! But at least the results were left for the public record.

In the article, Senator Chesley W. Carter observes, "the cost of the radionics method is only a fraction of the cost of chemical spraying and the potential savings alone justifies a fuller investigation into the radionics method. If there is truth in it, sooner or later, the truth will come out, because the truth cannot be suppressed forever."

The article ends, however, with the concept that the theory of radionics has been known for years, but it was discredited 50 years ago. "Like electricity, no one can explain it."

A typical reaction of the provincial authorities is that of Vincent MacLean, Nova Scotia Minister of Lands and Forests, while admitting that his province, a neighbour of New Brunswick had decided against the use of chemical insecticides and that they are "doubly interested in any or in all acceptable protection alternatives," the Ministry relies mainly on the federal Canadian Forestry Service, "for research into protection and control of forest insects and disease." They were leaving up to another level of government to act on this breakthrough. This is quite typical. There are many letters of this nature, all indicating the inability of local government to implement the positive nature of radionics.

Another letter was written by Senator Carter, who was clearly pro-radionics, to Roméo LeBlanc, future Governor General of Canada, and Environment Minister. Carter observes, "it is my understanding that the experiment was started too late in the year to achieve maximum success," yet it "*was already extremely successful*." The line of thinking suggests that the radionics method would have been more successful had all the protocols and appropriate timing been implemented.

Senator Carter continues, "The reports, some of which I have seen, indicate that there was marked improvement." "The principle of radionics is not new. It was very much in vogue 50—75 years ago (written in 1977) and was discarded because scientific theory and technology had not advanced to the point where it could be understood. Consequently, it was looked upon as being more in the realm of magic, and people tended to make exaggerated claims for it, which could not be substantiated. . . . However, modern science has verified that the theory on which it was based is sound, and since it offers a viable alternative to chemical spraying, I feel that the use of radionics as an alternative should be more fully explored."

Among the other senators who took considerable interest in radionics for a long time were of course, Senator Margaret Norrie, the enthusiastic lady I met on the plane from the Prairies, who started all of this, and Senator Bruce McCallum, who was considered to be the most senior and respected senator from the maritime provinces.

Here we are, almost twenty years later, and it is clear that radionics is not applied in Canada. The people who were closely related to episode, the senators and scientists have retired from the stage. Mr. Klich is reluctant to be involved with radionics anymore. In the late 1970s, the chemical industry lobby was able to convince the Canadian Forestry Service not to be getting involved in radionics. It made sure that money would spent on spraying – which by the way have killed many children and adults in New Brunswick, and became a very serious problem. They made sure that radionics, due to its novelty and simplicity would look very ridiculous, bordering on magic. So I feel that this is a tragic outcome for such a promising safe technique.

Let us look what Ted Klich learned about radionics prior to this over-reaction. Naturally, he was very elated with the New Brunswick results. He experimented with various radionic treatments, and succeeded saving individual and groups of Dutch Elm trees that were being destroyed by a fungus. The species is pretty well extinct by now in much of Canada. His results were remarkable because nothing seems to work against Dutch Elm fungus.

Ted Klich observed, after extensive trials, that:

1) Radionic treatments using the complementary rate (that cancel out the basic frequency rate of the insect, or fungus) were more effective than treatments using only a reagent in the treatment.
2) Treatments against insects and fungus were found to be more effective if put broadcast for 30 minutes or so, and repeated at 24-hour intervals and repeated 3 or 4 times. The decreasing vitality of the insect and fungus follows a step function with some bounce-back occurring once treatment stops.
3) Specifically targeted fungus colonies are not exterminated. Instead, they stop growing and expanding, and then decay

rapidly. This sequence is corroborated by an interruption of the developmental stages of the Spruce Budworm.

4) Radionic treatments must be carefully designed for proper protocol.

Experimental protocol must also ensure that the results will be accepted and not dismissed merely an anecdote. The New Brunswick experiments were done properly. The checkerboard pattern ruled out the possibility of wind as being a contributing factor for success. When you go along a lane and you have trees in bad shape on one side and on the other side in good shape, and you see this 4 or 5 times, you have a strong case

We must remember that It is difficult to foresee progress in radionics via the normal channels. I have tried some years ago to steward institutional acceptance of radionics when an Ottawa colleague, a microbiologist, found a laboratory post within the Canadian Forestry Service. Her assignment was to evaluate the different pest management systems. The fashionable tendency was at the time to go for sex attractants and like sophisticated systems. So I suggested to her, "Couldn't you at least add on radionics as an alternative? And here are all the facts from our New Brunswick experience." By the next day, after consulting with her supervisor, she came back and stated that this was not a right idea, and resigned from our learned society! This example only indicates how preconceived notions in the scientific community determine what is and what is not acceptable to study. It's a very difficult hurdle. We no longer have people like Senator Carter to ensure follow-up by government bodies.

However it is true that back in 1970s, there was a bad attitude towards radionics, because of the *DDT* lobby, [See the full-page ad in *TIME*, June 30, 1947 entitled "DDT is good for me-e-e!" by Pennsalt Chemicals. It wasn't until the 1980's that the U.S. discontinued the use of DDT after *biological magnification* was proven to be a serious threat to mammals. Everyone born in the U.S. after 1946 carries DDT in their bodies.—Ed.

note] *Myrex* and like companies, who were stamping out radionics, not only in Canada, but also in the United States, too. But that's changed now. They're out of business now. The U.S. Government, the U.S.D.A., and the Canadian authorities have put them out of business, because of all of the pesticides that were killing the birds, the eagles, and the children, and all of that. Now these agencies now are looking at alternatives. It has been suggested that since the governments won't do it, maybe the people need to take responsibility. If we could get some practitioners who understand what's going on and have a little group, and everybody tune in their instrument to take care of their particular problem.

But we must face the reality that the pest management alternatives that tend to be examined by the authorities and the hi-tech investment community are still enshrouded in vested interests. For example, a university will have a laboratory with good microbiologists, who are strongly motivated to show off how gifted they are in making fantastic sex attractants. Then there will be competition between 2 and 3 universities all vying to develop the most marketable, and patentable process. In such an environment, you cannot visualize world-class academics competing for prima donna spotlight on the radionics platform. Radionics is too simple. It does not require any genius to operate. Even I, after only 3 hours of getting a handle on a Hieronymus machine, was stunned how precise were the results obtained in my research. The technology is too simple and personal for a worldview that delights in the decadence of complexity! Today's society is not geared for easy things.

Radionics is an easy process. When you work with farmers and people in the field – you have to make it simple. Radionics was used among the Pennsylvania Dutch farmers and Quakers. They need a simple process, and so it is. You just put a witness on the unit and broadcast it. And that is as simple as can be.

VEGETABLE WEEVIL ADULTS ON LEAF

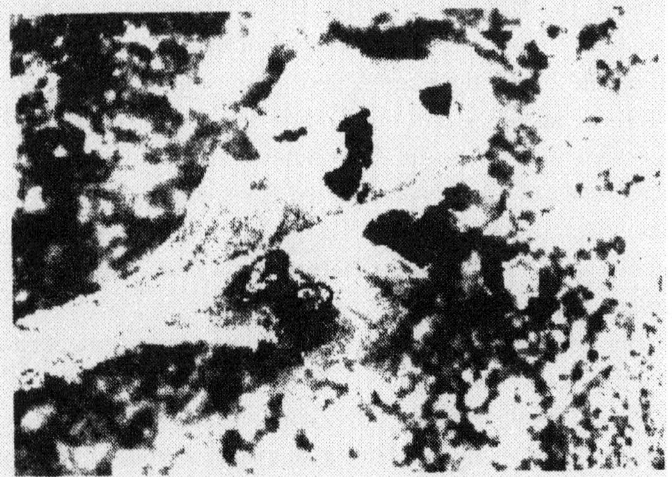

Photo by: Mr. David Jones, UGA Extension Entomologist

VEGETABLE WEEVIL LARVA ON TOBACCO LEAF

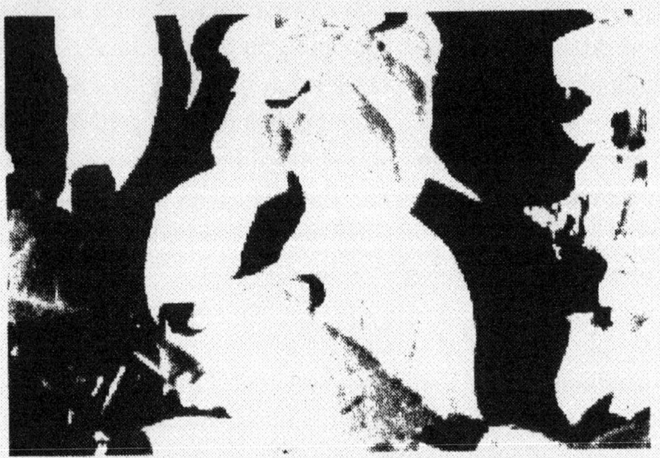

Photo by: Mr. David Jones, UGA Extension Entomologist

THE SENATE
CANADA

Ottawa, March 7, 1977.

The Hon. Roméo LeBlanc, P.C.,M.P.,
Minister of Fisheries and the Environment,
House of Commons,
O t t a w a.

Dear Roméo,

RE: The spruce budworm problem
<u>Hazards of chemical spraying</u>

I am in receipt of a letter from the Editor of the King's County Record of Sussex, New Brunswick, re the above.

It appears that the main chemical used in spraying the forests for protection against the budworm is known as fenitrothion which is manufactured in Japan and not licensed for any purpose in the United States. Canada's National Research Council has officially reported (publication No. 14104, NRCC) that this chemical has never been properly tested and that its full potential for harm, by itself, or in combination with other chemicals is not known.

The fact that several children in New Brunswick, between the ages of 8 and 11, have contacted Reye's Syndrome (a brain disease akin to encephalitis), while the disease is unknown in the other Maritime provinces, Newfoundland and the Eastern States, raises a grave suspicion that it could be due to the chemical used in spraying the budworm.

However, the letter from the Editor of The King's County Record emphasizes the point that the chemical used in spraying the budworm is also responsible for killing numerous birds of various species which are protected under the Migratory Birds Treaty to which Canada is a signatory. It appears therefore that the use of this chemical in New Brunswick is a violation of the Migratory Birds Convention Act, the enforcement of which is the responsibility of the federal government.

This raises the question as to why the federal government is not enforcing the Act in this instance and the corollary as to what is being done by federal and provincial governments to find an alternative to chemical spraying.

... 2

In this connection I should like to bring to your attention the possibility of solving the spruce budworm problem by means of radionics.

As I understand it, radionics operates on the theory that every plant (indeed every living thing) has its own characteristic vibration by which it receives or gives off energy. Radionics employs a device which pin-points the wave lengths and frequency of the plant's vibrations and transmits energy using the earth as a conductor. The plant, acting as a tuned receiver, picks up this energy which reinforces its vitality and its natural immunity against disease and insects.

This does not kill the spruce budworm but it makes the plant or the tree a much less attractive host for the insects and consequently the insects avoid them.

It was my understanding that an experiment employing the radionics method was carried out last year under the auspices of the University of New Brunswick on certain sections of forests owned by the K.C. Irving Interests. The experiment was started too late in the year to achieve maximum success, but the reports, some of which I have seen, indicate that there was marked improvement.

The principle of radionics is nothing new. It was very much in vogue 50 to 75 years ago and it was discarded because scientific theory and technology had not advanced to the point where it could be understood. Consequently, it was looked upon more as being in the realm of magic and people tended to make exaggerated claims for it which could not be substantiated. Quacks use it as a cure-all and in the hands of wrong people it was used for other wrong purposes so that in time it became discredited.

However, modern science has verified that the theory on which it is based is sound and since it offers a viable alternative to chemical spraying, I feel that the use of radionics as an alternative should be more fully explored.

For further information I would refer you to Dr. Edward J. Klich of Klimac Associates Limited, 2 Demaris Avenue, Downsview, Ontario, M3N 1M1. His telephone number is: 416/633-2215.

Trusting that you will look into this matter as well as the violation of the Migratory Birds Convention.

Yours sincerely,

C.W.C.

C. W. Carter.

KLIMAC MOTH REPELLANT TEST JULY 5/1976

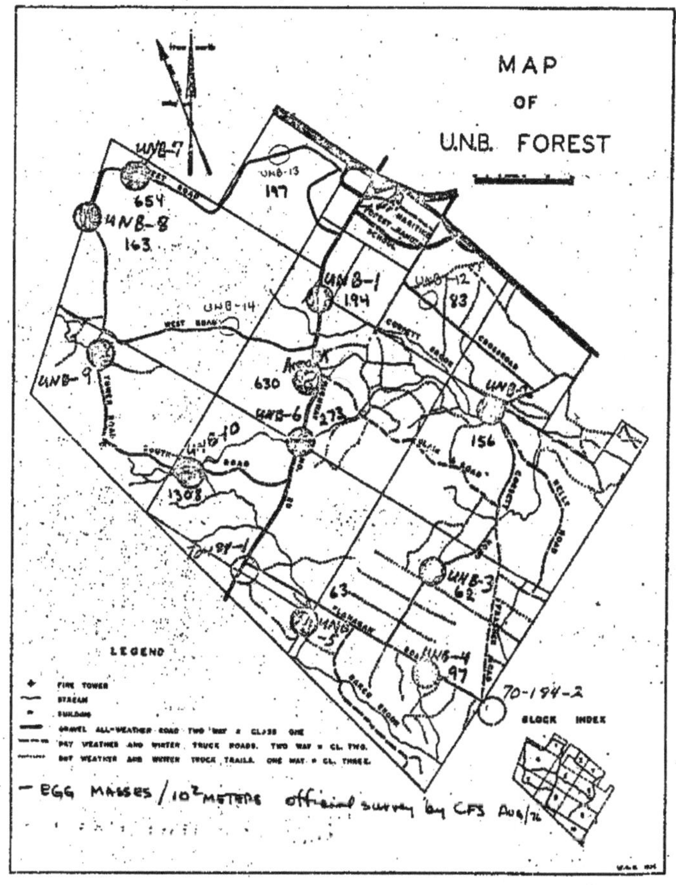

The Kings County Record,
Sussex, N.B. Wednesday, July 13, 1977

Radionics: here's what tests showed

By JON EVERETT

A report on radionics testing in Kings County in 1976 indicates that the experimental treatment of trees affected by spruce budworm had some influence on the trees.

The report was prepared for the radionics company, Klimac Management Associates Ltd, of Downsview, Ont., by Maritime Pest Control Ltd., of Fredericton, and made available to The Record. The report was written by N. R. Brown, of Fredericton, a University of New Brunswick forestry professor.

Radionics is based on the theory that plants emit distinctive impulse the same way that radiation impulses are emitted throughout nature. A machine pinpoints these wave lengths and the frequency of the plant's vibrations and transmits energy using the earth as a conductor. The plant, acting as a tune receiver, is strengthened against disease, or, in this case, the attacks of the budworm.

The original plan was to conduct the tests in an area located at White's Mountain near Sussex, made available by J. D. Irving Ltd. But on May 25, 1976, the area was sprayed with fenitrothion so it was abandoned.

Next 150 acres located on Route 880, Lester Road, near Berwick, were selected. After an initial malfunction of equipment on May 30, T. J. Klich, an officer of the Klimac Company, reported treatment had taken place June 11-13 on some 200 trees.

The report concludes that while spruce budworm populations were roughly equal on both trees treated with radionics and those in the "control" or untreated areas, the treated trees were able to produce better foliage.

Specifically eight trees from each of the treatment and control areas were sampled. The report said: "For eight trees in each there was no appreciable difference in spruce budworm populations".

Estimates of defoliation in trees sampled were divided into 10 categories depending on the percentage of defoliation. The categories were: O — no defoliation; T — one to 5 per cent defoliation; one-six to 15 per cent; two-16 to 25 per cent; three-26 to 35 per cent; four-36 to 45 per cent; five-46 to 55 per cent; six-56 to 65 per cent; Seven-66 to 75 per cent; eight-76 to 85 per cent; nine-86 to 95 per cent; 10a-96 to 100 per cent (needles almost all missing but some shoot axils remaining); and 10b-96 to 100 per cent (nearly all needles and axils destroyed).

The report said: "Despite similar spruce budworm population of the treatment and control areas, current defoliation on the trees sampled in the treatment area ranged from Category 1 ((6 to 15 per cent) to Category 4 with two trees in Category 1. On the control area, current defoliation on the trees sampled ranged from Category 5 to Category 8 with five trees in Category 5 and one each in Categories 6, 7 and 8.

"Vigor or recovery on the trees sampled in the treatment area was fair on seven of the trees and good on one tree. All eight trees sampled on the control area showed poor recovery as compared

MINISTER OF LANDS AND FORESTS
PROVINCE OF NOVA SCOTIA

P. O. Box 698
Halifax, Nova Scotia
B3J 2T9
March 18, 1977

Honourable C. W. Carter
The Senate
Ottawa, Canada

Dear Senator Carter:

Thank you for your letter of March 6, 1977, concerning the spruce budworm problem.

Since the Government of Nova Scotia has decided against the use of chemical insecticides in 1977, we are doubly interested in any and all acceptable protection alternatives.

In this connection I find your comments and suggestion concerning radionics most interesting. Accordingly, I am passing your letter on to my Department officials for follow-up. I should mention that we rely mainly on the Canadian Forestry Service, Department of Fisheries and Environment for research into protection and control of forest insects and diseases. Accordingly, I would expect that our follow-up will be through Canadian Forestry Service.

Yours sincerely,

Vincent J. MacLean.

13927-VALO

16

Extremely Low Frequency Magnetic Fields and EEG Entrainment: A Psychotronic Warfare Possibility?

Robert C. Beck, B.E., D.Sc.
Annual Conference of the U. S. Psychotronics Association, 1978, Dayton, OH

Introduction

Well-documented clinical research suggests that between 25% and 75% of human and animal subjects exhibit psychophysiological sensitivity to magnetic and electrical fields in the extreme low frequency (ELF) ranges corresponding to brain-wave spectra. Neuronal synchronization/desynchronization and brainwave entrainment can be demonstrated clinically in cats, monkeys and human sensitives in the presence of ELF oscillations of both natural and man-made signals, including pulse-modulated radio frequency carriers.

There is additional evidence that the naturally occurring earth-ionosphere cavity oscillations (known since 1952 as the "Schumann resonance") can affect moods, states of consciousness and health cycles of all life forms. Prior to 1975 or 1976, the Soviets began transmitting pulsed electromagnetic signals over broad frequency ranges (from approximately 4 MHz to beyond 18 MHz) of sufficient power (measured at 40 MW peak) to disrupt lawful radio communications globally.

Fundamental frequencies of the higher harmonics as well as the pulse repetition rates (of 5 to 15 Hz) of the Soviet EM transmissions fall precisely within the "window" of neuronal psychoactivity and have been observed to alter human EEG traces. Speculation arises as to whether this potentially devastating problem is intentional or an unfortunate side effect of the Soviet's highly advanced global radar holographic imaging technology and undersea magnetic communication pulses.

This personal communication is an overview of my investigation and discoveries in this area since 1970, a discussion of my instrumentation approaches, and projections for possible future research. Brain-wave entrainment can be demonstrated electroencephalographically when subjects are in the vicinity of oscillations in the frequency range of approximately 3-20 Hz at intensities below 100 nT (nanoteslas), where 1 Tesla = 10,000 Gauss. [This is also naturally true for those living in the country away from electropollution because human magnetoencephalogaphic (MMG) fields are in the *picotesla* range, making the earth's 8-10 Hz Schumann resonance field about 1000 times stronger than 8-10 Hz alpha brainwaves, causing natural entrainment and accentuated alpha rhythm. – Ed. note]

ELF fields of 6.67 Hz, 6.26 Hz and lower tend to produce symptoms of confusion, anxiety, depression, tension, fear, mild nausea and headaches, cholinergia, arthritis-like aches, insomnia, extended reaction times, hemispheric EEG desynchronization, and many other vegetative disturbances. H and B field (magnetic vector) oscillations of 7.8, 8.0, and 9.0 Hz produce anxiety-relieving and stress-reducing effects that mimic some meditative states. It has been speculated that frequencies in this range may be the universally permeating "clock frequencies" or carriers on which "mind" or "consciousness" states can be impressed and in which they may interact with other life-forms in the nebulous realms of ESP psychotronics, distant healing, radiesthesia, and related paranormal, but anecdotal phenomena.

Coherent ELF energies have the unique and interesting property of almost loss less propagation within the earth-ionosphere cavity waveguide, and attenuation of these signals due to distance from transmitter sites is negligible. Power losses are 0.8 dB per Mm (million meters). The magnetic vectors, unlike electrical (E-wave) components, permeate any substance and cannot be effectively shielded, even by iron, mu-metal, lead, copper, "Faraday cages," etc. [Dr. Bob Beck demonstrated this Faraday cage penetration of ELF more than once to industrial SQUID "experts" and even showed how to detect such ELF waves without a SQUID. See his amazing 1985 USPA presentation and slideshow. – Ed. note]

The established physics of radio propagation therefore suggests that vast geographical areas can be readily mood-manipulated by transmissions of EM energy within the earth-ionosphere cavity waveguide.

The "Luxemburg effect," by which a transmitter of relatively low power, fed to an antenna array producing a circularly polarized signal, can "piggyback" to any preexisting RF energy source and produce disturbances of the ionosphere at any frequency desired (which then "modulates" all other energies within that waveguide), was discovered accidentally in 1938. It is fully described in the literature of 40 years ago, but has probably been forgotten or is overlooked by today's technologists.

History and Background

My personal interest in EEG and consciousness dates back to 1969, when I became fascinated with the (re)discoveries of Joe Kamiya and the conscious control of brain waves through biofeedback. I developed sensitive and reliable, monopolar instrumentation for this purpose under the Alpha-Metrics trademark.

In the course of travelling, lecturing teaching classes, and demonstrating this EEG equipment, and because one of my personal interest was in parapsychology and consciousness research I had the unique opportunity (and reliable instrumentation at hand) to make electroencephalographic recordings of the brainwave patterns of a number of truly exceptional subjects in the United States and Hawaii, who were famous or had established reputations as psychics, healers, shamans, dowsers, etc. Since I, had a wealth of personal contacts in both the scientific establishment and the "psychic underground," I was fortunate to be allowed to meet and to wire up and instrument a cross section of "sensitives" from vastly different disciplines, ranging from charismatic Christian faith healers to an authentic Hawaiian kahuna, to practitioners of wicca, Santeria, radiesthesia and radionics, to seers, ESP "readers " and psychics.

A striking number of these authentic "sensitives" exhibited a nearly identical EEG signature when reporting that they were in their "working" state of consciousness, a state persisting from one to several seconds intermittently during the "altered state of consciousness" phase of the paranormal activity. The signal appeared to be an almost pure sine wave of up to 25 mV (read monopolar, frontal to occipital, midline) and 7.8-8.0 Hz in frequency (on the "alpha-theta" borderline). This serendipitous discovery was unexpected, in that—although the subjects were practising opposing disciplines, and came from totally disparate teachings and held opposing viewpoints, and would barely acknowledge the existence or authenticity of practitioners outside their belief systems—they all appeared to be marching to the sound of the same "cosmic drummer" when in an altered state of consciousness. After replicating this observation a number of times at sites thousands of miles apart, the obvious question arose that if these exceptional people, unknown to one another, were falling into the same "cosmic consciousness" mode, what or where was the signal to which their brain waves became entrained? What was the "drummer"? Was there a "clock" or "synchronizing" signal present?

In 1952, physicist Schumann postulated mathematically that our earth and ionosphere constituted a cavity waveguide whose physical constants and magnetic field would oscillate at a resonant frequency identical to the range of human brain waves. [W.O. Schumann published in the German journal, *Z. Naturforsch*, 72, 149, 1952, "On the radiation free self-oscillation of a conducting sphere, which is surrounded by an air layer and an ionospheric shell" –Ed note] In 1962, the National Bureau of Standards division of Radio Propagation reported the actual physical detection and instrumental recordings of these signals; and, as predicted, tracings were indistinguishable from encephalographic recordings from human brain waves. This newly discovered phenomenon was dubbed the "earth brain wave. "

Since there is a pronounced node in these "Schumann resonances" at 7.8-8.0 Hz, the question of possible EEG and ELF interconnectedness appeared to be an irresistible area for investigation.

In 1973, a professional coil fabricator duplicated the "Schumann pickup" (described on p. 313 of the *Journal of Research of the National Bureau of Standards, Division of Radio Propagation.* V. 66, 3, May-June 1962), and I perfected an extremely low-noise, highly filtered amplifier capable of recording and displaying the naturally occurring magnetic oscillations surrounding our biosphere.

My intention was to recontact as many of the "sensitive" subjects from my first study as was feasible and this time to make simultaneous EEG and ELF records and compare the signals for frequency and phase coherency. This was done on a more limited scale than in the original investigation. In a few instances, careful analysis revealed episodes of absolute brain-wave entrainment during the brief seconds when sensitives reported being in their altered states of consciousness. Unexpected variables emerged, such as reliability factors dependent on lunar phases and time of day.

This study was extended to test the theory that if a very small percentage of subjects, by virtue of hereditary factors, religious or metaphysical disciplines, or meditative practices, had sensitized some portion of their minds or brains to act as extremely sensitive "dual-conversion superheterodyne receivers," it might be possible to sense remotely, amplify, and display this real-time drummer." The Schumann magnetic oscillation, to less sensitive subjects (whose brains were as unresponsive and unselective as a crystal set) "so that, they too could" mimic the highly organized "psychic" abilities of the trained "seer."

Late in 1973, apparatus was built for pulsing a miniature lamp held in an empty eyeglass frame to be"a real-time photic stimulus that would cause an evoked potential, in step with the ELF"cosmic drummer" This was moderately promising but only marginally successful because of the individually variable delay-line (of about 100 ms) between the onset of the stimulus and its response.

The next effort at inducing psychic awareness was to place a coil 9 ft in diameter of about 100 turns of #28 magnet wire on the floor of the laboratory and expose subjects to the real-time magnetic replica of the highly amplified "Schumann" signal sensed at a remote location to avoid feedback. Results with individuals and groups experiencing this "magic circle" were dramatically successful. The third-generation investigations were extended to determine if subject's brain waves could be influenced by artificially generated magnetic oscillations of sine waves of low intensity and at specific frequencies within the ranges occurring naturally.

Some subjects exhibited absolute brain-wave entrainment over the range of approximately 6-14 Hz and at signal strengths of approximately 100 nT. Onset of phase/frequency lock-on averaged from 1-4 s from the time of switching on the artificial ELF generator and would sometimes last for the duration of the stimulus, usually a 10 s episode.

13927-VALO

One subject (Mr. A.P., aged 54) displayed absolute entrainment when he was placed inside a triple-shielded magnetic (iron) and triple electrostatic (copper) Faraday cage. The artificial ELF stimulus was originating from a pocketsize battery-powered device positioned outside the shielded room and 12 ft removed from the subject. Tuning the device over a wide frequency range caused subject's EEG to follow the stimulus exactly.

After demonstrating the neurological responses of sensitive individuals, and doing preliminary mapping of subjective states as reported for various specific frequencies (defined to 0.01 Hz on a digital frequency counter attached to the ELF generator), experiments were undertaken on a broader scale with totally unaware subjects, such as customers at local coffee shops during rush hours. This obviated the variables of "suggestion, " "expectancy, " or "hypnosis. "

Anecdotal data was amassed suggesting that a pocket-size transmitter at power levels of under 100 mW could drastically alter the moods of unsuspecting persons, and that vast geographical areas could be surretitiously mood-manipulated by invisible and remote transmissions of EM energy. Tests were rapidly abandoned after dramatic proof because of ethical considerations.

It is well known that naturally occurring earth-ionosphere magnetic oscillations will vary slightly in frequency diurnally, monthly (full vs. new moon), and in definite cycles related to sunspot activity. This may well explain observable "full moon craziness. "

We are aware that tides in the ocean are affected by lunar vectors. Resonant frequencies are also affected by Earth/Venus/ Mercury/Moon/ Jupiter/Sun gravity vectors. And there is well-documented correlation between these geophysical phenomena and episodes of political unrest, mood alteration, and health cycles, as supported by a vast technical and medical literature. Our "drummer" seems to affect all life-forms. An excellent reference source of widely unrelated phenomena that are dramatically tied to our earth's geomagnetic cycles is Petersen's book, *Man, Weather, Sun* cited in the bibliography.

By artificially amplifying or altering these geomagnetic fields or by transmitting specific and coherent frequencies, vast segments of earth's population could be affected. This now becomes an attractive modality for psychological or psionic warfare or for intentional modification of moods, which could reflect in areas ranging from time-specific insomnia to stock market fluctuations. (There have been recent epidemics of "worry insomnia" between 4:00 and 5:30 A.M., coinciding with the "Schumann resonance" signal dropout, as observed in journals of geomagnetic research.)

On several occasions within the last few years, our laboratory began to detect wave trains in the ELF ranges that could not have been of natural origin. These may or may not be related to recent Soviet transmissions of radio energy spread over broad segments of the frequency spectrum ranging up to 28 MHz. Danish monitoring stations report that peak powers of these signals are on the order of 40 Transmitters are presumably located near Riga or Gomel. Transmissions have disrupted lawful radio communications throughout the world and have been protested by several nations. The Soviets have not given an adequate explanation of.the purpose of these tests. An early theory assumed Soviet experiments with over-the-horizon radar; perhaps the psychoactive EM components are unexpected side effects of these tests.

Canadian Department of Transport monitoring sources have established that spectrum analysis of these strange signals indicate that they may be higher harmonics of a fundamental frequency of 6.67 Hz (the Tesla frequency). The signals are modulated with pulses with repetition rates of 5-15 prf, usually 10 Hz. Besides modifying the electrical, ionic, and stratospheric jet-stream equilibrium weather-motion factors, the signals fall precisely within the "windows" known to be psychoactive. The Canadians also report alarming mood alterations in certain areas of eastern Canada, such as near Timmins and Kirkland Lake, Ontario, which observers believe are linked to Soviet transmissions.

Since both theory and laboratory tests prove that magnetic (H-wave) shielding is impossible at these psychoactive frequencies, even with highly sophisticated multiple iron or mu-metal shielding, it can be speculated that ELF signals can be a powerful potential weapon with global capabilities in psychophysiological warfare. (The wavelength of an 8 Hz signal is 22,159 miles.)

I feel that tests should be undertaken with a number of remote ELF sensors that can be made directional in order to establish by triangulation the sources of these recently detected man-made disturbances, whether originating from offshore or on land. ELF data should be correlated with data monitored from Soviet transmissions detected on short-wave receivers. These can then be correlated with human or animal EEG recordings. (This was done May 25, 1978, with positive correlations.)

ELF as a modality for mood manipulation is a demonstrated reality. And there is a strong possibility that it has been implemented since 1976 by the Soviets, intentionally or accidentally, as an unpredicted side effect of local standing waves or reradiation of power lines. [See historic reprints at end of this article regarding the Soviet signal, which was active for about ten years. –Ed note] This speculation is currently being explored by a network of independent scientists working in the disciplines of psychophysiology, geophysics, radio propagation, pharmacology, physics, electronics, and psychotherapy. Possible countermeasure proposals embrace psychopharmacology, adaptive desensitization, and the utilization of personal low-powered (milliwatt) magnetic oscillators, which—by the law of inverse square—will override hostile signals, man-made or natural, with beneficial frequencies.

An interesting device of this nature with possible "countermeasure" capabilities is the "Vitasette" instrument, designed by W. Ludwig for limited distribution and testing in West Germany. One model of this device is the size of a cigarette lighter and has a claimed battery life of 2 years. Frequencies are user-programmable over the range of 1.25-19 Hz by activating specific combinations of switches. This "transmitter" generates spike-wave pulses when a mu-metal core of extremely high permeability is driven to beyond saturation with a single transistor and coil. Effective range is claimed to be about 1 m. This is sufficient to ensure proper synchronization of the wearer's "biological clocks," circadian rhythms, and possible coherence of left and right hemisphere neuronal firings. Ludwig claims cures for a broad spectrum of vegetative disturbances. The brain cells appear to "latch on" to the highest amplitude pulses in their proximity in a manner similar to the characteristics of a frequency-modulation discriminator (Foster-Seeley). Unlike audio modulation detectors, however, they will reject background noise and pulses of lower intensity. The analogy is that a small transistor radio held up to a listener's ear will drown out a nearby rock band with thousands of watts of audio amplification. Similarly, a milliwatt device worn on the body can override a hostile transmission of megawatt power at a distance.

While almost everyone is familiar with electronic heart pacemakers capable of ensuring proper heart rhythms, few are aware of recent research establishing brain waves and other biological functions can be influenced at great distances by magnetic pulses of'critical frequencies.

There is promise that such devices, when tuned to highly specific "beneficial" rates, could be of value in stress modification, tension and anxiety relief, dyslexia, insomnia, "confusion" states if caused by right and left hemisphere desynchronization, headaches, sexual dysfunction, and many other conditions. However, as was the case with the initial application of atomic energy, the first large-scale implementations of ELF discoveries appear to be destructive.

I invite other interested investigators to replicate and verify my observations. A brief disclosure of my procedures follows.

A human subject, selected for sensitivity, is wired to a battery-powered totally isolated EEG amplifier. The output is recorded on one or more channels of chart or (preferably) fed as an FM/VCO to channel(s) of magnetic tape. Monopolar electrodes were frontal to occipital, midline. Simultaneously, but with electrical or optical isolation sufficient to eliminate cross talk, the output of a magnet signal detector (Schumann coil) is chart-recorded or fed to its separate magnetic tape channel. .

The Schumann coils typically consist of 50,000-250,000 turns of # 38 to #44 magnet wire wound on a ferrite, soft iron, or mu-metal core. Coil axis is oriented to magnetic N-S and connected to a separate amplifier having a band pass of 2—40 Hz, a noise figure capable of seeing 0.1 mV rms at Z = 100 kW and 100 dB-or-better rejection of frequencies of 60 Hz and higher.

With proper subjects, phase, and frequency, EEG "lock-ons" can easily be observed by inspecting the chart recordings or, if measurements are made in the field, by later observation of the magnetic tape records after signal recovery on paper charts or dual-trace storage scopes (Tektronix 214).

My initial transmitter of magnetic ELF signals consisted of a phase-shift, modified sine wave oscillator whose output was fed to a 10 Hy soft iron core inductance of 1200 W DC resistance. Power level was 9 V at 0.7 mA or 6.3 mW. This device could cause EEG modification and mood alteration in subjects at up to 10 ft. A higher power device con-structed in 1973 provided greater effective range, as was to be expected. Highly specific modulating and carrier frequencies were obviously withheld for fear of potential misuse, as are "keyhole" and waveform data, as well as details of the multiple-source devices producing "soliton" ELF magnetic standing waves.

My investigations began in 1970. Early research in consciousness modification by external nonchemical stimulus was undertaken in the following areas:

1) Photic stimulation of the subjects by miniature lamps, both cold cathode (phosphors) and filament and "strobe." These light sources were either driven by oscillators or by the subjects' amplified brain waves in real time and (later) with delayed and phase-modified pulses to "pump" EEGs.

2) Exposure of subjects to voltage-gradient oscillating fields and electrostatic (modulated) fields.
3) Exposure of subjects to pulse-modulated negative ion generators, typically (-)20 kV DC sources of corona discharge modulated by mechanically rotating screen shields or by carefully adjusted spark gaps that would arc over and short the output at frequencies centering on the 8 Hz range.
4) Exposure of subjects to actinic stimulus of nearly monochromatic red-green-blue pulses of light through a fiberoptic display device held close to the left or right eye. Phase and frequency of each channel was selectively varied in efforts to excite red-green-blue rod and cone receptors independently and to evoke "standing wave" potentials in specific sites of "the occipital cortex". By selective excitation of both eyes with delayed pulses, evoked "standing waves" occurred.
5) Exploration of audible "click" stimulus, as well as infrasonics, ultrasonics (28 kHz), and phase-shifted sound fed to left and right ears. Audio-modulated 100 kHz electrostatic fields were tested.
6) In two series of tests, the amplified, filtered, and clipped (about 200 mV) real-time Schumann signals were fed directly to the head via surface electrodes. This approach was dramatically psychoactive, and was abandoned in 1974 as dangerous after subjects experienced LSD-type visions.

At this time, we prefer sinusoidal waveforms (not pulsed, triangular, square, sawtooth, or other waveforms). Fundamental frequencies are psychoactive, but can be enhanced by audio-modulating them onto compound carrier frequencies, heterodyning multiple sources, or generating "soliton" waves. We feel that much data has been overlooked by other researchers, not specifying the precise frequencies under investigation to accuracies of 0.01-0.001 Hz. There is evidence that long-chain molecules near liquid crystal boundaries may simulate coherent dipole arrays with very high Qs. Biological signals are, after all, at the opposite end of the electromagnetic spectrum, where communications frequencies in the VHF and UHF bands are specified to 0.005% and better. These investigations have been undertaken privately as a personal interest by the author. They have been totally funded by myself, and are in no way connected with any outside interests, either governmental or commercial.

Results have been reported on an informal basis via limited personal communications with other interested parties. Highly specific frequency and advanced waveform data are proprietary.

Precise technical details on low-noise biological and geomagnetic amplifiers, filters, Schumann detector coils (now into our fourth-generation devices), practical and inexpensive voltage-controlled oscillator and FM discriminator circuits for cassette tape recording of ELF and EEG signals and data, practical and inexpensive modifications to digital frequency counters with extended ranges and accuracies of 0.005 Hz, suggestions for recording, displaying, and analyzing these signals, etc. can be made available to other serious and informed research workers who have a responsible interest in this subject. We feel it wise to withhold only the data on hemispheric desynchronous frequencies. The instruments and hardware used in this study may be made available for inspection and evaluation.

ROBERT C. BECK, B.E., D.Sc., is widely known for his Instrumentation of altered states, his development of state-of-the-art medical electrostimulators, and his investigation of Tesla electromagnetics. Mr. Beck has been a consultant to Sandia Corporation, The USN Office of Surface Weaponry on the subject of E.L.F. detection, and was a Senior Staff Scientist at Eyring Research Institute. He was Acting Chief of Radiological Defense, OCD, In Los Angeles from 1958 through 1963. He has designed and built extremely sensitive magnetometers for the Navy. He has been a senior lecturer in the graduate school, University of Southern California. Dr. Beck is founder of Monitor Electronics Research Corporation and the Alpha-Metrics Company (1969-?), a firm manufacturing ethical EEG biofeedback Instruments. Bob owns the basic patents on low-voltage electronic flash (Strobelights, 1946-'55) and several other patents involving electro-optical systems. He is currently investigating psycho-physiology and electromedical modalities.

1984

Weather Modification Causes "Siberian Express"

Evidence suggests that the weather disturbances are the result of deliberate manipulations by the Soviet Union. Using extremely low frequency (ELF) radio waves projected into the upper atmosphere with a transmitter based on discoveries by Nikola Tesla, the Soviets, experts believe, have been able to create giant standing waves that block or alter the path of upper atmosphere air currents. This, in turn, is changing the weather across the globe, bringing rain during dry seasons, super cold to North America and an unusual warm wave in Europe—including, no doubt, the European portion of the Soviet empire and its satellite nations.

What the Soviets want—and what they are apparently getting this winter—is warmer weather in their "breadbasket," consisting of the European USSR. That includes Captive Nations such as Ukraine and the Russian part of the USSR, at least as far north as Moscow.

Weather reports from the Soviet empire are government censored. But if the weather is unusually warm on the northern borders of Poland, Romania, Czechoslovakia and Hungary then it must be relatively warm in the European USSR.

The movement of the jet stream, pushing the cold toward America and away from Siberia, from which European USSR gets its winter weather, has left a "vacuum" into which warm air from Africa is sucked.

The Soviets, desperate for more arable land, have been experimenting with weather modification since the inception of the communist dictatorship. More recently, the United States has been more involved in both overt and covert attempts to modify the weather, going so far as to conduct talks with the USSR about possible joint weather projects.

What the Establishment media isn't telling you is that just such an effect was reported more than six years ago. Dr. Andrew Michrowski of the Canadian State Department, in 1978, exposed the Soviet ELF "war" against North America.

Michrowski, in a letter, said: "In the case of the winter of 1976-77, the Soviets have managed to establish terrestrial electric resonance, and then to learn how to establish relatively stable and localized ELF magnetic fields, which were able to hamper or divert the jet stream flow in the Northern Hemisphere."

Michrowski described how stationary fronts were set up over the West Coast of North America, between Baja California and Alaska, which "permitted great diversion of air movement and the maintenance of high and low pressure areas."

Early in 1977, a U.S. scientist was quoted as saying that there was evidence the Soviets were using high-intensity radio wave broadcasters to move Arctic air masses away from their coastline—and toward North America.

In 1979, Harry T. Everingham, publisher of the "Fact Finder," wrote: "Is it true that Soviet scientists, with our help and technology, have succeeded in shifting the jet stream so that the winter weather that would normally fall on Siberia now falls instead on the United States to immobilize us?"

Weather is affected by the jet stream, seven to 10 miles above the Earth. Weather modification can be accomplished by regulating the movement of the electrically charged particles in the upper atmosphere. That will result in changing the direction of the jet stream to some degree, Everingham wrote in the "Fact Finder."

It is no secret that the Soviets are investigating the theories of Nikola Tesla.

In 1900, Tesla proved that the Earth could be used as a conductor of electricity and would respond to electrical vibrations of a certain frequency. His experiments succeeded in lighting 200 electric lamps 25 miles away without wires.

Tesla gave a number of possible uses for his discoveries, including weather modification.

Throughout 1983, many disturbances in the upper atmosphere were reported in the Establishment media, these disturbances always associated with "freak" weather conditions. Michrowski, who helped to establish the Planetary Association for Clean Energy (PACE), said, in 1982, that the new frequency of Soviet ELF pulses at 31.5 hertz caused "giant standing wave 'troughs' in the Rocky Mountains" from Alberta to New Mexico, and another giant trough in the East.

The scientist reported that the new Soviet Hertzian wave broadcasts go higher and "really raise havoc with the jet stream, which normally goes from west to east as the Earth turns."

Although Tesla was ignored (at best) and vilified (at worst) by the Establishment in the United States, his adopted country, his ideas received a much warmer reception in the Soviet Union. Much of Tesla's work was never completed. His notebooks are on file in the Tesla Museum in Belgrade, Yugoslavia.

But from Canada come reports that a Soviet scientist spent several months in Quebec in 1976 interviewing Tesla's last known living assistant, Arthur Matthews.

Is it so hard, then, to extrapolate a connection between the Soviet interest in Tesla's work and his assertions that the upper atmosphere could be altered, and a report given at the 1981 conference of the U.S. Psychotronics Association (USPA)? Electrical engineer Al Bielek delivered a lecture titled "Natural and Artificial ELF Signals in the Pacific Northwest and Psychic Phenomena" at that conference.

The engineer also reported that the Soviets have established an additional site for their ELF Tesla magnifying transmitters. He said the original sites were at Riga (in Latvia) and Gomel (in Byelorussia). Bielek said that in July of 1979, large-amplitude 30-hertz and 15-hertz electromagnetic signals were measured in the Pacific Northwest.

"A later examination of some of the wave characteristics implied in Nikola Tesla's description of his magnifying transmitter led to calculations, which implied that a Soviet magnifying device near the Usts/Urt Plateau, or Usturt Plateau (between the Caspian and Aral seas), as they now call it, could have generated the large-amplitude 30-hertz waves found in the Pacific Northwest," he said.

(Above article reprinted from The SPOTLIGHT.)

Aviation Week & Space Technology
November 8, 1976

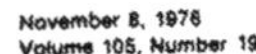
November 8, 1976
Volume 105, Number 19

Powerful Soviet Radio Signal Protested

Washington—Federal Communications Commission has sent several protests to the USSR over interference caused by powerful pulsed high-frequency radio signals that may be coming from a Russian over-the-horizon radar.

So far the Russians have not replied nor have they halted the transmission of the pulsed signals. As a result, the FCC recently lodged a protest with the International Frequency Registration Board, an element of the International Telecommunications Union.

However, there are no reports of interference on the HF frequencies used over the North Atlantic for airline communications.

The pulsed signals have a repetition rate of 10/sec., but their bandwidth, which is extremely wide, changes from time to time. FCC said the signal bandwidth varies from 30 kc. to more than 300 kc. at some times.

Engineers familiar with U.S. techniques for over-the-horizon radar are impressed by the extremely wide bandwidth of the signals, which could be used to obtain high target resolution.

On the other hand, the pulse repetition rate of 10/sec. is believed by one U.S. specialist to be too slow to permit the use of target Doppler shift techniques, which would be desirable to detect high-speed targets such as aircraft or missiles. If it is a pulse-type radar without Doppler, the slow repetition rate would be useful only against slow-moving targets such as ships, one engineer believes.

The interference from the pulsed signals was first brought to the FCC's attention this past July, with complaints coming principally from radio amateurs.

The FCC sent a cable to the Soviet Ministry of Post and Telecommunications in July, bringing the interference matter to its attention.

When the USSR ministry failed to take corrective action or to respond, the FCC sent three follow-up cables, with similar results.

On Oct. 7, the FCC notified the International Frequency Registration Board of the matter.

FCC direction finders indicate the source of the pulsed signal is in the general vicinity of Minsk, not far from the Polish border.

The intermittent nature of the pulsed signals and the change in frequency are compatible with the theory that they come from a new, experimental over-the-horizon radar.

An FCC official said the signal may be received for a few seconds and then be turned off, only to come on a few minutes or an hour later and remain on for 30 min. The longest time of signal observed has been several hours.

When the pulsed signal is shut off at one frequency, it may appear a short time later at another frequency, according to an FCC engineer. Signals have been monitored over almost all of the HF band of 3-30 mc.

The performance of an over-the-horizon radar, like HF radio, is very much affected by the choice of frequency and the time of day, because the signals must be reflected off the ionosphere.

If the signals are coming from a Russian over-the-horizon radar, it is not clear whether the system is intended primarily to detect surface shipping and aircraft over the North Atlantic or whether it is intended to detect a ballistic missile attack over the Arctic.

The U.S. Air Force's new over-the-horizon radar, being constructed in Maine by General Electric, is intended primarily to detect a Soviet missile attack from the northeast. However, because of the broad beam coverage, the USAF radar also will be able to detect aircraft flying over portions of the North Atlantic.

13927-VALO

THE INDIANAPOLIS NEWS — Thursday, December 29, 1977

Healing Device Could Do Evil, Too

The News Photo By John Flora

Jerry Gallimore with his radionics instrument

By JOHN FLORA

If what he says is true, Jerry Gallimore, a quiet and unassuming man who lives in a modest eastside apartment, could be one of the most powerful — and dangerous — men on the planet.

Gallimore, 37, who lives at 5637 E. Julian, claims to have designed and built a device which can heal any physical ailment of any specific person anywhere on earth.

The author of four weighty volumes (the most recent is "The Relationship Between Parapsychology and Gravity"), Gallimore calls his device a radionics instrument and plans to manufacture and market it for $429.

Since builders and operators of radionics apparatus made outrageous curative claims for their devices in the 1920s, Gallimore said, the Food and Drug Administration has prohibited their sale as therapeutic devices.

"That's why I'm selling them as peanut butter mixers," Gallimore said with a grin, adding, "They're not very efficient as peanut butter mixers, though."

With the exception of a 9-volt battery which runs a transducer in the instrument, Gallimore said, his device is completely without conventional power.

The radionics instrument transmits impulses through the earth's gravitational field — impulses which he says can be tuned to the specific frequencies of any single individual's body.

The attache case-size machine has two recepticles — labeled "positive" and "negative" — into which Gallimore says he inserts a blood sample, bit of hair or even a photograph of the individual who needs healing. This, he says, attunes the device to the specific person's vibrations.

By manupulating the 18 dials, Gallimore says he can fine tune the machine and send out harmonious, curative impulses tuned precisely to specific organs of the patient's body.

Since the device uses the forces of gravity, Gallimore said, its reach extends to everyone within the gravitational field of the earth.

But, he said, the radionics instrument can also be used for evil.

Gallimore, who says he has been visited by representatives of all of the branches of the armed forces, said he was recently asked by Secret Service agents if the machine could be used to harm the President.

"I told them anytime I wanted Jimmy Carter, his — was mine in three hours," Gallimore said.

The principle of killing with the radionics instrument, Gallimore said, involves sending out-of-phase signals to the victim's vital organs, causing a stroke, heart attack or some other such fatal organ malfunction.

Gallimore said governments have shown more than a passing interest in his work. He said the Central Intelligence Agency has ordered five units and he has an order from the government of Brazil for 25.

Gallimore, who worked for a number of different electronic firms until 1970, quit work that year to devote his time to his radionics instrument and other research.

17

Physics and Consciousness: A Study of Opposites

Thomas Valone, M.A., P.E.

Integrity Research Institute
1220 L Street NW Suite 100-232
Washington, DC 20005

Presentation to the Annual Conference of the U.S. Psychotronics Association, 1987, and to the Analytical Psychology Society of Western New York (transcript of lecture)

Introduction

All of you must be wondering how anything meaningful can be said about the realm of the psyche (as in psychology) and the realm of matter (as in physics) in the same discussion, when everybody knows they are opposites and have nothing to do with each other! Furthermore, the psyche is associated with the human soul, the mind, and intelligence. The word comes from the Greek meaning "soul" or "breath of life" and is often regarded as including both the conscious and unconscious parts of the mind. The dictionary goes so far as to say that in psychoanalysis, the psyche is often thought of "as an entity functioning apart from or independently from the body."{1} Now, you might ask, how can something so light and airy and without substance have anything in common with something so dense, inert, and lifeless as matter?

Greek History

In the Western world, the Greek philosophers influenced our early concepts of mind and matter. For the Pythagoreans, the universe was most fundamentally based on a mathematical, musical structure of harmonia. Number was seen as the key to nature. Parmenides, in the 5th century B.C. was the first philosopher to distinguish explicitly between the sensible and the intelligible. It is interesting to note that even when the material and the spiritual were distinguished later, "Plato usually preferred to call them sensible and intelligible."{2} The word "arche" was used by Anaximander in this period to describe a sustaining power or origin of natural phenomena. Later on, however, the Pythagoreans tried to remove the notion of arche from anything physical. They restricted it to the origin of the number series. The trend toward developing incompatible opposites affected the use of the word arche. It was hard to put it on one side of the matter-spirit duality that was developing and it found no use in Plato's thought.

For Plato, the realm of imagination was more fundamental than the manifested, sensible reality. Both spirit and form had their essence in his realm of ideas. Plato and Aristotle saw the form of an object more fundamental than its material substance. "Primary matter" for Aristotle was devoid of form and closely connected with "not-being." Isn't that curiously different from today's orientation? If we progress a few hundred years, we find that the Alchemists of the era from 200 B.C. to 300 A.D. harmonized with the Aristotelian view. They had spirits naturally floating toward the heavens and corporeal bodies sinking toward the earth.

The Middle Ages

For the next thousand years, science and religion or matter and spirit were discussed in the same text. St. Thomas Aquinas in the 13th century wrote about the metaphysics of matter and form as well as of the spirit. Around 1600, Johannes Kepler pioneered the use of mathematical proof and discovered three major laws of planetary motion. He believed that, "*Geometry is the archetype of the beauty of the world.*"{3} (Kepler's use of the word archetype, by the way, was in the sense of "primary images which the soul can perceive with the aid of an innate instinct."{4} It closely agrees with Dr. Carl Jung's use of the term in Analytical Psychology.) Dr. Carl Jung, the founder of Analytical Psychology, also co-authored a book (Ref. 3) with the famous physicist, Wolfgang Pauli, which inspired me to research the present paper with boldness. Along with Kepler's scientific theories, he also regarded the earth as a living thing and the planets endowed with individual souls. He mentioned too, the alchemical world soul, the "anima mundi" that sleeps in matter.

Galileo's Archetypal Struggle

Now if we look at how Galileo was doing in the 1620's, we find that his telescopes were broadening his horizons in the solar system. He was a professor of mathematics and pretty systematic about things. As he discovered more evidence for the sun being the central body around which the planets revolve, he mentioned this in a book on sunspots. The only problem was that this Copernican system was denounced by the Church in Rome and he was admonished for defending it. He had even tried to show that there was scriptural confirmation for the Copernican system!

In 1624, Galileo visited Rome and obtained permission to write on the earth-centered and the solar-centered theories, provided that the treatment was impartial. Yet, when the book, *Dialogue Concerning the Two Chief World Systems,* was published in Florence in 1632, it was declared a heresy. The publisher was ordered to stop publication and Galileo was summoned to Rome to face the Inquisition. There is one copy of his book at the library at my alma mater, the University of Buffalo. I think they smuggled it out from Florence!

Today it's hard for us to believe that Galileo was sentenced to life imprisonment in spite of the efforts of the Grand Duke Ferdinand II and others to free him. (He was put under house arrest.){5}

Descartes and Newton Create Materialism

We can see now why there was a general abandonment of authority as a criterion for truth from that period onwards. Science was coming into its own and discovering facts that were unknown to philosophers and religious people. Specialization was born and men chose to narrow their vision. Galileo, Newton, and others didn't bother to compose books on the general nature of man because they were so enveloped in their single approach to reality. As the 1700's progressed, science and philosophy, the objective and subjective both became more separate as Newtonian physics influenced people's view of nature. Definitions became tied to equations, space had an empty quality, time was performing some type of uniform flow, and causality had a firm foundation with material connections. Even the philosophers like Descartes joined in to help create the consciousness of polar opposites.

Dr. Carl Jung says that just before the emergence of materialism, everything was accounted for in terms of spirit and the soul was believed to be a real substance. He continues with a passage that I really like:

"When the spiritual catastrophe of the Reformation put an end to the Gothic Age, with its impetuous yearning for the heights, its geographical confinement, and its restricted view of the world, the vertical outlook of the European mind was cut across by the horizontal outlook of modern times. Consciousness ceased to grow upward, and grew instead in breath of view, geographically as well as philosophically. This was the age of the great voyages, of the widening of man's mental horizon by empirical discoveries. Belief in the substantiality of things spiritual yielded more and more to the obtrusive conviction that material things alone have substance, till at last, after nearly four hundred years, the leading European thinkers and investigators came to regard the mind as wholly dependent on matter and material causation."{6}

Modern Physics Affects Consciousness Studies

Now, to introduce Dr. Fritjof Capra, he is a physics professor at UCLA who has done research in theoretical high-energy physics in Paris, London and presently at the Lawrence Berkeley Laboratory. He gave a talk at the Science and Spirit Symposium in New York. Dr. Elisabeth Kubler-Ross was there and made the audience spellbound. Dr. Karl Pribram's discoveries, concerning holographic storage of information in the brain was also exciting.

Many organizations are interested in Fritjof Capra's book including the C.G. Jung Foundation in New York who is offering it for sale on their book list. It's a book that explores the parallels between modern physics and Eastern philosophy. It has a nice beginning that devotes a chapter each to Hinduism, Buddhism, Chinese Thought, Taoism, and Zen. Dr. Josephson, a Nobel Prize winner says of his book, "Readers will find much of interest in Dr. Capra's clear explanations of the basic ideas behind the various forms of Eastern Mysticism, and of the paradoxes of modern physics which seem to have been anticipated in the paradoxes of mysticism. It is likely that when the relations between them are well understood, the time will be ripe for considerable advances in our comprehension of the universe."{7}

First of all, when Dr. Capra talks about wave-like patterns of probability that don't exist at any one place with certainty, it's very hard for anyone to be convinced that it is really, physically true. In Fig. 1, we have the results of an experiment that shows not only the wave nature of particles but also the fact that they cannot exist in any one spot with certainly before interacting with matter.

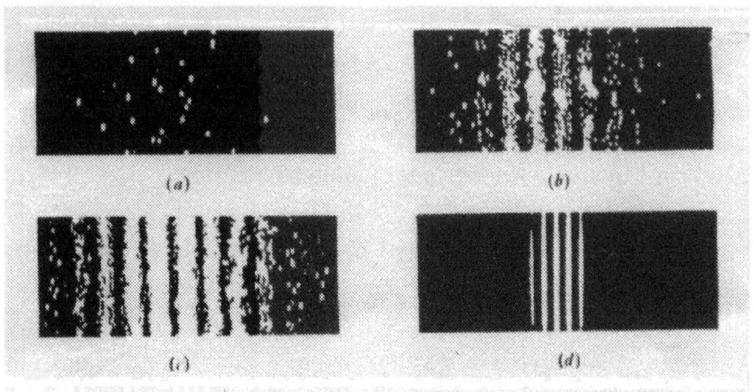

FIG. 1 Double slit experiment with single photons or electrons going through one at a time.

The interference pattern shown in picture (d) is usually obtained by shining a single frequency light source such as a laser, through a double slit. I did the experiment once with a Helium-Neon laser and the resulting parallel lines spread out onto the screen with a diameter of about a foot before they diminished.

Now the reason why this electron experiment is so important is that each electron must have a different form when it passes through one hole of the double slit. The quantum mechanics describe it as a wave-packet that diminishes to zero only at infinity. This electron was really a wave that was pretty wide when it came in. [Paul Dirac's statement "each photon interferes with itself" has been verified by this low light level experiment by Pfleegor & Mandel, *J. of Optical Soc. Of Amer.*, V.58, N.7, 1968, p.946] I did some calculations that showed an electron could actually have its "consciousness" spread over a couple of millimeters, which is huge compared to its particle size. Its interference pattern could then still be seen with a microscope. When an electron or any particle is forced to choose an opening or hit a screen, then the wave-packet squeezes together. This collapse makes us think that it is always localized in a small area of space but when it's free of material influence, it spreads out as much as it can. In fact, quantum mechanics requires that the wave packet extend to infinity!

This behavior reminds one of the Eastern description of meditation. When the person's consciousness is on the material body alone, it seems limited and defined. However, in meditation, the experience of expansion is very prominent.

Another property of matter that relates to the behavior of a single particle is its restlessness. When you try to confine a particle to a smaller and smaller space it displays more and more energy. It's as if the particle jiggles around faster and faster though really it's the wave-packet trying to spread out and maybe get out of its confinement. This reminds us of a psychological feeling that's associated with being tied down or trapped in some way. Our mind starts to race in an effort to find a way out. Well most mater in nature is confined. Electrons are confined in certain configurations in a molecule, etc. We are led to the question of *what is the way out for confined matter and confined psyches?*

Now another property of matter that shows there are no smaller units inside particles, is when they disintegrate. This leads us into Einstein's contribution to physics with $E=mc^2$. In Fig. 2, we see two cloud chamber pictures. Cloud chambers can be seen up at the Ontario Science Center in Toronto. They are boxes with glass tops containing a liquid that's just about to boil. When any small particle comes in disturbing the liquid, it does boil in that spot creating bubbles. Now these bubbles are many times larger than the particles but they show us where the particle went and what happened to it on the way.

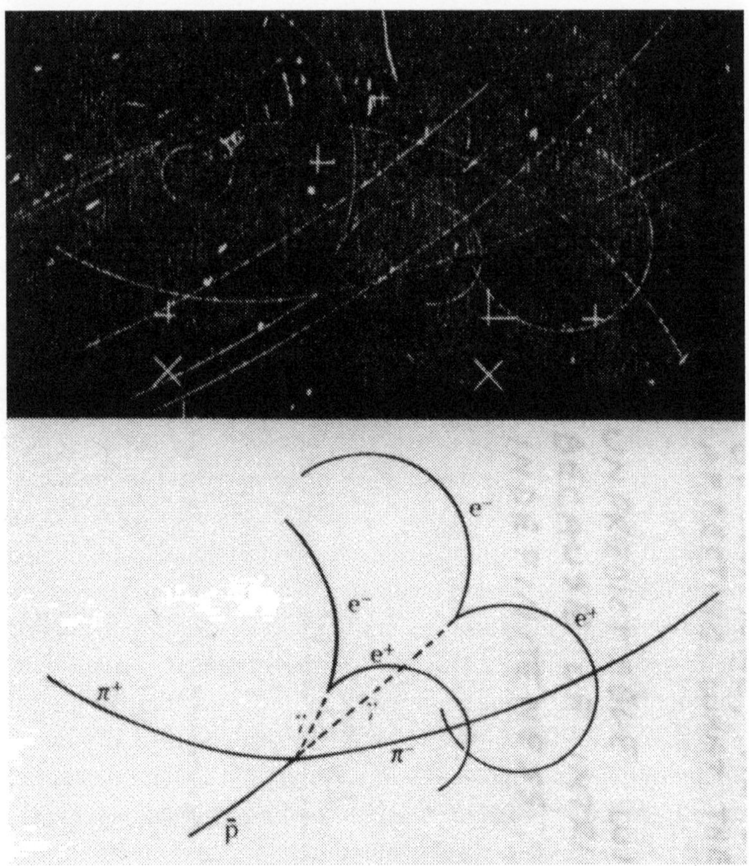

FIG. 2 Cloud chamber picture of e-,e+ particles being created from the vacuum.

What we see in the picture on the left is one result of a collision between a proton and an antiproton. Two particles called pions are created along with two wave packets of light called photons. Then we see a curious phenomenon. After the photons travel a small distance, they both transform into the matter of an electron and antielectron, (also called a positron). Using $E = mc^2$, we could find the energy of the photon that was transformed into the mass of each particle. If you look closely at the cloud chamber picture above the drawing you can see there are no tracks created where the photon's dotted lines are. Then all of a sudden two circular tracks appear where the positron and electron are created. Now the cloud chamber picture on the right shows another result from a collision between a proton and antiproton. In this case, simply eight pions are created with no protons. Nature displays many more forms when greater kinetic energies are involved. This vividly shows the dynamic, changeable quality of matter and its equivalence with energy.

How does the equivalence of matter and energy affect the psyche or involve human beings? Well, it may give us an explanation for such phenomenon as the Catholic Stigmatist Therese Neumann. Therese Neumann for example, who died in 1962, baffled doctors by the fact that this saint did not eat or drink for the last 36 years of her life. In the book, *The Story of Therese Neumann*, the author describes a scrupulous experiment in 1927 during which she was kept under constant observation by doctors for two weeks. Afterwards they testified under oath in a Munich court that she took neither food nor liquid yet remained healthy and did not lose weight.{8} She stated that she lived by "God's light." Now understanding $E = mc^2$ we know that it is possible for light energy to be converted into matter. Many physicists believe it is happening all of the time in our bodies. With the work of Dr. Andrija Puharich, later verified by Russian (1996) and Japanese (1998) experiments, we also find that biological transmutation can also occur in vitro and in vivo. This explanation is bolstered by the fact that in her later years Therese lived in a cottage that possessed a glass-roofed section to afford her plenty of light.{9}

Thanks to Einstein, we have found that matter itself is really made up of bundles of energy. To quote from Dr. Capra's book, "These dynamic patterns, or 'energy bundles,' form the stable nuclear, atomic and molecular structures which build up matter and give it its macroscopic solid aspect, thus making us believe that it is made of some material substance. At the macroscopic level, this notion of substance is a useful approximation, but at the atomic level it not longer makes sense. Atoms consist of particles and these particles are not made of any material stuff. When we observe them, we never see any substance; what we observe are dynamic patterns continually changing into one another – a continuous dance of energy."{10}

We can look at energy as a measure of activity. The more energy a system has the more activity it's capable of. Now why can't we tap this energy when we need it the most? Yogananda, an Eastern mystic, used to say, "There is enough latent energy in one gram of your flesh to supply the city of Chicago with electricity for a week. Yet you imagine yourselves powerless in the face of a few difficulties!"{11}

Another yogi, Swami Kriyananda, shows a practical application of this idea in his book, *The Path*. He says, "I had an interesting experience a few years ago relative to this energy-drain. Having, as I thought, seriously overextended myself in my work, I had reached a point of exhaustion. One evening, I had a class to give, and half an hour before leaving for it (I) lay down to rest, But I didn't sleep; instead, I reviewed in my mind as dispassionately as I could all the reasons I had for feeling so tired: the endless activities (daily lectures, classes, a radio program), the unceasing stream of correspondence, the constant telephone calls, the numerous request for interviews, the incessant demands for decision from people who could have made just as good decisions on their own. As I recalled each reason to mind, I reacted with an instinctive feeling of rejection: 'Oh no—it's just too much!'"

"But then came the dispassionate challenge: 'Is it? It is a fact of your life now, whether you like it or not. Why not simply accept it?' In each case, as I applied this advice, I felt as though I had closed some psychic door through which energy had been pouring from me in my anxiety to push the unwanted experience out of my life. As each door closed, I found more energy being retained in myself."

"The results were extraordinary. By the end of that half-hour my exhaustion had completely vanished; I was fairly bursting with energy! A friend who had seen me earlier that day and pleaded with me to cancel my class, saw me now and exclaimed, 'What a wonderful sleep you must have had. You look so refreshed!' Interestingly enough, the subject of my class that evening was, 'Energization.' It was perhaps the best I have ever given on this subject. Afterwards I still felt so full of energy that I stayed up until two o'clock the next morning, talking, reading, then meditating."{11}

Now how does the psyche interface with the material brain? Is there any evidence for an energy transfer and how is it made? Carl Jung refers to this area when he says: "We can judge the magnitude of the error, which our Western consciousness commits when it allows the psyche only a reality derived from physical causes. The East is wiser, for it finds the essence of all things grounded in the psyche. Between the unknown essences of spirit and matter stands the reality of the psychic—psychic reality, the only reality we can experience immediately." {12}

Neurophysiology and the Understanding of the Brain

The application of physics to the operation of the brain, under the heading of neurophysiology, is an interesting aside. Dr. John Eccles, a Nobel Prize winner was a resident professor at U.B. for several years. I became interested in his theories when he gave an alumni lecture in 1975. He mentioned then, "We see the results of the mind searching the brain storage banks for data but we don't know what is directing it." In his book *The Understanding of the Brain*, Dr. Eccles says that *the mind is the non-physical entity acting upon the physical brain through the area of the speech center in the left hemisphere.* (It is also likely that there are more than one sites in the brain for multiple interface—see discussion about the medulla oblongata.) The main reason he gives for this is that for the past twenty years, he has worked on tracing neuron paths, among other things. He found that when neuron pulses go to the region of the speech center, the pulses just end in neurons fibers (called modular columns) that become finer and finer. These modular columns terminate singly in the upper cortex. Instead of finding a complex nerve center like the motor cortex, he found the speech center curiously incomplete. Therefore, he says that we must put together our experiences in the mind and transfer information through the speech center. For the incoming transfer, her describes the neurons as "critically poised" requiring an extremely small force to cause them to fire.{13}

Before going on, I'd like to add that there have been patients who have undergone complete *hemispherectomies* of the right or left hemisphere of the brain. They did not lose their basic self-identity and in time usually regained any lost functions using the remaining half of their brain.{14} These cases seem to correlate with an Eastern Yoga belief that a more basic psyche-matter transfer occurs deep within the brain in the medulla oblongata, which is the first layer on top of the spinal column and the deepest part of the brain.

Causality Analysis by Way of Aristotle's Quaternary

Now, one of the most important consequences of modern physics has been to completely alter our notion of causality. In the two leading theories today, quantum mechanics and Einstein's relativity theory, neither one can include causality. Quantum mechanics cannot tell what causes an atom to emit light energy for example, it can only attribute a certain probability to it happening. This is generally not regarded as a failing of quantum mechanics but more fundamentally as a limitation set by nature under the uncertainty principle. Today, physicists generally agree that spontaneous emission is actually "stimulated emission" caused by the fluctuations of the zero point field. Because of the wave nature of matter, we cannot predict with certainty the physical behavior that men have always dreamed about knowing. Causality used to be related to the proximity of two events in space with one event occurring before the other in time. However, the new framework that relativity theory has provided us with is a four-dimensional space-time continuum. The direction of time no longer has a preferrence and time itself is simply regarded as another axis equivalent to the other three. We measure time by macroscopic changes in matter. Quantum mechanics is in agreement when it allows, for example, the behavior of a positron (or anti-electron) to be identical to an electron going backwards in time. The two events are physically equivalent. This might involve something like a *future cause*, to borrow a phrase from Aristotle.

Now to explain some of this heavy stuff, let me challenge you with some every day examples. Would you be satisfied with someone telling you that the cause of a baseball being hit into the bleechers in Yankee Stadium was the bat that hit it? How about a more personal example: what if someone struck you with their hand. You ask, "Why did you do that?" He or she explains that their arm muscles contracted in a certain way and you happened to be in the way. Lastly, a good example that touches our creative side is: "What is the cause of a statue?" Just posing such a question sounds confusing, yet the hammer, chisel, and muscle contractions are about all that classical physics will allow.

Well, Aristotle covered this scene pretty well a few thousand years ago when he proposed a quaternary of *four basic causes* for an event. Two have a mental quality and the other two have a physical quality (after his teacher, Plato, who only talked about mental and physical causes). Taking the example of a statue, the block of marble is called the *material cause*; the artist is labeled the *efficient cause*, being the force of the event; then the shape or form of the statue is the *formal cause*; and the concept of beauty, being the end or purpose of the whole process is called the *final cause*.

It is important to mention that two of these causes are only manifested in physical reality *after the event is completed*. The form of the statue can only be seen by others when the statue is near completion. The final cause, being the concept of beauty, is better expressed by the statue's completion but still escapes our definition. Both final and formal causes give meaning to the event while the material and efficient causes only answer "how did it happen?" When we ask "why?" we are asking for something meaningful. You may be as amazed as I was to learn that the dictionary definition of "meaning" is "*that which is intended*."{15} Again, this refers to something manifested in future. In other words, by definition, we cannot have a meaningful life if we do not set goals and reasons for our actions!

Referring to a physical causality, Carl Jung explains: "Causality is only one principle and psychology essentially cannot be exhausted by causal methods only, because the mind (= psyche) lives by aims as well. Psychic finality rests on a 'pre-existent' meaning. . . . In that case we have to suppose a 'knowledge' prior to all consciousness."{16}

We find physicists saying very similar things in describing four-dimensional space-time. In the words of Louis deBroglie: "In space-time, everything which for each of us constitutes the past, present, and the future is given en bloc. . . . Each observer, as his time passes, discovers, so to speak, new slices of space-time which appear to him as successive aspects of the material world, though in reality the ensemble of events constituting space-time exist prior to his knowledge of them."{17}

It's much like the person in the book, *Flatland* who becomes aware of another dimension of space above and below his world. We get glimpses of this more fundamental framework when events in our lives synchronize without any apparent cause, yet produce meaningful and sometimes beneficial results. An example might be picking up a friend hitchhiking who I had met the month before in Pennsylvania and became close with during that time. Obviously, precognitive experiences would also fit into the realm of "meaningful cross-connection" or synchronicity. These events give us an insight into a unitary reality because psyche and matter are both involved in something that strikes us as beyond simple cause and effect. In referring to synchronicity, Jungian analyst, Mary Gammon says, "meaning can be considered as being synonymous with the self-fulfilling pattern of relationships which creates the event."{18}

New Physics Principles Must Change Our View of Reality

Now, I'd like to look over the chart (Table 1 at the end of this paper) showing a comparison between the *Old Physics* and the *New Physics.* As we focus on these comparisons and notice their disparities and the essential qualities of opposites, let us consider Dr. Capra's words regarding disciplines outside physics: "The natural sciences, social sciences and the humanities have all modeled themselves after physics. They've taken physics as the shining example of a hard science. But what they've done is taken the old Newtonian physics as their example. They had to do so because when these sciences, like biology or psychology were developed, this was the only physics that was available—17th century Newtonian, classical physics."{19}

Therefore, for your own good, the next time you go to the doctor, notice what type of physics he uses to analyze you: A holistic practitioner will consider the entire person in the analysis of a "dis-ease" whereas the Newtonian, Old Physics, allopathic doctor will only consider the body part, exclusively treating the symptom with material causes.

One thing that I forgot to mention in regards to the new physics is an aspect of general relativity that reinforces the picture of an interconnected whole. First of all, referring to inertia, the resistance a body feels in response to a change in movement, Einstein believed in what is called Mach's principle. The philosopher, Ernest Mach held that we feel inertia because of the interaction of our mass with all of the other massive bodies in the universe, particularly the ones farther away. The ones farther away are considered fixed from our perspective. We would still feel inertia out in space, when turning or accelerating, but if all of the stars and galaxies disappeared, there would be no way to tell that you were changing your direction or speed. It's all relative in relativity!

Now it's hard to believe that gravity would be responsible for such an interaction over a large distance. However, space-time is regarded as having a "generalized" gravitational field everywhere so that there is no space that is "empty of field". Thus where there is a large planetary body, the field curves the space-time around it and it has been verified that even a light path is bent. The conclusion of general relativity is in the words of Albert Einstein: "We may therefore regard matter as being constituted by the regions of space in which the field is extremely intense. . . . There is no place in this new kind of physics both for this field and matter, for the field is the only reality."{20}

So on your diagram, you could put "force" in the column on the left and the word "field" in the right hand column. The next time someone says, "May the force be with you" you can answer with new awareness, "And may the field be with you!"

To finish up with, I'd like to read a selection of quotations that go from materialism to holism. First of all, here's one from Einstein, which concurs with Dr. Mindell's point, "The physicist seeks to reduce colors and tones to vibrations, the physiologist thought and pain to nerve processes, in such a way that the psychical element as such is eliminated from the causal nexus of existence, and thus nowhere occurs as an independent link in the causal associations. It is no doubt this attitude, which considers the comprehension of all relations by the exclusive use of only (classical) concepts as being possible in principle, that is at the present time understood by the term, 'materialism.'"{21}

What is the Secret of Life?

Next is a short story from the first issue of *Synthesis* magazine by the man who discovered Vitamin C. Albert Szent-Gyoergyi entitled the article, "Drive in Living Matter to Perfect Itself." This story is a story of his whole life:

> Any level of organization is fascinating and offers new vistas and horizons, but we must not lose our bearings or else we may fall victim to the simple idea that any level of organization can best be understood by pulling it to pieces, by a study of its components—that is, the study of the next lower level. This may make us dive to lower and lower levels in the hope of finding the secret of life there. This made, out of my own life, a wild goose chase. I started my experimental work with rabbits, but I found rabbits to complex, so I shifted to a lower level and studied bacteria; I became a bacteriologist. But soon I found bacteria too complex, and shifted to molecules and became a biochemist. So I spent my life in the hunt for the secret of life.
>
> It is most important for the biologist to give himself an account of these relations when he asks himself on which level of organization to work when embarking on research with the desire to understand life. Those who like to express themselves in the language of mathematics do well to keep to lower levels.
>
> We do not know what life is but, all the same, know life from death. I know that my cat is dead when it move no more, has no reflexes and leaves my carpet clean – that is, no longer transforms chemical energy into mechanic, electric or osmotic work. These transformations of energy are most closely linked up with the very nature of life. We, ourselves, get our energies by burning our food and transducing its chemical energy into heat and various sorts of work.
>
> So for twenty years I studied energy transformations by going to the source of the vital energies and worked on biological oxidation on the molecular level. These

> studies netted me a Nobel Prize (which was most pleasant) but left me eventually high and dry without a better understanding.
>
> So I turned to muscle, the seat of the most violent and massive energy transformations. This study led me and my associates to the discovery of a new muscle protein, and we could then ourselves make little muscles and make them jump outside the body. To see these little artificial muscles jump for the first time was, perhaps, the most exciting experience of my scientific life, and I felt sure that in a fortnight I would understand everything.
>
> Then I worked for twenty more years on muscle and learned not a thing. The more I knew, the less I understood; and I was afraid to finish my life with knowing everything and understanding nothing. Evidently something very basic was missing. I thought that in order to understand I had to go one level lower, to electrons, and—with graying hair—I began to muddle in quantum mechanics. So I finished up with electrons. But electrons are just electrons and have no life at all.
>
> Evidently on the way I lost life; it had run out between my fingers.{22}

Now one step higher to include the psyche, here is Dr. Carl Jung relating physical and the psychological in dreams. "Not infrequently the dreams show that there is a remarkable inner symbolical connection between an undoubted physical illness and a definite psychic problem, so that the physical disorder appears as a direct mimetic expression of the psychic situation. I mention this curious fact more for the sake of completeness than to lay any particular stress on this problematic phenomenon. It seems to me, however, that a definite connection does exist between physical and psychic disturbances and that its significance is generally underrated, though on the other hand it is boundlessly exaggerated owing to certain tendencies to regard physical disturbances merely as an expression of psychic disturbances, as is particularly the case with Christian Science. Dreams throw very interesting sidelights on the inter-functioning of body and psyche, which is why I raise this question here."{23}

Lastly, to sum up, let me quote Fritjof Capra's ending to his masterpiece *The Tao of Physics*, connecting the Eastern and Western traditions: "The parallels between the views of physicists and mystics become even more plausible when we recall the other similarities which exist in spite of their different approaches. To begin with, their method is thoroughly empirical. Physicists derive their knowledge from experiments; mystics from meditative insights. Both are observations, and in both fields these observations are acknowledged as the only source of knowledge. The object of observation is of course very different in the two cases. The mystic looks within and explores his or her consciousness at its various levels, which include the body as the physical manifestation of the mind. The experience of one's body is, in fact, emphasized in many Eastern traditions and is often seen as the key to the mystical experience of the world. When we are healthy, we do not feel any separate parts in our body but are aware of it as an integrated whole, and this awareness generates a feeling of well-being and happiness. In a similar way, the mystic is aware of the wholeness of the entire cosmos which is experienced as an extension of the body. In the words of Lama Govinda, 'To the enlightened man . . . whose consciousness embraces the universe, to him the universe becomes his body while his physical body becomes a manifestation of the Universal Mind, his inner vision an expression of the highest reality, and his speech an expression of eternal truth and mantric power.'"

"In contrast to the mystic, the physicist begins his enquiry into the essential nature of things by studying the material world. Penetrating into ever deeper realms of matter, he has become aware of the essential unity of all things and events. More than that, he has also learnt that he himself and his consciousness are an integral part of this unity. Thus the mystic and the physicist arrive at the same conclusion; one starting from the inner realm, the other from the outer world. The harmony between their views confirms the ancient Indian wisdom that Brahman, the ultimate reality without, is identical to Atman, the reality within.

"A further similarity between the ways of the physicist and mystic is the fact that their observations take place in realms which are inaccessible to the ordinary senses. In modern physics, these are the realms of the atomic and subatomic world; in mysticism they are non-ordinary states of consciousness in which the sense world is transcended. Mystics often talk about experiencing higher dimensions in which impressions of different centers of consciousness are integrated into a harmonious whole. A similar situation exists in modern physics where a four-dimensional 'space-time' formalism has been developed which unifies concepts and observations belonging to different categories in the ordinary three-dimensional world. In both fields, the multi-dimensional experiences transcend the sensory world and are therefore almost impossible to express in ordinary language."

"We see that the ways of the modern physicist and the Eastern mystic, which seem at first totally unrelated, have, in fact, much in common. It should not be too surprising, therefore, that there are striking parallels in their descriptions of the world. Once these parallels between Western science and Eastern mysticism are accepted, a number of questions will arise concerning their implications. Is modern science, with all its sophisticated machinery, merely rediscovering ancient wisdom, known to the Eastern sages for thousands of years? Should physicists, therefore, abandon the scientific method and begin to meditate? Or can there be a mutual influence between science and mysticism; perhaps even a synthesis?"

"I think all these questions have to be answered in the negative. I see science and mysticism as two complementary manifestations of the human mind; of its rational and intuitive faculties. The modern physicist experiences the world through an extreme specialization of the intuitive mind. The two approaches are entirely different and involve far more than a certain view of the physical world. However, they are complementary, as we have learned to say in physics. Neither is comprehended in the other, nor can either of them be reduced to the other, but both of them are necessary, supplementing one another for a fuller understanding of the world. To paraphrase an old Chinese saying, mystics understand the roots of the Tao but not its branches; scientists understand its branches but not its roots. Science does not need mysticism and mysticism does not need science; but man needs both. Mystical experience is necessary to understand the deepest nature of things, and science is essential for modern life. What we need, therefore, is not a synthesis but a dynamic interplay between mystical intuition and scientific analysis."

"So far, this has not been achieved in our society. At present, our attitude is too yang—to use again Chinese phraseology—too rational, male and aggressive. Scientists themselves are a typical example. Although their theories are leading to a worldview, which is similar to that of the mystics, it is striking how little this has affected the attitudes of most scientists. In mysticism, knowledge cannot be separated from a certain way of life, which becomes its living manifestation. To acquire mystical knowledge means to undergo a transformation; one could even say that the knowledge is the transformation. Scientific knowledge, on the other hand, can often stay abstract and theoretical. Thus most of today's physicists do not seem to realize the philosophical, cultural and spiritual implications of their theories. Many of the actively support a society which is still based on the mechanistic, fragmented world view, without seeing that science points beyond such a view, towards a oneness of the universe which includes not only our natural environment but also our fellow human beings. I believe that the worldview implied by modern physics is inconsistent with our present society, which does not reflect the harmonious interrelatedness we observe in nature. To achieve such a state of dynamic balance, a radically different social and economic structure will be needed: a Cultural Revolution in the true sense of the word. The survival of our whole civilization may depend on whether we can bring about such a change. It will depend, ultimately, on our ability to adopt some of the yin attitudes of Eastern mysticism; to experience the wholeness of nature and the art of living with it in harmony."{24}

TABLE 1

OLD PHYSICS	NEW PHYSICS
Hard Matter	Matter = Energy
Atom = Ultimate Part	No Ultimate Part
Cause Precedes Effect	Interconnected Events with Future and Material Causes
3-D Space = Empty Container	4-D Space-Time With Bidirectional Time
Understanding = Reductionism (Breaking Up Into Parts)	Understanding = Synergy (Whole Greater Than Sum Of Parts)
Mechanical Universe (Materialism)	Dynamic Universe (Vitalism)
People = Detached, Objective (Observers of Nature)	People = Integrated, United (Necessarily Influencing Nature)
Predictable Behavior (Certainty and Determinism)	Unpredictable Outcomes (Because Of Intrinsic Indeterminism)

References

1. Funk & Wagnall's, *Standard College Dictionary, 1963, Funk & Wagnalls Company*
2. Guthrie, WKC, *Encyclopedia of Philosophy*, Macmillan, 1967,V.6 P.443
3. Pauli W & Jung, C., *Interpretation of Nature & the Psyche,* Bolligen Foundation NY, 1955 P.156
4. Ibid, P.153
5. Caponigni, R, *Encyc. of Philosophy,* V.3, P.263
6. Jung, C. *Structure & Dynamics of the Psyche,* in the *Collected Works of Carl G. Jung (CW)* V.8 1964 P.338
7. Josephson, B., quoted on the back coverof *Tao of Physics* (Capra) Shambala 1975
8. Schimberg, A P, *Story of Therese Neuman*, Bruce Publishers 1947
9. Yogananda Paramahansa, *Autobiography of a Yogi*, Self Realization Fellowship L.A., CA 1950 P.425
10. Capra, F., P.203
11. Kriyananda, S. The Path Ananda Publications, Nevada 1977 P.453
12. Jung, C., *CW*, V.8, P.384
13. Eccles J., *The Understanding of the Brain,* McGraw Hill, 1973 (see also, Eccles, J., "Cerebral Activity and Consciousness" in Philosophy of Biology, McMillan Press, 1974, p.87 and Eccles, J., "The Physiology and Physics of the Free Will Problem" in *Progress in the Neurosciences and Related Fields*, Mintz and Widmayer, Plenum Pub.)
14. Puccetti R. "Brain Bisection & Personal Identity" *B. J. Phil. Sci.*, 24, 1973, P.339
15. Funk & Wagnall's *Standard College Dictionary*
16. Jung, C., *CW* ,V.8, P.516
17. Capra, F, P.185
18. Gammon Mary, "Window on Eternity", *J. Analytical Psychology,* March 1975, P.13

19. Capra, F., *Human Behavior*, Oct 1978, P.30
20. Caprek, M, *Philosophical Implications of Contemporary Physics,* Van Nostrand 1961 P.319
21. Einstein, A. *Relativity, Special & General Theory,* Crown Publishers NY 1961 P.142
22. Szent Gyoergyi, *Synthesis 1*, Synthesis Press, Redwood City, CA No.1, P.16
23. Jung, C., *CW* V.8 P.261
24. Capra, p.304

THOMAS VALONE is a retired college physics and engineering teacher and President of Integrity Research Institute. He is the author of the *Homopolar Handbook, Energy Crisis,* and editor of *Electrogravitics Systems* and *Future Energy* all of which concern emerging energy technologies. He can be reached through *iri@erols.com* and *www.integrity-research.org*

18

Volitional Effects of Healers on Bacterial Systems

Beverly Rubik, Ph.D.

Institute for Frontier Science
6114 LaSalle Avenue, PMB 605
Oakland, CA 94611

Abstract

The effects of volition accompanied by 'laying on of hands' of Olga Worrall and other self-proclaimed healers on normal, chemically inhibited, or nutritionally starved cultures of Salmonella typhimurium were measured in a series of controlled experiments. The participants treated the bacteria by placing their hands near but not touching microscope slides or racks of test tubes containing liquid bacterial cultures with the intention to heal them. Bacterial culture growth was measured at various time intervals by light scattering using a double beam spectrophotometer. Motility was quantitated by photographing the bacteria under dark-field microscopy illuminated by a strobe lamp, such that tracks of swimming bacteria could be counted from the microphotographs. Naive participants who similarly placed their hands near the cultures for identical time periods but without intention to heal were used as controls in addition to untreated control cultures.

The results with Worrall are summarized as follows. (1) Various levels of enhancement of the growth of treated cultures over controls were observed on those cultures to which growth inhibitors chloramphenicol or tetracycline were added. The magnitude of the effects observed depended on the concentration of antibiotic used, and ranged from small to moderate. In general, a greater volitional effect was observed for low concentrations of growth inhibitors that did not completely inhibit growth. (2) No effect on culture growth over controls was apparent under optimal laboratory culture conditions of logarithmic growth phase in minimal media. (3) Bacterial motility in Worrall-treated cultures was observed to be enhanced over controls for bacteria completely paralyzed with phenol. (4) No growth was observed for a met(-) mutant starved for methionine in either test or control cultures.

In a few experiments with Worrall, no volitional effects were observed over controls. Nonetheless, the results obtained were generally consistent with her intention to heal or protect the bacteria from harsh environmental conditions. At the same time, Worrall was occasionally able to ascertain remotely the conditions of the various cultures as well as predict results of particular test tube aliquots. She spontaneously spoke about this throughout the experiments, although this was not part of the experimental design.

Three other participants reputed to have healing abilities were also tested using the same protocol for measuring culture growth. Two of these manifested similar small enhancements of bacterial growth consistent with their intentions. However, the results for one of the participants was insignificant compared to controls.

The experimental results of volitional effects on bacterial cultures generally show small effects on bacterial growth and motility consistent with participant volition. One may speculate that a signal emitted from the participants in the form of a specific low-level non-thermal electromagnetic field associated with a 'healing' state of consciousness stimulates bacterial vitality.

This experimental design is exemplary in being a simple, relatively inexpensive, quantitative measure of volitional effects on a well-characterized biological system. Nonetheless, there are shortcomings to such experiments which neglect the inner states of the participants and the experimenters. A more balanced and complete approach to the effects of volition would address both the inner states as well as measurable physical interactions. Recommendations for a new paradigm for the human sciences are offered. [Invited paper, updated by the author. – Ed. note]

Introduction

Persons with reported healing abilities have apparently existed in every culture, and ours is no exception. There have been laboratory examinations by others of purported abilities to remotely affect biological systems, for example, on wound healing in mice{1}, plant growth{2}, and enzyme activity{3}. Whereas those studies involved effects on complex phenomena in multicellular organisms or on enzymes, non-living components of cells, this work examines the subtle interactions of humans with the bacterium, Salmonella typhimurium (ST). This bacterium is closely related to the ubiquitous Escherichia coli which inhabits the human gut. More physiology and biochemistry is known about it than any other organism. The motility (swimming behavior) and growth rate of ST cultures as affected by so-called "healers" were measured in comparison to control cultures.

The purpose of this work is: (1) to see whether volitional life-enhancing effects could be observed on a simple, classical biological system; (2) to investigate the possibility of measurable bioeffects of 'laying on of hands'; (3) if volitional healing effects are found, to work toward elucidating their *modus operandi* on a well characterized organism; and (4) if positive effects are ob-

13927-VALO

served, to see whether this methodology yields phenomena that could be replicated over time.

The experimental design involves a number of considerations. It is very important to take into consideration the attitude and belief system of the participant because the psychological conditions can possible enhance or inhibit any positive experimental results. The participant that was studied first and most extensively over a four-year period is the late Olga Worrall. She had worked as a spiritual faith healer in Baltimore and was internationally known for her purported healing abilities. In the early stages of the experimental design, she expressed interest and enthusiasm in the possibility of treating a biological target, as she had already demonstrated volitional interactions with several physical targets in tests conducted by other experimenters.

The biological system should be well-characterized. That is, there should be a compilation of data from controlled experiments without the participant present to provide an adequate baseline. As I had already completed four years of experimental research involving the motility behavior and growth rate of ST prior to my studies on volitional effects, it was an ideal system for me to use. It is relatively simple to prepare identical control and test samples, and the results on control cultures are replicable over years.

It should be possible for the participant to receive immediate feedback as to the state of her intervention in the system. If possible, the experimenter should be able to observe the effects of this feedback on the participant and the system. The motility of ST can be directly observed by using a double-ocular microscope so that both participant and experimenter can readily observe motility changes in real time. However, the growth rate experiments do not lend themselves to immediate feedback.

The system should have a rapidly varying parameter that is well characterized, in which one can measure change or rate of change. Motility changes and culture growth rate represent rapidly changing parameters in ST that are easily measured.

It should be possible to make a permanent record of both the test and control measurements. The motility measurements can be permanently recorded using dark-field microphotography at the same time that a sample is observed. The growth rates of liquid cultures can be recorded as absorbance over time using a recording spectrophotometer.

A variety of tests to study volitional effects should be available to stimulate the participants and prevent boredom. Moreover, as the nature of specific participant effects are unknown or may vary, a variety of tests is needed to best capture a participant-associated phenomenon, if any. In the case of ST, which is a weak pathogen in humans, a variety of tests was especially important, as it was unclear exactly how participants might react to the organism. Some might try to produce detrimental effects on the bacteria, whereas others might try to produce life-enhancing effects. Furthermore, by using specific chemical inhibitors and various mutants in the various test designs, the specificity, if any, of volitional effects on the bacteria might be observed. For example, a participant's ability to overcome the effects of one particular chemical inhibitor would provide a clue as to a specific mechanism for that participant's effect. The tests using a met(-) auxotroph, a mutant requiring methionine (an animo acid) for growth, starved for methionine was designed to show whether participants might affect the bacteria by increasing the background mutation rate of DNA.

It is typical in biology or medical research to choose a simple cell or animal model to study a new phenomena, and bacterial systems are among those traditionally used. They have been selected for their relative inexpensiveness and ability to yield rapid results that are easily replicated over time and reproducible by others. Because this system is relatively simple and already well-characterized, it maximizes the potential toward understanding the nature of volitional effects, if any, on life processes. Furthermore, such an understanding may lead to predictions as to the nature of the interactions that may be observed on more complex systems such as volitional healing effects in animals or humans. The experimental results with Worrall as participant have already been reported elsewhere {4,5}.

Experimental Methods

A wild type strain of Salmonella typhimurium (ST1) was grown in Vogel-Bonner citrate medium, an aqueous mixture of buffered salts to which 1% glycerol was added as a carbon source. This is a minimal medium favored by ST that supports growth of flagella (organelles for motility). Bacteria were grown to mid-logarithmic growth phase (active growth), resuspended in fresh media, and used directly for experimentation. The details of working with this bacterial system are described in the literature{6}. Olga Worrall as participant performed what she described as "healings" for up to two minutes in which she held her hands with the palms facing near to (up to 2") but not touching the closed containers of liquid bacterial cultures with an expressed intention to heal them. From changes in her face and tone of voice during these treatment intervals, she appeared to be in an altered, trance-like state.

In the first type of experimental test, volitional effects on the growth of chemically-inhibited cultures were measured. The participant treated plastic-stoppered glass or plastic test tubes containing 15 milliliters (ml) of liquid cultures of ST171, another strain of Salmonella typhimurium, the population density being 3×10^8 bacteria per ml, to which was added various doses of the bacterial antibiotics, chloramphenicol or tetracycline, immediately prior to the treatment. These antibiotics inhibit protein synthesis in bacteria and thereby stop culture growth to some degree, depending upon their concentration. Control cultures prepared in exactly the same way were removed from the room prior to treatment of the test cultures. Naive participants also served as additional controls. Samples were run at least in triplicate.

The second type of experimental test involved treatment of normal cultures to see if any growth enhancement would occur. The participant treated test tubes containing 15 ml of medium either with ST1 in early logarithmic growth phase or freshly inoculated with ST1. Control cultures prepared in exactly the same way were removed from the room prior to treatment of the test cultures, to prevent any possible 'field effects' associated with participant treatment. A naive participant who had no prior experience was also used as an additional control. Samples were run at least in triplicate.

In the third type of experimental test, volitional effects on bacterial motility were determined. The biological target was in the form of three microliters of bacterial culture on a glass microscope slide under a glass coverslip. Prior to preparation of the slide, phenol was added to the bacterial suspension to a final concentration of 50 millimolar (mM). This high concentration of phenol is sufficient to paralyze ST1 in all control cultures by destroying the energy source for motility. I had previously used 50 mM phenol in over four years of experimentation on ST1 with the result of completely immobilizing the bacteria. Both participant-treated and-untreated control samples were run in triplicate. Treatment by a naive participant served as an additional control. Control cultures prepared in exactly the same way were removed from the room prior to treatment of the test cultures, to prevent any possible 'field effects' associated with participant treatment. The slides were observed under a dark-field microscope at 600X magnification both by experimenter and participant and at the same time photographed using a one-second time exposure to a 5 Hz xenon stroboscopic lamp. Motility was calculated from the microphotographs that showed sequential patterns of rod-like tracks characteristic of motile bacteria, easily distinguishable from the fixed or blurred rod-like images characteristic of immotile bacteria. Tracks were counted and motility expressed as a percentage of total bacteria present. From a series of such photographs, the percentage of motile bacteria at specific times up to

15 minutes after treatment was calculated and compared to controls.

In the fourth type of experimental test, the participant treated test tubes containing 15 ml of minimal medium lacking methionine in which 3 X 10^8 met(-) bacteria per ml were suspended. This is a mutant strain of ST that requires methionine in order to grow. Furthermore, this particular mutant was previously characterized as being a "nonsense" mutant, i.e., having a point mutational defect in a single base pair in its DNA. Not only is it one of the simplest mutations, but a further single mutation induced at that point in the DNA would cause it to revert to normal, whereby it could grow normally without methionine. The aim of this test was to see if the participant could effectively cause point mutations above and beyond the normal background mutation rate of about 1 spontaneous mutation in 10^6 bacteria per generation time. Control cultures prepared in exactly the same way were removed from the room prior to treatment of the test cultures. Samples were run in triplicate.

In the experimental tests involving culture samples in test tubes, aliquots of bacterial cultures were taken from the tubes using standard sterile technique and placed in 1 ml glass cuvettes in order to measure the density of bacteria optically by means of a standard technique. The absorbance at 620 nanometers in a spectrophotometer was determined for each bacterial sample using the growth medium as a blank. The absorbance measurement or optical density, related to the light scattered from the bacterial cells, was previously experimentally correlated with bacterial cell density.

Most of the experiments were performed in an electromagnetically shielded 30°C constant temperature room, in which cultures were aerated by mechanical rotation at 20 rpm, conditions optimum for the motility of the strains used. Double-blinded or at least blinded conditions were utilized in all experiments.

Results

Table 1 gives a summary of the results of three experimental studies conducted with Worrall as participant. The results shown are calculated differences from controls averaged for at least triplicate samples. Particular time points were selected in each case to show the maximum differences from the controls. In all cases, naive participant controls did not differ significantly from other controls, and the data is not shown. Thus, Worrall-treated samples are compared directly to untreated controls.

The data for the growth studies compiled in the table are expressed as the percent difference of Worrall-treated samples over controls, calculated from the numbers of bacteria present at the same bacterial generation times. The bacterial generation time was determined to be about 1 hour under normal growth conditions by measuring the time in which normal cultures (without antibiotics present) double in opacity, as optical density is proportional to cell number.

Table I

Summary of Results from 1979, 1980, and 1981 Studies with O. Worrall as Participant

Bacterial Culture Conditions	Generation time, hrs.	Per Cent Average Difference of Healer-Treated over Controls*
Normal, 1981	24	+23%
Normal, 1979	16	0%
Growth Inhibition Using Antibiotics 1 microgram/ml tetracycline, 1981	23	+121%
10 microgram/ml tetracycline, 1980	21	+28%
10 microgram/ml chloramphenicol, 1981	22	+70%
100 microgram/ml chloramphenicol, 1979	16	+22%
100 microgram/ml chloramphenicol, 1980	21	+24%
Methionine Auxotroph Starved for Methionine, 1980	23	0%
Motility Inhibitor Present, 1979 50 mM phenol	-	+7%

* % difference is defined as (T-C)/C x 100%, where T = average number of bacteria in healer-treated samples, and C = average number of bacteria in control samples.

Effects of Worrall Treatment upon Bacteria in the Presence of Antibiotic Growth Inhibitors

Although the two antibiotics, chloramphenicol and tetracycline, differ in their mode of action in stopping bacterial protein synthesis, the experiments in which they were used yielded quite similar results, in that the Worrall treatment apparently did not discriminate between them. Also similar was the apparent dose-response trend for each particular antibiotic. That is, for smaller concentrations of either antibiotic, the healer treatment enhanced bacterial growth more than it did on larger concentrations of the same antibiotic. As a dose-response effect is one criterion for a definitive result in biomedical research, this is an important result. It appears that the bacteria respond more positively to the Worrall treatment when they are less thwarted by chemical inhibitors.

In each of the three studies performed in different years, it was also found that the time course of the effects of Worrall's treatment on bacterial growth rate was relatively constant. Thus, for each Worrall-treated bacterial sample, the features of the viability curve (numbers of bacterial survivors over time) are similar for both antibiotics at comparable doses. This indicates that there is some measure of constancy and reproducibility in these experiments.

The application of 10 micrograms/ml tetracycline completely inhibits bacterial growth after about four hours in the absence of participant intervention. Treatment by Worrall apparently inhibited the effect of tetracycline, producing a maximum difference from controls of 121% more bacteria surviving in the presence of 1 microgram/ml tetracycline at 23 generation times. The viability curves is shown in Figure 1. The maximum difference observed in the Worrall-treated cultures with 10 micrograms/ml tetracycline was 28% more bacteria at 21 generations. These figures show significant differences between control and participant-treated cultures, as the random error in the control samples is only 2%. Although the random error in the treated samples ranged from 2 to 20%, the treated samples were always observed to possess more viability than the controls. These data demonstrate a dose response trend.

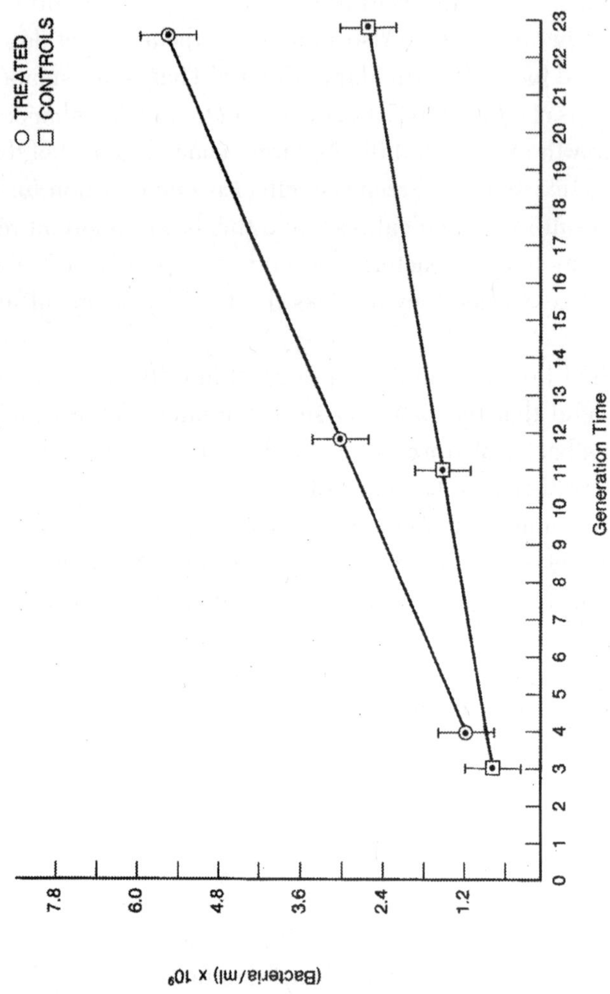

Fig. 1. Viability curve for bacteria in the presence of 1 microgram/ml tetracycline (1981).

The application of 100 micrograms/ml chloramphenicol completely inhibits growth of ST after about four hours in the absence of participant intervention. Worrall's treatment inhibited the effect of this particular dose of chloramphenicol to the effect of 22 to 24% more bacteria surviving over controls, and in the case of 10 micrograms/ml of the drug, an enhanced growth rate of 70% over controls. These data also show a dose-response trend. As the results from the naive participant controls are the same as untreated controls, one cannot account for the Worrall effect by a warming effect of the bacteria by human hands.

In the 1979 and 1980 studies, very similar results were obtained for the growth enhancement of participant-treated cultures containing 100 micrograms/ml chloramphenicol. The 1979 experiments yielded a 22% enhancement of treated over controls, and the 1980 experiments yielded a 24% enhancement. This indicates some degree of replicability of this approach. Note that in Figure 2 where standard deviations are not displayed, they are equal to or smaller than the circles or squares around the data points.

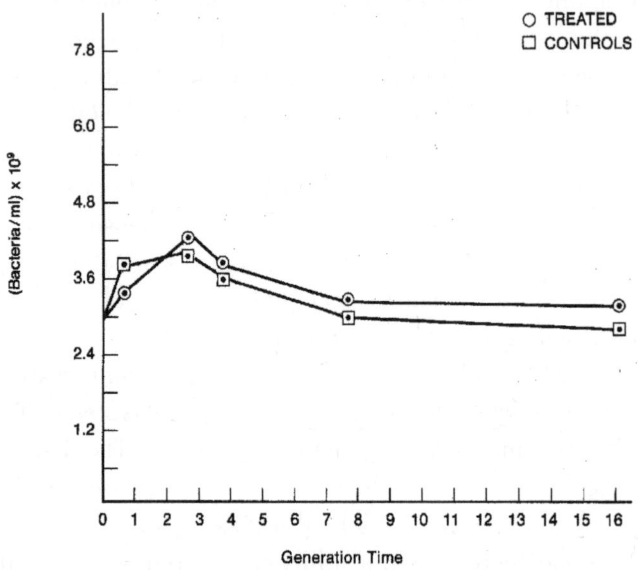

Fig. 2. Viability curve for bacteria in the presence of 1000 micrograms/ml chloramphenicol (1979).

Effects of Worrall Treatment upon Normal Bacterial Cultures without Inhibitors

Two sets of experiments were done to examine Worrall's interaction with the growth of normal bacterial cultures. The 1979 experiments yielded no difference in growth between control and treated samples when the organisms were treated early in their growth phase, the so-called lag phase. In 1981, participant treatment was performed while the bacteria were in mid-logarithmic growth phase (actively growing), and led to a 23% increase in numbers of bacteria over controls. One major difference between these two experiments is the culture conditions. In lag phase, conditions are optimal for growth with no accumulation of bacterial wastes. However, in logarithmic phase, the culture medium may be less than optimum, since bacterial wastes have accumulated. Thus, the difference in the results obtained between these two different experiments may be significant, indicating the possibility of an optimum state of health for the bacteria beyond which healer intervention has little or no effect.

Effects of Worrall Treatment upon Bacterial Cultures Treated with a Motility Inhibitor

Application of 50 mM phenol completely paralyzes the bacteria within 1 to 2 minutes. Worrall's treatment inhibited this effect on ST1, such that on the average up to 7% of the bacteria continued to swim after 12 minutes exposure to phenol compared to the control groups which were completely paralyzed in all cases. This is highly significant, for motility had never been observed in over four years of biophysical experiments using ST1 in 50 mM phenol.

Effects of Worrall Treatment upon Met(-) Auxotrophic Strains Starved for Methionine

No effects of Worrall treatment above controls were observed in this case. That is to say, no culture growth occurred for the mutant bacteria starved for methionine and requiring methionine for growth, either in controls or Worrall-treated cultures. This result is consistent with the apparent inability of the Worrall treatment to increase the spontaneous mutation rate of ST.

Additional Observations in Experiments with Olga Worrall as Participant

On two occasions, Worrall spontaneously produced information during the experiments which subsequently or cotemporaneously proved to be true. Upon placing her hands near the met(-) bacterial auxotrophs which were methionine-starved and unable to grow, she exclaimed that these were like

13927-VALO

"starving children". Since all of the bacterial samples appeared identical as opalescent liquid suspensions, there were no cues to suggest this. On other occasions, she put her hands near a test tube labelled #20, and said that it was anomalous and that she felt much "energy" associated with it. Data gathered subsequently on the growth of sample #20 indeed proved that it was an anomaly, showing growth several times faster than all other samples. Such unplanned occurrences, however, have no place in the scientific literature, but nonetheless appear to be significant demonstrations of psi.

Volitional Effects of Others Performing 'Laying on of Hands' on Bacterial Growth

Three other participants who are purported healers have been studied to date. Only two of these were able to produce positive volitional effects on the growth of the bacterial cultures in the presence of the same antibiotic inhibitors under the same conditions of the experimental design (data unpublished). The results suggest similar trends of a dose-response effect. However, rapid-onset effects of growth stimulation within 10 minutes were observed in the case of one participant who also predicted this type of effect. As with Olga Worrall, no participant effects were observed on the met(-) auxotroph starved for methionine.

These findings also offer considerable support for the results obtained with Worrall. They suggest that the phenomena observed are not merely isolated anomalies, but that a distinctive pattern of results may be obtained using this experimental protocol with purported healers as participants.

Conclusions

Results indicate that volitional participant treatment associated with 'laying on of hands' produces typically small but significant bacterial culture growth and motility increases over controls in the presence of a variety of chemical inhibitors, without any apparent specificity. These results suggest the hypothesis of a generalized effect of healer intervention upon bacterial cultures.

There is the possibility that specific signals that are low-level non-thermal electromagnetic (EM) fields may be associated with volitional 'laying on of hands'; for example, specific EM frequencies that produce enhanced vitality of the bacteria. For example, in bioelectromagnetics, specific resonant frequencies of extremely low-level microwaves have been shown to stimulate in vitro growth of yeast{7}. Because naive participants did not produce any net effects above untreated controls, such specific frequencies, if they are present, would be physiological correlates to specific states of consciousness, i.e., healing states, and not associated with ordinary states of consciousness. This is consistent with the fact that human nervous system activity, as shown by electroencephalography or magnetoencephalography, consists of extremely low frequency activity whose patterns are known to change with altered states of consciousness. However, particular patterns of extremely low frequency fields have not yet been reported in association with 'laying on of hands' treatments. Moreover, such experiments to measure low-level extremely low frequency EM fields are difficult to do, requiring special conditions and equipment.

On the other hand, studies with Worrall done by other experimenters demonstrated long distance effects on organisms, suggesting that local electromagnetic fields associated with particular states of the body-mind may not be involved in these types of healer treatments. Alternatively, it is possible that more than one type of modus operandi may be involved in participant effects on biological systems, i.e., for local and nonlocal.

The studies described here examine the effects of a purported psychic and spiritual healer, the late Olga Worrall, on rapidly growing, motile bacteria with controls, direct feedback to the participant, and a permanent recording system. It is important to consider the attitude of the participant, which may be critical to the experimental outcome. Prior to the experiment, Worrall was informed that ST is a weak pathogen for humans, capable of causing dysentery. Their motility behavior was shown to her through a microscope. She was asked whether her intention would be to heal or harm the bacteria. Upon seeing the swimming bacteria under the microscope, she responded with, "cute little critters". She also said that she would enhance their motility and growth because her healing abilities could not be used to the detriment of any organism. The feedback which Worrall received during the motility experiments was positive in terms of her having an effect on the motility. This enhanced her already positive attitude toward the experiment. Most of the experimental results obtained here are consistent with Worrall's stated intentions and expressed attitudes.

This bacterial system appears to be a most suitable one by which to study intention to heal or other volitional effects under controlled laboratory conditions on a well-characterized organism. Like most experiments on microbial systems, these are relatively inexpensive, technically simple, and involve basic parameters associated with the living state—growth and motility. Furthermore, others may attempt to replicate them by using the same bacterial strains and laboratory conditions.

Discussion

Reflecting several years later on these experimental studies raised several issues about the approach used here as well as in psi research, research on paranormal abilities in general. For example, the fact that Worrall was able to ascertain remotely information about the status of the bacteria, despite the double-blinded conditions of the experiment, was significant and meaningful, even if unquantifiable. Since it was not anticipated or controlled for in the experiments, it is not considered to be reportable scientific evidence. It suggests that further experiments be set up to measure these apparent psi abilities by an appropriate methodology. However, psi may manifest more readily under conditions of natural spontaneity than focussed attention. Can psi research really ever meet this level of spontaneity?

There were also uncontrollable differences in the psychological atmosphere from one experiment to another, which occasionally appeared to correlate with Worrall's performance in the laboratory. But contemporary science largely ignores the psychological aspects of both experimenters and participants, assuming that its validity depends only on operations for gathering evidence. In general, psi research results suggest that the psychological conditions prior to and during the experiment are of critical importance. This is not surprising, since such research is intimately involved with particular states of consciousness and intention. But how can we adequately control for subjective aspects we cannot measure, such as states of consciousness? Can the subtle realms of mind be contained by experimental boundary conditions? What about psychological effects of others present or not who have vested interests in the experimental outcome? Are we deluding ourselves when we close the laboratory door in a psi research experiment, in believing that we are isolating ourselves from other influences? What about the possible effects of other nonlocal influences on psi, such as geomagnetic field variations and other natural cosmic cycles?

Humans may be regarded as dynamical dissipative biological structures that are always changing. Of all aspects of life, consciousness may be the most fleeting, since we cannot easily control our own rambling thoughts or inner states. For psi research, this makes the scientific validating criteria of reproducibility and replicability difficult, if not impossible. However, since the living state is dynamic, not static, in the limit these criteria may need to be reexamined for the life sciences in general.

It appears that quantitative data gathering and statistics dominate contemporary psi research. It may seem easy enough to put psi participants through numerous trials to generate a large amount of data. However, it may be statistically significant but humanly insignificant. Boredom, fatigue, alienation, or mistrust may affect the participant, destroy the psychological rapport, and yield a lower psi score. It is well known that any psi effect is effectly lost upon numerous subsequent trials, just as habituation results with any repetitious human activity. In my research with Worrall, by the third study she expressed her reluctance to repeat what she had already done twice before, and some of the data reflected this. Novelty was clearly important in maintaining her interest and ability.

These questions lead to the deeper issue of developing a more appropriate paradigm for psi research. One possible framework is general systems theory. The experimental human system may be considered to be composed of all the researchers and participants, with psi a property of the whole system. In addition, psi events from a system's view may be regarded as dynamical spontaneous features of the cosmos at large, analogous to Mach's Principle in physics in which things are related to the system of all other bodies in the cosmos. Rather than putting all the emphasis on the participant, acknowledgment of a holistic ideology may be an important step forward for psi research both philosophically and methodologically. The specific location and time of the experiment, people present, and other subtle factors including geo-cosmic rhythms may be important considerations toward optimizing the experimental outcome.

Although conventional science requires replicability by any scientist, this may be an extreme requirement for psi research considered from a systems view. All scientists are not equivalent in psi research because each has a unique presence that would create a distinctly different experimental experience for the participant. If the psi-challenging magician, James Randi, had repeated the experimental protocol with Olga Worrall, it is conceivable that he would not obtain the same results. None of us are impartial observers. We have interests, even passion, in proving or disproving our hypotheses. In one sociological study on scientific falsifiability{8}, hypotheses were assigned to groups of scientists and clergymen that were entirely false, although they did not know it. They were asked to perform a simple experimental test of their hypotheses to see whether they would conclude that the hypotheses were indeed false. The results indicated denial, as most of the scientists refused to admit that their hypotheses were false. However, the clergymen more frequently reported that theirs were false! Nonetheless, there is a myth in the scientific community, an undercurrent of expectation, that scientists function as intelligent extensions of machines. Given the complexity of conscious and unconscious factors, are we deluding ourselves in considering that we could even attempt impartiality in any experiment?

From examining the literature on research methodology in psychology, one of the most notable omissions is any indication of how the psychological researcher is supposed to think. A search uncovered only one paper that indicated that the role of intention on the part of researchers is a significant component of the process and outcome of research in psychology{9}. If the consciousness of the experimenter is important, what is the appropriate state and relationship to the participant in psi research? Will a scientist who believes strongly in psi affect the outcome of the experiment? From a holistic systems viewpoint, new properties emerge at new levels of order, which is in this case, the new whole comprised of persons and target systems together in a psi research experiment. Just as powerful effects of collective or coherent phenomena are observed at molecular and cellular levels, one might expect strong synergistic effects of collective, focussed attention associated with the mind-body of a coherent group of people. These could be explored experimentally.

Human systems are interactive, mutually causal systems{10}. There are different ways of interacting with participants under study. One way is to render them naive and uninformed about the experiment. Another is a more cooperative inquiry between researchers and participants, allowing both to contribute directly to hypothesis formation and experimental design. The latter was utilized in the studies with Worrall as participant. This interaction may be more appropriate for psi research and may enhance the results obtained. Analogous situations in education and business show that people perform better when interactive or participatory management is employed.

The main reason that I stopped doing research in this area was that I felt that the real challenge for psi research was not to refine a method for reproducibly measuring and documenting psi, but to develop a new paradigm that is appropriate. In my opinion, the conventional paradigm is inadequate for psi research and has perhaps impeded its progress. Modern parapsychology has suffered from what I call 'physics envy'. The main approach, adopted from the physical sciences—object-oriented, behaviorist, quantitative, and statistical—has been applied by psi researchers sincerely in a valiant effort to scientifically validate their work, but apparently without sufficient examination of basic epistemological methodological issues.

A whole new basis for the life sciences, particularly the human sciences, is needed. The humanistic psychologists have pointed out this need for decades{11,12,13,14}. A truly human science emphasizing human experience as its subject matter is now beginning to emerge{15}. Some new methodologies include qualitative approaches{16}, heuristic methods{17}, perceptual psychological methods{18}, contemporary hermeneutics{19}, and phenomenological methods{20}. One important point of agreement is that there is no one best method. Research methods are becoming more appropriately seen as tools. The methodology selected is appropriate to the research question; e.g., qualitative questions require qualitative methods. However, humanistic and transpersonal psychology have not made significant impacts on mainstream academic psychology. They remain a small voice largely unheard within the scientific community at large.

New findings in other frontier areas of science such as bioelectromagnetics, the interaction of electromagnetic fields with living systems, consist of anomalies that also challenge the dominant paradigm. Together with psi research, these are beginning to fit together like pieces of a puzzle demanding a larger scientific worldview to accommodate them. Collectively they specify the features of an emerging paradigm which addresses new realms of the living state: new informational capacities, interactions with electromagnetic fields, and subtle interrelationships between mind and matter{21,22}. New developments in the frontier sciences may help pave the road toward a new paradigm for psi research as well as a post-modern science.

In order to develop a new paradigm for psi research, we need a new way of looking at the world and interpreting it. "The most important task today is perhaps to learn to think in a new way . . . if we don't learn to think clearly and appropriately in a way that suits our subject matter and our approach, we run the risk of simply doing analytical science badly." {23}

However, it is extremely difficult to see that there are alternatives to our traditional ways of thinking when our ordinary states of consciousness are so entwined with accepted modes of scientific thinking. Although conventional science does not admit to notions of meaning, a human science cannot ignore it. Psi research should encompass the meaning and value of the psi experience and experiment for both researchers and participants. Data on the "inner dimensions" are just as important as on external phenomena. In this regard, I have some interesting anecdotal data. In an experiment I conducted using one of Helmut Schmidt's random event generator devices with Terry Ross as the operator, I saw from the visual feedback that his scores were insignificant from the very beginning. Terry also seemed frustrated during the experiment. When I asked Terry about his attitude toward the device, he replied that he disliked it. I asked him whether there was any way that he could change his attitude toward it, even for a moment, and immediately try another run. In a moment of apparent inspiration, he picked up the device and cuddled it like a puppy dog, and in the next run achieved a positive score over three standard deviations above the mean value, the most significant positive data that I ever obtained.

Experiential and phenomenological research could have important interplay with research designs in a new paradigm for psi research. High calibre experiential research would be most valuable because it is closest to 'real life'. However, use of subjective experience as a source of knowledge requires high standards of the scientist. It is a paradigm for a "state-specific" science, i.e., a science in which you have to shift your state of consciousness in order to do the research, communicate it, and understand communications about it {24}. "Sciences appropriate to different systems levels may be qualitatively different"{25}.

In my opinion, psi phenomena manifest from our deepest, most intimate realms of being, and an appropriate science of psi must include not only the psychological but the spiritual domain to accommodate its full depth and breadth. An appropriate new paradigm for psi research will emphasize the integrity, authenticity, and personal commitment of the scientist in addition to a revisioned scientific philosophy and methodology.

"Scientific methodology needs to be seen for what it truly is, a way of preventing me from deceiving myself in regard to my creatively formed subjective hunches which have developed out of the relationship between me and my material."{26}

We cannot study human potential except as humble and aware human beings in pursuit of knowledge as well as self-knowledge.

Acknowledgments

The late Olga Worrall first inspired me to the possibility of volitional interventions to promote healing. I am grateful to the Ernest Holmes Foundation of Los Angeles, CA, for supporting the experimental research with Olga Worrall as participant. I also wish to acknowledge Elizabeth Rauscher who assisted me in the experiments with Olga Worrall, and with whom I co-authored earlier reports on those experiments.

References

1. Grad, B., Cadoret, R.J., et al. (1961). The Influence of an Unorthodox Method of Treatment on Wound Healing in Mice. *International Journal of Parapsychology*, 3, 5-24.
2. Grad, B. (1964). A Telekinetic Effect on Plant Growth. II. Experiments Involving Treatment of Saline in Stoppered Bottles. *International Journal of Parapsychology* 6, 472-498.
3. Smith, M. J. (1972). Paranormal Effects on Enzyme Activity. *Human Dimensions* 1, 15-19.
4. Rauscher, E. and B. Rubik (1980) Effects on motility behavior and growth rate of Salmonella typhimurium in the presence of Olga Worrall, *Research in Parapsychology* 1979, London: Scarecrow Press, 140-2.
5. Rauscher, E. and B. Rubik (1983) Human volitional effects on a model bacterial system, *Psi Research* 2(1), 38-48.
6. Rubik, B. A. (1979) *A System's Approach to Bacterial Chemotaxis*. Ph.D. Dissertation (University of California, Berkeley, CA).
7. Grundler, W. and F. Keilman (1989) Resonant microwave effect on locally fixed yeast microcolonies. *Z. Naturforsch.* 44c, 863-866.
8. Truzzi, M. (1990) Reflections on the reception of unconventional claims in science. *Frontier Perspectives* 1(2), 12-25.
9. Weiss, A. and B. Kempler (1986) The role of intent in psychological research, *J. Hum. Psych.* 26(1), 117-125.
10. Rowan, J. (1981) A dialectical paradigm for research, in *Human Inquiry: A Sourcebook for New Paradigm Research,* P. Reason and J. Rowan (ed.), New York: John Wiley and Sons, 93-112.
11. Rogers, C. (1964) Toward a science of the person, in *Behaviorism and Phenomenology: Contrasting Bases for Modern Psychology*, T. Wann (ed.), Chicago: Univ. of Chicago Press.

12. Rogers, C. (1968) Some thoughts regarding the current assumptions of the behavioral sciences, in *Man and the Science of Man*, W. Coulson and C. Rogers (ed.), Columbus, Ohio: Charles Merrill.
13. Rogers, C. (1985) Toward a more human science of the person, *J. Hum. Psych.* 25(4), 7-24.
14. Maslow, A. (1966) *The Psychology of Science.* New York: Harper and Row.
15. Barrell, J., Aanstoos, C., et al. (1987) Human Science Research Methods, *J. Hum. Psych.* 27(4), 424-457.
16. Van Maanen, J. (ed.) (1983) *Qualitative Methodology.* Beverly Hills, CA: Sage Publications.
17. Douglass, B. and C. Moustakas (1985) Heuristic inquiry: the internal search to know, *J. Hum. Psych.* 25(3), 39-55.
18. Combs, A., Richards, A., et al. (1976) *Perceptual Psychology: A Humanistic Approach to the Studying of Persons.* New York: Harper and Row.
19. Bubner, R. (1988) *Essays in Hermeneutics and Critical Theory.* New York: Columbia University Press.
20. Giorgi, A. (1985) *Phenomenology and Psychological Research.* Pittsburgh: Duquesne Univ. Press.
21. Rubik, B. (ed.) (1990) From the Editor's Desk. *Frontier Perspectives* 1(2), Philadelphia: Center for Frontier Sciences, Temple University.
22. Rubik, B. (1991) Life at the Edge of Science: The Center for Frontier Sciences at Four Years. *Raum & Zeit* 3(1) 59-64.
23. Bateson, G. (1972) *Steps to an Ecology of Mind.* San Francisco: Chandler.
24. Tart, C. (1972) States of consciousness and state-specific sciences, *Science* 176, 1203-10.
25. Harman, W. (1981) Science and the clarification of values: implications of recent findings in psychological and psychic research, *J. Hum. Psych.* 21(3), 3-16.
26. Rogers, C. (1961) *On Becoming a Person: A Therapist's View of Psychotherapy.* London: Constable.

BEVERLY RUBIK, Ph.D. is the Founder and Executive Director of the Institute for Frontier Sciences, a biophyscist, researcher, author, and educator. She is the author of Life at the Edge of Science. She is a member of the Program Advisory Council of the Office of Alternative Medicine at the U.S. National Institute of Health. She can be reached at *www.concentric.net/~explore* and *explore@concentric.net*

13927-VALO

19

On the Principles of Permissible Overunity EM Power Systems

Thomas. E. Bearden

CTEC, Inc.
Fellow Emeritus, AIAS

26th Annual Conference of the U. S. Psychotronics Association, Columbus, OH

Abstract and Summary

We develop the major principles of emerging overunity EM power systems as open systems far from thermodynamic equilibrium, freely receiving excess energy from the active vacuum. Such systems were arbitrarily omitted from Maxwell's theory by curtailment. Heaviside's reinterpretation and simplification of Maxwell's equations did retain such overunity EM systems as one major subset. Lorentz then regauged the Maxwell-Heaviside equations by arbitrary symmetrical regauging to provide still simpler equations and a further reduced subset of permissible Maxwell-Heaviside systems. Lorentz regauging erroneously discarded the entire class of

Maxwellian EM systems not in thermodynamic equilibrium with the active vacuum.

Generators and batteries do not furnish energy to their external circuits. Instead, the source dipole, once formed, extracts energy from the vacuum via the broken 3-symmetry of its constituent charges. The generators and batteries only perform work upon their internal charges to separate them and form the source dipole. Hence one does not input energy to a conventional power source to *power the circuit*; instead, the input energy is only for the power source to *create its source dipole*. Once made, the broken symmetry of the dipole extracts usable EM energy from the vacuum and pours it out the terminals of the power supply. The extracted energy from the vacuum is in the form of Heaviside/Poynting energy flow, consisting of two components. The portion striking the circuit and diverged into the conductors to power the electron current is the Poynting component. The remaining Heaviside nondiverged component misses the circuit and is wasted. Every dipolar power supply is already a COP>1.0 EM converter system. [COP is "coefficient of performance" and differs from efficiency. See page 434. – Ed. note]

Closed current loop design of present power systems insures that Lorentz symmetrical regauging is self-applied by every system. The depotentialized electrons in the ground return line are forcibly rammed back through the back emf of the source dipole, scattering the dipole charges and destroying the source dipole. This kills the flow of energy being extracted from the vacuum by the former dipole. Such systems use their collected energy to destroy their free energy mechanism (the source dipole) and its extraction of energy from the vacuum, faster than they can power their loads. Hence present EM power systems are self-crippling systems inherently self-limited to COP<1.0.

Classical EM still erroneously assumes any charge as existing in an inert vacuum and creating—right out of nothing—all the EM energy flow it continuously pours out in all directions across the entire universe, providing the EM energy in the fields and poten-

13927-VALO

tials associated with the charge. This erroneous assumption that every charge is a pure source and a perpetual motion machine was resolved over 40 years ago in particle physics. However, classical electrodynamicists have never changed their century-old model to incorporate the proven active vacuum exchange.

For circuits, electrodynamicists presently do not calculate the entire associated EM energy flow, which is large. Instead, they calculate the small Poynting component of the flow—that component of the flow that strikes the surface charges in the circuit and is thereby diverged into the circuit to power the electrons. The *non*diverged energy transport (Heaviside) portion of the EM energy flow that misses the circuit is arbitrarily discarded. Following Lorentz's method {1 }, electrodynamicists calculate the Slepian vector equivalent (i.e., the Poynting component) and erroneously label it the entire EM energy flow. Instead, it is the *energy dissipation flow* inside the circuit, not the entire EM energy flow associated with the circuit, both inside and outside it.

For a nominal circuit, the entire EM energy flow extracted by the source dipole from the vacuum may be on the order of 10^{13} times as great as the Poynting component actually intercepted by the circuit {2 ,3 } and then used to produce the Slepian vector and power the losses and loads while also killing the source dipole. (My calculation of the 10^{13} figure was admittedly very crude, but even if it is excessive by several orders of magnitude, the total amount of Heaviside energy flow in space around the conductors, not entering the circuit, is still formidable. We have nominated that nondiverged, unaccounted "dark" Heaviside energy as the agent producing the excess gravity in the arms of spiral galaxies and holding them together. See T. E. Bearden, "Dark Matter or Dark Energy?", *Journal of New Energy*, 4(4), Spring 2000, p. 4-11.)

Examples of legitimate overunity systems and processes developed by scientists (Sweet, Kron, Lawandy, Letokhov, Chung, Mandel'shtam and Papaleksi) are briefly presented. The Bohren experiment is repeatable and produces COP = 18.

A summary of the major principles and characteristics of permissible EM power systems with COP>1.0 is presented at the conclusion. The reader is directed to my website, *www.cheniere.org*, for appreciable additional COP>1.0 system information.

Introduction Beginning with Magnetics

Kinetic Magnets: Self-Oscillation in Magnetic Materials

The present author was for some years a colleague of inventor Floyd Sweet. In the 1980s and 1990s, the Sweet solid state vacuum triode amplifier {4} produced ordinary, standard EM energy (500 watts) unless specially rigged to do antigravity. A retired electrical engineer proficient on the bench, Sweet's power unit produced 500 watts with a COP = 1.5´10^6. The system used barium ferrite permanent magnets whose materials were conditioned into self-oscillation at an initiated ELF frequency. Such a magnet is loosely referred to as a "kinetic magnet".

Self-oscillation in permanent magnets is fairly well-known {5}, though not in electrical power system circles. Sweet's unique contribution was to stimulate self-oscillation at lower frequencies than what is ordinarily thought possible, and to do it more strongly than commonly found in the literature. The unit could also be rigged to do anti-gravity, and would reduce its weight on the laboratory bench by 90%, but that is beyond the scope of this present paper.

It should be obvious to the reader that a permanent magnet with self-oscillating fields can be surrounded by conductors or coils in which the kinetic fields "cut" the conductors and induce currents freely. A resistor can be connected in a closed circuit with the coils, and the resistor will be powered by the kinetic magnet so that free work is continuously performed. In short, any competent university laboratory can produce such a demonstrable little overunity EM power system with a little effort from presently known self-oscillation in magnetic materials. That alone is sufficient to prove that overunity EM power systems are permissible, since it only takes a single white crow to prove that not all crows are black.

Sweet activated his magnets by a proprietary process which he never fully revealed. Nevertheless, materials scientists competent in self-oscillation in magnetic materials can produce such an example magnet, which remains self-kinetic at somewhat higher frequency than the Sweet VTA for some period of time such as minutes, several hours, a day, or even a week.

Sweet's mentor was the great Gabriel Kron, whose negative resistor we discuss later. (A full bibliography of Kron's works is given in S. Austen Stigant, "Gabriel Kron on Tensor Analysis, A bibliographical record," *BEAMA Journal*, Aug. 1948. If one reads Kron's papers carefully, with the "supersystem" in mind, much of what Kron did in his negative resistor becomes apparent.) Sweet greatly admired Kron and knew the details of Kron's negative resistor. A possible connection between Sweet's VTA and Kron's negative resistor cannot be ruled out.

The Researcher Must Be Aware Of Numerous Magnetic Effects {6}

Overunity researchers into magnetic approaches must progress beyond the simplified notion that a permanent magnet is just a blob of uniform material with a magnetic pole at each end. One must be aware of a wide range of odd and unusual effects in magnetic materials {7}, if one wishes to address unusual magnetic engines.

Multivalued magnetic potentials (MVMPs) arise naturally in magnetic theory {8}, and such potentials can yield a nonconservative magnetic field. (A multi-valued magnetic potential has two values at a single point in space, one on the "right" and a different one on the "left". A rotor passing through the point thus sees a free and instantaneous change of magnetic potential, accompanied by a free and instantaneous change of magnetic force.) In that case, integration of F·ds around a rotation loop may permissibly be nonzero, producing an open system far from thermodynamic equilibrium, and permitting the system to exhibit COP>1.0. The MVMP "potential self-jump" is an asymmetrical self-regauging. (We point out that the gauge freedom axiom in gauge field theory already assumes that the potential energy of an electromagnetic system can be freely changed at will, anytime, anywhere. It directly follows that, if we freely increase the potential energy of a system by asymmetrical regauging, the free nonzero force that results allows the excess regauging energy to be dissipated as free work in a load. That our present circuits do not do this, thus focuses attention that it is strictly a fault of the circuitry design. We speak more on this when we mention the concept of the "supersystem". Note that energy conservation requires that an energy transfer method exist for any such regauging under the gauge freedom axiom.)

Many magnetic materials are also photorefractive, and readily produce nonlinear optical effects at various frequencies. As one example, multivalued phase conjugate reflection can occur {9}. Such effects did occur in the Sweet vacuum triode amplifier.

If the magnetics researcher doesn't know what a Wiegand wire{10} is or the Dromgoole {11} effect is, or what the exchange force is, he needs to read the literature. The Wiegand effect occurs in a magnetic pulse wire which, in a magnetic field of a certain size, will self-reverse its dual magnetic state and deliver a very sharp, free magnetic pulse. By surrounding the wire with a coil of many fine turns, one can get a 12-volt pulse of electrical energy, for free. These assemblies are widely used as sensors and switching initiators.

The Dromgoole phenomenon is an interesting effect whereby a voltage placed on a solenoid wrapped around an iron wire may be increased up to 300 times as much by twisting the wire through 90 degrees.

The exchange force is a result of nearly instantaneous "spin flipping" of electrons in the magnetic material, producing a sharp change in magnetic field, both in magnitude and orientation. (For an introduction, Feynman, Richard P., Robert B. Leighton and Matthew Sands, *The Feynman Lectures on Physics*, Addison-Wesley, New York, 1963, Vol. II, Chapter 37 covers magnetic materials including exchange forces, spins, and spin effects.)

There are hundreds of other novel magnetic effects in magnetic materials, many of them involving unusual spin effects. The serious overunity researcher needs to laboriously compile a set of references on such topics. One never knows in advance when one may meet one or more of these phenomena in magnetic experiments with odd devices. About half the known magnetic phenomena are well understood; the remainder run the gamut from "somewhat understood" to "not understood at all".

A Caution on the Rare Production of Higher Polarization EM Energy

With great rarity, some novel uses of stresses and opposing forces in highly nonlinear electromagnetic circuits can produce and have produced "unusual" forms of EM energy. I am occasionally asked about these anomalous phenomena experienced by an experimenter encountering one or more of them. Let me explain these "unusual EM energies," at least what I understand of them from limited experience with them.

In quantum field theory {12} and quantum electrodynamics, there are four photon (EM energy) polarizations {13}. The x-and y-polarizations or any combination of the two are where the 3-space energy transported by the photon (or transported by a transverse EM wave comprised of such photons) is oscillating perpendicularly in 3-space to the line of propagation of the photon or wave.

If vibrations in the x-and y-directions are "frozen" so that the spatial energy cannot oscillate laterally, the transported energy will pulsate longitudinally like an accordion, back and forth along the propagation line of motion. That's called a "longitudinal" or "longitudinally polarized" photon (or EM wave). Most of the "unusual EM energy" effects produced in various nonlinear coils and other devices have involved the inadvertent production of such longitudinal EM waves (LWs). Irradiation by LWs can be detrimental to the body if too powerful. (This is because, unknown prior to 2000, the longitudinal EM wave in 3-space is always accompanied by a companion longitudinal EM wave in the time domain. Strong irradiation in the time-domain can interfere with body and cellular processes.) Irradiation by weaker longitudinal EM radiation can make one ill {14}, while stronger LW radiation can maim or kill {15}, particularly if strongly pulsed.

In theory a purely longitudinal EM wave would have infinite velocity and infinite energy. In the real world, however, one can only make "partial" LWs, with some transverse wave residues. These "imperfect" LWs are known as *Undistorted Progressive Waves* (UPWs) {16}. In theory at least, a UPW can travel either slower than light (in which case it's called an *electromagnetic particle*) or faster than light (then it's a *superluminal wave*). Most major weapons laboratories of the world either have already discovered or are now discovering and using longitudinal EM waves. But back to our basic longitudinal EM wave, for further development.

If we now "freeze" the z-direction as well, then the *3-space* energy in the wave does not oscillate at all, but just moves along as a slug of spatial energy. However, photons carry not only a piece of *spatial energy*, but also a piece of *time*. Time is actually spatial energy compressed by the factor c^2. With the spatial energy component "frozen", now the time component oscillates its magnitude. In short, that is called a "time-polarized" or "scalar" photon (or, if waves are used, a *time-polarized* or *scalar* EM wave.).

EM waves also carry not only spatial energy but also time-energy, since they transport photons. However, presently physicists just ignore and do not model the energetics of the time-component transported by the wave in spacetime (vacuum). They—usually unwittingly—portray only the 3-spatial intersection of the wave after observation (*observation* is a d/dt operator invoked on spacetime L^3T, destroying the T and leaving the L^3. For that reason, all observation is spatial. No observable even "persists in time", since it is a frozen instant 3-snapshot of an ongoing 4-interaction). Rigorously, the "spatial" wave portrayed in the texts is the material force field wave in the detecting matter (as in the Drude electron gas in a detecting wire antenna). None of the dozens of texts checked shows the EM wave in *spacetime*, but only in 3-space.

(See particularly Robert H. Romer, "Heat is not a noun," *American Journal of Physics*, 69(2), Feb. 2001, p. 107-109. This is an editorial discussion by the Editor of AJP of the concept of heat in thermodynamics. Heat is not a substance, not a thermodynamic function of state, and should not be used as a noun. In endnote 24, p. 109, he also takes to task "*. . . that dreadful diagram purporting to show the electric and magnetic fields of a plane wave, as a function of position (and/or time?) that besmirch the pages of almost every introductory book. . . . it is a horrible diagram. 'Misleading' would be too kind a word; 'wrong' is more accurate.*" "*. . . perhaps then, for historical interest, [we should] find out how that diagram came to contaminate our literature in the first place.*" As one can see, even the illustration of an "EM wave in space" is totally ridiculous and wrong. Why such is not rooted out of the texts remains an enigma wrapped in a mystery, to adapt a phrase by Churchill.)

The time-polarized EM wave is the most powerful of all EM waves, and in pulses or with any substantial power can have quite lethal effects upon anything living. Mind operations are totally electromagnetic, but consist of time-polarized EM wave and photon operations rather than transverse.

The Russians, e.g., have long since developed weapons utilizing time-polarized EM waves and generators for them. Russian forces tested such a time-polarized EM weapon in Afghanistan, on two occasions {17}. A powerful pulse of time-polarized (scalar) waves instantly destroys all life of any kind in the struck area or object or zone. It does so by simply snapping the time-domain mind completely loose from the 3-spatial body, resulting in instant and total death (hence the name *mindsnapping*). Everything living, at cellular level or even much finer, has its own correlated "mind-part" in the time-polarized EM domain. So mindsnapping kills all living parts, from the finest level to the largest {18}.

Time can be taken to be spatial energy {19} compressed by a factor of at least c^2. So it has at least the same energy density as mass. When one uses time-polarized EM waves, one is using the time-components of the EM waves and photons, hence the equivalent of extremely powerful nuclear energy—one where *all* the mass can be converted to spatial energy! So a little bit of transduction of time-energy into spatial energy can produce enormous spatial energy {20}.

We previously extended the conventional conservation of energy law—which conserves the net total of the spatial energy and the mass-energy—to include conserving the net total of the spatial energy, mass-energy, and time-energy {21}.

Usually researchers stumble into weak LW emission phenomena (hopefully only mildly!) when experimenting with something like opposing or biwound coils with cores of various materials (especially mixed organic material cores) or with plasmas irradiated by multiple EM waves where the difference frequencies can serve as extremely active radiation {22}. Under the right circumstances, the peculiar actions of the *difference* frequency are directly amplified by all the EM noise present {23}. Certain plasmas also transform transverse EM waves to longitudinal EM waves. The conglomerated results of such phenomena can be hazardous if powerful.

I advise anyone against experimenting with such, unless he is a *very* experienced researcher, takes extreme precautions, and *uses very little power*. Since LWs can affect nuclear detectors, one is also advised to have several different types of them closely on hand and monitoring. One experiments with such effects at one's own risk, and the risk can be substantial if other than minimal power is used. Neither this author nor the publishers of this volume are responsible for accidents or effects suffered by experimenters in this area, who experiment at their own volition and risk.

Unless rigged for antigravity, the Sweet device did not produce or radiate longitudinal EM waves. Otherwise I would no longer be among the living, because I was closely exposed to it many times for long periods.

A Heat Pump Can In Theory Be Close-Looped

The common home heat pump with say, 40% efficiency, under ideal conditions has a COP = 4.0. Its maximum theoretical COP is 8.22, and probably a 6.0 heat pump could be designed for optimum conditions. The COP>1.0 is made possible by the heat pump extracting excess energy from its external environment (the heat energy gleaned from compressing environmental gas and extracting the heat).

In theory, one can "close loop" a motor-generator-heat pump combination of some sort, where the system will provide electrical power output while also running itself. That doesn't violate conservation of energy; all the energy for the outputs and the losses are in fact extracted from the external environment by the heat pump's COP>1.0 performance.

Of course the ambient air will usually not remain ideal. When the ambient air gets colder, its heat energy content reduces appreciably. The efficiency of the heat pump drops precipitously, until one must switch to the resistive heating elements to provide the necessary heating at COP<1.0. So close-looping the system isn't practical in most cases, and even when made practical by burying long air lines, etc. it is quite expensive. The complexity and maintenance also become burdensome. (If one wishes to experiment with close-looping a heat pump, then underground installation of the lines should be utilized in order to stabilize the heat pump's COP at a high level.)

Overunity Systems Are Already Known

Overunity systems are quite ordinary, nothing fancy, and no different from a waterwheel or a windmill or a sailboat. The only difference is that we're trying to do it with EM power systems, and unwittingly facing the anathema of the closed-loop circuit which guarantees COP<1.0. It follows that the first requirement is to produce an operation in the circuit which violates that "single closed-loop operation".

Overunity systems are already prescribed by physics and thermodynamics, already in the standard physics texts, and certain overunity processes are well-known in the literature—including some EM overunity processes which we've cited in many previous publications. The skeptic should refer to lasing without population inversion, the Lawandy patents, the Letokhov publications and processes, Letokhov's negative absorption of the medium (a medium can emit more energy than we input), negative resonance absorption (a particle can collect more energy than one would think impacts on it, and then emit that excess energy), the fiber fuse, Russian parametric oscillator power systems of the 1930s, Kron's negative resistor, etc.

In short, *as in any field of physics, one must read the literature and find out what physics actually says and already contains about overunity processes that have been proven experimentally.* It's not as simple as just having an EE degree or graduating from an electronics and motor course. None of the material taught in conventional educational institutions will explicitly tell one that an overunity EM power system is even possible, much less show what the principles of such a device are, or how to go about building one. One will have to discover the principles and methods oneself; there are no handbooks and there are no great experts—the present author included!

Also, contrary to prevailing opinion, real overunity EM systems *have* been built, including by leading scientists, and suppressed or abandoned for one reason or another.

13927-VALO

Gabriel Kron's Negative Resistor

One of the greatest electrical scientists of all time was Gabriel Kron. Kron built a true negative resistor in the 1930s, and it could power itself and the network analyzer at Stanford University, under a GE contract with the U.S. Navy. Here is a direct quote from Kron {24} to show what we refer to:

> *"When only positive and negative real numbers exist, it is customary to replace a positive resistance by an inductance and a negative resistance by a capacitor (since none or only a few negative resistances exist on practical network analyzers.)"*

In that sentence, Kron was required to insert the words "none or". In another quote, Kron {25} also revealed that he was not allowed to use the negative resistor to openly power the Network Analyzer. Quoting and reading through the spin-control:

> *"Although negative resistances are available for use with a network analyzer, in practice it is more convenient to use a second type of circuit, in which the positive and negative resistances are replaced by inductors and capacitors and the dc currents and voltages are replaced by ac currents and voltages of fixed frequency. The use of the second type of interpretation is equivalent to multiplying the wave equation by $i = \sqrt{-1}$."*

In that quotation, one should just extract what is said in the first part of the first sentence: "*Negative resistances are available for use with a network analyzer.*" And quoting Kron {26} from another publication as to what his overunity secret of the open path {27} was:

> *". . . the missing concept of "open-paths" (the dual of "closed-paths") was discovered, in which currents could be made to flow in branches that lie between any set of two nodes. (Previously—following Maxwell— engineers tied all of their open-paths to a single datum-point, the 'ground'). That discovery of open-paths established a sec-*

ond rectangular transformation matrix . . . which created 'lamellar' currents . . ." "A network with the simultaneous presence of both closed and open paths was the answer to the author's years-long search."

Kron's secret has never been released by General Electric, Stanford University, or the U.S. Navy (the work was done under a Navy contract). It has never been deciphered {28} outside those groups {29}, with the possible exception of Floyd Sweet, who worked in General Electric with Kron (but not on the Network Analyzer project).

However, we will point out that Lorentz discarded all the "open circuit" or "open path" Heaviside energy flow associated with a circuit, and energy flow that normally does not strike the circuit and power loads. It is a fact that this discarded energy flow is independent and open vis a vis the circuit ground and other parts. The entire "time current" domain is also independently open. We personally believe the time-domain-induced energy currents may possibly account for at least a part of Kron's "open circuit path" discovery. Certainly there is enormous surplus EM energy flow there to be collected and used, in every electromagnetic circuit, and it is presently just wasted.

The present scientific community simply will not allow funded research and publication in such "out of the box" energy research areas. From time to time scientists still try, but are viciously attacked and suppressed for their impudence. Cold fusion research is a primary example; there are many others. This is sad, because the Maxwell-Heaviside equations, *prior to Lorentz's symmetrical regauging circa 1886*, include both COP < 1.0 and COP ≥ 1.0 Maxwellian systems. Lorentz symmetrical regauging changed the equations so that the COP > 1.0 systems—which are *disequilibrium* systems a priori—were just arbitrarily discarded.

Chung's Negative Resistor

Professor Deborah Chung {30} at University of Buffalo also has invented a true negative resistor utilizing crossed carbon filaments, and thoroughly tested it. The university filed a patent application and moved toward licensing for commercial applications. However, the university's web site abruptly pulled off the University's offer of a technical package to companies signing nondisclosure and wishing to license the technology. Chung's paper was submitted to a journal and after a protracted period in review has finally been published: Shoukai Wang and D.D.L. Chung, "Apparent negative electrical resistance in carbon fiber composites," *Composites, Part B*, Vol. 30, 1999, p. 579-590. For related work, also see Deborah D. L. Chung, "Superconductor-metal laminates and method of making," U.S. patent #5,059,582, issued Oct. 22, 1991. A superconducting laminate having at least one layer of metal and at least one layer of superconducting material. The metal layer and the superconducting layer are bonded. The metal later may also include carbon fibers from various precursors. The superconductor may be a composite material. The invention also includes a method of making the laminates. Assigned to "The Research Foundation of State University of NY," Albany, NY. It appears that the university has classified defense contracts, and the Chung negative resistor may have been classified or made totally proprietary. However, J.-L. Naudin in France has replicated the Chung-type negative resistance experiment, as well as several versions which can be performed by experimenters much more readily. The reader is referred to his website. (For replication and tons of related technical information on Chung's negative resistor and negative resistors in general, see J.-L. Naudin's website at *http://jnaudin.free.fr/cnr/*. We carefully point out the difference between the "differential" negative resistor—which continuously "eats" more power than it provides to the circuit and therefore is a net load rather than a net source—and the *true* negative resistor, which furnishes excess power to the circuit and is a net internal source.

Other Overunity Systems

Lawandy's Processes and Lasing Without Population Inversion

Lasing without population inversion is always overunity in optical gain. It is underunity overall, so long as the stimulation input power remains externally provided. It does not take a genius to examine the latest experiments confining over 1,000 "random" photon interactions inside the optically active material—both in the forward time and time-reversed paths—to see that self-stimulation and self-oscillation is inherently possible. The simple Lawandy experiment {31} itself can be done in any university nonlinear optics laboratory, and the experiment works every time. It's also quite spectacular visually. Why the Lawandy and related work—including his several patents {32} and marvelous results by others {33}— is not being explored for power system applications is a deep mystery. There is a growing body of literature on this area.

A closely related phenomenon is the emission of excess energy from a stimulated medium due to resonant particles sweeping out a greater "reaction cross section area" in the prevailing Heaviside energy flow {34}.

Self-Powering Russian Overunity Parametric Oscillator Power Systems

In leading physics institutes and laboratories in the 1930s, the Russians built overunity parametric oscillators—and some pretty big ones. That work is fully documented {35} in the Russian scientific literature and in the French scientific literature. The devices were developed and tested in several physics institutes and laboratories. With linear loads the oscillators would progressively build to self-destruction. With nonlinear loads, the devices would stabilize and power themselves and their loads.

This work appears to have been deliberately suppressed by the Communist regime just prior to WW II. After the war all such technology passed under the ruthless control of the KGB, and into the special weapons research and development area, still highly classified and KGB-controlled to this day.

The Seiko Kinetic Wrist Watch

Rigorously, any overunity system—electrical or otherwise—must be an open thermodynamic system far from equilibrium. I wear such a little system on my wrist, in my wristwatch, which taps the mechanical energy in its dynamic environment (my arm movements) to move a little mass, which operates a little electrical generator, which charges a little capacitor, which powers a little motor operating the watch. It's a neat little watch and a clever design by Seiko. It exhibits a broken symmetry in its energy exchange with its active environment (my arm movements). Effectively it receives "free" energy and uses that to power itself and its load.

Miscellaneous EM Overunity Power Systems

A solar cell is a perfectly valid EM overunity EM power system, as is any windmill-powered generator. Any receiving wire antenna of itself is a free energy "electrical" system whenever it freely receives and outputs its received signal. It receives energy from its environment and outputs most of it, with some scattered as heat. A hydroelectric turbine-driven generator is also an overunity EM power system.

The *operator himself* does not have to input energy to any of those systems. They are in fact all "energy converters", freely converting the form of some energy they freely receive from the environment, so that the output is electrical energy.

However, those systems suffer from the common pandemic of modern EM power systems: the design of the electrical portion so that it rigorously enforces Lorentz symmetry during excitation discharge, by self-regauging itself to implement it. Hence these systems are not good solutions of the "energy crisis", nor do they solve the ever-increasing problem of polluting the biosphere with hydrocarbon combustion products and nuclear wastes.

The Mead-Nachamkin Zero Point Energy Converter

In 1996 Mead and Nachamkin {36} were granted a patent on an overunity EM power system process for extracting zero-point energy of the vacuum. If one closely examines the patent wording, the device is patented as an energy converter and does not overtly state that it is a free energy system. It is, since the input energy is freely received.

Because energy cannot be created or destroyed, any "free" energy system *a priori* is a *converter*. It must receive the energy from its active environment, and convert that energy to a form usable to power its loads and losses.

Indeed, it turns out that all EM energy in 3-space comes from the time-domain, and the charge or dipole absorbs time-energy, converts it to 3-space energy, and emits it in 3-space in all directions. See T. E. Bearden, "Giant Negentropy from the Common Dipole," *Journal of New Energy*, 5(1), Summer 2000, p. 11-23. On DoE open website *http://www.ott.doe.gov/electromagnetic/* and *www.cheniere.org*. After publication, we discovered very powerful additional support in Mandl and Shaw, *Quantum Field Theory*, Wiley, 1984, Chapter 5. Mandl and Shaw argue that the longitudinal and scalar polarizations of the photon are not directly observable, but only in combination, where they manifest as the "instantaneous" Coulomb (i.e., electrostatic) potential. Our comment is that this argument, translated from particle terminology to wave terminology, directly fits my re-interpretation of Whittaker's 1903 decomposition of the scalar potential. However, Mandl and Shaw fail to account for the interaction of the detecting/observing unit point charge (which is the "combining" mechanism), and thus fail to account for the absorption of the incoming time-polarized wave or photon, the transduction of that excitation energy of the charge into longitudinal EM wave/

photon energy, and the subsequent emission of that excitation energy in 3-space. Thus they missed the time-excitation charging via absorption of the "coupled" time-polarized EM wave/photon, and the decay by emission of 3-space longitudinal EM wave/photon. This interaction has been erroneously omitted in physics prior to our recognition of it. So Mandl and Shaw do not account for photon (or wave) polarization transduction, where the "causal" time-polarized EM wave or photon comes in and is absorbed by the detecting charge or dipole, then re-emitted as the longitudinally polarized EM wave or photon in 3-space. Recognition of these missing facts allowed at last a solution to the long-vexing problem of the source charge, often called the greatest problem in both quantum and classical electrodynamics.

Open Systems Far from Thermodynamic Equilibrium

In any overunity system, the total of the *operator's* energy input and the *environmental* energy input is always equal to the total of the energy output in the load and the energy dissipated in the system's losses.

The thermodynamics of such systems has been well-known for decades {37}. As an example, Ilya Prigogine was awarded the Nobel Prize in chemistry in 1977 for his contributions to that kind of thermodynamics.

The tired old classical thermodynamics with its infamous second law—which only applies to a closed system or a system in equilibrium with its environment, is all that the skeptics ever seem to have studied or know about. One would wish the arch skeptics would find out what has happened in physics and thermodynamics in the last 40 years! Classical thermodynamics does not apply unless the given system is *in equilibrium* with its active environment. It does not apply to any system *out* of equilibrium.

E.g., see Robert Bruce Lindsay and Henry Margenau, *Foundations of Physics*, Dover, New York, 1963. Quoting p. 213: "*Equilibrium states are the only ones that are capable of explicit analysis in thermodynamics . . .*" Quoting p. 217: "*Non-equilib-*

rium conditions cannot be specified by variables of state, and their entropy cannot be computed. . . . the condition of equilibrium is the condition of maximum entropy." It follows that (i) the disequilibrium state is an excited state, (ii) it has decreased its entropy and thereby increased its entropy, and (iii) classical thermodynamics does not and cannot describe systems which operate in disequilibrium with their active environment. It is very interesting that U(1) electrodynamics assumes the external environment of the Maxwellian system is inert, hence the system is in equilibrium. Accordingly, U(1) electrodynamics as developed and used in electrical engineering does not even apply to open dissipative systems, which are systems in disequilibrium with their active environment, in this case the active local vacuum and the active local curvatures of spacetime.

A common example of such a disequilibrium system is the windmill, or the waterwheel, or the sailboat—all used for thousands of years. Each of those three overunity systems rigorously obeys the conservation of energy law while it's doing free work. It just gets that free energy from its environment, and converts it to a form useful to its owner/operator. The operator does not have to furnish the input energy to it.

The greatest of all overunity systems far from thermodynamic equilibrium, however, is the ubiquitous charge. Every electrical or magnetic charge in the universe is already an overunity EM power system, freely receiving a flux of virtual energy from its seething vacuum environment, converting a portion of it, and outputting that portion as a Poynting energy flow across the entire universe. Presently we crudely harness these natural free energy systems in our rather inept power systems.

In the future we must learn to apply them in far more efficient ways. Presently we build only systems which kill the free "source dipole converters" faster than they power their loads.

Energy Conservation and Its Relation to Work Obtainable

Much stuff and nonsense have been written about the conservation of energy in physics and electrical engineering.

The primary and *master* law of conservation of energy is this: *Energy cannot be created or destroyed.* But it certainly can be converted in form!

Let us be rigorous. We have great difficulty in trying to *define* energy. It isn't the "capacity to do work," because it isn't capacity. *Having* capacity and *identically being* capacity are two quite different statements!

Ultimately energy represents a change in a potential (potential state, condition, vacuum, whatever) which, however, is itself a collection of energy and thus just a form of energy. So, we can also reverse ourselves and interpret the potential as a change in the energy state. Regardless of how we proceed, effectively we just wind up stating that energy—whatever it might be—can always be changed in form. Perhaps the closest approach to defining energy can be taken from general relativity, where it can be argued on one hand that energy *is* a curvature in spacetime, and on the other hand that energy *causes* a curvature in spacetime, and on yet another hand that energy is *whatever acts* upon uncurved spacetime to curve it. And there is about where the matter rests. As Nobelist Feynman {38} stated,

> " *It is important to realize that in physics today, we have no knowledge of what energy is.*"

Along with Feynman, we have to admit that no one *really* knows what energy *is*, and this author does not claim to be an exception. We just know a lot of things that energy *does*. However, we do know what work is, once we assume energy as a given. *Work identically is the changing of the form of energy*, rigorously.

So a standard question I always ask new researchers is this: "Suppose we have one joule of collected energy. What is the maximum work we can do with that joule of energy?"

Almost invariably the answer is, "One joule of work." That is quite wrong.

If we change the form of all that joule of collected energy, we have done one joule of work. But afterwards we still have precisely one joule of energy remaining! It's just in a form differing from the form it was in when we started. *Energy is never consumed, and never destroyed.* Use it to do work, and we just have all of it left in a different form.

But we've done one joule of work from our original joule of energy, and we've still got one joule of energy remaining. If we then change the form of *that* joule of energy yet another time, we get yet another joule of work. And so on, as long as we can design an "energy-form changing" system that will not just let the energy completely escape after each transformation of the form of the energy.

Here is a great secret, known to Nikola Tesla: all you really must have is two entities or functions that change the energy's form back and forth between two states or types. The first one receives the energy in form A, and changes it into form B, doing work, but also feeds the form B energy to the second function. The second function changes the B-energy back to form A, doing work, but then feeds this A-energy back to the first function. And so on. If one could do that without "spilling" any of the energy from the reverberation process, one could simply create work continually and indefinitely, from any charge of energy. There is no conservation of work law, and the work-energy theorem has been arbitrarily interpreted only for one single change of form of the energy. The universe does this "iterative reuse" of energy; it is just that we've concentrated on changing the form of energy once in our circuits (i.e., in the load), and more or less letting it escape our system (the load) after that. Tesla surged the energy back and forth between special accumulators at the two ends of a single wire, to accomplish the necessary reverberation. This reuse of energy by reverberation between two states was one of his secrets.

In theory, a single joule of energy can do any number of joules of work, if we change its form repeatedly and if we continue doing that indefinitely. In short, energy can be—and is—recycled and reused, over and over without end. (This specifically includes as the primary change, the change between time-energy and 3-space energy, and vice versa.)

In the prevailing Big Bang theory, every joule of energy in the universe was there shortly after the big bang began. Since then, every joule of that energy has been doing joule after joule of work. And all of it is still here, and still doing more work!

There is no conservation of work law! All that means is that there is no limit on the number of times a given joule of energy can be changed in form or "transduced." Run some energy through a resistor, and produce heat. Retroreflect all the heat somewhere into some chemicals, and change it all into chemical energy. Let that chemical energy do some more work on some plates, and get some more electrical energy. And so on. Such serial form-converting reactions producing more than one joule of work from one joule of energy do not violate the conservation of energy law, the laws of physics, and the laws of thermodynamics. *One is permitted indeed to get more than one joule of work from one joule of energy.* (Again, see my "Giant Negentropy" paper. The easiest thing in all the world to do, is to engineer negentropy, simply by making a little dipole. That blasts the daylights out of classical 3-equilibrium thermodynamics, because 3-symmetry of energy flow is broken by any dipole. Instead, 4-symmetry between inflow of time-energy and outflow of 3-space EM energy applies, and there is no 3-space EM energy input to the dipole at all.)

But not in a *single* energy-form conversion! In only one conversion, one can only get one joule of work from one joule of energy—but one also still has a joule of energy remaining . If one does not further convert that remaining joule, that's the end of it. In short, one then collects a joule of energy, does a joule of work with it, and then one wastes (dissipates) the joule of energy remaining in its different form.

Most of our professors in university were not quite clear on this subject, although at least some of them understood it. But many did not, and many still do not today.

A Surprising Thing about Thermodynamics and Reservoirs

It is quite fashionable to state that one cannot take energy from a reservoir at constant temperature. Well, that is not quite true as stated. More rigorously, we cannot take energy from a reservoir *in equilibrium* at constant temperature. We can indeed take energy from a reservoir at constant temperature but *not in equilibrium*. That is, from a nonhomogeneous reservoir at constant temperature.

We quote Hsu-Chieh Yeh {39} for a vivid statement of this fact:

> *From Planck's statement of the second law of thermodynamics it is generally inferred that it is impossible to construct an engine which produces work at the expense only of heat taken from the air or the ocean. . . . [It is demonstrated that] . . . when the air and the ocean are combined as a nonhomogeneous reservoir of uniform temperature, it is possible to construct an engine which produces work by extracting heat from the said reservoir. This does not constitute a violation of the second law of thermodynamics, rather that the "reservoir" in the Planck's statement must be clearly stated as being in equilibrium."*

The proof and a schematic diagram of a machine to successfully do that energy extraction process is shown by Yeh {40}.

The "Final Word" On the Conservation of Energy Law

Some arch skeptics are fanatically die-hard—and a real pain in the neck as well.

To be absolutely precise, they have no leg to stand on, if they accept what physics ultimately says on the subject of energy conservation.

Before one gets too adamant about the universality of energy conservation, here's a most astonishing thing, but quite true: *In general relativity there is at basis no such thing as conservation of energy at all, unless one first makes some assumptions to inject it artificially so as to avoid facing the sheer terror of the collapse of energy conservation!*

The great Hilbert pointed this out shortly after the advent of Einstein's theory of general relativity. E.g., quoting from Logunov and Loskutov {41}, p. 179:

> *"In formulating the equivalence principle, Einstein actually abandoned the idea of the gravitational field as a Faraday-Maxwell field, and this is reflected in the pseudotensorial characterization of the gravitational field that he introduced. Hilbert was the first to draw attention to the consequences of this. In Ref. 2 [D. Hilbert, Gottingen Nachrichten, Vol. 4, 1917, p. 21] he wrote: 'I assert . . . that for the general theory of relativity, i.e., in the case of general invariance of the Hamiltonian function, energy equations . . . corresponding to the energy equations in orthogonally invariant theories do not exist at all. I could even take this circumstance as the characteristic feature of the general theory of relativity.' Unfortunately, this remark of Hilbert was evidently not understood by his contemporaries, since neither Einstein himself nor other physicists recognized the fact that in general relativity conservation laws for energy, momentum, and angular momentum are in principle impossible."*

For situations where serious general relativity is not terribly involved, then we can legitimately speak of conservation of energy. Even so, one should not be too hasty to leap forth with the old *equilibrium* thermodynamics and pontificate that "there's no such thing as an overunity EM system because that would violate the infamous second law". If it's an open system far from equilibrium, classical thermodynamics and that second law do not even apply. The skeptic then objecting on the grounds of equilibrium thermodynamics is revealing that he doesn't know the difference between systems in equilibrium and open systems not in equilibrium. In short, he simply does not understand thermodynamics, and it is useless to argue with such a critic.

Before one gets overly confident about ordinary electrical and electronic circuits, and concludes that it's the rarest thing in all the world to have out-of-equilibrium operation in them, one should read the literature carefully. To the contrary, in all sorts of circuits, equilibrium often is unexpectedly departed from, leading to chaotic operation and a highly increased degree of system complexity. E.g., quoting from Ogorzalek {42}, p. vii:

> *"All real systems are nonlinear in nature. This simple observation is true also for electrical and electronic circuits even though many of them are designed to perform linear transformations on signals. . . . in many cases the designed circuit, when implemented, performs in a very unexpected way, totally different from that for which it was designed. In most cases, engineers do not care about the origins and mechanisms of the malfunction; for them a circuit which does not perform as desired is of no use and has to rejected or redesigned. . . ."*
>
> *". . . electrical and electronic circuits constitute a group of real physical systems in which observations and measurements are relatively easy to make. ..Such an 'experimental comfort' enabled thorough studies confirming the existence of strange unexpected behavior in almost every type of electronic circuit – oscillators, filters, instrumentation circuits, power supplies, PLLs, electric machines, microwave circuits, electro-optic systems, etc. The main problem remains in interpreting experimental data."*

In other words, normal circuits indeed do often depart from expected equilibrium behavior. Engineers just shrug and "fix the circuit where it doesn't do that". The scientists are aware of such occurrences, but have not yet fully deciphered all the ramifications or the wild phenomena that result. But they are working on it!

Seemingly Random Behavior Can Be Adaptively Controlled

One has to be extremely careful these days about many of the old statements that were drummed into us as axioms. Some of them no longer hold, or are even true. Others have to be modified from their "absolute" form.

Such a dead notion is the belief that randomness cannot be controlled. That is no longer true. In modern adaptive nonlinear control theory combined with nonlinear oscillation theory, random oscillations can indeed be brought under control and used.

We do not intend to belabor this fairly recent development, but just state that it casts a quite new eye on the notion in some quarters that random fluctuations of zero-point vacuum energy can certainly not be "controlled". That statement is no longer absolute, and must be modified in the light of new knowledge. In fact, we propose that the ordering by a charge of a portion of its received disordered or random virtual energy, is just such an adaptive control mechanism, "controlling" part of the disorder by adapting to it so as to cohere and integrate a portion of it into observable form.

We leave this interesting but complex subject by quoting from the very first scientific work successfully combining both nonlinear control theory and nonlinear oscillation theory. Quoting from Fradkov and Programsky {43 }, p. 8:

> *"In fact, the fields of nonlinear control and nonlinear oscillations were developed surprisingly independently. The present book is perhaps the first one to bring together these two important branches of nonlinear science."*

And again, quoting from Fradkov and Programsky {44}, p. 359-360:

> *"1. There is . . . great benefit of using the modern nonlinear and adaptive control theory. . . . 2. There is no need to distinguish periodic and chaotic behavior. Accurate control is possible without accurate prediction. . . . 3. There is no need to define chaos in order to control it. . . . 4. There is no need to use probability in order to control systems with seemingly random behavior."*

We must leave further investigation of this promising avenue to far better theorists than the present author! We mention it, however, because if the random perturbations of the vacuum energy interaction can be controlled, obviously one can extract EM energy from the vacuum. A simple charge or dipole already possesses the ability to do just that.

The Unresolved Problem of the Source Charge and Its Field Energy

But to return to the so-called "source charge". In the rigorous sense, there are no energy sources and there are no energy sinks. For example, quoting from Semiz {45}, p. 151:

> *"The very expression 'energy source' is actually a misnomer. As is known since the early days of thermodynamics, and formulated as the first law, energy is conserved in any physical process. Since energy cannot be created or destroyed, nothing can be an energy source, or sink. Devices we call energy sources do not create energy, they convert it from a form not suitable for our needs to a form that is suitable, a form we can do work with."*

So there are "charge field-energy gates" and charge "field-energy converters", but there are no "source charges" and there are no energy sinks. We have already pointed out that the notion of "energy source" hides a very special kind of energy and a very special kind of EM energy flow symmetry. The same is true for the notion of "energy sink", but this cannot be further discussed until certain patent applications in process of being filed are secured. We merely note that the gauge freedom principle of quantum field theory, applied to "source" and "sink" concepts, tells us already that we can change the form of the energy involved in a "sink" to the form of energy involved in a source". For the rest, one must wait for my forthcoming book, T.E. Bearden, *Energy from the Vacuum: Principles and Concepts*, World Scientific, 2002 (in process).

However, one must keep one's sense of humor. Ironically, classical electrodynamicists may already be the most dedicated perpetual motion machine "advocates" in the world! In the overunity researchers' wildest nightmares, we could never begin to approach the vast scale of perpetual motion machines that the electrodynamicists already accept and prescribe.

It's that totally false concept of "source charge" that they advocate! They would have us believe that the source charge continually *creates right out of nothing* that enormous EM energy it continuously pours out across the universe in all directions. They would have us believe that a fearsome energy output is generated by the "source charge" without any input of energy from the environment to that charge. Classical EM assumes the inert vacuum, and nothing at all furnishing the energy to that source charge.

Of course that violates the most sacrosanct conservation law of all: that energy cannot be created or destroyed. But many electrodynamicists just "hide" that little problem and seldom state it explicitly. When pressed, they do—as stated by Sen {46}— admit that,

> *"The connection between the field and its source has always been and still is the most difficult problem in classical and quantum electrodynamics."*

In short, the electrodynamicists haven't solved the "source charge problem" yet. My comment is a question: How many more decades should it take, just to read the solution already arrived at by the particle physicists, and accordingly change the flawed classical electrodynamics by adding in the required active vacuum and the broken symmetry of the source charge?

Classical EM seriously errs in ignoring the active vacuum. It's well known that no mass system can even *be* in equilibrium without the presence of the vacuum interaction. So just to observe a power system sitting in equilibrium on the floor, is to automatically "prove" that vacuum interaction is occurring with it.

Particle physicists solved that "source charge" problem over 40 years ago, but the electrodynamicists have not yet changed their 137-years-old {47} seriously flawed theory accordingly. One simply has to include the active vacuum exchange with the charge and the dipole, and the broken symmetry of the charge and of the dipole, since *a priori* any energy source is actually an *energy converter*.

Particle physicists proved (both theoretically and experimentally) that the vacuum is active, highly energetic, etc. Nobel prizes were awarded, such as to Lamb and to Lee.

(For Lamb's work that led to his Nobel prize, see Willis E. Lamb, Jr. and Robert C. Retherford, "Fine structure of the hydrogen atom by a microwave method," *Physical Review*, 72(3), Aug. 1, 1947, p. 241-243. Lamb received the 1955 Nobel Prize in physics jointly with Polykarp Kush for experiments measuring the small displacement later called the "Lamb shift" of one of the energy levels in atomic hydrogen. The reader should be advised that, even though this is a small effect, the *energy density* involved is greater than the surface energy density of the sun. In

1956, Lee predicted broken symmetry. In 1957, Wu et al. proved it experimentally, whereupon the Nobel Prize was awarded to Lee in the same year, 1957. Two charges of opposite sign, separated, do constitute such a broken symmetry in the vacuum flux. See T.D. Lee, "Question of Parity Conservation in Weak Interactions," *Physical Review*, 104(1), Oct. 1, 1956, p. 254-259; T. D. Lee, Reinhard Oehme, and C. N. Yang, "Remarks on Possible Noninvariance under Time Reversal and Charge Conjugation," *Physical Review*, 106(2), 1957, p. 340-345; T. D. Lee, "Weak Interactions and Nonconservation of Parity," Nobel Lecture, Dec. 11, 1957; C. S. Wu, E. Ambler, R. W. Hayward, D. D. Hoppes and R. P. Hudson, Experimental Test of Parity Conservation in Beta Decay," *Physical Review*, Vol. 105, 1957, p. 1413.)

The particle physicists also proved that any charge is a broken symmetry in the fierce virtual energy exchange between the seething vacuum and that charge. The very definition of broken symmetry means that something virtual has become observable. In other words, *some* of that enormous virtual disordered energy that the charge absorbs from the vacuum, is *not* reradiated as virtual and disordered energy at all. Instead, that component is first organized by the charge (by its spin?) into observable size groupings. This component is reradiated as the energy flow pouring continuously out from that "source charge" across the entire universe in all directions, thereby providing the energy in the fields and potentials from that charge. Again, every energy "source" is *a priori* an energy converter! So is an energy "sink". Note that one does not calculate "the magnitude of the field", but only the intensity of the field at a point occupied by it. The field itself may extend across all space, from its "source charge". Similarly one does not calculate the "magnitude of the potential", but only it's intensity at a point occupied by it. Many electrical engineers are nonplussed to realized that they have never calculated the magnitude of either a potential or a field. They also are often startled to realize that, from any nonzero potential φ, one may intercept and collect any amount of energy W from φ by using sufficient intercepting charge q. The formula is $W = \varphi q$. That is because both the field and the "static" or scalar potential actually involve continuous energy flow.

The charge does not *create* the energy it continuously emits, but *gates* and organizes some of the energy it continuously receives from its vacuum exchange. It is not a *source* charge, but an *ordering and gating* charge.

The charge is thus an open system far from thermodynamic equilibrium. Since one has lots and lots of such charges in an EM power system, and every one of them is an open system freely receiving and gating energy from the vacuum, *a priori* it should be possible to tame and use some of that observable Poynting energy that the charges freely pour out, to power loads and run the system, without the operator having to continually input additional energy to the system!

That we do not do so is not a commentary on nature's prohibitions, but a commentary on the inadequacy and wrong direction of our scientific research on EM power systems.

The Marvelous "Source Dipole" Overunity Power System

It follows that a dipole, being two separated charges, is also a broken equilibrium in the vacuum energy flux, and thereby it also gates out EM energy flow in all directions in 3-space, continuously. It too is an open system not in thermodynamic equilibrium. In short, it's a wonderful little overunity EM power system! It's one that every circuit contains, and may contain a very large number of them.

It is well-known that an open system not in thermodynamic equilibrium is permitted to perform five magical functions: It can (1) self-order, (2) self-oscillate, (3) output more energy than the operator inputs (the excess comes from the active environment, in this case the vacuum), (4) power itself and a load simultaneously (in this case all the energy comes from the active environment/vacuum, and the operator need not furnish any),

13927-VALO

and (5) exhibit negentropy. Every charge and dipole in the universe already does all five functions. Contributions to the theory of such open systems far from equilibrium with their active environment is what earned Prigogine a Nobel Prize. (See Ilya Prigogine (with G. Nicolis), *Self-Organization in Non-Equilibrium Systems: From Dissipative Structures to Order through Fluctuations*, Wiley, New York, 1977; Ilya Prigogine with D. Kondepudi, *Modern Thermodynamics: From Heat Engines to Dissipative Structures*, Wiley, Chichester, 1998.)

Perpetual Motion Debunkers Begrudgingly Recognize Overunity Systems

Note that even those determined fellows who make a career out of debunking overunity EM systems as "perpetual motion machines" (but never debunk *themselves* or the classical electrodynamicists advocating *charges* as perpetual motion machines on a breathtakingly large scale!) do admit that such overunity systems exist!

They call such permissible overunity systems *false perpetual motion machines*—because, they say, those systems are not closed systems {48}. They themselves begrudgingly admit that a proper open system, receiving and using energy from outside, can indeed produce COP>1.0.

We free energy researchers never said we have classical *equilibrium* systems! It's the *skeptics themselves* who keep setting up that tired old "closed system" strawman {49} and knocking it down—and that strawman has nothing at all to do with permissible overunity in open EM systems far from thermodynamic equilibrium.

We also clear up another great misunderstanding that is widespread: the difference between efficiency and coefficient of performance. The efficiency of a system is determined by how much useful work it provides, or useful energy it outputs, divided by how much input energy it receives *from all sources*. No system, either in equilibrium or in disequilibrium, can exceed 100% efficiency. If it has any internal losses, etc., any EM system will always have efficiency less than 100%. However, coefficient of performance compares the useful work provided, or the useful energy the system outputs, to the operator's input of energy. Thus a system can indeed have a COP>1.0, even if its efficiency x < 100%. An example is the common home heat pump, which has a COP = 4.0 or so in ideal operating conditions, while at the same time having an efficiency of less than 50%.

We in fact advocate the very kind of so-called "false perpetual motion machines" that the skeptics already admit can legitimately exhibit overunity COP and are permissible.

So eerily, if one cuts through the jargon and lack of understanding, that brand of skeptic unwittingly supports our position, though it may tear his vitals and he will never admit it. As we said, one must keep one's sense of humor. It's truly amazing how classical thermodynamics is used so ubiquitously to object to COP>1.0 electrical systems, when such systems are open dissipative systems and not even described by classical thermodynamics.

Generators and Batteries Do Not Output Energy to the External Circuit

Now here's a real shocker: Generators and batteries—i.e., so-called "power sources"—do not furnish energy to their external circuits! Well, how could they! We already pointed out that there is no such thing as a source, but only a "gate" or transducer. So rigorously, batteries and generators *must* be receiving and gating or transducing that energy from their "external environment" The gating for the energy furnished to the external circuit is from the source dipole converter. It receives the EM energy from the time domain, transduces it into 3-space, and outputs the flow of 3-space EM energy from the source dipole converter through all space surrounding the external circuit. The small flow component striking the system conductors, potentializes the surface charges in the conductors and components. Those surface charges serve as energy converters locally powering the Drude electrons. (For the several functions played by the surface charges and their excitation energy, see J. D. Jackson, "Surface charges on circuit wires and resistors play three roles," *American Journal of Physics*, 64(7), July 1996, p. 855-870.) The external circuit is powered by its own surface charge converters, freely receiving excess energy from the impinging EM energy flow existing in their immediate spatial environment.

To understand how the external circuit is powered, we must therefore pay attention to all the source charges (energy converters) in the circuit, receiving excess EM energy from their environment, converting it to usable energy form, and powering the elements of the circuit.

The external circuit itself can be nothing but a "receiver/converter" receiving, collecting, and converting some of that Poynting energy flow in its immediate environment.

We reiterate: *Generators and batteries do not furnish energy to their external circuits!* If one does not know that, then one needs to go back and seriously reflect upon the processes inside batteries and generators, including what particle physics has to say about the source dipole's broken symmetry in its vacuum interaction.

More rigorously, we introduce the concept of the *supersystem*, which consists of three components: (i) the physical electrical system and its dynamics, (ii) the local active vacuum and its components, and (iii) the active local curvatures of spacetime and their dynamics. All three components of the supersystem interact with each other. No circuit analysis is actually complete until the supersystem has been analyzed. U(1) symmetry electrodynamics arbitrarily and falsely assumes that the local vacuum is inert, so that no broken symmetry with it exists, and falsely assumes that the local spacetime is flat. Hence it discards the two components of the supersystem that comprise the "active environment" of the physical electrical system. In such case, by assuming equilibrium with the active environment, U(1) electrodynamics arbitrarily discards all overunity electrical power systems, which a priori must be in disequilibrium with an active environment, receiving and using energy from that environment.

Lorentz Procedure for Electromagnetic Fields

The actual Lorentz procedure—which he did originally circa 1886—is contained in H. A. Lorentz, *Vorlesungen über Theoretische Physik an der Universität Leiden*, Vol. V, *Die Maxwellsche Theorie (1900-1902)*, Akademische Verlagsgesellschaft M.B.H., Leipzig, 1931, "Die Energie im elektromagnetischen Feld," p. 179-186. Figure 25 on p. 185 shows the Lorentz concept of integrating the EM energy flow vector around a closed cylindrical surface surrounding a volumetric element. This is the procedure which arbitrarily selects only the *diverged* component of the energy flow associated with a circuit—specifically, the small Poynting component striking the surface charges and being diverged into the circuit to power it—and then treats that tiny component as the "entire" EM energy flow. Thereby Lorentz arbitrarily discarded all of the extra Heaviside *nondiverged* energy transport component which does not strike the circuit at all, and is just wasted.

One really needs to ponder what Lorentz did to snarl the EM energy flow theory, essentially substituting the tiny Slepian vector (for the energy flow dissipated in a circuit) for the monstrously large energy flow vector of the flowing energy in space surrounding (and associated with) the circuit—and treating the Slepian vector as the entire energy flow vector because all the rest was "physically insignificant" (Lorentz's actual phrase, translated, was that the discarded nondiverged EM energy flow "has no physical significance." To falsify that statement, refer to Craig F. Bohren, "How can a particle absorb more than the light incident on it?" *American Journal of Physics*, 51(4), Apr. 1983, p. 323-327.) {34}.

Here's how a generator works, highly simplified. *It generates the source dipole converter!* Consider a generator, e.g., one that is steam turbine-powered. We burn a little coal to heat the water in a boiler to form the steam to power the turbine to rotate the generator's shaft. With rotation, a magnetic field is formed in the generator. In that magnetic field, the negative charges are forced in one direction and the positive charges in the other, separating the internal charges inside the generator and forming the source dipole converter.

Now that's all a generator does. It performs work on its own internal charges to form that source dipole. It cannot do anything else except scatter some extra energy in its other internal losses. It doesn't furnish *current* to the external circuit, because it doesn't furnish the electrons that form the current in the external circuit. Those electrons mostly come from the materials in that external circuit. In a copper wire, e.g., there is just about one electron free and bumping around like a gas molecule, per copper atom. Considered as a sort of gas, those free electrons from the circuit materials are referred to as the *Drude electron gas*.

What comes out of the generator's source dipole—once it is formed—is the enormous energy that the dipole converter extracts from its broken symmetry in the vacuum interaction. *That's* where the energy flow component comes pouring out from and goes roaring out through all space surrounding our external circuit. It's gated from the vacuum by the source dipole converter, by the proven broken 3-symmetry of the dipole.

A battery dissipates chemical energy to accomplish the formation of its source dipole on the plates. We have to *pay* for the initial formation of the dipole, whether it's in a battery or a generator. But once made, the dipole converter will furnish energy continuously and indefinitely, so long as it exists, if we do not let it be perturbed. The energy for every EM circuit is taken straight from the active vacuum, classical electromagnetics and its mindset notwithstanding!

Once the source dipole is formed, particle physics assures us that the broken symmetry of that dipole, in its fiery exchange with the vacuum, orders and gates out a fierce flow of organized EM energy. This energy roars out through all space along (and generally parallel to) the external conductors attached to the generator terminals. John D. Kraus {50} shows a good drawing of the how the *Poynting* component of the energy flow is actually withdrawn from surrounding space around the external conductors, by the surface charges as the absorb energy and move into the interior of the conductors radially, drawing in the immediate near-field portion of their fields extending out into space. Almost all that huge energy flow is not intercepted by the circuit (not drawn into the conductors) at all and thus is not diverged into the circuit to power it. Instead, most of the energy flow misses the circuit entirely and just roars on off into deep space and is "wasted."

The entire energy flow is enormous, filling all space surrounding that circuit, out to an infinite perpendicular radius away. *Both individual and collected charges modify the entire vacuum potential across the universe*. There's about 10^{13} times as much energy flow now zipping through space (for a nominal simple circuit) as the feeble little "sheath" of energy flow against the conductors. This small "sheath of flow" strikes the circuit's surface electrons and thereby gets diverged into the circuit to power the electrons and form the Slepian vector **j**φ.

All the rest of that enormous *free* Poynting energy flow extracted from the seething vacuum by the source dipole converter just passes on off into space and is lost.

Lorentz Arbitrarily Discarded All Overunity Maxwellian Systems

Lorentz found that enormous amount of energy—most of it missing the circuit and just wasted—to be very, very embarrassing! It was perhaps irritating to him that we build such puny "intercepting and collecting" electrical power systems. We build them with a laughable energy collection efficiency of some 10^{-13} or so. Hardly something to brag about!

If the truth hurts, it is often buried with a non sequitur. That is a human trait, and it applies to scientists as well as to lay persons. In modern times it's called "spin control".

So Lorentz fixed the problem with a little scientific spin control! He placed a little spherical surface mathematically around each element of those conductors, and integrated the Poynting vector around that surface. Voila! All Poynting energy flow *missing* the circuit and therefore wasted, gets mathematically cancelled in that neat little mathematical trick {51}. It is not canceled in the real world, just in Lorentz's little trick. The result of the Lorentz surface integration of the Poynting vector is that only the tiny Poynting component of that energy flow—the component that struck the surface charges and got diverged into the circuit, forming the Slepian vector $\mathbf{j}\varphi$, is retained mathematically.

All the rest is just *arbitrarily* discarded. It's "out of sight, out of mind!"

Of course our instruments measure dissipation of energy. They indirectly measure how much energy is diverged into the circuit and collected (intercepted) there, because they measure the energy dissipation from the circuit. What is *dissipated from* an otherwise inert circuit must first have *entered* it. The instruments measure nothing of the non-intercepted, nondiverged Heaviside energy flow that does not enter the circuit.

So Lorentz's trick does retain how much energy is intercepted, diverged into the circuit, collected on the electrons to power them, and dissipated in the loads and losses. And that does match our instrumental measurements. However, that *is not* the total EM energy flow connected with a circuit, but only a small component of it.

Classical electrodynamicists dutifully continue to follow Lorentz's little trick and call that Poynting component the "entire energy flow." Then they caution against thinking too deeply about the energy flow subject.

In the text by D.S. Jones, *The Theory of Electromagnetism*, Pergamon Press, Oxford, 1964, p. 52, we see: *"It is possible to introduce the Poynting vector S, defined by S = E x H, and regard it as the intensity of energy flow at a point. This procedure is open to criticism since we could add to S any vector whose divergence is zero without affecting [the basic integration procedure's result]."* Obviously if we have such a nondiverged additional EM energy flow there, the Poynting nondiverged energy flow is not the *total* energy flow at all. Quoting J. D. Jackson, *Classical Electrodynamics*, Second Edition, Wylie, 1975, p. 237: "*. . . the Poynting vector is arbitrary to the extent that the curl of any vector field can be added to it. Such an added term can, however, have no physical consequences.*" Note that the divergence of a curled field is zero. So Jackson has also stated that a nondivergent energy flow accompanying the diverged Poynting component can have no physical significance. That is in error. It has no physical significance for the specific diversion process by that specific diverger that is diverging the particular Poynting flow component. However, we may place an *additional* interceptor/diverger outside the functional region of that first divergence, and collect (diverge) additional EM energy from that "component that can have no physical significance." It can indeed have physical consequences for other divergers (other collection processes outside that volume inclosed by the little Lorentz surface where the energy flow vector is integrated.

As a result of this *faux pas* by Lorentz, physicists are politely debating even today about just what the "Poynting" vector really is, and what it should be, and is it the Slepian vector, and so on. They've been quietly doing that in *American Journal of Physics*, e.g., for more than 30 years now. Compare with C. J. Carpenter, "Electromagnetic energy and power in terms of charges and potentials instead of fields," *IEE Proceedings A (Physical Science, Measurement and Instrumentation, Management and Education)*, (UK), 136A(2), Mar. 1989, p. 55-65. Carpenter advocates that $j\varphi$ be used as the energy flow vector. For a refutation of Carpenter's argument, see J. A. Ferreira, "Application of the Poynting vector for power conditioning and conversion," *IEEE Transactions on Education*, 31(4), Nov. 1988, p. 257-264.

The Effect of Lorentz's Closed Surface Integration of the Poynting Vector

Lorentz stated that all the rest of that wasted EM energy flow was "physically insignificant" (because it did not hit the circuit). Well, contrast this to the ocean wind on a sailing ship. Lorentz's statement is analogous to arguing that the huge component of the wind that does not strike the ship's sails is "physically insignificant". However, if we put some more ships with "intercepting and collecting sails" alongside our ship, or at a distance, they will be powered quite well with a little more of that "physically insignificant" wind. Lorentz's "physically insignificant nondiverged energy flow component" is insignificant only if we assume one and one only interceptor/collector charge which does not interact with it. For other interceptor/collector charges which do interact with it, the discarded flow is significant because it will then be diverged and do work. So Lorentz really did advance a non sequitur of first order.

However, Lorentz thus avoided having to try to explain how the source dipole in every generator and battery outputs far more energy flow than the amount of shaft energy input to the generator, or chemical energy dissipated in the battery.

The electrodynamicists repeat that deceptive little Lorentz integration trick to this very day, in all the texts and all the papers. As a result, most electrical engineers and even many electrical physicists have thoroughly confused electrical energy and energy flow with electrical energy dissipation and the flow of that dissipation energy component. A confusion in electrical engineering exists between EM work and EM energy, and every leading sophomore physics book shows this confusion. One cannot "draw power" from a generator, e.g. Power is the rate of doing work, and work is the change of energy form, so power is the rate at which the form of energy is being changed. *A priori*, that can only occur in the component where the form of the energy is actually being changed. The energy pouring from a generator's terminals has absolutely no "power" until it is intercepted and diverged or changed in form.

Let me put it this way. A flow of a trillion joules of energy per second, none of which is intercepted, diverged, or changed in form, rigorously has absolutely zero power. In the trillion joules per second example, no rate of change of the form of the energy is occurring, hence there is no power. However, one cannot logically ignore that it is still there as energy flow, as Lorentz did, even though it is not doing any work.

The textbooks will usually submit that the trillion-joule-per-second energy flow has a power of a trillion watts. Quite wrong. It has zero power {52}.

We do not "draw power" from a battery or generator. Power is ongoing right where the energy is being changed in form, in the component changing the energy's form and performing work. One cannot "draw it" from the source. One draws (receives) *energy* from the source dipole gating. But how tangled the lexicon for power systems has become, and how filled with non sequiturs!

Heaviside and Poynting independently and essentially simultaneously discovered the flow of EM energy through space, after Maxwell was deceased. We use Poynting's theory because Poynting published more prestigiously. However, to his credit Poynting always gallantly credited Heaviside with being first {53}. Also, Heaviside gallantly credited Poynting with being first.

From the beginning, Poynting considered only that component of the energy flow that actually enters the circuit {54}.

On the other hand, Heaviside pointed out that the diverged (Poynting) component was only a small component of the energy flow {55}. However, Heaviside could not explain what was producing such a startlingly large flow of energy from the terminals of the battery or generator. Heaviside was self-taught and never

13927-VALO

attended university. Consequently, he was acutely aware of his lack of the formal Ph.D., and therefore his role as an outsider or near-hermit. Mathematicians had objected to some of the operational methods Heaviside originated, and attacked him resoundingly. Later, these methods were soundly justified and adopted. However, in the 1880's Heaviside was still a very cautious man around academics. He therefore did not plainly state how much larger the remaining component of the energy flow was, but merely referred to it obliquely in terms of angles to a reference. This way, he was not violently attacked as a "perpetual motion nut." In the 1880s, neither the electron nor the atom had been discovered, there was no knowledge of an active vacuum since quantum mechanics was not born yet, and there was no knowledge of curved spacetime since neither special or general relativity had been born.

He thus spoke cautiously in terms of the "angles" the two components—diverged and nondiverged—made with some reference direction. The Lorentz "solution" to the problem—just ignore all that extra nondiverged energy flow—matched the fundamental instrumental measurements in the dissipating circuit. So today all the texts and engineers calculate "*the* energy flow" as just that feeble little Poynting fraction of it caught by our circuits and dissipated in them. That's a non sequitur of first magnitude which—*inexplicably!*—continues to be perpetuated throughout electrodynamics, and *particularly* throughout electrical engineering. The electrodynamicists actually calculate only a tiny bit of the total energy flow already extracted—by the source dipole in our circuits—from the vacuum, and do not recognize the actual vacuum source for the energy that powers every electrical circuit. They continue to mistake the part for the whole, and continue to eliminate the active vacuum from their discipline, nearly half a century after the discovery of the interaction of the vacuum with that source dipole and the dipole's broken symmetry in it. Literally hundreds of texts and technical books, and thousands of scientific papers, contain these glaring foundations error. It is ironical that not a single electrical engineering department in the United States teaches how an electromagnetic circuit is actually powered.

Scientists must think logically, and construct the theory logically. Else it isn't science.

There Is No Energy Problem, Just an Energy Intercepting and Using Problem

But back to our generator or battery. Once the source dipole converter is formed, the energy flow along the circuit, powering the electrons, is for free. The energy is already freely extracted (actually *gushing in a torrent*) directly from the vacuum. We have never built anything *but* an electrical power system driven by electrical Poynting energy extracted from the vacuum!

Yet following Lorentz, and considering an EM power system theory from which the active vacuum is excluded, most scientists continue to believe that it's *terribly difficult if not impossible* to extract electrical energy from the vacuum. What a colossal joke! None of our electrical power systems ever did anything else *but* extract and convert all the energy furnished to the external circuit, directly from the vacuum. And they actually extract and convert a great deal more EM energy that misses the circuit and is wasted. All we have ever built is an inherently free energy, overunity power system (if one accounts just the *energy conversion* process that is ongoing between the system and the other two components of the supersystem), once we paid to form the source dipole converter in the generator or battery. It is just that we have *crippled* every one of the myriads of free energy power systems we have ever built!

Here's how "difficult" it is to build a free energy flow generator. Take a charged capacitor. Lay it across a permanent magnet so that the **E**-field of the capacitor is at right angles to the **H** field of the magnet. That maximizes the Poynting EM energy flow, which is expressed as $\mathbf{S} = k(\mathbf{E} \times \mathbf{H})$ by orthodox theory. That silly thing sits there and pours out energy indefinitely {56, 57}. Substitute an electret for the capacitor, and you don't even have to recharge it. That's a *certified* free energy generator. The only problem is in how to *capture the steadily flowing energy and use it*.

There is no *energy* problem per se! One can get all the *energy* one wishes, anywhere in the universe, directly from the vacuum's interaction with a source dipole, easily and simply. Just make a little dipole and pay peanuts for it. And have a developed technology that can catch a great deal of the resulting energy flow and use it effectively, without destroying that dipole.

The problem is only in how to (1) intercept and use an appreciable or useful bit of the free energy flow so easily gated from the active vacuum, and (2) dissipate the captured energy in loads (and some system losses) *without* using half of it to destroy the source dipole, as all our present circuits and power systems are designed to do.

There are two other associated problems: (3) the continuing advocating of a seriously flawed energy flow theory and electrical power system theory, and (4) the influence of very large international energy cartels with deeply vested economic commitment to the present course of power system research, development, and engineering. Still another related problem is (5) the resulting intense economic control of science and of energy research and policy, constraining it into "accepted" directions. In short, "thinking outside the box"—the present buzzword for highly innovative thinking— is almost ruthlessly excluded in the field of EM power system theory and technology.

Try it and see. Just visit the websites of the National Academy of Sciences and the National Science Foundation, and see if they are doing any work in this area.

How EM Power Systems Enforce Symmetrical Self-Regauging

So why do not our present "inherently free energy" power systems exhibit COP>1.0?

Quite simple. We are all trained to build the systems as closed current loop circuits, where all the spent electrons in the ground return line (from all loads and losses) are forcibly rammed right back through the source dipole charges in the generator or battery. That knocks the end charges every which way, scattering them and destroying the dipole converter—and thereby shutting off the free gating of energy from the vacuum.

It is easy to show that precisely one half the captured free energy in the circuit is utilized to continuously destroy the source dipole. The other half is distributed amongst the loads and losses. That means that less than half the captured free energy is available to do work in the loads. So the circuit kills its own source dipole faster than it powers its load.

In short, we only build symmetrically regauging Maxwellian EM power systems. We deliberately design them so that they *forcibly* self-regauge symmetrically.

We Pay the Power Company for a Sumo-Wrestling Match Inside Its Generators

One of the Lorentz asymmetrical self-regaugings in the EM power circuit is used to destroy the source dipole converter and shut off its gushing Poynting energy flow from the vacuum interaction. The other Lorentz asymmetrical self-regauging is the dissipation of captured EM energy in the external system loads and losses. The two are equal, so the net regauging is symmetrical.

In the generator, once the source (gating) dipole converter is destroyed, we have to burn some more fuel to get the generator shaft rotated a bit more, making the magnetic field inside the generator and expending that magnetic energy to do work on the internal charges of both signs, to re-separate them and reform the dipole converter. Which the circuit promptly kills again, so we have to burn some more fuel to rotate the shaft to get the dipole converter reformed—and so on and so on. One gets the picture.

13927-VALO

We pay the power company to engage in a giant and continuous Sumo wrestling match inside its own generators, and to *always lose* that wrestling match. Our universities proudly keep training our engineers to specifically design our power systems that way, so they proudly keep building them that way. And the power meter stays on the houses and factories, the gas pump meter stays on the gas pump, and we keep burning train loads of coal and oil from fleets of tankers to maintain this mess.

If it were not so tragic scientifically and responsible for the resulting gigantic pollution of the biosphere by hydrocarbon combustion byproducts and nuclear wastes, it would be a cosmic joke. For such an inane power system theory and technology, one is even tempted to paraphrase Tesla's {58} infamous statement—more a fervent hope—that

> "*. . . . [I]n a short time it will be recognized as one of the most remarkable and inexplicable aberrations of the scientific mind which has ever been recorded in history.*"

Of course we do not wish to antagonize the electrodynamicists, but only wake them up to what has been done to all of us by the serious flaws and arbitrary changes implemented in their classical electrodynamics model. And we also wish to alert them to the fact that the Sachs unified field theory provides an excellent framework to deal with and analyze the supersystem, which must be done to design and build overunity EM power systems. Further, higher symmetry electrodynamics is required rather than U(1) electrodynamics. The O(3) electrodynamics originated by Evans and Vigier, and further pioneered by Evans, is ideal for engineering such overunity systems and understanding them{78}. After all, it is the electrodynamicists themselves whom we are urging to make the necessary corrections to the theory.

In a battery-powered system, the battery has to keep furnishing chemical energy to keep doing work on the internal charges to keep reforming the source dipole converter, that we ourselves design the circuit to keep destroying. Eventually the battery chemistry is all changed (e.g., the lead plate surface is all converted to lead oxide in a lead-acid battery) and the battery chemistry can no longer furnish chemical energy to do the work in separating the internal charges to reform the source dipole. So we must get a new battery, or if rechargeable we must send some current back through it to do work on that chemistry again to change it back (to reconvert the lead oxide back to lead). Since every system has some inefficiencies and losses, we will pay for more energy to recharge the battery than the work we get back in the load {59}.

So that's why we continue to universally build underunity power systems.

Off there in the distance, one can hear Lorentz laughing, and laughing, and laughing. . . . .Meanwhile the strangling creatures in our biosphere now becoming a sewer, are crying, crying, crying. . . . and dying, dying, dying. . . . .

What Lorentz Symmetrical Regauging Technically Is and Does

Lorentz was and remains one of the truly great scientists of all time, and his magnificent accomplishments in physics are renowned and well-known. Yet ironically he also gave us the two major changes to EM theory that for a century have prevented overunity EM power systems from being developed and utilized.

Lorentz's symmetrical regauging is a mathematical operation invoked on the Maxwell equations to simplify them. So what were Maxwell's *original* equations?

Maxwell's equations are some 20 quaternion and quaternion-like equations in 20 unknowns. Heaviside changed them into what today is four equations, or in potential form is two equations with variables coupled. In that form the equations are referred to today as "Maxwell's equations".

Consider the potential form.{60} The Heaviside-Maxwell equations are difficult to solve in that coupled condition, and one must most often use numerical methods. So to mathematically produce equations with the variables decoupled, and therefore far, far easier to solve, Lorentz just arbitrarily and symmetrically regauged them (changed the potentials). In short, he assumed that the potential energy of the system is arbitrarily and freely changed twice.

We should not criticize Lorentz too much! Everyone at the time believed that the potentials were not real anyway, but only mathematical conveniences. So—it was universally thought—changing them mathematically was of no physical consequence, so long as the *real* EM causative agents—thought to be the force fields—were not changed overall. In other words, if changes of the potential generated no net forces when completed, it was believed that one could freely change potentials at one's whim, without changing the system. We know today that such a notion is quite false, but eerily there is still great attachment to that very notion. For example, quoting p. 67 of Bloch and Crater {61}:

> *[It is usually] ". . . assumed that the magnitude of potential energy is irrelevant, being arbitrary to the extent of an additive constant."*

Understand what is being said. It is being assumed that the potential energy of a system is irrelevant and arbitrary! Cheez! The entire notion of "powering a circuit" is to get some potential energy transferred to it, so that potential energy (collected energy) can be dissipated in the load to power it! The magnitude of how much energy we have available to discharge into loads and power them, is *most certainly not* irrelevant!

Again, quoting Goebel {62} p. 1137:

> *"[T]he zero of both scalar and vector electromagnetic potentials is irrelevant; the addition of a constant to an*

> *electromagnetic potential is of no consequence (so-called gauge invariance of the first kind).*

Lorentz used two simultaneous regaugings. Each regauging alone is *asymmetrical*; that is, it produces not only a free potential energy change (in the system, e.g.), but also a free new force (in the system) which could be used to dissipate that newly collected potential energy into a load, yielding overunity. Ah, but that would never do! So Lorentz simultaneously changed the other potential, but precisely selected the change *just so* that the new free force was the exact equal and opposite of the first one. This zero-summed the two new free forces, so there were no *net* translation forces remaining. In short, the combination was and is a *symmetrical* regauging.

But the two net forces did not vanish; they are still there, as a "stress". So the two asymmetrical regauging forces fight each other to a Sumo wrestling draw. There is no *net* translation force to do external work. Hence the net effect is that the system has been *symmetrically* regauged {63}. It has also had its internal stress changed.

All the free system potential energy—the two changes of same—is thereby converted into pure stress energy inside the system, stressing the system but doing no external work! There is no net force left after Lorentz symmetrical regauging which can be used to dissipate that free regauging energy upon a load and do work for free.

In short, Lorentz retained only that very small subset of Heaviside-Maxwellian systems wherein all the systems are forcibly brought into thermodynamic equilibrium with their environment i.e., with the active vacuum. For those systems, classical equilibrium thermodynamics rigorously applies. Lorentz just arbitrarily and unwittingly discarded *all* the Heaviside-Maxwell systems in disequilibrium—the very Maxwellian systems which could exhibit COP>1.0. He retained *only* those systems that are in equilibrium and can only exhibit COP<1.0 (assuming a little internal losses for any real system).

For Overunity Systems, One Must First Undo the Lorentz Condition

The Heaviside-Maxwell equations do indeed include vast numbers of systems not in thermodynamic equilibrium, *before* Lorentz did his "symmetrical regauging" and arbitrarily changed those equations.

To simplify the mathematics and restore beautiful symmetry (which historically mathematicians worship), Lorentz arbitrarily discarded far more Maxwellian systems than he retained. He unwittingly taught electrodynamicists to simply discard and ignore all permissible overunity EM systems.

It follows that the very first thing we must do to an EM power system, to make it possible for the system to produce COP>1.0, is arrange for the system to violate that arbitrary Lorentz condition. Actually, breaking the Lorentz condition is designing the system so that it does not forcibly pass all the "spent electrons" from the loads and losses, in the ground return line back through the primary source dipole converter, destroying it. The ramifications of doing this have been pointed out in a paper by the AIAS {64}.

Electrodynamicists already assume one can asymmetrically regauge any EM system—that is, freely change its potential energy, which in electromagnetics is just changing the voltage that is then applied to the charges. However, seemingly one is expected to love mathematics and symmetry so much more than the physics that one will (1) inanely regauge that system again in a peculiarly restrained manner to "thwart" any ability of the system to discharge its excitation energy in the load without destroying its source dipole, and (2) carefully choose and apply a second regauging so that it precisely cancels out all "work-producing capability" of the first one.

Now other than mathematical convenience, why would anyone wish to destroy a perfectly good and already accepted free energy process, or cripple it so that the excess energy could not be utilized to do some free work? From a power system viewpoint, that is total insanity {65}.

Meanwhile, true to Lorentz our scientists and engineers have been building electrical power systems precisely so they symmetrically regauge themselves forcibly. And meanwhile the scientific community, environmental community, and governmental community have been decrying that we have a great energy problem in modern society and a great biosphere contamination problem. We do not. Instead, we have a formidable *scientific mindset* problem.

Hope for the Future: Poor but Growing

As the reader can see, there is a quite rigorous basis for overunity EM power systems. The gist of overunity operation—*asymmetrical self-regauging*—is already accomplished in every power system:. Unfortunately, the engineers have given us power systems (energy converters) that also continually perform a *second* countering asymmetrical regauging, precisely designed to kill the useful results of first one. We will never produce overunity electrical power systems unless we design and build systems that deliberately violate symmetry (violate Lorentz regauging), and use *net asymmetrical* regauging.

Frankly, the scientific community seems almost beyond hope on this, because it rather adamantly insists on upholding equilibrium systems and classical thermodynamics, behaving as if open disequilibrium EM systems do not exist (in the face of extensive published experimental proof that they do).

This may change, however, with continued pressure from the environmentalists and the coming decline of oil supplies in about year 2030 or so. (The supply of cheap, low sulphur oil is declining *now*.)

Also, hopefully there is now slowly rising an understanding of what Lorentz symmetrical regauging did to us, and what the real principles of permissible overunity power systems are. Particularly the younger researchers, still not so brainwashed, are willing to look at the references themselves and see precisely what was done to the earlier Maxwellian EM models and how the theory they have been taught to apply was actually derived.

Some of the Flaws in Foundations of Electrodynamics

As a parting thought, we leave the reader with this startling statement: No Western electrodynamicist—with the possible exceptions of Lorentz and Heaviside—appears to ever have calculated the magnitude of the scalar potential, even though every professor teaches "how to do it" and every text purports to show how to do it! We've all been taught to calculate the *reaction cross section* of the potential, not the magnitude of the potential itself {66}. The reaction cross section of the potential is a scalar value, but the potential itself *is not a scalar entity*.

Think of it closely. The so-called "magnitude" of the so-called scalar potential at a point, is defined as the joules of energy that will be *diverted from* the potential and "collect" upon a unit point static charge assumed to be located at that point. Sorry, but that's not the magnitude of the potential (which may occupy all spatial points), but rigorously that is its reaction cross section at that point! So when we express this so-called "scalar potential" function which gives a scalar value at every spatial point, we are expressing the function that gives its reaction cross section at every spatial point.

The so-called "scalar" potential itself is not even a scalar entity, as rigorously shown by Whittaker {67} in 1903. Whittaker rigorously demonstrates that the potential is a harmonic bundle of bidirectional EM longitudinal wavepairs. Each wavepair is comprised of a longitudinal EM wave and its phase conjugate replica. So the so-called "scalar" potential is a bundle of special EM waves, going in both directions. It's an entire giant collection of EM energy flows in higher EM polarization form, reaching across the entire universe in all directions from that "source charge". It's an ongoing change to the entire vacuum potential of the universe, across all space. And it's a multiwave, multivectorial entity.

It's also a closed feedback loop. The vacuum feeds energy to all the charges, and all the charges "feed" a mix of ordered and disordered energy back to the vacuum. This was beautifully expressed by Puthoff {68} as a *self-regenerative cosmological feedback cycle.*

At any spatial point, of course, the combined *reaction cross section* of all those composite waves is a scalar value—which has nothing at all to do with whether or not the potential itself is a vector or a scalar entity.

Again, we have to have a sense of humor! If the scalar potential were really a scalar entity, then when one set it onto a transmission line, it would just sit there like an old scalar boot. It doesn't do that at all, but takes off down the line like a scalded hog, revealing its vector nature. And if one sets it onto the middle of the transmission line, it takes off in both directions at once like two scalded hogs, showing its bidirectional vector nature.

Isn't it odd that such a simple gedankenexperiment alone proves instantly that the "scalar" potential isn't a scalar entity? Yet the electrodynamicists have not changed that horrible non sequitur in the nearly 100 years since Whittaker {69} clearly showed it with mathematical rigor.

It indeed often requires the Western scientific community from 40 to 100 years to do what should be done in four.

The amount of water one dips from a rushing river in a standard bucket, or diverts in a swirl around a fixed standard rock on the bottom, is not the magnitude of the river! What is collected from or diverted from something, is not the something but only a component of it. The part is not the whole.

From any "potential" that is nonzero (i.e., that has a nonzero cross section, no matter how small), one can collect as much energy as desired, at least in theory. W = Vq is the simple equation where W is the energy collected in joules from potential V (cross section V) upon charges q, covers the situation. As can be seen, from a microvolt potential (cross section) one can collect a trillion joules of energy, if one sets sufficient collecting charges into it where the cross section is one microvolt. And if one sets even more collecting coulombs in space occupied by that potential, one will collect another appropriate number of joules.

In placing intercepting/diverging/collecting coulombs, one is placing interceptor/collectors in a myriad rushing bidirectional rivers of energy, fed by the entire energy of the universe (the simple potential is a change across the entire universe to the ambient vacuum potential). So the *actual* magnitude of any finite potential itself is so great that we may consider it infinite.

There are many other flaws in electrodynamics. The entire model needs a vigorous overhaul. To quote Bunge {70}, p. 182:

> "*. . . the best modern physicist is the one who acknowledges that neither classical nor quantum physics are cut and dried, both being full of holes and in need of a vigorous overhauling not only to better cover their own domains but also to join smoothly so as to produce a coherent picture of the various levels of physical reality.*"

I'm pleased to report that Dr. Myron Evans {71}, President of the Alpha Foundation's Institute of Advanced Study (AIAS), and other AIAS advanced theorists such as Dr. L. B. Crowell {72}, together with other eminent theorists such as Barrett {73}, are now moving electrodynamics to a much more modern non-Abelian theory in higher gauge such as O(3). The first major steps toward Sachs's unified field theory have also been taken {74}. While Evans himself cautions that this extended O(3) electrodynamics is still not the perfect step, it provides a dramatic new electrodynamics far superior to the U(1) electrodynamics presently in vogue. And it can be used to directly engineer much of Sachs's unified field theory.

The AIAS theoreticians have also elegantly pointed out serious failures of the present U(1) electrodynamics {75}, as have Barrett {76} and others {77}. Many of these shortcomings of the present electrodynamics are being rectified in the new O(3) electrodynamics.

In Summary

In closing, we summarize the bottom line for overunity EM power systems as the following list:

(1) There already do exist overunity EM processes, recognized in physics and in the leading journals. That alone proves one can build overunity EM systems, since it only takes one white crow to prove that not all crows are black. Specifically, every charge and dipole in the universe is already a legitimate COP>1.0 Maxwellian system.

(2) Classical electrodynamics is thoroughly fouled, and actions have been performed decades ago to arbitrarily limit it to a small subset and exclude all overunity Maxwellian systems.

(3) The Heaviside-Maxwell equations indeed prescribe and contain overunity EM systems, including overunity EM power systems, before Lorentz's arbitrary symmetrical regauging just to simplify the mathematical labor and thereby discard all the overunity systems.

(4) The reduction of Maxwell's EM theory to a subset and the discarding of overunity EM systems is documented in the standard literature, once one comprehends what the curtailing actions actually represented in supersystem terms. One must keep a sense of humor and not treat classical electrodynamics and equilibrium thermodynamics as religious law brought down from the mountain by Moses on his stone tablets.

(5) Any overunity system *a priori* is an open system far from thermodynamic equilibrium.

(6) If one wishes to build an overunity self-powering electrical power system, one must build the system so that it or some part of it violates Lorentz *symmetrical* self-regauging and uses net *asymmetrical* self-regauging.
(7) The free change of the potential energy of a Maxwellian system is already assumed by all electrodynamicists to be possible at will.
(8) Orthodox power systems are specifically designed to forcibly self-restore Lorentz symmetrical regauging by passing all the spent (depotentialized) electrons in the ground return line back through the primary source dipole converter to destroy it.
(9) It is radically easy and operationally simple to extract all the electrical energy one wishes, directly from the vacuum, anywhere in the universe.
(10) Particle physics has proven the basis for the active vacuum and any dipole's broken symmetry in it for over 40 years, but classical electrodynamicists have not yet changed the classical EM U(1) model's assumption of an inert and empty vacuum, much less a broken symmetry in the ongoing vacuum exchange.
(11) Batteries and generators utilize their internal energy to continually restore their continually destroyed source dipole converters, but do not furnish energy to the external circuit including to the loads. Once formed, the source dipole converter receives vacuum energy and converts some of it to Poynting energy flow furnished to the external circuit and to all surrounding space.
(12) The external circuit itself contains a conglomerate of source charge converters called "surface charges". The surface charges intercept and receive energy from the immediate energy flow environment in space, converting it to circuit energy and powering the circuit elements.
(13) Any proficient magnetics laboratory can build a self-oscillating permanent magnet via present thin film techniques

and surround it with conductors to freely power a small load, thereby instantly establishing overunity EM power systems and extraction of usable EM energy from the active vacuum.

(14) Well-known scientists have indeed previously built overunity power devices, such as negative resistors, and such as devices with stimulated media producing excess emission.

(15) Practical overunity EM power systems can be developed whenever sufficient funding for a carefully selected team and dedicated laboratory along the lines of this paper are provided—and the research is allowed to proceed by the scientific community.

Epilog

In a strange sense we just wish to free the overunity EM power systems the orthodoxists already build, but then invariably have the systems fight themselves to the death. There really is a hidden free energy genie in the bottle, waiting to be released.

In a more humorous vein, I recently checked with my friend Rajah, in India, who moves logs with elephants in his logging business. Rajah is an expert on asymmetrical self-regauging systems called "elephants". His elephants forage for their feed, freely taking on excess energy from their environment and storing it, thereby asymmetrically regauging themselves. Then Rajah takes one elephant (one net force with some regauging energy to expend) and uses it to lift and carry one or more logs. He has to pay a little to direct the elephant, of course, by hiring the trainer. But the elephant produces far more work output than the work done on the elephant by the trainer/rider. In fact, the elephant expends some of the free energy it has received from the environment in its foraging and asymmetrical self-regauging.

I discussed the problem of Lorentz symmetrical regauging with Rajah, and explained that in his business it would require that he always use his elephants in opposed matching pairs, straining fiercely one against the other. He exclaimed that such a scheme was utter nonsense, because then he himself would have to furnish the energy to drag both the struggling elephants and the logs to the loading dock! It was immediately obvious to him that such a proposed system was the worst of all possible solutions.

Rajah was astounded at my suggestion for such a thing, and asked me what on Earth prompted the Western scientists to make such a strange proposal. I explained to Rajah that all our own Western power systems were already built that way, and the electric companies were very proud of the fact that they therefore continually burned fuel by the trainloads to keep the Western "logging operations" and "paired elephants inside the generators" going furiously to move the loads.

Rajah looked at me intently for a long moment, saw that I was not joking even though my eyes were twinkling, then laughed uproariously for an extended period.

"That is very, very strange!" he exclaimed. "Never have I heard such a bizarre tale. I think that I will never understand your Western science and its insane way of trying to use its elephants!"

Rajah then asked a simple question, "How many logs have they moved with their elephants alone?" And I replied, "Not a single one! They constantly drag two opposing elephants and their load of logs around at the same time, sweating and puffing and blowing and burning fuel to do so. And our universities continue to assure us that such is the will of God and the laws of nature."

When I left, Rajah was still laughing uproariously, as he approvingly watched his own elephants working steadily and efficiently in singles.

Notes and References

1. W. K. H. Panofsky and M. Phillips, *Classical Electricity and Magnetism*, Addison-Wesley, Reading, MA, 1962, 2nd edition, p.

181 shows the Lorentz closed cylindrical surface integration trick that erroneously discards most of the Poynting energy flow vector while retaining only that small component striking the circuit and being diverged into it—in short, the component of the Poynting vector that is equal to the Slepian vector.

2. For a calculation of this nominal 10^{-13} factor, see T. E. Bearden, "Energy Flow, Collection, and Dissipation in Overunity EM Devices," *Proceedings of the 4th International Energy Conference*, Academy for New Energy, Denver, CO, May 23-27, 1997, p. 5-51. In Figure 5, p. 16 the fraction of the energy flow that is intercepted and collected by the circuit—i.e., the Poynting component—is roughly shown to be on the order of 10^{-13} of the entire energy flow available. We welcome a more careful functional representation by skilled electrodynamicists!
3. Most of the energy flow filling space surrounding the circuit will miss the circuit entirely, and just roar on off into space and be wasted. For a view showing that the intercepted and diverged Poynting component actually enters the conductors from the surrounding space, see John D. Kraus, *Electromagnetics*, Fourth Edn., McGraw-Hill, New York, 1992, Figure 12-60a and 12-60b, p. 578.
4. Floyd Sweet and T. E. Bearden, "Utilizing Scalar Electromagnetics to Tap Vacuum Energy," *Proceedings of the 26th Intersociety Energy Conversion Engineering Conference (IECEC '91)*, Boston, Massachusetts, p. 370-375.
5. For a good scientific book on the subject, see V. S. L'vov, *Wave Turbulence Under Parametric Excitation: Applications to Magnets*, Springer Series in Nonlinear Dynamics, Springer-Verlag, New York, 1994. This book covers self-oscillation in permanent magnets and magnetic materials. Professor L'vov is with the Department of Physics, Weizmann Institute of Science, Israel.
6. For an excellent advanced treatise on magnetic materials and the novel effects exhibited in them, see Robert C.

O'Handley, *Modern Magnetic Materials; Principles and Applications*, Wiley, New York, 1999.

7. Here are two very good references: (1) B. D. Cullity, *Introduction to Magnetic Materials*, Addison-Wesley, Reading, MA, 1972. Out of print, but a classic—and wonder of wonders, it's written in clear English so one can actually understand it; (2) Harry E. Burke, *Handbook of Magnetic Phenomena*, Van Nostrand, New York, 1985; this is a one-of-a-kind, indispensable handbook on magnetic effects and magnetic phenomena.
8. For a discussion of multivalued magnetic potentials with appropriate references, see T. E. Bearden, "Use of Asymmetrical Regauging and Multivalued Potentials to Achieve Overunity Electromagnetic Engines," *Journal of New Energy*, 1(2), Summer 1996, p. 60-78.
9. e.g., see S. Itoh *et al.*, "Simulational and experimental studies on anomalous reflectivity of phase conjugate wave," *Ferroelectrics*, Vol. 170, 1995, p. 209-217. The appearance of multivalued conjugate reflectivities produced by the photorefractive effect was investigated.
10. "Wiegand effect: A new pulse-generating option," *Automotive Engineering*, 86(2), Feb. 1978, p. 44-48; SAE paper 780208, "The Wiegand Effect and its Automotive Applications," by J. David Marks and Michael J. Sinko, The Echlin Manufacturing Co.; "The Wiegand Effect. Some Properties of Wiegand Wire under Asymmetric Sine Wave Drive," by R.C. Barker and J.H. Liaw, Dept. of Engineering and Applied Science, Yale University; D. Botnick, "Access control systems offer programming flexibility," *Bank Systems and Equipment*, 21(8), Aug. 1984, p. 66-68; J. Buj, "The 'Wiegand effect' enables various devices to be operated with the minimum of electric power," *Revista Espanola de Electronica* (Spain), 24(267), Feb. 1977, p. 14-17; Phillip E. Wigen, "Wiegand Wire: New Material for Magnetic-Based Devices," *Electronics*, July 10, 1975, p. 100-105.; Gerald M. Walker,

"Wiegand's Wonderful Wires," *Popular Science*, May 1979, p. 102-104, 109; B. Dance, "The Wiegand effect – its applications," *Electron* (UK), No. 139, June 5, 1978, p. 23-24; H.J. Gevatter and W.A. Merl, "The Wiegand wire—a new magnetic sensor," *Regelungstechnische Praxis* (Germany), 22(3), Mar. 1980, p. 81-85 [In German]. See also Guenter H. Kuers, "Wiegand effect in theory and practice," *Proceedings of SPIE*, vol. 392, *Proceedings of the 2nd International Conference on Robot Vision and Sensory Controls*, Stuttgart, West Germany, Nov. 2-4, 1982, p. 123-132.

11. G. W. O. Howe, "Effect of Torsion on a Longitudinally-Magnetized Iron Wire," *Wireless Engineer* 29(344), May 1952, p. 115-117.
12. See F. Mandl and G. Shaw, *Quantum Field Theory*, Wiley, 1984.
13. For a good introduction to the four photon polarizations, see Lewis H. Ryder, *Quantum Field Theory*, Second Edition, Cambridge University Press, 1996, p. 147+.
14. As witnessed by some 60 ground workers who became ill, some permanently, while handling the debris of the Arrow DC-8 at Gander, Newfoundland which was killed with a Russian longitudinal EM wave interferometer on Dec. 18, 1985. The actual strike of the "ball of glowing EM energy" was witnessed. A photograph of the hole burned through the side of the right fuselage ahead of the engines was later published in *Aviation Week & Space Technology*. The struck parts of the aircraft were time-charged, and the decay of that charge produced longitudinal EM wave irradiation for some days. Ground crew exposed to that irradiation developed debilitating syndromes such as chronic and severe fatigue, nausea, dizziness, blood changes, chronic headaches, etc.
15. Several nations of the world appear to have secretly weaponized longitudinal EM wave weapons for more than two decades, and one of them (Russia) deployed such weapons as early as 1963. These weapons, e.g., have been tested

to generate large earthquakes. For a confirmation of the quake-producing EM weapons and that they have been used, we cite the following statement by Secretary of Defense Cohen: *"Others [terrorists] are engaging even in an eco-type of terrorism whereby they can alter the climate, set off earthquakes, and volcanoes remotely through the use of electromagnetic waves… So there are plenty of ingenious minds out there that are at work finding ways in which they can wreak terror upon other nations…It's real, and that's the reason why we have to intensify our [counterterrorism] efforts."* Secretary of Defense William Cohen at an April 1997 counterterrorism conference sponsored by former Senator Sam Nunn. Quoted from DoD News Briefing, Secretary of Defense William S. Cohen, Q&A at the Conference on Terrorism, Weapons of Mass Destruction, and U.S. Strategy, University of Georgia, Athens, Apr. 28, 1997.

16. A good overview is given by W. A. Rodrigues, Jr. and J.-Y. Lu, "On the existence of undistorted progressive waves (UPWs) of arbitrary speeds $0 \nleq v < \infty$ in nature," *Foundations of Physics*, 27(3), 1997, p. 435-508. A slightly corrected version is downloadable as hep-th/9606171 on the Los Alamos National Laboratory web site. It includes corrections to the published version. See also W. A. Rodrigues, Jr. and J. Vaz Jr., "Subluminal and Superluminal Solutions in Vacuum of the Maxwell Equations and the Massless Dirac Equation," *Advances in Applied Clifford Algebras*, Vol. 7(S), 1997, p. 457-466.
17. See Yossef Bodansky, "Soviets testing chemical agents in Afghanistan," *Jane's Defence Weekly*, 1(3), Apr. 7, 1984, p. 508. The Mujahedin (freedom fighters) thought this was some strange new gas that killed instantly and silently, and called it "smerch" (wind of death) gas. I personally spent two hours in Washington, D.C. with the representative of the Mujahedin to the U.S. government. The Mujahedin saw the silently struck bodies just suddenly drop like limp dishrags, never making

a single twitch thereafter. They were totally and instantly dead, down to every cell. The bodies did not decay in the desert sun during the 30 days required for the Mujahedin to fight their way back . No predators or bacteria or insects bothered the bodies where they lay. What the Mujahedin did not know was that the various particles of the struck bodies had been "time-charged" (see my "Giant Negentropy" paper) and a time-charge slowly decays, emitting longitudinal EM radiation. Any predator etc. approaching the bodies would sicken from the LW radiation, fall, and soon expire. The longitudinal EM radiation dies away slowly, the half-life depending upon the degree of initial time-charging. Hundreds of other cases of the use of LW weapons can be given.

18. T. E. Bearden, "Mind Control and EM Wave Polarization Transductions, Part I, *Explore*, 9(2), 1999, p. 59; Part II, *Explore*, 9(3), 1999, p. 61, Part III, *Explore* (in publication).
19. This can be understood as follows: The fundamental units used in one's physical model are arbitrary and chosen for convenience. (The arbitrariness of the number of fundamental units utilized is shown by the example of the "natural" system of units used by physicists and having only a single fundamental unit, usually chosen to be mass.) So one can model physics in terms of a single fundamental unit—say, *energy*. In that model, all other entities are functions of energy, in which case time becomes a function totally of energy. The resulting model would be a nightmare for learning, visualizing, and calculating, but it would yield all the correct results. In such case, time turns out to be spatial energy compressed by c^2, and thus has the same energy density (in the 4th Minkowski axis) as mass has in 3-space. To ease understanding, think of it this way: If I compress some spatial energy (say, EM energy in space) by the factor c^2, and leave that highly compressed EM energy in 3-space, it is called *mass*. If I put the compressed spatial energy over into the fourth Minkowski axis, it is called *time*. One second

of time, if "decompressed" and thereby turned back into 3-space energy, yields some 9 x 10^{16} joules of spatial energy. As can be seen, active spacetime hardly misses the time-energy extracted by even the largest electrical power plant.

20. Note that time and spatial energy in the photon are canonical; their product equals a constant. So the lower the spatial energy (the lesser the photon frequency), the greater the time component, which in energy equivalents is multiplied by nearly 10^{17}. So ironically, low frequency EM waves and photons have far greater energy than the conventional "high energy" (high frequency) photons so valued by physicists. We have previously pointed out that the low (spatial) energy nuclear reactions (LENR) experienced in cold fusion experiments, are in fact extremely high energy interactions, of greater energy density than used in the most powerful supercollider, when the time-energy is taken into account. See T. E. Bearden, "EM Corrections Enabling a Practical Unified Field Theory with Emphasis on Time-Charging Interactions of Longitudinal EM Waves," *Journal of New Energy*, 3(2/3), 1998, p. 12-28.
21. T. E. Bearden, "Toward a Practical Unified Field Theory and a Deep Experimental Example," *Proc. INE Symposium*, Univ. Utah, Aug. 14-15, 1998; — "EM Corrections Enabling a Practical Unified Field Theory with Emphasis on Time-Charging Interactions of Longitudinal EM Waves," *Explore*, 8(6), 1998, p. 7-16.
22. See Owen Flynn, "Parametric arrays: A new concept for sonar," *Electronic Warfare Magazine*, June 1977, p. 107-112. Any two sine-wave frequencies as simultaneous drivers combine to produce a sine-wave difference frequency propagating in water (or in an isotropic nonlinear medium), essentially without sidebands or reverberations. Its pattern has a main lobe approximately equal to that of the high frequency drive, but devoid of sidelobes. The level of the propagating difference frequency is proportional to both the product of

the two fundamental drive levels and to the square of the desired value of difference frequency.

23. M. I. Dykman *et al.*, "Noise-enhanced heterodyning in bistable systems," *Physical Review E*, 49(3), Mar. 1994, p. 1935-1942.
24. Gabriel Kron, "Numerical solution of ordinary and partial differential equations by means of equivalent circuits." *Journal of Applied Physics*, Vol. 16, Mar. 1945a, p. 173.
25. Gabriel Kron, "Electric circuit models of the Schrödinger equation," *Phys. Rev.* 67(1-2), Jan. 1 and 15, 1945, p. 39. See also S. Austen Stigant, "Gabriel Kron on Tensor Analysis, A Bibliographical Record," *BEAMA Journal*, Aug. 1948, for a full bibliography of Kron's outstanding publications.
26. Gabriel Kron, "The frustrating search for a geometrical model of electrodynamic networks," Journal unk, circa 1962, p. 114. See also Gabriel Kron, "Invisible dual (n-1) networks induced by electric 1-networks," *IEEE Transactions on Circuit Theory*, CT-12(4), Dec. 1965, p. 464-470.
27. John Bedini and I have filed a patent application on the flow of a novel kind of EM energy current between any two points at different potentials in an EM circuit. This also includes a process for converting that novel (and in an overunity system, detrimental) energy current into ordinary electrical current fed into the input section of the overunity system. Thus we are in patent pending status on the major method for close-looping a COP>1.0 EM system. Details cannot be provided until our foreign patent filings are secured. We will caution all overunity researchers that the simple-minded notion that ordinary clamped positive feedback can close-loop a COP>1.0 electrical power system is naïve to the extreme. Unless one understands the supersystem (noted elsewhere in the footnotes), one cannot understand Kron's statement of his open path, and one cannot begin to understand close-looping an electrical power system for self-powering operation. This entire area is of the utmost importance to physics; e.g., it

appears that the strange energy flow we discovered in overunity systems is responsible for the antigravity that is causing the acceleration of the expanding universe.

28. See P.L. Alger, Ed., *The Life and Times of Gabriel Kron*, or *Walking Around the World, and Tensors*, Mohawk Development Services, Inc., Schenectady, NY, 1969; Banesh Hoffman, "Kron's Non-Riemannian Electrodynamics," *Reviews of Modern Physics*, 21(3), 1949, p. 535-540; K. Kondo and Y. Ishizuka, "Recapitulation of the Geometrical Aspects of Gabriel Kron's Non-Riemannian Electrodynamics," Research Association of Applied Geometry, *Memoirs of the Unifying Study of Basic Problems in Engineering and Physical Sciences by Means of Geometry*, Gakujutsu Bunken Fukyukai, Tokyo, Vol. I, 1955, p. 185-239 (particularly see footnote 1, p. 222).
29. However, it may have involved multiply-connected spacetime, in which a single bit of energy can be in two different spatial locations (to the external observer) simultaneously. In short, the external observer sees a direct and unique "energy amplification" since he sees twice as much energy existing in his frame. In theory any number of spatial points in a normal frame can be multiply connected, similar to a quantum potential. Energy appearing at one MCS-point will simultaneously appear at every other, since in MCS all the points are superposed. For the connection to Kron's work, we quote J. W. Lynn and R.A. Russell, "*Kron has never published details of his method of making the polyhedron self-organizing, although his published results show that in this state it has some remarkable properties, associated with harmonic integrals on multiply connected spaces.*" [J.W. Lynn and R.A. Russell, "Kron's Wave Automaton," Journal unk, date unk., p. 131.]
30. For a skeptical reference, see K. C. Cole, "Experts Scoff at Claim of Electricity Flowing with 'Negative Resistance'," *Los Angeles Times*, July 10, 1998. I wrote a rebuttal to the editor, but it was not published. Professor Chung is a leading scien-

tist in "smart materials" (materials that act similar to electronic circuits) in the United States and she is widely published.

31. Nabil M. Lawandy, M. Balachandran, A. S. L. Gomes and E. Sauvain, "Laser action in strongly scattering media," *Nature*, 368(6470), Mar. 31, 1994, p. 436-438. For a good lay article complete with color pictures, see Ivars Peterson, "Boosted light: Laser action in white paint," *Science News*, 145(15), Apr. 9, 1994, p. 228-229. See also P. Mandel, "Lasing without inversion: A useful concept?" *Contemporary Physics*, Vol. 34, 1993, p. 235; O. Kocharovskaya, "Amplification and lasing without inversion," *Physics Reports*, Vol. 219, 1992, p. 175.
32. For example, see Nabil M. Lawandy, "Optical Gain Medium Having Doped Nanocrystals of Semiconductors and Also Optical Scatterers," U.S. Patent No. 5,434,878, July 18, 1995. A pending co-patent application serial No. 08/210,710, filed Mar. 19, 1994 entitled "Optical Sources Having a Strongly Scattering Gain Medium Providing Laser-like Action" has also probably been granted.
33. Diederik Wiersma and Ad Lagendijk, "Laser Action in Very White Paint," *Physics World*, Jan. 1997, p. 33-37. A slight update of the article, along with other pertinent and updated references is given on website *http://www.wins.uva.nl/research/scm/adlag/articles/dgain.htm*.
34. Craig F. Bohren, "How can a particle absorb more than the light incident on it?", *American Journal of Physics*, 51(4), Apr. 1983, p. 323-327. In the same issue, see independent confirmation of Bohren's work by H. Paul and R. Fischer, "Comment on 'How can a particle absorb more than the light incident on it?'," *American Journal of Physics*, 51(4), Apr. 1983, p. 327. Under nonlinear conditions, a particle can absorb more energy than is in the light incident on it. Metallic particles at ultraviolet frequencies are one class of such particles and insulating particles at infrared frequencies are

another. Bohren shows an experiment that outputs 18 times as much energy as is input to it via "conventional" calculations. The absorbing particles are simply resonated, so they sweep out a greater reaction cross section than the static charge by which the field, potential, and field intensity is defined. So the resonant charges sweep past the normal Poynting-diverged" zone into the usually nondiverged Heaviside zone, and absorb additional energy—some 18 times as much, which is then re-emitted as real energy. This is a verifiable overunity process which any good university nonlinear optics laboratory can easily perform. Other pertinent references are V.S. Letokhov, "Laser Maxwell's demon," *Contemporary Physics*, 36(4), 1995, p. 235-243; — "Generation of light by a scattering medium with negative resonance absorption," *Soviet Physics JETP*, 26(4), Apr. 1968, p. 835-839; — "Double g - and optical resonance," *Physics Letters A*, Vol. 43, 1973, p. 179-180.; — "Stimulated emission of an ensemble of scattering particles with negative absorption," *ZhETF Plasma*, 5(8), Apr. 15, 1967, p. 262-265. Pappalardo, R. and A. Lempicki, "Brillouin and Rayleigh Scattering in Aprotic Laser Solutions Containing Neodymium," *Journal of Applied Physics*, Apr. 1992, p. 1699-1708.

35. See L. Mandelstam [Mendel'shtam, L. I.], N. Papalexi, A. Andronov, S. Chaikin and A. Witt, "Report on Recent Research on Nonlinear Oscillations," Translation of "Expose Des Recherches Recentes Sur Les Oscillations Non Lineaires," *Technical Physics of the USSR*, Leningrad, Vol. 2, 1935, p. 81-134 [NASA Translation Doc. TT F-12,678, Nov. 1969]. See also A. Andronov, "The limiting cycles of Poincare and the theory of self-maintained oscillations," *Comptes-Rendus*, Vol. 189, 1929, p. 559; — and A. Witt, , "On the mathematical theory of self-excitations," *Comptes-Rendus*, Vol. 190, 1930, p. 256; — On the mathematical theory of self-excitation systems with two degrees of freedom," *Zhurnal Tekhnicheskioi Fiziki*, 4(1), 1934.

36. Franklin B. Mead and Jack Nachamkin, "System for Converting Electromagnetic Radiation Energy to Electrical Energy," U.S. Patent No. 5,590,031, Dec. 31, 1996.
37. E.g., see G. Nicolis and I. Prigogine, (1987), *Exploring Complexity*, Piper, Munich, 1987; — *Exploring Complexity: An Introduction*, Freeman, New York, 1989. For a good layman's treatise, see Gregoire Nicolis, "Physics of far-from-equilibrium systems and self-organization," Chapter 11 in Paul Davies, Ed., *The New Physics*, Cambridge University Press, Cambridge, 1989, p. 317-347. See particularly Ilya Prigogine, *The End of Certainty: Time, Chaos, and the New Laws of Nature*, Free Press, New York, 1996, 1997; — *From Being to Becoming: Time and Complexity in the Physical Sciences*, W.H. Freeman and Company, San Francisco, 1980.
38. Richard P. Feynman, Robert B. Leighton, and Matthew Sands, *Lectures on Physics*, Addison-Wesley, Reading, MA, Vol. 1, 1964, p. 4-2.
39. Hsu-Chieh Yeh, "Remark on the second law of thermodynamics," *American Journal of Physics*, 52(8), Aug. 1984, p. 720+.
40. *Ibid.*, p. 721.
41. A. A. Logunov and Yu. M. Loskutov, "Nonuniqueness of the predictions of the general theory of relativity," *Sov. J. Part. Nucl.*, 18(3), May-June 1987, p. 179-187.
42. Maciej J. Ogorzalek, *Chaos and Complexity in Nonlinear Electronic Circuits*, World Scientific, New Jersey, 1997.
43. Alexander L. Fradkov and Alexander Yu. Pogromsky, *Introduction to Control of Oscillations and Chaos*, World Scientific Series on Nonlinear Science E, Series Editor Leon O. Chua, World Scientific, New Jersey, 1998, p. 8.
44. *Ibid.*, p. 359-360.
45. Ibrahim Semiz, "Black hole as the ultimate energy source," *American Journal of Physics,* 63(2), Feb. 1995, p. 151-156.
46. D.K Sen, *Fields and/or Particles*, Academic Press, London and New York, 1968, p. viii.

13927-VALO

47. Maxwell's seminal EM paper was J. C. Maxwell, "A Dynamical Theory of the Electromagnetic Field," *Royal Society Transactions*, Vol. CLV, 1865, p 459. Read Dec. 8, 1864. Also in *The Scientific Papers of James Clerk Maxwell*, 2 vols. bound as one, edited by W. D. Niven, Dover, New York, 1952, Vol. 1, p. 526-597. In the latter, two errata are given on the unnumbered page prior to page 1 of Vol. 1. In this paper Maxwell presents his seminal theory of electromagnetism, containing 20 equations in 20 unknowns. His general equations of the electromagnetic field are given in Part III, General Equations of the Electromagnetic Field, p. 554-564. On p. 561, he lists his 20 variables. On p. 562, he summarizes the different subjects of the 20 equations, being three equations each for magnetic force, electric currents, electromotive force, electric elasticity, electric resistance, total currents; and one equation each for free electricity and continuity. In the paper, Maxwell adopts the approach of first arriving at the laws of induction and then deducing the mechanical attractions and repulsions.
48. e.g., see Stanley W. Angrist, "Perpetual Motion Machines," *Scientific American*, Vol. 218, Jan. 1968, p. 114-122. Angrist gives a typical critique using classical equilibrium thermodynamics. He calls *permissible* overunity systems (open dissipative systems receiving excess energy from an external source) *false perpetual motion machines*. See also Angrist's article, "Perpetual Motion," *Encyclopaedia Britannica*, Bicentennial Edition, Macropaedia Vol. 14, 1976, p. 102-105. Here he gives a very good summary of the subject as ordinarily posed, with precise definitions included for perpetual motion machines of the first, second, and third kinds and for fictitious perpetual motion machines. Unfortunately his argument is completely irrelevant to permissible overunity machines, which he already labels "fictitious perpetual motion machines" and admits they exist. The substance of his argument then is that systems in equilibrium cannot power

themselves. That is quite true, but is a mere tautology and has no relation to an open system in disequilibrium, receiving excess energy. So he demolishes a dummy strawman, while ignoring the Statue of Liberty under his very nose.

49. Indeed, once the active vacuum is considered, there is no such thing as a "closed system" in all the universe. Every system is open, at least to the vacuum exchange. So the most that can be legitimately raised as a question is the matter of a system in equilibrium. Even so, the system is subject to individual fluctuations, and may thus be subject to nonlinear oscillations, chaotic operation, etc.
50. John D. Kraus, *Electromagnetics*, Fourth Edn., McGraw-Hill, New York, 1992, Figure 12-60, a and b, p. 578.
51. e.g., the trick can be seen in Wolfgang Panofsky and Melba Phillips, *Classical Electricity and Magnetism*, Second Edition, Addison-Wesley, Menlo Park, CA, 1962, third printing 1969, p. 181, or in W. Gough and J.P.G. Richards, *European Journal of Physics*, Vol. 7, 1986, p. 195.
52. As an example, the various dipoles in the human body extract from the vacuum and output an energy flow rate of about 10^{15} joules per second. However, the body's reaction cross section is about 10^{-13}, so it actually intercepts, collects, and utilizes about 100 joules per second. So its power output is about 100 watts, about like powering a room light bulb. If the body caught all of that energy, it would instantly explode like a huge bomb with a sudden surge of enormous power. So life as we know it could not exist unless that Poynting reaction cross section were very, very small—which it fortunately is.
53. Editorial, "The Transfer of Energy," *The Electrician*, Vol. 27, July 10, 1891, p. 270-272.
54. See J. H. Poynting, "On the transfer of energy in the electromagnetic field," *Philosophical Transactions of the Royal Society of London*, Vol. 175, Part II, 1885, p. 343-361.
55. Quoting Oliver Heaviside, *Electrical Papers*, Vol. 2, 1887, p. 94: *"It [the energy transfer flow] takes place, in the vicinity*

of the wire, very nearly parallel to it, with a slight slope towards the wire.... Prof. Poynting, on the other hand, holds a different view, representing the transfer as nearly perpendicular to a wire, i.e., with a slight departure from the vertical. This difference of a quadrant can, I think, only arise from what seems to be a misconception on his part as to the nature of the electric field in the vicinity of a wire supporting electric current. The lines of electric force are nearly perpendicular to the wire. The departure from perpendicularity is usually so small that I have sometimes spoken of them as being perpendicular to it, as they practically are, before I recognized the great physical importance of the slight departure. It causes the convergence of energy into the wire."

56. Often we hear naïve objections to the notion that a "static field" or "static potential" is actually an ongoing continuous flow. To answer that, we refer to an admirable explanation; see Tom Van Flandern, "The speed of gravity – What the experiments say," *Physics Letters A*, Vol. 250, Dec. 21, 1998, p. 1-11. Quoting p. 8-9: *"To retain causality, we must distinguish two distinct meanings of the term 'static'. One meaning is unchanging in the sense of no moving parts. The other meaning is sameness from moment to moment by continual replacement of all moving parts. We can visualize this difference by thinking of a waterfall. A frozen waterfall is static in the first sense, and a flowing waterfall is static in the second sense. Both are essentially the same at every moment, yet the latter has moving parts capable of transferring momentum, and is made of entities that propagate.*

As this applies to gravitational fields for a fixed source, if the field were static in the first sense, there would be no need of aberration, but also no apparent causality link between source and target. If the field were static in the second sense, then the propagation speed of the entities carrying momentum would give rise to aberration; and the observed absence of aberration demands a propagation speed far greater than lightspeed.

So are gravitational fields for a rigid, stationary source frozen, or are they continually regenerated? Causality seems to require the latter."

57. Indeed, astronomy experiments have now verified that gravity's speed v_g is enormous, being $v_g \geq 2 \times 10^{10}$ c. See Tom Van Flandern, ibid. Quoting Van Flandern, p. 10: "*To many, this result* [astronomy's verification that gravity's speed $v_g \geq 2 \times 10^{10}$ c] *is so contrary to 'common sense' in the light of relativity theory as to be absurd. But Thomas Kuhn has cautioned all scientists to avoid the trap of becoming so steeped in a prevailing paradigm that it starts to seem like common sense and makes other ideas sound and feel wrong. Eventually, even one's professional status can become linked to a prevailing paradigm.*"
58. Nikola Tesla, "The True Wireless," *Electrical Experimenter*, May 1919.
59. That is, unless we utilize the Bedini method for creating a negative resistor in the charging battery, and supercharging the battery while also powering the load. See T. E. Bearden, "Bedini's Method For Forming Negative Resistors In Batteries," *Journal of New Energy*, 5(1), Summer 2000, p. 24-38. The paper is also carried on *http://www.cheniere.org* and also on DoE website *http://www.ott.doe.gov/electromagnetic/papersbooks.html.*
60. e.g., see J. D. Jackson, *Classical Electrodynamics*, Second Edition, Wiley, New York, 1975, p. 219-221.
61. Ingram Block and Horace Crater, "Lorentz-Invariant Potentials and the Nonrelativistic Limit," *American Journal of Physics*, Vol. 49, No. 1, Jan. 1981, p. 67.
62. Charles J. Goebel, "Symmetry Laws," in *McGraw Hill Encyclopedia of Physics*, Sybal B. Parker, Editor-in-Chief, McGraw Hill, NY, 1983, p. 1137.
63. One can see the Lorentz regauging and how it is done in J.D. Jackson, *Classical Electrodynamics*, Second Edition, Wiley, New York, 1975, p. 219-221; 811-812.

64. P. K. Anastasovski; T. E. Bearden; C. Ciubotariu; W. T. Coffey; L. B. Crowell; G. J. Evans; M. W. Evans; R. Flower; S. Jeffers; A. Labounsky; B. Lehnert; M. Meszaros; P. R. Molnar; J. P. Vigier; and S. Roy; "Classical electrodynamics without the Lorentz condition: Extracting energy from the vacuum," *Physica Scripta* 61(5), May 2000, p. 513-517. It is shown that if the Lorentz condition is discarded, the Maxwell-Heaviside field equations become the Lehnert equations, indicating the presence of charge density and current density in the vacuum. The Lehnert equations are a subset of the O(3) Yang-Mills field equations. Charge and current density in the vacuum are defined straightforwardly in terms of the vector potential and scalar potential, and are conceptually similar to Maxwell's displacement current, which also occurs in the classical vacuum. A demonstration is made of the existence of a time dependent classical vacuum polarization which appears if the Lorentz condition is discarded. Vacuum charge and current appear phenomenologically in the Lehnert equations but fundamentally in the O(3) Yang-Mills theory of classical electrodynamics. The latter also allows for the possibility of the existence of vacuum topological magnetic charge density and topological magnetic current density. Both O(3) and Lehnert equations are superior to the Maxwell-Heaviside equations in being able to describe phenomena not amenable to the latter. In theory, devices can be made to extract the energy associated with vacuum charge and current. More than a dozen potential methods of approaching the practical extraction of EM energy from the vacuum is presented.
65. We must admit that it may only be insanity in the view of the consumer and the environmentalist. It may be highly lucrative and desirable in the view of the "energy seller".
66. We also do an analogous thing for the fields, but the discussion for the potential will illustrate the point.
67. E. T. Whittaker, "On the Partial Differential Equations of Mathematical Physics," *Mathematische Annalen*, Vol. 57, 1903, p. 333-355.

68. H. E. Puthoff, "Source of Vacuum Electromagnetic Zero-Point Energy," *Physical Review A*, 40(9), Nov. 1, 1989, p. 4857-4862.
69. Whittaker, *Mathematische Annalen, ibid.*
70. Mario Bunge, *Foundations of Physics*, Springer-Verlag, New York, 1967, p. 182.
71. M. W. Evans and S. Kielich., (eds.), *Modern Nonlinear Optics*, Vol. 85 of I. Prigogine and S.A. Rice (series eds.), *Advances in Chemical Physics*, Wiley, New York, 1992, 1993, and 1997. See also M.W. Evans et al., "A General Theory of Non-Abelian Electrodynamics," Foundations of Physics Letters, 12(3), June 1999, p. 251. See particularly the collection of more than 30 AIAS papers, in press, to be published shortly as a Special Issue of *Journal of New Energy*. Presently more than 90 AIAS papers are carried on a Department of Energy website (limited access) for ongoing discussions with DOE scientists.
72. See Dr. Crowell's paper given at this conference.
73. T. W. Barrett and D. M Grimes.,[eds.], *Advanced Electromagnetism: Foundations, Theory, & Applications*, World Scientific, River Edge, New Jersey, 07661, 1995. See particularly T. W. Barrett, "Electromagnetic Phenomena Not Explained by Maxwell's Equations," in Lakhtakia, A. (ed.): *Essays on the Formal Aspects of Electromagnetic Theory*, World Scientific Publishing, River Edge, NJ, 1993, p. 6-86; T. W. Barrett, "Maxwell's theory extended: Part 1: Empirical reasons for Questioning the Completeness of Maxwell's Theory – Effects Demonstrating the Physical Significance of the A Potentials," *Annales de la Fondation Louis de Broglie*, 15(2), 1990, p. 143-183; Part II: Theoretical and Pragmatic Reasons for Questioning the Completeness of Maxwell's Theory." *Annales de la Fondation Louis de Broglie*, 15(3), 1990, p. 253-283.
74. L. B. Crowell and M. W. Evans, "SU(2) x SU(2) Electroweak Theory I: The B(3) Field on the Physical Vacuum," *Founda-*

tions of Physics Letters, Vol. 12, 1999, p. 373; — "SU(2) x SU(2) Electroweak Theory II: Chiral and Vector Fields on the Physical Vacuum," *Foundations of Physics Letters*, Vol. 12, 1999, p. 475; M.W. Evans and L. B. Crowell, *Classical and Quantum Electrodynamics and the B(3) Field*, World Scientific, Singapore, 2001. See also footnote 30.

75. e.g., Evans *et al.*, "Inconsistencies of U(1) Gauge Field Theory in Electrodynamics: The Inverse Faraday Effect," DOE web site; — "Interferometry in Higher Symmetry Forms of Electrodynamics and Physical Optics," *Physica Scripta*, 61(1), Jan. 2000, p. 79-82; — Inconsistencies in the U(1) Theory of Electrodynamics: Stress Energy Momentum Tensor," *Foundations of Physics Letters*, 12(2), Apr. 1999, p. 187; — "Empirical Evidence for Non-Abelian Electrodynamics and Theoretical Development," submitted to *Annales de la Fondation Louis de Broglie*; — "Equations of the Yang-Mills Theory of Classical Electrodynamics," *Optik* (in press).
76. e.g., see Terence W. Barrett, "Electromagnetic Phenomena Not Explained by Maxwell's Equations," in Lakhtakia, A. (ed.): *Essays on the Formal Aspects of Electromagnetic Theory*, World Scientific Publishing, River Edge, NJ, 1993, p. 6-86.
77. Such as Bunge (quoted in this paper), the great John Wheeler, Nobelist Richard Feynman, Cornille, etc.
78. Some pertinent papers and books are: M. W. Evans (Ed.), *Modern Nonlinear Optics*, Second Edition, Wiley, 2001, 3 vols. (in press), comprising a Special Topic issue as Vol. 114, I. Prigogine and S. A. Rice (series eds.), *Advances in Chemical Physics*, Wiley, ongoing. In that reference, particularly see M. W. Evans, "O(3) Electrodynamics," a review of some 250 pages; M. W. Evans, "The Link Between the Sachs and O(3) Theories of Electrodynamics," M. W. Evans, "Link Between the Topological Theory of Ranada and Trueba, the Sachs Theory, and O(3) Electrodynamics," T. E. Bearden, "Extracting and Using Electromagnetic Energy from the Active Vacuum," T. E. Bearden, "Energy from the Active

Lightning Source UK Ltd.
Milton Keynes UK
UKHW04f1129160718
325772UK00001B/174/P

9 781401 041137